"A gripp___ _____ ___ _____ _____
reader fron_ _____ __ _____ __. Michael Walters's
taut, literate prose _____ _____ _____ ernational
crime _____ _____ and very
scary __ __ ___ ____, __ ___ shadows, nothing is as it seems and
no one should be trusted."

—Margaret Coel, author of *The Girl with Braided Hair*

"Like the best of all crime fiction, Michael Walters's *The Shadow Walker* is as much about the place (Mongolia) as the plot, which makes it an exceptional read . . . In the land of Genghis Khan we're introduced to a fascinating new protagonist named Nergui . . . An exotic mystery by a writer to watch."

—C. J. Box, author of *Blue Heaven* and *Blood Trail*

"Nail-biting . . . It's a complex book, but compulsive reading, and the descriptions of Mongolia are richly enjoyable. I look forward to another bloodthirsty visit with Nergui as my guide."

—*The Independent* (London)

"A sense of place has always been an important ingredient in crime fiction, with the descent into a different culture, time or environment key to establishing foreboding or atmosphere. This debut . . . chooses its locale well, a previously uncharted crime destination: Mongolia. Walters ably brings his uncommon setting to teeming life. A worthy new series in the making."

—*The Guardian* (UK)

"An intriguing police procedural, with a formidable sleuth . . . It's Nergui who is firmly in charge, assisted by his young protégé, Doripalam, as they slowly unravel a complex mystery. It's a promising debut."　　—*The Sunday Telegraph*

continued . . .

THE
SHADOW
WALKER

MICHAEL WALTERS

BERKLEY PRIME CRIME, NEW YORK

THE BERKLEY PUBLISHING GROUP
Published by the Penguin Group
Penguin Group (USA) Inc.
375 Hudson Street, New York, New York 10014, USA
Penguin Group (Canada), 90 Eglinton Avenue East, Suite 700, Toronto, Ontario M4P 2Y3, Canada
(a division of Pearson Penguin Canada Inc.)
Penguin Books Ltd., 80 Strand, London WC2R 0RL, England
Penguin Group Ireland, 25 St. Stephen's Green, Dublin 2, Ireland (a division of Penguin Books Ltd.)
Penguin Group (Australia), 250 Camberwell Road, Camberwell, Victoria 3124, Australia
(a division of Pearson Australia Group Pty. Ltd.)
Penguin Books India Pvt. Ltd., 11 Community Centre, Panchsheel Park, New Delhi—110 017, India
Penguin Group (NZ), 67 Apollo Drive, Rosedale, North Shore 0632, New Zealand
(a division of Pearson New Zealand Ltd.)
Penguin Books (South Africa) (Pty.) Ltd., 24 Sturdee Avenue, Rosebank, Johannesburg 2196,
South Africa

Penguin Books Ltd., Registered Offices: 80 Strand, London WC2R 0RL, England

Copyright © 2006 by Michael Walters.
Published in arrangement with Quercus Publishing, PLC.
Cover art by Richard Tuschman.
Cover design by Rita Frangie.
Text design by Kristin del Rosario.

PRINTING HISTORY
Quercus hardcover edition / November 2006
Quercus mass-market edition / May 2007
Berkley Prime Crime trade paperback edition / August 2008

Library of Congress Cataloging-in-Publication Data

Walters, Mike, 1960–
    The shadow walker / Michael Walters.—Berkley Prime Crime trade pbk. ed.
      p. cm.
    ISBN 978-0-425-22233-1
    1. Police—Mongolia—Fiction. 2. Geologists—Crimes against—Fiction. 3. British—Mongolia—
Fiction. 4. Mongolia—Fiction. 5. Serial murders—Mongolia—Fiction. 6. Serial murder
investigation—Mongolia—Fiction. I. Title.
    PR6123.A474S47 2008
    823'.92—dc22   2008060018

PRINTED IN THE UNITED STATES OF AMERICA

10   9   8   7   6   5   4   3   2   1

"In the country of the blind, close your eyes."
—Mongolian proverb

So that was it. Cleaned out again. Right down to the last *tugruk*.

He fell against the wall, nearly lost his footing, then staggered upright again and continued his uncertain way down the empty street.

What time was it? After midnight, for sure. The streetlights were on in the square, but the narrow side-streets were lost in darkness. And it was cold. Bone-chillingly cold, and winter was hardly here. He had tried to bet his coat on the last game—it was the only asset he had left—but thank blue heaven they'd just laughed at him. They usually laughed at him.

He tripped again, stumbling on an uneven paving stone, and felt suddenly nauseated. He should stop this. Stop the drinking. Stop the gambling. Yet again, he had left himself with nothing to live on till the next public handout, days away. But what else was there? Endless empty promises. That was the story of this country; everyone made promises. But nobody kept them. At least the cheap vodka always delivered.

He stopped suddenly, feeling sick, realising that his bladder was painfully full. The city lights swirled around him, a dizzying scatter of neon logos proclaiming a future he had no part in. He took a step back, trying to regain his equilibrium, the freezing cold aching in his limbs.

Where was he? Still a long way from home, a long way to go. He looked around, trying to find somewhere to relieve himself. There was a cramped side-street to his left, unlit, thick blackness only yards from the main street. He glanced back. The city centre and the main square in the distance were deserted, bleak and wintry in the thin glow of the streetlights.

He turned and began to make his way cautiously down the unlit street. Some lingering sense of propriety made him try to move further into the darkness—he had no desire to get himself arrested, on top of everything else.

He could barely see now, his eyes not yet accustomed to the dark. Tall blank buildings rose up on both sides of him, the lights of the main street lost behind him. He took another step, trying to regain his balance and his bearings, and then he stumbled again, his foot catching on something. Something heavy lying in the middle of the street. Something soft.

He fell headlong, his arm and his shoulder scraping on the rough ground, the impact agonising even in his drunken state. He rolled over, gasping, and lay on his back, trying to catch his breath. Above him, in the narrow gap between the high buildings, he could see a brilliant patterning of stars.

His eyes were adjusting to the darkness now, and he twisted around, trying to see what it was that had tripped him. At first, he couldn't make it out. Just a blank shapeless mound, spread across the frozen ground. And then he thought it looked something like a human figure, but not quite like one. He rolled over, trying to clear his head, trying to work out what was wrong.

And then, suddenly, he realised what it was, and he screamed, the nausea that had been building in his stomach overwhelming him, acid in his throat.

He was still lying there, moaning and retching, when the police patrol arrived fifteen minutes later.

PART ONE

ONE

It was like one of the gates of hell.

They drove at speed away from the airport, northeast towards the city, as the setting sun cast crimson shadows along the road ahead. As night fell and the sky filled with stars, the empty steppe was left behind, replaced by a vast industrial complex dominating both sides of the road. Endless blank buildings stretched into the thickening winter darkness, interspersed by networks of heavy pipe-lines, scatterings of pale orange lights. Somewhere in the centre, there was a single guttering flare.

Nergui followed Drew's gaze. "Mining. Mainly coal here, though there are gold reserves in the area also. A primitive operation. This would not now be allowed in your country, I think. The ugliness, pollution. But the Soviets were not too bothered about things like that. And neither are we, I suppose, so long as we maintain some kind of industry. We have been through difficult times." He shrugged, and then smiled. "But much of the country is unspoiled. I hope you will get the chance to see some of it while you are here."

"I don't know—"

Nergui nodded. "Of course, forgive me. Murder is not a trivial matter. Especially in a case like this. We will provide you with every support. This matter is a grave concern to us as well. I merely wish to be hospitable."

Drew shook his head. "No, that's fine. I'm keen to see something of the country while I'm here."

"I will be pleased to be your guide, Chief Inspector."

"Call me Drew, please."

The Mongolian nodded slowly, as though absorbing this request. He had given no indication of his own rank or position. At the airport, Nergui had introduced himself to Drew—one of a handful of Westerners on the in-bound flight—only by the single name. It had appeared, from the phone calls and e-mails exchanged prior to Drew's arrival, that Nergui was the officer in charge of the investigation, but he had not made this explicit. Instead, he had introduced the younger second officer, Doripalam, as the Head of the Serious Crimes Team.

But there was no doubt that Nergui was at ease in the back of this official car, with Doripalam in the front passenger seat and a silent underling driving them down this featureless road towards the city centre.

And there was no doubt, too, that Drew was a long way from home.

Home was five thousand miles away. Home was the soft chill of late autumn rain, not the harsh grip of approaching winter. It was the grey downpour that had greeted Drew as he crawled from his bed at some godless hour that morning, hearing the steady breathing of his sleeping wife, the softer synchronised breath of the children in the next room. The ceaseless torrent down the windscreen of the taxi thirty minutes later, the rhythmic sweep of the wipers. The overcheerful banter of the driver, on his last run of the night, looking forward to his own bed.

As always, Drew had arrived at the airport too early, with an age to wait after check-in, trying not to think about the hours of travel that lay ahead, about what might wait at the end of the journey. He was still barely awake as he boarded the flight to Heathrow, a compliant automaton, gripping his passport, fumbling for the hastily arranged visa, juggling his deck of tickets. The flight was, inevitably, late, stacked for long minutes over London, Monday morning congestion already building. He ended up with no time to spare, racing across the terminal for the connecting Lufthansa flight to Berlin, convinced he would be stopped at the gate. As he stumbled up the aisle of the plane, the other passengers had stared at him, no doubt recognising him as the one who had briefly delayed their flight.

This was, supposedly, the easier route to Mongolia. The alternative was a flight to Moscow and an Aeroflot connection to Ulan Baatar. The specialist travel firm that had organised the trip had warned against this, citing the inevitability of delays in Moscow and the notorious unreliability of the Russian carrier. Better to trust German efficiency and the enthusiasm of Mongolia's own state airline, MIAT, to bring tourists and their currency quickly into their country.

The advice proved sound. The Berlin flight was on time, and the transfer at Tegel smooth enough. Two hours later, he was sitting on MIAT's only 737, finally beginning to relax. This flight was also on schedule and the service was efficient, even if the style and catering were, to Western eyes, eccentric. The inflight meal consisted entirely of a selection of meats—cured, roast, perhaps boiled—accompanied by an apparently unending supply of miniature Mongolian vodkas. Drew drank two of these, enjoying the warmth and pepper taste, with a growing sense of ease that the hardest part of the journey was past. Three vodkas seemed too many for the early afternoon, and he slipped the last small bottle into his pocket as a souvenir. His neighbour, a middle-aged Mongolian man in a smart-looking black business suit, smiled at him and raised his own glass of vodka in silent greeting.

Unexpectedly—to Drew at least—the flight was interrupted for refuelling at Irkutsk, on the far eastern Russian border. The flight circled in over the vast white expanse of Lake Baikal, the dark Siberian forests stretched out ahead. There was more queuing to display passports and visas, the wooden-faced official peering suspiciously at Drew's documents.

"Police?" he had said finally, in heavily accented English.

Drew nodded, drawing a deep breath to launch into some kind of explanation. He had in his pocket the formal letter of invitation from the Mongolian government, though he had no idea how much weight this would carry this side of the border. But, after a lengthy pause, the man had just nodded and smiled faintly. "Good luck," he said. Drew suspected that he had used the only English words he knew.

Drew and the other passengers had sat in the empty airport, surrounded by cheap pine veneer and grimy plate-glass windows, drinking strong coffee from the primitive bar. At one point, seeking air, Drew had wandered out to join the cluster of smokers on a small wooden balcony, with views out over the woodlands and lake. Although it was mid-afternoon, it was icy cold, the Russian winter already biting. He stood for as long as he could, the frozen air harsh in his lungs, looking out at the dense Siberian forests, the trees black against the pure blue of the sky, the landscape deathly silent. He had felt then as if he was standing at the edge of the world, with no inkling of what might lie beyond.

Minutes later, they were shepherded back on to the plane. As they walked back out across the tarmac, Drew looked around at his fellow travellers. Most were Mongolian, with the distinctive broad features and dark skin, though there was a scattering of Westerners and some who looked, to Drew's undiscerning eye, to be Chinese. Most were dressed in conventional Western clothes—suits, jeans, sweatshirts—but two older men were dressed in heavy, dark coloured robes, wrapped around with brilliantly-patterned golden sashes.

Later, as they approached Ulan Baatar, the plane banked low over the steppes, turning in sharply towards the airport. The sun was low in the clear sky, casting deep shadows across the endless green plains. Even the shape of the hills was different here—softer, rounder, distinctively Asian. As the plane descended, Drew glimpsed, startlingly close to the runway, scatterings of nomadic camps, round grey tents, figures wrapped in traditional robes, tethered horses, flocks of sheep and herds of horned cattle.

The sight was unexpected, but this was how the people lived here. The population was sparse—little more than one person per square kilometre of land—and half still lived in the traditional *ger* tents. Half of those remained nomadic, tending their herds, moving with the seasons, coping with the extremes of an intense continental climate. It was a basic lifestyle unchanged for a thousand years. And over the past decade, unemployment and poverty had driven increasing numbers back out to the steppes, struggling to eke out an existence from the inhospitable grassland, rediscovering traditional ways of living, the lure and challenges of the endless plains.

Minutes later, the plane landed and, as incongruous as if from another age, there were the strings of landing lights, the formalities of passport and customs, the baggage carousel that, to Drew's mild surprise, rapidly disgorged the luggage he had checked in hours before. All around, there was the anonymous glare and bustle of a shabby airport terminal that might have been anywhere in the world.

"Drew," Nergui said. "Drew McLeish. That is a Scottish name, yes?"

Drew looked across at the heavily built figure beside him. "My father was from Glasgow. But my family moved to Manchester when I was a boy, so I lost the accent long ago. You know the UK?"

Nergui nodded. "I spent a year there. Studying."

"Your English is excellent."

"Thank you. I also spent some years in the US, so I talk about sidewalks and elevators." Nergui laughed. "But I liked England. A beautiful country."

"We have our own ugliness and pollution," Drew said. "But some of it is beautiful."

"We will show you some of the attractions of our country while you are here." Nergui paused. "It is good of you to come. We will need all the help and advice you can give us. You will find us very amateurish, I am afraid."

This seemed unlikely. The police might be short of resources and experience, but it was clear, even from their brief initial contact with Drew, that Nergui and Doripalam were anything but amateurs. "I don't know that there's much I'll be able to teach you," he said. "But I'll give whatever help and support I can."

"This kind of crime is new to us, Chief Inspector. Drew." He said the name as though trying it out, but seemed satisfied with the effect.

Drew shrugged. "Thankfully," he said, "none of us comes across this kind of crime very often."

*   *   *

That was true enough. Crime wasn't supposed to be like this, not here. Crime here could be violent and sometimes complex— which was when Nergui tended to get involved these days—but mostly it was trivial stuff. Nergui had read in the newspaper only a few days before that the single most common crime in Mongolia was the theft of cattle. A few months earlier, an English journalist had had his bicycle stolen by a man on a horse, though Nergui had no idea how this could have been done. And there was always the drunkenness, worse when the nights lengthened and the weather became cold, and worst of all among the growing numbers without jobs or prospects. The levels of alcoholism and drug abuse in the capital mounted with every passing month.

But, even in these dark times, crime was not like this.

When they found the first body, nobody was surprised. These things happened from time to time. They had always happened, even in the old days, though then the authorities had made sure they were never reported. In these more liberal times, the privately owned scandal sheets picked up on stories like this and tried to stir up some trouble. But such incidents were usually soon forgotten, either because the police knew immediately who was responsible or because they were never likely to find out.

The body had been found in one of the narrow unlit side-streets near the city centre, in the shadow of a long-abandoned clothing factory. Cocooned in his new role, Nergui had had no reason to be involved. But he felt some frustration that this potentially interesting case had arisen so soon after his detachment to the Ministry. Bored and curious, he had used his new-found authority to request a copy of the scene-of-crime report. To his surprise, it arrived promptly and without question. One of the minor privileges available to those who no longer had to deal with policing on the front line.

Not for the first time, reading through the turgid account, Nergui wished that the police were able to demand a higher standard of literacy from their frontline officers. But the basic narrative was clear enough. A local drunk had found the body, while making his way home in the small hours after a night spent gambling in some illegal bar.

Nergui had seen more than enough dead bodies in his career. He could only hope that, when the drunk realised what lay beside him, alcohol had lessened the shock. But he suspected not, given the copious amounts of vomit apparently spread across the body when the police arrived. The pathologist, faced with an already unpleasant task, had expressed outrage at this further disruption of the evidence. On the other hand, as Nergui glanced through the crime-scene photographs he had to admit that, even for a sober person, vomiting would have been an understandable response.

The body was severely mutilated; it had been decapitated and was missing its hands, the neck and wrists savagely chopped as though with a heavy blunt blade. There were multiple lacerations to the chest as if the killer had been unable to stop, slashing savagely at the body, tearing repeatedly through its thin clothing, long after life must have departed. There was no sign of the missing body parts.

The pathologist had concluded that, in fact, all this mutilation had occurred after death. The most likely cause of death itself was strangling or asphyxiation. There was little other visible evidence. The body was dressed in Western-style clothes—cheap trousers, a thin cotton shirt, a rough jacket. Apart from the tearings and blood stains, the clothes were clean and looked new. They were mass-produced items that could have been purchased anywhere; although this late in the year, it was difficult to imagine that anyone had willingly gone outside dressed like that. The pockets were empty.

The local police had, characteristically, stumbled into the incident more or less by accident. A passing patrolman, shining his flashlight down the side-street, had been startled by the scene—the twisted body, the prone drunk. His first reaction was to call for back-up, and then to apprehend the still retching drunk who had offered little resistance.

It was a natural assumption. Most deaths and criminal injuries in the city were the result of drunken brawls. But a moment's glance at the corpse had been enough to tell the patrolman that, though the drunk might be a witness, he was unlikely to be the perpetrator. There was little blood surrounding the body, and it was clear that the murder and dismemberment had taken place elsewhere and some time before.

Apart from the additional lacerations, the murder had all the signs of a professional killing. The removal of the head and hands had presumably been intended to conceal the victim's identity, the clothes had been stripped of identifying marks. The body had been dumped here, in the dark but just off the main drag, so there had been no concern about its being found. It might even be that the discovery of the body, and its inevitable reporting in the media, was intended as a warning to someone.

The murder might have been committed for any number of reasons. The drugs trade had made its inroads here as it had in most impoverished Soviet satellites, especially among the younger unemployed. There were the usual networks of organised crime—much of it with its roots over the borders in China and Russia but gaining an ever-stronger foothold in the capital. This was a country with no money but plenty of potential. The perfect buyer's market for anyone looking to get a piece of the future action.

And, of course, there was no shortage of home-grown corruption. It was only a few years since the Mon-Macau Casino scandal had resulted in the trial and imprisonment of a prominent group of politicians on bribery charges. And that case had been just one high-profile example of what was becoming an endemic problem—a seeping corruption evident in all parts of public life. Even, as he knew only too well, among the police themselves.

The police would make a show of investigating, but they would probably make little progress. For all its horror, this was the kind of crime that wouldn't justify much investigative time; the chances of resolving it were too small and it was in nobody's interest to dig too deeply. And even the most honest policemen might think that the victim, whoever he might be, probably deserved his fate. Which, Nergui conceded, could well be the case.

So, after a small flurry in the press, the case aroused little interest. Nergui had the details logged in the Ministry files on the off-chance there was some connection to any of the fraud or other cases they were already investigating, but he didn't seriously expect any link, he had already dismissed the murder as just another manifestation of the criminal underclass that infested this city.

And then, a week later, they found the second body.

"You are something of an expert in this field, I understand?" Nergui said. Outside, the night and guttering lights rolled past them as the car entered the city outskirts. The heavy industrial sites gave way to row after row of featureless low-rise apartment buildings, a familiar testament to ugly Soviet pragmatism. Most looked neglected, paint peeling, the occasional window smashed. But virtually all seemed to be inhabited—there were lights at the windows, occasional lines of washing hanging limply in the cold evening.

Then, unexpectedly, in an open space between the tightly packed apartment blocks, there was another clustering of *gers,* a nomadic camp somehow lost in the urban anonymity. Drew stared out at the neat lines of identical round grey tents, the smoke rising steadily from their central chimneys. There were ranks of old-fashioned, brightly polished Russian motorbikes and a lone tethered horse, its breath clouding the night in the pale orange of the streetlights. As if to compound the incongruity, a group of denim-clad teenagers stood chatting around a single streetlight in the heart of the camp, cigarettes glowing in their hands, as though transported there from some Western inner city.

He looked back at Nergui. The Mongolian was watching him closely, as though his response might be significant. Nergui's face remained expressionless, his flat features and dark skin looking almost as if they might be carved from wood.

"That would be an exaggeration," Drew said. "But I've had to deal with a lot of violent crime. Including murder."

"Serial killings?"

"It depends what you mean. I handled one case where we had a genuine psychopath. He killed twice before we got him, but if we hadn't, I don't doubt that he'd have killed more. And I've handled several multiple killings, but those were mostly professional hits."

Nergui nodded. "Which may be what we have here."

"I wouldn't like to speculate," Drew said. "From what I've read, the whole thing is just—well, bizarre. It doesn't sound like the random killings of a psychopath, but it's a strange way to organise any kind of professional hit."

"Yes, indeed," Nergui said. "Well, we welcome your help. And we will do all we can to reciprocate. We understand that this matter is a concern to both our countries."

In truth, it wasn't clear why Drew had been sent here. It was not unusual, when a serious crime had been committed against a British subject, for an investigating officer to be sent to work with the local police. Often, it was little more than a token gesture, a demonstration to the public that the matter was being taken seriously. This was probably the case here. The brutal murder of a British businessman in a remote and largely unknown country was always going to create a stir in the tabloids, even though the full details of the murder had not been released.

The victim had been a Manchester resident, and Drew, as one of the more experienced investigating officers, had been offered the opportunity to make the trip. It was a difficult offer to refuse, although Drew could see little that he could bring to this particular party. Investigating any crime, even murder—especially murder—was generally a matter of routine, of systematically exploring every avenue, sifting each bit of information, until you began to make the connections. There was little doubt that Nergui and Doripalam would be organising that side of things very efficiently. Drew might facilitate some contacts in the UK, if there turned out to be any significance in the last victim's identity, but that was probably about it.

They had now entered the city centre. The road widened into a brightly lit avenue, lined with a mix of official-looking buildings, many studded with communist emblems, and newer commercial offices, some with Korean, Japanese or even American business names that Drew recognised. This could be any Eastern European city struggling to come to grips with life after the Soviet Union—the first shoots of Western capitalism alongside drab weathered concrete, poorly maintained roads and streetlights, shabby squares and inner-city parks. Familiar logos, neon-lit on the summits of office buildings, competed with stylised images of soldiers and stars—the fading murals of communism. And then, off to the right, there was a sudden glimpse of a very different building, the monastery of Choijin Lama, palely illuminated against the dark sky—a jumble of curving gilded rooflines, copper and crimson colourings, towers and short golden spires.

It was not late, but the streets were largely deserted, except for an occasional passing truck or car—mostly old-fashioned former Soviet or Eastern European models. Nergui pointed to an imposing building on the right. "The British Embassy," he said.

Drew nodded. "The ambassador wants to see me. I've an appointment for tomorrow."

"For lunch?"

Drew laughed. "I don't think so. I'm due there at ten. I'm probably not important enough to merit lunch."

"A pity," Nergui said, as if he really meant it. "He gives a good lunch."

Drew was vaguely wondering how often this senior policeman had cause to lunch with the British ambassador when the car pulled to a halt outside the hotel Chinggis Khaan.

Nergui gestured towards the extraordinary towering pink and black glass monolith, set incongruously among the featureless Soviet-style architecture that otherwise dominated much of the city centre. "I hope you don't mind staying here," he said. "I was unsure whether it was tactful to place you so near the scene of the crime."

Drew shrugged. "At least I'll be on hand for the next one," he said. Even as he spoke, he felt that his words were glib and inappropriate.

But Nergui gazed at him impassively, as if taking his statement seriously. "Let us hope," he said, "that your help will not be needed."

TWO

At first, the second killing changed little. The circumstances were different, and nobody connected the two deaths. The body was found in the early morning, sprawled in a narrow alley at the rear of the Hotel Bayangol, by a hotel cleaner heading in to work. She had nearly walked past, mistaking the corpse for one of the huddled homeless drunks commonly found sleeping in the meagre warmth of the hotel's rear entrance or scavenging in its kitchen bins. But as she got closer, she realised that the distorted angle of the limbs and the surrounding splashes of blood indicated a fall from a much greater height than street level. Her screams were loud enough to bring out a group of the hotel's kitchen staff who had been smoking by the rear exit.

By the time Doripalam arrived an hour later, the body had already been removed. One of the local officers was standing within the police cordon, apparently directing activities. Doripalam hoped, without much confidence, that everything had been done by the book. More likely, the priority had just been to clear up the mess.

"What's the story?" he asked.

The local man shrugged, looking mildly irritated at Doripalam's arrival. Doripalam was growing accustomed to this. He had once naively assumed that local forces—with their limited resources always stretched to the limit—would welcome the involvement of the Serious Crimes Team. Now he realised that as far as the locals were concerned, his arrival simply heralded more complications and more work.

"Who knows?" the man said. "Suicide, probably, or a drunk trying to close his bedroom window. We're checking the hotel guest list. Shouldn't take long." He turned away, the s̶e̶n̶s̶e̶ ̶o̶f̶ dismissal almost palpable.

But, by the end of the morning, when the case remained unresolved, the local team had itself been dismissed and Doripalam's men had taken over. Doripalam established a temporary base in the hotel manager's office, and sat with Batzorig, one of his junior officers, working through the data that had been collected. They were no closer to identifying the victim or to determining the circumstances of the death. Batzorig, with his usual blend of enthusiasm and rigour, was working painstakingly through his notes. "It looks as if we've accounted for all the guests and hotel staff. We thought at first that one of the night porters was missing but he was just sleeping off a hangover."

Doripalam looked up and raised an eyebrow. "A hangover? Was he on duty?"

"Supposedly. I don't think our investigation has done his employment prospects a lot of good."

Doripalam nodded. It was this kind of thing that made his team so unpopular. Solving serious crimes usually meant uncovering a raft of more trivial misdemeanours along the way. "So what do we know, then?"

"Well, we know that the victim didn't fall through a bedroom window—all the rooms on that side of the hotel were either occupied or locked, and there's no sign of any disturbance. It looks as if the body must have fallen from the hotel roof."

"Is the roof accessible?"

"Not easily, but you can get up there through a maintenance area on the top floor. You'd have to know about the access, though—it's not the sort of thing you'd just stumble across."

"So this isn't just some drunk who went up to look at the stars and took one step too many?"

"It doesn't look like it. And, since he wasn't staying at the hotel, we don't know how or when he got in. But security wasn't particularly tight. They usually lock the doors at midnight, but if he'd come in before that he wouldn't necessarily have been spotted. We're checking the security cameras, but I'm not hopeful. We're still waiting for confirmation of the time of death—it's not easy to be precise because it was so cold out overnight—but it could have been midnight or even earlier."

"And nobody saw anything?"

"We're interviewing all the guests and the staff. But so far nothing."

"But this still could just be a suicide?" Doripalam was playing devil's advocate, but everything had to be checked. After all, suicide was not exactly unknown in the city, or indeed anywhere else in the country. Unemployment had been running at forty per cent or more in the post-Soviet era. Poverty levels were similar, although less severe in the urban areas. Many people were living at barely more than subsistence levels.

Batzorig shrugged. "Well, yes, it could be. But the puzzle is the anonymity. We've got a body dressed in cheap, mass-produced clothing—empty pockets, no documentation, no identifying labels. Why would a suicide bother to clear his pockets? For that matter, why would he bother to break into a hotel to kill himself? I can think of plenty of easier ways to do it. It doesn't feel right to me."

Batzorig's instinct proved correct; the body remained anonymous. The fingerprints matched nothing in the police records. The dental records provided no clues. The victim was confirmed as a male, in his late thirties, medium height, heavily built, and appeared to be a Mongolian national. Beyond that, there was no information. The story was reported in the media, and the police hoped that someone would come forward to identify him, but there was little else they could do.

The post-mortem revealed that the victim had died from the massive trauma caused by the impact of hitting the hard concrete. But, although the state of the body prevented a definitive judgement, the victim appeared to have been involved in some sort of violent struggle prior to death, and there were traces of a strong sedative in the victim's blood. There seemed little doubt that the man had been murdered.

To his surprise, Nergui had found that a copy of the scene-of-crime report arrived on his desk in the Ministry, this time unrequested. Clearly his authority was now such that his arbitrary demands were immediately interpreted as essential departmental routines. After all these years, he was finally beginning to understand the attractions of power.

Nevertheless, the coincidence of the two unexplained deaths sparked his interest. Murders happened in the city more frequently than most people liked to admit; but this was still a relatively stable society. Most killings were sordid and straightforward—crimes of passion, drunken brawling, domestic violence. Even the unexplained murders could usually be categorised fairly easily. If a small-time local hoodlum was found murdered, it might be difficult to identify the individual perpetrator, but the police would generally have a good idea why the killing had happened and what sorts of people were involved.

But this was different. His curiosity aroused, Nergui took the opportunity to set up an informal meeting with his former deputy, Doripalam. Doripalam was young and relatively inexperienced, at least compared with his predecessor, but Nergui respected his intelligence and judgement. He had tried to keep some distance since Doripalam's promotion, anxious not to be seen as interfering, but offering support and advice when requested.

For his part, Doripalam seemed happy still to treat Nergui as a mentor, and was keen to draw on the older man's experience. They had developed a routine of meeting once a month, in one of the new American-style coffee houses that were beginning to spring up around the city centre. Nergui was intrigued that, despite the chaotic state of the economy, money was still available to spend in places like this.

They had arranged to meet early, but the place was already busy with a mix of young people—students, for the most part, chatting and smoking between lectures—and serious-looking businessmen in dark suits, earnestly discussing business deals or making apparently urgent calls on mobile phones. There was a rich smell of coffee and the cloying scent of baking pasties.

Outside the sun was shining and the sky was an unsullied blue. Across the street, at the edge of the square, crowds of men clustered round tables, playing chess or chequers, taking advantage of what might turn out to be one of the last temperate days of the year. Some of the older ones were dressed in traditional robes, but most were in heavy overcoats, with berets or American-style baseball caps pulled down over their eyes against the glare of the mid-morning sun. The fog of countless cigarettes hung around them like a localised cloud.

Nergui looked with some displeasure at the large foaming

cup that Doripalam placed in front of him. "This isn't coffee," he said. "It's a nursery drink."

Doripalam shrugged. "It's what the Americans drink. Apparently."

"So we must get used to it." Nergui took a mouthful and grimaced. "Though that may take some time, I think. But thank you anyway."

Doripalam sat down opposite and sipped at his own drink. "So how are you finding life in the corridors of power?"

"I think the power must be in another corridor. All I do is attend meetings and sign forms. While you get all the good fortune."

"Do I? Remind me."

"Two homicide cases in a week. And both of them more interesting than anything I had to deal with in the last five years."

"Oh, yes, that good fortune. How could I forget?"

"What's your view? Do you think they're linked?"

Doripalam looked at Nergui for a second, then he smiled. "This is a fishing expedition?" he said. "Surely the Minister isn't interested in anything as trivial as murder?" He was still smiling, and his wide-eyed features seemed innocent of anything more than mild curiosity, but Nergui knew better than to underestimate him.

"This is purely on my own account," Nergui said. "I'd like to be able to claim some official justification, but it's just idle curiosity. Wishing I was back in the old routine." He stared gloomily down at the absurd coffee, and, for a moment, Doripalam felt some sympathy for his former boss. Sitting here, his austere dark grey suit off-set by a characteristically garish orange tie, his large body hunched awkwardly over the table, Nergui looked uncomfortably like a man who no longer had a purpose in life.

Nergui's detachment to the Ministry of Justice and Internal

Affairs had been a substantial promotion, requested by the Minister himself. Nergui had always been an aloof figure in the police department, well respected but not widely liked among the team. There had been too many rumours about his past, too much suspicion about his real motives. And, of course, Nergui had always made very clear his intolerance for the incompetence and petty corruption that was endemic in the civil police.

For many in the team, Nergui's transfer to the Ministry had been a confirmation of their long-held assumptions—that all along he had been an authority lackey, delegated to strip away the few meagre perks associated with their thankless job. Or, worse, that he was simply another opportunist, adept at riding the waves of political change, with no loyalty except to his current paymaster.

But Doripalam hadn't shared these views. He had no doubt about Nergui's professional commitment or dedication, and he shared the older man's distaste at the endless petty corruption that seemed to be taken for granted by most of his colleagues. On a personal level, he had always found Nergui straightforward and trustworthy, if enigmatic, and he had been grateful when Nergui had actively endorsed his own promotion to head of department.

He was not surprised that the Minister, looking for a trustworthy ally in an increasingly turbulent political world, should have seen Nergui as one of the few individuals with the necessary abilities and personal integrity. And, in the circumstances, he could hardly be surprised that Nergui had found the offer impossible to refuse. But he suspected that, for all the prestige and material rewards associated with his new role, the old man would never be comfortable shuffling papers.

"For what it's worth," Doripalam said, in response to Nergui's question, "I don't think the murders are linked. I think it's probably just coincidence. It's unusual to have two such murders in close proximity, but that doesn't mean it can't happen. Or maybe it's some small-time feud. If so, I don't think anyone other than maybe their mothers will be grieving too hard."

So, in the face of this summary dismissal, Nergui's interest had remained casual. There were no evident tie-ups with the other cases that his team in the Ministry was currently investigating—the largest of which was a complex corruption case in the taxation office. In truth, there was no reason to justify even the limited amount of time he had spent on the murder cases. He told himself that it was useful to keep in touch with developments in other areas of the Ministry. But he knew he was fooling himself, trying to find some justification for dabbling again in his old area of expertise.

But that all changed when they found the third body.

It was discovered three days after the second, and Nergui took the call within thirty minutes of the body being found. It was not merely the usual routine passing on of information, but the Minister himself, clearly agitated. Nergui spoke with him frequently, often two or three times a day, and he knew that the Minister was not easily rattled. On the whole, Nergui had little sympathy with either the Minister's politics or his ethics, but he had already learned to be grateful for the politician's calmness in the face of crisis.

"You've heard they've found another body, Nergui?"

"Another body? When?" Nergui assumed that the Minister had only just learned about the second killing. His staff tended to brief him only on the day's essentials, and it was reasonable to assume that a sordid street murder would not rate highly in the Minister of Justice's priorities.

"This morning."

"No, I hadn't heard yet." He wondered how long it would be before the neatly typed scene-of-crime report dropped unbidden on to his desk.

"This is becoming a dangerous place to live, Nergui."

Nergui sighed inwardly. He knew that the Minister's primary interest would be how this would play in the media. Under the old regime, this would not have been a problem. These days, although the state still owned the radio and television, the clusters of privately owned newspapers made old-style censorship virtually impossible. There were times when Nergui wondered whether this was entirely a positive outcome. At least in the old days you knew where you stood, even if it was in a state of blind ignorance. Today, the media agenda was more subtle but equally pernicious, as a multitude of owners—from individual entrepreneurs to political parties—made sure that their own perspectives were appropriately represented.

"Does there seem to be a link to the other murders?" Nergui asked.

"To the first, anyway," the Minister said.

"The decapitation?"

"Exactly."

"Any clues on identity?"

"None, apparently. Just like the others."

"Right. I assume you've spoken to Serious Crimes—"

"Nergui," the Minister said. "You know as well as I do that the state police department, Serious Crimes or otherwise, is divided pretty equally between the corrupt and the inept. They could barely cope with the theft of a tourist's bicycle. Why do you think I was so keen to co-opt the one decent brain I found in the place? From where I'm sitting, this is a priority. No, this is *the* priority. Forget all the banking and state corruption stuff. We can afford to let them steal a bit more. I want you back there to sort this one out."

Despite himself, Nergui momentarily felt his spirit lighten, but his better judgement prevailed. "I really don't think that's a good idea. And, with respect, your comments aren't entirely fair. Doripalam's an excellent man—"

"Which is why, if I recall, he got the job as your successor with barely five years' experience under his belt. As I understand it, he was the only one there with a degree of integrity and two brain cells to rub together. But he'll be out of his depth with this, and I want it sorted quickly. I've already told them you're going back. I've told them to give you whatever you need. But get it dealt with."

Thanks, Nergui thought. The police always love being told what to do by politicians. Especially when it's the prodigal son returning from his cushy billet as the Justice Minister's favoured lackey. And for all their friendship and mutual respect, Doripalam was unlikely to be first in the welcoming committee. He was already fighting an uphill struggle to gain credibility with the longer-serving but much less able officers who were now reporting to him. The enforced return of Nergui at the first sign of difficulty was hardly likely to strengthen Doripalam's position in the team.

Nergui couldn't help feeling some irrational guilt. In his heart, he knew—and he suspected that Doripalam would also know—that this was exactly the development that he'd been quietly fantasising about throughout the whole of the last six mind-numbing months.

"Okay," he said at last. "If you say so, Minister. I'll do my best."

The Minister hung up. Nergui stared for a moment at the receiver, wondering why it was that the politician judged it appropriate to dispense with all the standard courtesies in his dealings with others. Then, hesitating only momentarily, he dialled Doripalam's number.

"It's okay," Doripalam said, before Nergui could launch into an explanation. "I've already been told. At least now I know why you were so keen to meet for coffee."

"Doripalam, that's not—"

"No, I know. I was joking. I'm not exactly overjoyed, but I don't imagine this is your fault. At least I hope not. We have to make the best of it."

"I'll try to make it as painless as possible," Nergui said. "Really."'

"Yes," Doripalam said. "I'm sure you will."

An hour later, Nergui stood silently with the young man, examining the desolate spot where the third body had been found. The body itself had been taken away for the post-mortem. Nergui had seen it briefly, but it had told him nothing except how disgusting a mutilated human body can look. Which was something he already knew too well.

They were on the edge of the city, the dark green mountains rising behind them. This was one of the areas where the population still lived largely in the traditional round nomadic tents, rather than in the endless rows of faceless apartments that had grown during the Communist era. The presence of the tents was commonplace, even in this urban environment, but Nergui, after his time in the West, found it jarring.

It was tradition, of course, a way of life uniquely appropriate to the climate and lifestyle of the country. But it was a strange way to live, he thought, as though the inhabitants were trying to deny the city's existence, desperate to be up and on the move instead. Or perhaps that was not so odd. In this land, it was the city, the presumption of permanence, that was the aberration. And there was no question that the tents were solid and comfortable enough with their wooden frames and brightly painted doors, the thick felt and canvas of the walls. With the central stove burning, a few glasses of vodka, and the shared body heat of a family, it was possible to repel even the harshest of Mongolian winters. And Nergui had to acknowledge that the clusterings of family groups, the *ails*, offered a sense of community that was different from anything he had ever known.

But the body had been found outside all of this, dumped in a scrubby knot of fir trees in a small ravine. It was a bleak spot, especially so late in the year when, even at midday, the low sun barely penetrated its shadows. There had been a stream running through here, but the dry autumn had left the ground parched and cracked. The trees and bushes were scattered with garbage, rusting tins and rotting cardboard discarded from the camp above.

Earlier that morning, an ageing guard dog, left prowling by the edge of the camp while its owner sat outside his tent boiling water for tea, had suddenly raced off into the ravine, barking endlessly. By the time the owner had caught up, the dog had been snarling at a bundle dumped in some bushes. Even without touching the object, the owner had had some premonition about its contents and had backed up the slope to track down the local police.

It was fortunate that he had not looked more closely. The state of the body was even worse than that of the first. The head and hands had been removed, the severed neck and wrists yawning bloodily, and there were similar large knife wounds to the chest, this time cut savagely down to the bone. There was little blood and the body had not yet begun to decay. The murder had clearly happened in some other location, and relatively recently. The pathologist had quickly concluded that death had been caused by the stab wounds, but that again the removal of the limbs had taken place after death. Given the cold weather, it was difficult as yet to pinpoint the time of death precisely, but the killing had probably taken place overnight or even earlier that morning, perhaps only some six or seven hours before. It was not clear how the body had been transported to this spot, although it would not have been difficult to get a van or truck close to the edge of the ravine.

The victim was dressed in a heavyweight burgundy *del*, the traditional garb of the herdsmen out on the steppes, a heavy robe wrapped around the body, tied with an ornate but faded belt, designed to combat the rigours of the Mongolian winter. Such clothing was still commonplace even in the city, particularly among the older residents.

"Can we identify the clothing?" Nergui asked. "This isn't one of those mass-produced Chinese suits."

Doripalam shrugged. "We might. But I'm not optimistic. The *del* and the boots are both years old, though they've worn well. The labels have been removed. That stuff could have been made or purchased anywhere in the country. Probably goes back to Soviet times."

"So what else do we have?"

"Not much. Another male, probably in his late forties, fairly short and stout, and definitely Mongolian. There are no other identifying features. No other possessions. In a word—nothing." Doripalam shook his head and then kicked at the hard ground in frustration. "Just another nameless corpse."

It was a cold clear morning, and the temperature had dropped from the brief Indian summer of the previous week. Winter was on the way, and the young man had a heavy black overcoat pulled tightly around him. He was a slight figure, constantly full of nervous energy. He took several steps out into the scrubby wasteland and then turned back, as though pacing a room. His dark hair, Nergui noted, was perhaps slightly too long.

"They weren't making any attempt to hide the body," Nergui said. It was a comment rather than a question.

"If they'd wanted to conceal it, they wouldn't have chosen this spot." He gestured up at the rows of *gers* visible above the ravine. "There are people down here all the time. People with their dogs. Children playing."

"Lucky it was a dog found it, then," Nergui said grimly.

Doripalam nodded. "But you have to say," he added, "that it's as if they wanted it to be found."

"That seems a potential link between the three killings," Nergui said. "The bodies were left in places where they were bound to be found quickly, even though in two cases the murders took place elsewhere. But the killer has gone to great lengths to make sure we can't easily identify the bodies. So why not hide the bodies as well?"

Doripalam shrugged. "I couldn't begin to imagine the thought processes of someone who does this."

Nergui had been peripherally involved in a couple of serial killer cases while liaising with his Russian counterparts, and he was well aware of the confused psychology that underpinned such acts. That, of course, was to assume that these murders were indeed the work of a psychopath. Taken in isolation, the apparent professionalism of the murders would have suggested something more cold-blooded, more calculated; a commercial transaction. But three professional hits in two weeks seemed unlikely.

"Do you seriously think they're linked?" asked Doripalam, reading Nergui's thoughts. He knew well enough why the Minister had requested Nergui's return. And, as Nergui had half-suspected, while Doripalam had been far from pleased at the implied judgement of his own abilities, he had to admit some private relief that if they really were facing a serial killer, it would be Nergui's handling of the case under scrutiny. "I mean, the second body as well?"

Nergui shrugged. "I don't know any more than you," he said. It was always worth saying that, even though Doripalam wouldn't believe him. The police always assumed that the Ministry was privy to information denied to ordinary officers. If only they realised how rarely that was the case, Nergui thought. "It's difficult to imagine that this one isn't linked to the first, but the second—who knows? But, given the timing, I guess there are enough similarities for us to at least bear it in mind until we've got some better ideas."

They trudged back up the steep slope to where the *gers* were clustered. After the gloomy shadows of the ravine, the bright morning sunshine created at least an illusion of warmth. A group of middle-aged women, mostly dressed in dark-coloured felt robes and heavy boots, were standing talking, watching the two policemen with apparent suspicion. Other women were sitting at the south-facing doors of their *gers,* washing clothes in plastic bowls or carefully chopping vegetables, peering at the two men from under their tightly bound headscarves.

There was a man, a heavyweight brown *del* pulled tightly around his body, a grey beret clamped firmly on his head, crouching by the engine of an old Russian IJ Planeta motorbike, carrying out some kind of work on the engine. He had a lit cigarette dangling from the corner of his mouth, apparently unconcerned about his proximity to the bike's fuel tank. A small group of children, dressed mostly in Western-style jeans and thick sweaters, were gathered round him, watching intently as if he were some form of street entertainment. There was a radio playing in the distance, a keening traditional tune probably playing on the state channel. In counterpoint to the plangent music, a dog barked shrilly and incessantly. From somewhere, there was the rich smell of roasting meat and the softer scent of wood smoke. It was difficult to imagine a psychopath stalking this community.

"You've made enquiries among this lot?" Nergui asked.

"We've started," Doripalam said. "Nobody saw or heard anything last night, so they say."

"Nothing?"

"So they say."

Nergui nodded. It was always the same. It had, apparently, been the same at the hotel. No one had seen or heard anything. "Still, we have to keep asking. We may get something eventually."

"You never know," Doripalam said.

Nergui shook his head. This was going nowhere. It was all just routine stuff, which Doripalam would handle as well as, if not better than, he could. Forensic examination of the victims' bodies. Attempts to gather any relevant data they could from the records. Links to any previous killings—though Nergui could think of no obvious ones. Routine questioning of possible witnesses. The usual grind of investigative work. But, unless they could begin to unravel the mystery of who the victims were, Nergui couldn't see them making any headway. It wasn't the kind of thing he would say to the Minister, but the best hope of their making further progress would be for the killer to strike again. Ideally, he added to himself as an afterthought, without actually succeeding.

As it turned out, Nergui's unexpressed wish was soon granted, though only in part. The killer struck again, and unexpectedly quickly. Unfortunately, he was all too successful.

The call came at around eleven the following morning. Nergui was in his new office in police HQ, reading and re-reading through the police reports on the previous killings. He had not thought it appropriate to turf Doripalam out of the office that had previously been his own, and had been quite happy to lodge himself in a small, unused room at the end of the corridor, with only a cheap desk and an empty filing cabinet for company. He hoped that this was at least sending the right message to Doripalam and the rest of the team.

Even before he picked up the phone, his instincts were telling him that this was not good news.

"Nergui? It's Doripalam."

"What is it?"

"There's been another one."

"Already? The Minister was right for once—this is getting to be a dangerous place to live. Where?"

"The Chinggis. In one of the bedrooms."

"You're joking."

"I don't hear you laughing."

Nergui was silent for a moment. The Chinggis Khaan was one of the city's newest hotels, built in response to the growing business and tourist trade in the city. Any incident there would have major repercussions, maybe even international repercussions. The Minister, it was safe to predict, would not be happy.

"Do we think it's linked to the others?" Nergui asked.

"It's difficult to say," Doripalam said, after a pause. "This one's different."

"Different how?" Nergui asked, already dreading the answer.

"I think you'd better come and see for yourself."

It took only minutes for Nergui to reach the hotel in an official car, sirens screaming. The Chinggis was a striking building, a successful attempt to bring Western-style service and luxury to the city. Some of the other hotels, including the Bayangol, had subsequently emulated its style, upgrading their previously basic facilities to something that might begin to meet Western expectations.

Nergui waved his ID pass at the reception and was directed across the expansive lobby to the lifts. He glanced around him at the dark mirrored walls, the thick-piled carpet, the clusters of Japanese and Western tourists waiting to start their morning's excursions. He'd been in the place a few times before for conferences and formal meetings, but hardly knew his way around. Nevertheless, it wasn't hard to find the room number that Doripalam had given him. There were officers dotted throughout the lobby and by the lifts, discreetly deflecting guests to ensure they didn't approach the crime scene accidentally. They nodded to him as he passed.

The bedroom also had an officer stationed outside. Nergui was glad they were doing this by the book, but hoped that the police presence didn't itself stir up concerns. Still, the hotel had more than its share of high-profile visitors from overseas. Probably the other guests would simply assume that some international celebrity was among them.

Doripalam waved him in. The room was impressive, Nergui thought, and compared favourably with those he had seen on his travels in Europe and the US. In other circumstances, he would have thought it luxurious, with its wooden panelling and plush king-size twin beds. As it was, his attention was entirely dominated by what lay on the nearest of those beds.

For all his experience, Nergui almost found himself gagging. The rich smell of blood was overwhelming, even though the scene-of-crime officers had thrown open the windows in an attempt to render the atmosphere of the room bearable. The two officers had stationed themselves, understandably enough, by the open window.

The white cotton sheets of the bed were thoroughly soaked with blood, and there were further splashes on the carpet and pale walls. The blood was beginning to turn from red to brown, but clearly the killing was relatively recent. The chambermaid had discovered the body when entering to clean the room in the mid-morning. Nergui thought that she could never have imagined how much her cleaning skills might be required, though he guessed she wouldn't willingly be back in this room for a long time.

The body was spread-eagled on the bed, dressed in blood-caked cotton striped pyjamas. Nergui would have described the body as lying face up, except that the face was definitely not looking upwards. The head had been severed from the body, but this time had not been removed from the scene. Instead it had been placed neatly on top of the television set, gazing impassively at its former owner on the bed.

Nergui opened his mouth but could think of nothing to say. Doripalam and the other officers stood silently, looking almost smug that for once there was a sight that had rendered the legendary Nergui speechless.

In fact, Nergui had been struck by two overwhelming thoughts almost simultaneously. The first had been sheer mindless horror at the enormity of the sight that lay before him. The second was the realisation that the mutilated figure before him was a Westerner.

What, he thought before he could stop himself, would the Minister have to say about this?

THREE

"I'm impressed," Drew said. "This is excellent. A lot better than most of the hotels I get to stay in."

Nergui gestured him to sit down. "I hope beer's okay. We still have good contacts with Eastern Europe, so can get some decent stuff." He lifted the glass and gazed thoughtfully at the contents. "Czech. They know how to make beer."

"Beer's perfect," Drew said, with complete sincerity. His early-morning departure from Manchester seemed a lifetime away, and the long and fragmented journey had only compounded his sense of disorientation. And now, in a country where half the population lived in tents, he was drinking beer in the kind of anonymous hotel bar that might be found in any capital city in the world. Soft piped music was playing in the background, a piano version of some pop tune that Drew half-recognised.

"Your room is okay?"

"Fine," Drew said. "Excellent."

Nergui nodded. "I should not say this, perhaps. But your room is very similar to the one where—well, where we found the body."

Drew nodded slowly, unsure how to respond. It was difficult to imagine the plush bedroom despoiled by the scene he had read about. He looked at Nergui, sitting magisterially in the corner of the hotel bar, and wondered how seriously he should take him. He was an impressive figure, heavy-set and tall by Mongolian standards, with a stillness and physical presence that somehow enabled him to dominate the room. His even features were distinctively Mongolian, wide-eyed and broad-cheeked, his clean-shaven skin dark and almost leathery, as though it had been burnished by the sun and wind of the desert. His dress was mildly eccentric—a plain, dark, good-quality suit contrasting with a shirt and tie both in what Drew supposed was salmon pink. But it would not be difficult, Drew thought, to imagine him, centuries before, riding out as a member of Genghis Khan's armies, leading the conquest of the known world.

Nergui's bright blue eyes watched Drew intently, his blank face giving no clue to his thoughts or feelings. Doripalam sat beside him, a slighter and paler figure, toying aimlessly with a menu from the table, apparently disengaged from the conversation.

"I'm sorry," Drew said. "Is it okay if we speak in English?"

Doripalam glanced up, smiling faintly, brushing his thick hair back from his forehead. He had the same wide-eyed features, but on this young face the effect was of openness and eagerness, perhaps even naivety. "We will teach you some Mongolian while you are here," he said. "My English is not so good as Nergui's but if you speak slowly I can follow."

"I can translate for Doripalam if we need to," Nergui said. "But he is too modest. His English is really very good. More and more of us are trying to learn, since it seems now to be the international language." He turned to Doripalam. "We should tell Drew what we know so far about our fourth victim."

"Well," Doripalam said, "as you know, his name was Ian Ransom. He was a geologist in the mining industry, with a contract with one of our mining consortia. He had been in the country before, on two occasions I think, working on contracts. We spoke to the company involved. They say he was an excellent employee—a specialist in his field, a hard worker, all of that. But we see no motive for the killing. He was not robbed—there was a wallet with currency and credit cards in his jacket in the wardrobe."

"What about the work he was engaged in?" Drew said. "Any possible motive there?"

Nergui shrugged. "Mining is a difficult industry here. Rapid growth. Lots of money to be made. New players coming into it all the time. Massive foreign investment, not all of it particularly legitimate. We're a mineral-rich country and everyone would like a slice of it. So, yes, it's possible. But we can see no real evidence in this case. Ransom was a specialist, a scientist. He wasn't senior enough to get involved in anything risky, I would have thought." He took a mouthful of his beer. "But we're keeping an open mind."

"There's not a lot I can add," Drew said. "We looked at Ransom's domestic circumstances, in case that shed any light. He was divorced, two children—two girls who live with his wife, who's remarried. He lived in Greater Manchester—decent house, decent area so presumably did all right financially. He seemed to have lived alone and, as far as we know, wasn't in any kind of relationship, maybe because he travelled so much. He had a doctorate in geology, and started his career after university with British Coal—that was our state mining industry, now largely closed down—"

"Ah. Your Mrs. Thatcher," Nergui said.

"Our Mrs. Thatcher," Drew agreed. "Ransom took early retirement from British Coal about fifteen years ago, and has worked as a consultant since then, largely overseas. Worked in India, Australia, South Africa, China and, of course, here. Seems to have been a bit of a loner."

"But nothing there that would provide a motive?" Nergui said.

"Not that we can see. I suppose when someone travels like that there's always the possibility that they might have got involved in something dodgy—"

"Dodgy?" Nergui asked. It was the first time he had shown any uncertainty in following Drew's English.

Drew laughed. "Dodgy. Um—dubious, criminal. That kind of thing."

"Ah," Nergui said. "I understand. Dodgy," he repeated slowly, as though committing the word to memory.

"So, yes, it's possible. But there's no evidence of it. He didn't seem to be living above his means, for example, so there's no sign of him having an income from another source."

Nergui nodded slowly. "So we both seem to have arrived at the same conclusion," he said. "It's quite possible that there's no significance at all in Mr. Ransom's unfortunate involvement in this."

"You mean he was just selected at random?"

"Well, of course that is possible. If we really are dealing with a psychopath here, then it may be that the killings are simply opportunist. Perhaps the killer just spotted Ransom in the street. He would have—how do you say it?—stood out in the crowd here."

"He certainly would," Drew said. It was an unnerving thought, given that his own Caucasian features would presumably draw the same attention. He looked around the bar. Four men, all Mongolians, dressed in Western-style business suits, had come in and were drinking beers at the far end of the room. One of them glanced over and smiled vaguely in Drew's direction. Drew looked down at his beer, feeling inexplicably vulnerable.

The restaurant maintained the standard of the rest of the hotel. The food was nothing special, but certainly comparable with that provided by most business hotels in Europe. The atmosphere was pleasant enough—dark wood, dim lights, attentive service, even a cocktail pianist meandering though a selection of familiar melodies. Nergui remained an entirely charming host, advising on the food, suggesting they stick with beer rather than moving on to the mediocre and highly priced wine list. "It's your choice," he said. "But the beer is better."

In other circumstances, Drew would have found the experience thoroughly enjoyable. Here, though, it was impossible to ignore the looming presence of the killer. Drew looked uneasily around the busy restaurant, with its chattering mix of locals and Westerners, and hoped that the presence was only metaphorical. He couldn't understand why he felt so rattled—after all, in his time he had strolled willingly, if not always comfortably, around some of the rougher parts of inner-city Manchester. It was odd to feel this level of discomfort in an upmarket hotel dining room.

Nergui carefully dissected his prawn starter. "I suppose that is the place we have to start—whether there is any significance in Ransom being the victim." He shook his head. "If he was simply chosen at random, then our difficulty is even greater."

Drew could see the problem. The worst possibility, from the police perspective, was that they were dealing with a psychopath with no rational motive but a high level of lethal professionalism. There would be no way of knowing where the killer might strike next, and the likelihood was that the killer would be adept at minimising any potential leads or evidence.

The only hope would be to wait until the killer made an error. And with the earlier victims still unidentified, at present the only possible lead lay with Ransom.

"You're not likely to identify the earlier victims?" Drew asked.

Nergui glanced at Doripalam, who shook his head. "Who knows? We have gathered the forensic information. Perhaps there are more sophisticated tools in the West, but I do not know that they would tell us much more. We know as much as we can about the bodies, but we have no identities to link them to."

"But you've had coverage in the media? Surely someone must know who these people are?"

Nergui smiled. "This is not like your country. A quarter of our population is nomadic. Of course, there are close family ties in many cases, and these days most people are formally registered with the state for voting and social security purposes. It's easier than it used to be. But with all the troubles we've had over the last decade, there has been a lot of movement. In both directions. Nomadic people coming to the cities seeking work. And unemployed city dwellers moving out to try their hands at herding or farming—usually without much success. Some of those have lost touch with their families or friends. Some have drifted into crime or more marginal ways of surviving." He finished the prawns and placed his knife and fork, with some precision, across the plate. "It is most likely that the victims here were not from our stable middle classes. They will probably be from our growing underclass—criminals or those on the edge of criminality. We are trying to match them up with our missing person records and we may hit lucky, but I'm not too optimistic. If someone was missing these people, we'd have heard from them by now."

It was a desolate but logical conclusion. "And you're sure the four deaths are related?"

"Again, who knows? It's reasonable to assume that the first

and third are related—the characteristics of the killings were identical. And the characteristics of the Ransom killing are sufficiently similar for us to assume a link. But the second killing was different—really, the only common factor was the timing and the anonymity of the victim. If you're asking whether we have only a single killer—well, I hope so. I don't like the idea of one murderer stalking the city, let alone two. But, yes, it's quite possible that the second killing was simply a coincidence, and we have to keep that in mind."

"There's no possibility that the later murders were copycat killings?"

"Copycat killings?" Nergui frowned, puzzled at the terminology. "That is one of your tabloid phrases, no?" He translated the phrase briefly for Doripalam's benefit.

Drew laughed. "I suppose so. I just meant, well, that a second killer might have copied the characteristics of the first killing. It's not unknown."

"No, I imagine not," Nergui said. "But it sounds unlikely in this case, unless we have two psychopaths on the loose."

"Or someone who wants you to think that the subsequent killings were random," Drew said. But even as he spoke he was aware that this was becoming fanciful, the terrain of crime fiction rather than real life. "No, forget it. It's nonsense."

Nergui shook his head. "No, we need to remain open to every possibility, no matter how unlikely. As your Sherlock Holmes so rightly says." He laughed. "Although I think this is verging on the impossible, in fact. We have not published the full details of the earlier killings—the decapitation and so on. No doubt rumours have leaked out, but no one could have the full details except from the police. Though, of course," he added, as an afterthought, "the police themselves do not always demonstrate the highest levels of integrity. Another legacy of our recent history, I'm afraid."

"What about some sort of gangland feud? Is that a possibility?"

"Of course. That may be the most likely explanation. Crime here has not tended to be that organised, but we cannot discount the influence of our friends across our two borders. Real organised crime is, sadly, becoming more prevalent. And it brings us back to Mr. Ransom. If this is the fallout from some sort of feud, how did an apparently unimportant geologist get caught up in it?"

"There've been no further murders or similar assaults since Ransom's death?" Drew asked.

"Nothing. We have four brutal killings in less than two weeks, and then nothing. I'm glad to say," Nergui added, in a tone that suggested this was perhaps only half true. Another killing or assault would be dreadful, of course, but might at least help to provide some further leads. "No, I'm glad there have been no more, but it makes me uneasy. I'm waiting for—" He paused.

"For the second shoe to drop?"

"A graphic expression. Yes, precisely that. A sense of something incomplete." He shook himself, and began to attack the mutton dish which had just been placed before him. "We should stop talking shop and find something more pleasant to discuss. You enjoy football? Manchester United?"

"Manchester City, I'm afraid," Drew said. "The bitter rivals."

"Ah, but not so successful, I believe?"

"You could say that. But we've had our moments. Do you play football here?"

Nergui nodded. "Yes, we play. It's becoming more and more popular. And rugby. People still like the traditional sports—horses, archery, wrestling. The three manly sports, as we call them. But every day we become more part of the global community."

"Do you want that?"

Nergui shrugged. "What I want is neither here nor there. Compared with the vast majority of people in this country, I am a global citizen. I've lived in Europe and the US. I've travelled regularly across Asia, the Middle East, Australia. I can see all the benefits of the changes that are taking place here. But I also see many losses."

"What kinds of things?"

"Well, the losses are obvious. We're losing our traditional ways of living, of thinking. We're losing traditional family ties. This country has been through many changes over the last century. Things are improving now, but these are still difficult times. We have the potential to be a wealthy, successful economy, but we live in poverty and we are surrounded by predators. Not just Russia and China, but the West, too."

"Predators?"

"Maybe I exaggerate. But I think not. I'm a patriot at heart, probably all the more so since I have travelled so widely. Most of my fellow countrymen take this country for granted. They have seen nothing else. They complain about the government. They complain about the police. They complain about the economy. All very understandable. They have been through difficult times. But I think they do not realise how much they could still lose." He laughed suddenly. "I am sorry. We start to talk about football, and immediately I plunge you into despair."

"You get used to that," Drew said, "supporting Manchester City."

Nergui laughed appreciatively. "I'm sorry," he said again. "I am being selfish. You must be tired and I just sit here rambling on about the state of our nation."

"It's very interesting," Drew said, honestly. He found himself wondering again about this man's role and rank, and also, for the first time, wondering about his background. Mongolia had been, in effect, a satellite of the USSR until the beginning of the

1990s. It was unlikely that Nergui had risen to a senior role in the police without being part of the previous regime, particularly since the Communist Party, with its new-found enthusiasm for democracy, had remained in power here for much of the past decade. Drew's understanding was that the police, in its current civilian form, was a product only of the mid-1990s, so it was likely that Nergui's career had been formed in the government militia.

"Well, we will have more time to discuss such things this week, no doubt. I am at your service as your host. But, equally, please tell me if you desire time to yourself. I know how oppressive such trips can be."

"Thank you," Drew said. "So what's on the agenda for tomorrow?"

"Well—" Nergui waited while coffees were placed before them. "You have your meeting with the ambassador at ten?" Drew nodded. "You saw the embassy as we passed—just a few minutes' walk away. There's probably not much point in your coming to police headquarters till after your meeting, so we can arrange a car to collect you from there once you're finished."

"I don't know how long the meeting's likely to take, I'm afraid. Probably just half an hour's courtesy chat, but you never know."

Nergui smiled. "The ambassador will assume you know things he doesn't. Which is no doubt true, but not about this case—he's been kept fully informed. He'll also want to make sure you know which side you're on."

"I'm not aware I'm on anybody's side," Drew said.

"We don't even know what the sides are," Nergui agreed. "But he will remind you, very discreetly, that the British Government is your paymaster, just in case there should be any—conflict of interest."

"Is there likely to be?"

Nergui shrugged. "Not from me. But we are involved in politics here. Politicians think differently from the rest of us. They perceive conflicts where we do not."

Drew nodded, not sure if he was really following this. He recalled Nergui's earlier words: "I'm a patriot at heart."

"You seem to know the ambassador well?" he said.

"I come across him from time to time. In the course of duty. He's a likeable enough person." Nergui left the comment hanging in the air, as if there were more he could say. "Well," he said, at last, "tomorrow, then—I'll give you my office and mobile numbers, and then you can call me when you've finished and I'll send a car over."

Drew found himself absurdly surprised that the country had mobile phone coverage. But, of course, in a remote country like this a mobile infrastructure made more sense than fixed lines.

"I think the best use we can make of tomorrow is for us to give you a short tour of the city, and show you where the four bodies were found. Doripalam can also talk you through the various crime reports and witness statements. They're not in English, of course, but we can give you the gist easily enough." Nergui paused. "There is nothing we can do, really, but press on and hope something turns up. And maybe we can throw a few stones into the pond and see what ripples we cause."

Drew wasn't entirely sure what he meant but nodded anyway. He noticed that Doripalam was watching the older man closely.

Nergui rose slowly to his feet. "But, as I say, you've had a long day. We will let you get some sleep. Give me a call as soon as you're free in the morning."

Drew watched Nergui and Doripalam walk slowly across the restaurant, Nergui pausing to speak briefly with the head waiter. Suddenly, sitting alone, Drew thought about Ian Ransom, who had presumably eaten alone in this very room the evening before he was killed. Drew would shortly have to make his way through the silent hotel corridors to a room identical to that where Ransom met his brutal death. The thought was far from comforting.

FOUR

It was stupid, he knew, and he'd spent the first three or four months trying to resist it. He knew what they thought, and told himself that he didn't care. After all, why should he have any respect for them? He recognised what they were, most of them, and given half a chance he'd have had them out of the place. But it was impossible; there were no alternatives. That, of course, was precisely why he had been given the job in the first place. Because, everywhere you looked, this place was desperately short of alternatives.

So he should have just ignored them. That was the advice that Nergui had given him, and it was the advice he would have given anyone else in the same position. But it was much easier to say than to do. He knew how much they despised him—almost, he supposed, as much as he despised them. He knew that they were watching, waiting for him to make his first slip. And he was determined not to give them the satisfaction.

So, against his better judgement, he found himself arriving

earlier and earlier each morning, getting in before any of the others arrived, making sure he was fully on top of everything. And of course Solongo, who had initially seen his promotion as finally proving him to be a husband potentially worthy of her social aspirations, now began to complain bitterly about the amount of time he was spending in the office. There was, he thought, no way of pleasing everyone, but at the moment he felt he was pleasing no one, least of all himself.

And now, on top of all that, Nergui's return had made everything ten times worse. He didn't entirely blame Nergui himself, though he knew full well that Nergui would have been unable to resist the prospect of returning to the scenes of his former glory. But that didn't help his own position. To the rest of the team, Nergui's arrival had simply confirmed their view that Doripalam had never been up to the job in the first place. Solongo had tried hard to conceal her disappointment when he had informed her, but he was clear that she too now assumed that his promotion was only a stopgap and that Nergui would be kept in the role until a more suitable candidate was found. She had never really believed that her husband was senior management material.

In the face of all that, he should have told them what to do with their job. Or at least he should have ceased putting in all the extra effort that had become the norm over the past few months. And yet here he was again, stumbling into the building at six-thirty in the morning, the day not even light, preparing for another day of minimal achievement.

As he made his way along the corridor, he was surprised to see that the lights were already on in one of the other offices. The night shift would have been on duty, of course, but they were unlikely to have ventured up to the management offices. Then he realised. Even now, it seemed, Nergui couldn't resist demonstrating that he was always one step ahead of everyone else. Knowing Nergui's domestic circumstances, though, Doripalam wasn't sure whether to feel irritated or pitying.

He tapped lightly on Nergui's door and poked his head around. "Good morning, Nergui. See you haven't changed your habits."

Nergui looked up from the mass of paperwork. "Usual story about old dogs and new tricks, I'm afraid."

Actually, Nergui was sorry that Doripalam had found him here so early in the morning. He had always had a reputation for working absurdly long hours, which others found intimidating and which he knew wasn't particularly justified. There was nothing wrong with intimidating people now and again, but Nergui didn't want Doripalam to think he was engaged in some egotistical game. There was enough tension between the two men already.

The truth was that Nergui needed little sleep. He had a suspicion that he could probably survive with virtually no sleep at all. But over the years he'd gradually settled for around four hours a night, generally between around one and five a.m.

This morning, he had thought it worth getting in early. Although he had been through the case papers countless times, he wanted to re-read them before they met Drew again later in the morning. Nergui had no illusions as to why Drew had been sent here. He knew it was a token gesture aimed largely towards the victim's family and the UK media. He also recognised that there was probably little that Drew could add to the investigation in the limited time he was here.

However, his years of working in this environment had taught Nergui that it was worth making best use of whatever resources were thrown in his direction. At the very least, Drew would bring another perspective to the case—and a fairly astute one, as far as Nergui could judge—which might complement his own experience and Doripalam's perspicacity. More importantly, Drew was an experienced investigating officer, of a kind all too rare in this country. Nergui wanted to extract whatever value he could from his brief presence.

Since arriving in the office at five-thirty, he had read painstakingly through the case documents, highlighting apparently important points, making detailed notes, producing short English translations of anything he felt might be of interest to Drew, and reviewing again the innumerable, largely unpleasant photographs.

Doripalam gestured to the mounds of papers and files in front of Nergui. "Surprised you managed to keep awake," he said. "Find anything new?"

"What do you think?" At least Nergui now felt that he was thoroughly up to speed with everything in the notes. Nevertheless, the overwhelming impression that he was left with was an absence of any serious leads, nothing they could pursue with any feeling of confidence. "Apart from the usual routine stuff, which you've clearly got well in hand, I can't see anywhere else to go."

Doripalam nodded. "Well, I'm disappointed to hear you say that, but I wouldn't have been pleased if you'd found something I'd missed."

"I'd have been astonished. I didn't see it in the notes, but I take it we've done DNA testing on the victims' clothes?"

Doripalam raised an eyebrow in mock reproach, though he accepted that Nergui was only checking that all avenues had been covered. "Official reports aren't back yet," he said, "but unofficially they've told me there's nothing. There is some extraneous matter on the clothes but nothing that's consistent between the victims or that matches any or our records."

Nergui nodded and sat back in his chair, looking vaguely around the office as though seeking inspiration. His temporary office here was smaller and more functional than his room in the Ministry, but only marginally so. He was not a man who sought comfort or domesticity in the workplace, or, for that matter, even in his home life, but just for a moment he was struck by the bleakness of the room—the cheap functional desk, the pale green Ministry-issue paint on the walls, an old metal filing cabinet, a two-year-old calendar on the wall. Suddenly he felt as if the state of this room simply demonstrated how thin their resources were, how pitifully ill-equipped they were to face whatever it was that lay out there.

Nergui did not underestimate his own capability, he knew he was ideally suited to the role to which he had, for the moment, returned. He hadn't always been successful. But where he had failed he was confident that few could have done more.

So normally, even in these circumstances, he would be approaching this job with relish and optimism, particularly after the deadening experience of recent months. He knew the pressures he was under; he knew that the Minister's job—and therefore his own—might depend on the outcome of this case. That didn't worry him. It was the price of entry to this level of the game.

But what did worry him, as he sat here looking at Doripalam's tired but still enthusiastic face, were the implications of this case for the city, maybe for the country. This was a fledgling nation in its current form, struggling to find an identity. It was still a primitive state in many ways—its people fearful after decades, even centuries of repression and hardship, where for generations life had been scraped daily from the bare earth, where nothing lay between man and heaven except a thin protection of wood and felt.

There was something about these killings that stirred a primordial unease in Nergui. It was not simply that the streets of the city might be stalked by a psychopath, killing randomly and brutally, Nergui could deal with that. Such a killer would eventually make an error, and might even choose to reveal himself. But what really disturbed Nergui about the killings was the sense of purpose. The sense of deliberate, planned savagery. The sense of some narrative, moving slowly towards its dark resolution.

He slammed shut the file in front of him. "Come on," he said. "Let's get some coffee. I think we both need it."

"I'm a United man myself, I'm afraid."

"Oh, well, we all have our crosses to bear." Drew wasn't surprised. Like all City fans, he believed that Manchester United had been invented for people who didn't really like football.

The ambassador laughed. "I thought it was you lot who bore the stigmata." Which, Drew noted, was exactly the kind of thing you would expect a United fan to say. Upper-class public school toffs who had never even visited Manchester, except maybe for a champagne dinner in the executive box at Old Trafford.

"Takes me back," the ambassador mused. "I was brought up in Wythenshawe, you know. Seems a long way away now."

I bet, thought Drew, who had grown up in the neighbouring but substantially more upmarket suburb of Hale. Wasn't that just typical? You couldn't even be confident in your prejudices these days.

"Coffee?"

And it was true that the ambassador did seem to have left Wythenshawe a long way behind, as they sat in apparently antique armchairs in this oak-panelled room, a silver tray of fine china set out on the low coffee table between them. Drew wondered vaguely where Mongolia sat on the hierarchy of ambassadorial assignments. He couldn't imagine it was one that they were all clamouring for at the Foreign and Commonwealth Office. On the other hand, it was an interesting enough place, and pretty stable compared with some of the options on offer. It was probably the kind of posting they gave to the bright young things on the rise, or to the loyal servants on the way to retirement. Judging from his white hair and tweed-jacketed manner, it was safe to assume that the ambassador fell into the latter category.

"Thank you." Not only was the china very fine, the coffee was also predictably excellent.

"Well, Chief Inspector, thank you very much for sparing the time to see me this morning."

As if I had a choice, Drew thought. "Not at all. I was very keen to seek your opinion in any case, so thank you for the invitation."

"I'll be happy to share whatever insights I can with you. I've been here for a few years now, and this region has always been one of my areas of interest. Wrote a dissertation on it at Oxford, as a matter of fact. It's an extraordinary place in many ways. One of the few substantial countries that's still relatively untouched by the forces of globalisation."

"That must be changing, I imagine?"

"It is, but still relatively slowly. It's very remote here. There are still comparatively few tourists. Not that many nationals have travelled outside the country. Your man Nergui is something of an exception there."

"He seems to have travelled remarkably widely," Drew said. He had the sense that the ambassador was keen to impart information, presumably in the hope of receiving some back.

"So I understand," the ambassador said, in a tone that implied a fairly comprehensive knowledge. "Lived in the States for a couple of years, and in the UK, and he seems to have spent time in Europe, Asia—well, you name it."

"Seems a little odd for a policeman," Drew commented.

"Even a senior one. No one's offered to send me on my travels. Except here, of course."

The ambassador laughed. "Well, yes, I think it is a little odd for a policeman, especially here where they generally seem keen to ensure that the police are as insular as they can make them. But there's more to Nergui than meets the eye."

It was clearly a prompt, but Drew decided just to take a slow sip of coffee and let the ambassador approach this on his own. He knew from endless hours of interviewing suspects that there was nothing more effective than prolonged silence for encouraging others to speak.

"He's an interesting man is Nergui," the ambassador said finally, "and I'm not sure I've got anywhere close to fathoming him. But there are certain things you should be aware of."

Drew raised an eyebrow and reached out to take a biscuit. There was no point in making this easy for the ambassador, or in giving him any sense that Drew owed him any information in return.

"The first thing you should know is that he doesn't work for the police. Not formally."

"He doesn't? But I thought he was in charge of the investigation here—"

The ambassador nodded. "Oh, he's certainly in charge of the investigation. He has his remit from the Minister of Justice himself."

"Then—"

"But Nergui himself now works for the State Security Administration. Another arm, as it were, of the Ministry of Justice and Internal Affairs."

"And the State Security Administration is what?" Drew asked, already having a good idea of the answer.

"Essentially counter-intelligence, as I understand it," the ambassador said. "As a department, it deals with anything that potentially comprises a threat to the state. Terrorism. Espionage. Sabotage. All that."

"Like MI5?"

"As you say."

"So Nergui's a spy?"

The ambassador shrugged. "Well, I'm not sure that that's necessarily the terminology they'd use. But, yes, Nergui is a senior officer in the intelligence service."

"What's his background?" Drew asked, wondering what he'd got himself into here.

The ambassador frowned. "Well, that's one of the odd things about our friend Nergui," he said. "No one seems to know too much about him. Or at least no one's telling us." Drew was momentarily amused by the conceit that, since no one had told the ambassador, it must follow that nobody else knew either. "He's a mysterious fellow. Something of a state hero, for reasons that aren't entirely clear. He rose through the ranks of the government in the days when it was essentially an oppressive arm of the Communist Party, but seems to have avoided getting too tainted by all that. Mind you, the rise of democracy and the fall of the Soviet Union haven't prevented the Party from retaining a large majority here over most of the past decade. We now have a reformed Communist Party promising to govern like New Labour."

Drew resisted the temptation to ask whether the ambassador thought this was a good thing. "So what's he doing dealing with this case?"

"Well, when the civilian police was formed in the 1990s, he moved from the old militia to become head of the new serious crimes team. Then some months ago he moved back into the Ministry in what appears to be an intelligence role. He seems to have an awful lot of authority across all parts of the Ministry, and across the government in general. He appears to be trusted to get on with things in the interests of the government and the state—assuming that those are congruent, which isn't always the case. The Minister in particular uses him as a kind of right-hand man to deal with problems as they arise."

"You make it sound slightly sinister," Drew said. "As if he were a Mafia hitman."

The ambassador smiled, faintly. "Do I? I'm sorry, that's not intentional. I don't think there's anything particularly sinister about Nergui's role, though of course we always have to bear in mind that he's an agent of the state."

"And therefore not to be trusted?"

"Well, no, I wouldn't say that. But, as the Gospels say, no man can be the servant of two masters. If there were a conflict of interest, it's clear where Nergui's duty would lie."

"Is there likely to be conflict of interest?" Drew asked, finding himself repeating his question from the previous evening. "In this case, I mean?"

"I shouldn't think so for a minute, Chief Inspector," the ambassador said. "I'm talking generalities here."

"Of course. So what kinds of cases does Nergui get involved in? From what you've said, it seems a little odd to find him caught up in a murder case, even one on this scale."

"Well, I think this is where you have to recognise that priorities here are probably different from those you're used to. As I understand it, Nergui's remit covers anything that's a potential threat to the state. In the UK that would mean things like terrorism, subversion and so on. Lesser crimes—if I can call them that—although serious would not be construed as a threat to the state, and so would be handled by the police."

"The police handle terrorists," Drew pointed out.

"In terms of arresting suspects and so on, yes, of course," the ambassador said. "But you would be working on the basis of information and guidance from Special Branch, MI5 and so on."

If only, Drew thought, but didn't bother to interrupt.

"But here, you see, in what is still an emerging country, any kind of large-scale or serious crime can be a threat to the state—fraud, corruption, industrial sabotage—"

"And murder?"

"Well, not usually, because most of the murders are pretty mundane affairs. But this is different. Just the sheer scale of it. They don't know what they're dealing with, and my guess is that the Minister has intervened personally, which is why Nergui's involved."

Drew sipped on his coffee, mulling this over. "Do you think they know something they're not sharing with us?"

"I was hoping you might be able to give me some insights into that one. Not immediately, of course—I realise you've just got here. But it would be helpful to know how your thinking develops."

I bet it would, Drew thought. At least now he knew why the ambassador was being so open with him.

"My guess, though," the ambassador went on, in the tone of one accustomed to having his guesswork taken seriously, "is that that's not the case. Of course, they're quite capable of not sharing information with us." He shook his head, as if overwhelmed by the enormity of such behaviour. "But I've got one or two sources of my own, and my impression is that they're as baffled as we are by this." He paused. "What's your take on the whole thing, anyway?"

"So far? Well, I've not yet been through the case notes in any detail—they sent me over some stuff but most of it would need translating, of course. I'm meeting with Nergui after this to go through it all with him. But, on the face of it, it seems an odd one. The most straightforward explanation is that we're simply dealing with a psychopath, someone who's just picking victims at random. A Brady or a Sutcliffe."

"But do . . . those kinds of people genuinely pick their victims at random?"

"I'm not a psychologist, but I think there's generally more of a common pattern than would seem to be the case here. Though of course we don't really know if there is any pattern given that the first three victims are still unidentified."

"And if it's not just a psychopath killing at random?"

"The odd thing, I think, is how professional the earlier killings seemed to be. The removal of the identifying marks, emptying of pockets. The removal of the limbs apparently done with some precision—not that we're looking for a skilled surgeon, but I understand it doesn't look like the work of someone in a hurry, panicking at the scene of the crime. It's strange behaviour for a psychopath, but then I guess that psychopathic behaviour is strange by definition. Equally, the scale of the killings would be odd if this were some sort of professional hit—unless we're looking at some sort of tit-for-tat feud."

"What, organised gangs battling for turf? That kind of thing?"

Drew smiled. "Well, it happens in Moss Side all the time. It must be a possibility. But it does raise the question of why so much trouble was taken to hide the victims' identities. If you're sending a message, you'd surely want to make it as unambiguous as possible. Although, of course, the identities may be crystal clear to those involved. But, as Nergui rightly pointed out to me last night, this does take us straight back to the question of Ransom's involvement. From what we know of him, he doesn't seem the type to get caught up in a Mafia turf war."

"Stranger things have happened, I suppose."

"Of course. But if we are talking about some kind of local internecine struggle, I can't imagine that the parties would be keen to draw the attention of the Western media. Why go to all that trouble concealing the earlier victims' identities, then brutally murder a Westerner in his bed in the best hotel in town?"

"Perhaps that was the unambiguous message you were talking about?"

For the first time, Drew looked closely at the ambassador. Behind the externally amiable old duffer, there was a very sharp and no doubt highly political brain. Maybe it was the ambassador who knew something about this that he wasn't sharing. "Why do you say that?"

The ambassador shrugged. "Just my Foreign Office training, Chief Inspector." He laughed, though without obvious mirth. "If someone kills one of your citizens, particularly in this kind of brutal way, your first assumption is that they're trying to tell you something."

"Like what?"

"I haven't a clue in this case. Our relationships with the government are generally good. There's no great resentment to the presence of Westerners among the general population. On the contrary, they tend to see us as a source of prosperity and stability—better the West than the Russians or Chinese. I'm sure there are those who think differently, but not many. No, ignore me, Chief Inspector, like you I'm just floundering around in the dark trying to find a narrative that fits this dreadful set of incidents. In my role, I naturally gravitate towards a political interpretation first, but I suspect that in this case the truth will turn out to be much more mundane."

Drew was left with the sense that he'd just been given some sort of coded message but lacked the insight to decipher it.

"Well, Chief Inspector, I suppose I've taken up enough of your time. But I'm sure you'll agree that we need to keep in contact. Will you join me for dinner later in the week? Nothing fancy, but a change from the hotel. Thursday?"

"Yes, of course." It didn't sound like the kind of invitation one could easily refuse.

"I'll get someone to pick you up from the hotel—around seven? You're off to the police HQ now? Do you need a car?"

"Nergui suggested I call and he'd send one of theirs."

"Ah, very good. And do let Nergui know that he will be welcome to join us." The ambassador rose and led Drew towards the door. "I think it's very important that we keep all the lines of communication open here, don't you?"

Drew nodded, but with a strong sense that most of the current communications were probably going over his head. There were times when he was grateful to be nothing more than a policeman.

The ambassador stopped in the doorway, his hand on Drew's arm. He paused for a moment, as though considering the most appropriate form of words, then said: "Stick close to Nergui, won't you? And watch your own back."

Well, Drew thought as he made his way slowly down the embassy stairs, that sounded like another unambiguous message.

FIVE

"One of our local heroes," Nergui said, striding quickly ahead. Drew was finding it hard to keep up with him. Doripalam strolled some way behind them, clearly accustomed to Nergui's ways and apparently unconcerned by any need to match his pace. "Hero of the revolution."

"Ah. Right." Drew looked round the expanse of Sukh Bataar Square, dominated by the equestrian statue of the epony-mous revolutionary hero. It was perhaps not one of the world's great squares, he thought, but impressive enough. Here, Soviet-style functionality was replaced by something approaching grandeur—the squat white Parliament House, the palatial gov-ernment buildings, the imposing bulk of the city Post Office. The square was expansive but busy with people, some standing talking in the morning sun, most striding purposefully to or from the nearby shops and the open-air Black Market. The ma-jority were dressed in Western clothes although the older ones were often clothed in traditional robes and sashes. A group of young people, dressed in baggy sweatshirts and jeans with familiar designer labels, were gathered at one end of the square, eating ice creams from cardboard cones, outfacing the chill of the late autumn morning.

At this time of day, the streets were busy but free-flowing, the traffic moving slowly without the freneticism of a European capital. There were noisy buses, UAZ trucks and some old stuttering Lada or IZH vehicles, but also some newer-looking Korean Daewoos, Hyundais and Kias. Now and again, Drew caught sight of shiny Western cars—a BMW or Mercedes—indicative of the rising wealth of at least one category of Mongolian citizen.

"And our real hero," Nergui said, still walking. He gestured towards a large hoarding depicting the squat image of Genghis Khan. "He'll be watching you everywhere you go."

Drew had already noticed this. The standard image was everywhere—in pictures in the hotel lobby, painted in large murals on the sides of buildings, inked in tiny faded posters pasted across concrete walls. Here in the city centre his ubiquitous image competed incongruously with the lingering emblems of communism and the familiar global logos, neon signs and advertising hoardings that, as capitalism had taken hold, had come to dominate the city skyline.

"I think he still has something of a negative public image in the West, no?" Nergui said over his shoulder. "But not here. And in part perhaps rightly so. He was a ruthless conqueror, but a remarkable man."

Drew was feeling too breathless to respond. He had already discovered that it was difficult to keep up with Nergui, both figuratively and literally. He had called Nergui on leaving the embassy that morning, and a car had been sent over with remarkable efficiency to take him to the police HQ.

He had found Nergui and Doripalam sitting in a small,

anonymous office, with a deskful of files and papers in front of them.

"Welcome," Nergui said. "Please, sit down. How was the ambassador?"

"Fine," Drew said, warily. He was still mulling over the implications of the ambassador's final words. "He sends you his regards. Oh, and we're invited to dinner on Thursday. He made a point of inviting you." Drew looked across at Doripalam with mild embarrassment. "Just Nergui, I'm afraid."

Doripalam made a mock grimace of disappointment, then laughed. "I will contain my disappointment," he said. "Although if you could arrange an invitation for my wife she might appreciate it."

Nergui smiled at him. "It is the British way, of course. There is no situation so bad that it cannot be remedied with a good dinner. But I am invited only because he hopes for some gossip from the Ministry."

"So long as it *is* a good dinner," Drew said. "I have my standards."

"The ambassador will not let you down," Nergui smiled. "Not with regard to dinner, anyway."

Nergui had carefully prepared all the files, and Drew was impressed by the Mongolian's detailed familiarity with all aspects of the case. The three men worked painstakingly through all the material, Nergui translating as necessary, highlighting any points which seemed significant or interesting. Despite their scrutiny, the process appeared to add little to their understanding of the case. Drew had expected this, he was far too experienced in such matters to imagine that some major lead would have been overlooked. Equally, though, he knew that this kind of repeated, exhaustive examination of the facts was the only practical way to proceed. Even if there were no new leads at this stage, there was always the possibility that some new development might provide some illumination to the mass of material in front of them.

"The other question," Drew mused as they finished working through the papers, "is where did the first and third murders actually take place?"

Nergui nodded. "It could be anywhere in the city. There are plenty of deserted or partially demolished buildings where you could commit an act like that. We've had a couple of officers investigating some places, but it's an impossible task. Unless someone stumbles on it accidentally, we're not likely to find it. And it could have been in the back of a van or truck, somewhere like that. Or some old slaughterhouse or yard that could easily be hosed down. Anywhere."

"So not likely to be much help there, then. I suppose the next thing for me would be to have a look at the sites where the bodies were found. I don't know what it's likely to tell me, but it would be helpful to get a sense of the places."

"Of course," Nergui said. "I could arrange a car, but it might be better for us to walk. We can try to give you a feel of the city."

If Drew had realised quite how quickly Nergui walked, he might not have taken him up on this suggestion. As it was, he found himself almost jogging behind him as they strode through the city streets, Doripalam ambling casually behind both of them. The city itself was initially unremarkable—a mix of blank-faced low-rise commercial buildings, concrete tower blocks, and the occasional striking new building. They passed stalls selling snacks and, around the square, tourist souvenirs such as the traditional brightly coloured *loovuuz* hats, apparently identical to that sported by Sukh Bataar's statue. Beyond, there was a large mural, formed in muted shades of brown, depicting stylised martial and equestrian images with, bizarrely, the words "Welcome to Mongolia" emblazoned in English across the top.

But the overall effect was typical of a former Soviet satellite making its painful way into the free-enterprise world of the twenty-first century. They passed through Sukh Bataar Square, and then walked down one of the side streets. Nergui moved quickly ahead, and then stopped suddenly, turning to face Drew. "There," he said, pointing.

Drew caught up with him and followed the direction of Nergui's finger. Another, smaller street led off from where they stood, dark between what appeared to be a residential tower block and an abandoned factory, its large windows long boarded up.

"That was where the first body was found," Nergui said, walking slowly into the dim side-street. He walked twenty or thirty yards, then stopped.

"Just here," he said. "You can still see some of the blood-stains."

Drew looked down. The street was paved at the junction with the main road, but within yards degenerated into hard-packed earth. But Drew could make out the darker stains on the ground in front of them. He looked up and around at the looming building on each side of the street and shivered inwardly. It was not pleasant, even for an experienced policeman, to think of the headless, handless corpse being found in this bleak spot.

"And nobody from there witnessed anything?" he said, gesturing at the tower block. Rows of blank windows stared down at them.

"It seems not," Doripalam said, arriving behind them. "We have had officers going door to door, of course, but so far nobody saw or heard anything. It may just be true. This street is not lit at night. The streetlighting only goes as far as there." Doripalam pointed to the larger road they had just left. "So if the body was dumped in the hours of darkness, there is no reason why anyone should necessarily have witnessed anything."

"What's this place?" Drew asked, nodding towards the commercial building on the other side.

"Nothing now," Doripalam said. "It used to be a clothing factory. A state-run place. Made suits—like this one." Doripalam gestured ironically at his own cheap-looking blue outfit, visible beneath his heavy overcoat. "Not exactly your Savile Row, but the best we can get. But when the government pulled out of this one, it closed. So now the place is empty."

"And no sign of any activity inside?"

Doripalam shook his head. "We searched the place, of course. But no sign that it has been disturbed for months."

There was nothing else to be seen here. Drew and Doripalam followed Nergui as he strode swiftly back through Sukh Bataar Square, past the edifice of the Post Office building and down Lenin Avenue. Nergui pointed to the square tower of the Bayangol Hotel. "The second body was found by the hotel there," he said. "We concluded that the victim had fallen from the roof."

Drew looked up as they approached the looming shadow of the hotel. The building itself was another example of undistinguished Soviet-style architecture, through the hotel had obviously been extensively renovated in recent years to cater to an international market. Nergui led him into the alley at the rear where the body had been found.

"You said he was killed at night?" Drew said. "So how did he get into the hotel?"

Nergui shrugged. "We're still trying to find out. There are various possibilities. It's possible that the killers actually took a room there, and somehow brought him in during the day. We've been following up with all the guests who were booked in that day, which is taking a long time—a lot of them are international visitors. But I'm not optimistic. More likely they just bribed someone to let them in. We've interviewed the staff, but nobody's saying anything. Hotel staff are used to being discreet."

"Even in a murder case?"

"Especially in a murder case, I think. They don't want to get involved. They may even have been threatened."

"It just seems incredible that someone could be drugged and then taken up to the roof and, well, thrown off, and nobody saw anything."

"Not that incredible, really," Doripalam said. "It was a Saturday night. There are few places to drink in the city, especially if you are an expatriate. There would have been a lot of drunken people in the hotel. Who notices one more person being half carried along the corridor?"

Drew nodded. "And the third body? You said that was found in one of the *ger* camps?"

"I'll get a car to take us out there," Nergui said. "It is a little way from here, at the edge of the city."

The car arrived in minutes in response to Nergui's call, and they were driven a mile or so from the city centre to the *ger* encampment in the suburbs. For the first time, Drew found himself in an environment that seemed genuinely alien. The centre of the city had been distinctive, but the pervading atmosphere and architecture were reminiscent of those in much of the former Soviet Union. For Drew, who had travelled only a little in Eastern Europe, the city had recalled nothing more than the anonymous settings of 1960s spy films.

This, though, was very different. The car pulled up at the point where the metalled road gave way to a rougher track, and the three men climbed out. Ahead of them were rows of the traditional *gers,* forming what appeared to be an exceptionally neat and well-cared-for shanty town. A few men, women and children were visible between the constructions, chatting together like neighbours in any suburb, all dressed in the herdsmen's costumes, the thick felt pulled tight against the chill of the morning. There were tethered horses, dogs, even a goat. Farther along, there was a chicken run, the scraggy birds scratching at the dusty ground. As they emerged from the car, Drew was struck by the richness of the atmosphere, the mix of smells—the scent of wood smoke, the musky aroma of goats and horses, somewhere the acrid stench of burning oil or petrol, all interlaced with the enticing smells of cooking.

The camp was an extraordinary sight. To Drew, it appeared different in kind from the type of encampment which one might find in a Third World country or amongst displaced or refugee peoples. These people were living in this way apparently through choice, maintaining a lifestyle balanced between their nomadic roots and the increasingly urban demands of the twenty-first century. There was a sense that, for all the concrete and glass monoliths of the city centre, this community could, if it wished, simply pack up and move on.

"It is very different from Manchester, no?" Nergui smiled.

"It's different from—well, anywhere I've ever been," Drew said.

"For most people here, this is simply the natural way to live. They may be compelled to work in the city for economic reasons, but they retain their links to the steppes, to the traditional ways of living. They prefer to live here rather than in a bleak tower block in the city."

"Probably a sane decision," Drew said.

"Definitely. But, having lived in the West, I'm not sure I quite understand this lifestyle any more." Nergui laughed. "I like having my creature comforts too much."

"Where was the body found?"

"There." Nergui pointed to the ravine that lay beyond the rows of *gers*. "Come." He led them along the track until they were standing on the edge of the ravine. A line of *gers* stood immediately behind them.

"There was no attempt to hide the body?" Drew asked, recalling with a shudder the graphic photographs he had viewed of the exposed and mutilated corpse.

"It seems not," Doripalam said. "We think they drove a truck or van over to that point," Doripalam gestured to the metalled road that ran along the far side of the ravine. "And then they just tipped the body over. It would probably have simply rolled till it hit those bushes."

"But why leave it here?"

"I think it is the same as the first body. They probably wanted to take it somewhere where it could be disposed of quickly and easily, but where it would be found. The road over there does not run close to the *gers,* so no one would take any notice of a truck passing in the night. They probably barely stopped. As it happened, the body was not visible from this side, as the bushes shielded it. Otherwise, it would have been spotted an hour or two earlier."

Nergui began to lead them back past the *gers* to the waiting car. Although the summer was over now, the sky was clear and the day was growing warmer. Nergui had told him that the autumn weather could be changeable. There had been a few flurries of snow earlier in the week, the first signs of the approaching winter. They passed an old woman, wrapped in the now-familiar dark robes and sash, carrying a bucket of water. She smiled and nodded a greeting.

Drew had opened his mouth to make some comment about the *gers,* but at the same moment Nergui uttered an incomprehensible cry and flung himself backwards toward Drew. Drew stumbled, taken aback, and lost his footing, finding himself rolling on to the hard earth. Nergui flung himself across Drew, and then Drew felt the other man pulling hard on his jacket.

"What are you—?"

"This way!" Nergui said sharply, tugging harder. Drew rolled over, and ended up lying beside Nergui, who was rapidly shuffling back behind one of the *gers*. "Come!" he snapped, gesturing urgently at Drew. Drew crawled after him until they were both shaded by the tent. Doripalam had dropped to his knees at Nergui's shouted warning, and was now scrambling around beside them. Behind them, chickens clucked loudly, alarmed by the disturbance.

"What is it?" he said.

Nergui was breathing heavily. "There," he said, gesturing up at the front of the *ger*. "But keep your head down."

Drew peered tentatively around at the front of the *ger*. There, embedded neatly in the thick felt, was a crossbow bolt still vibrating from the force of impact.

It seemed ridiculous. More a scene from an old Hollywood Western than any kind of real threat. At the same time, Drew recognised rationally that the arrow was a lethal weapon. If there was someone out there shooting at them, their lives were in danger, as surely as if they were facing a sniper with a rifle.

"Where did it come from?" he whispered.

Nergui pointed to an apparently disused factory building that lay across a patch of empty ground. "Up there, I think. Somewhere on the first floor."

"Do you think they're still there?"

"I don't know. My guess is not. Too risky, even if they'd hit one of us. I think they'd have taken one shot then made a run for it."

"What if you're wrong?"

"I'm not planning to bet my life on it." Nergui carefully pulled his mobile out of his pocket, and dialled the number of the police officer driving the car. "He can get the car along this dirt track," Nergui said. He spoke briefly to the officer in Mongolian, and a moment later the car came bumping along the track towards them. As it stopped, Nergui pulled open the rear door, and he and Drew bundled inside. Doripalam clambered into the front passenger seat. The driver rapidly reversed towards the main road, and then pulled out in the direction of the factory.

Drew realised he was shaking. "Thanks," he said. "I thought you'd gone mad. How did you manage to see the bolt?"

"I don't know. Instinct, I think. I saw a movement in the air out of the corner of my eye, and somehow registered that it was something more dangerous than a bird. I wasn't sure where it was headed, but I threw myself back without really thinking." He laughed, humourlessly. "Mind you, if my instinct had been wrong, I might have thrown you into its path, so you shouldn't be too profuse with your thanks."

"Or worse still, you'd have messed up my suit for nothing," Drew smiled. Both of them were playing this down, but he suspected that Nergui's instincts were more finely honed than he was letting on.

"There is nothing worse that one could do to an Englishman," Nergui agreed.

The car pulled to a halt in front of the factory building. The ground-floor windows were boarded up, and there was no sign of life. Above, the windows had been left uncovered and most of the glass had been smashed. Presumably it was from one of those that the arrow had been fired. They pulled the car up close to the doors to minimise the risk of being shot at from above.

"What are you planning to do?" Drew asked, peering through the car window at the concrete building. "We can't risk going in there on our own."

Nergui shook his head. "Certainly not. It's bad enough that your life has been placed in danger once. The ambassador would never forgive me if I allowed it to happen a second time." Nergui remained blank-faced, and it took Drew a moment to realise that the Mongolian was joking. "I've sent for back-up," he said. "They will be here in a few minutes. We're risking allowing whoever it is to escape—I don't know if there's a rear entrance to this place, but I've asked for a car to go to the back. But we don't know what we might be facing here. If this is just some joker taking a pot shot at the police, then he'll be long gone anyway. But if it's our killer, and he's still in there, then we don't know what he might want."

The moments ticked by. This wasn't the first time that Drew had faced the prospect of entering a building with a potentially dangerous suspect inside, but here he felt absurdly vulnerable, because he had no idea what to expect, what the norms were. He had never, even in his most paranoiac policing moments, expected to have an arrow shot at him. And he had never faced a killer capable of mutilating his victims' bodies.

"What's your guess?" he asked to break the silence. "Do you think it's our killer?"

Nergui looked back from the window. "My guess is not. My guess is some joker."

"But why shoot at us?"

"You will be surprised to learn," Doripalam interjected, "that the police are not always popular here. I know that this is difficult for a British policeman to understand."

Drew regarded the young man's blank expression. "And you share our sense of irony, too," he said. "But how would he know you were from the police?"

"Probably recognised the car," Doripalam said. "Cars like this usually mean either police or politicians. A good target in either case. If it is just some idiot, he probably didn't mean to kill us anyway. Perhaps just to give us a fright."

"He achieved that objective, anyway. Speaking for myself, you understand."

"It was a good shot. He knew what he was doing. But we have many skilled archers in this country."

"You need to get yourselves some cowboys."

"Some would say," Doripalam said, "that the police are precisely that."

Behind them, two more official cars drew up. Nergui signalled for their occupants to remain in their cars for the moment, then he and Doripalam carefully opened their own doors. Nergui pressed himself against the concrete wall, edging back towards the other cars, protected by the building from any attempted assault from above, Doripalam following closely behind. Drew started to follow, but Nergui gestured him back. "As I say, the ambassador would not forgive me."

Nergui motioned to the other police officers to join them. The other cars had also been parked by the walls, and four officers climbed from each, pressing themselves against the walls by Nergui and Doripalam. Drew heard the sound of other cars, presumably lining up against the rear of the building.

There was an external entrance to the building a few yards further along the wall, fastened with a chain and a large rusty padlock. Gradually, the group of officers edged towards it. Nergui peered for a moment at the door fastening, and then spoke quietly to Doripalam behind him, who inched slowly back to one of the cars and returned, moments later, with a crowbar.

It looked as if the wood was rotten. Doripalam inserted the crowbar between the door and the frame, and pressed his weight against it. The door burst open with a splintering of wood, and the chain and padlock fell uselessly to the ground. He peered cautiously round the frame, pulling a flashlight from his pocket. He shouted something loudly in Mongolian, and then shone the torch inside, flashing it around the empty factory space beyond, clearly ready to pull back immediately if there was any response.

Drew realised he had been holding his breath, and let it out steadily. Everything seemed to be quiet. Nergui signalled to the men behind him, and he slowly followed Doripalam into the darkness.

Drew shook his head. It wasn't possible for him to sit here quietly in this car while Nergui and his team were potentially risking their lives. He opened the door of the car, and slipped out to join the police officers still waiting to enter the building. The officer at the rear turned and looked at him in surprise, but then gave a grin of welcome. Drew pulled out the pocket flashlight he always carried and held it as if it were a weapon.

Nergui called out something from inside. Drew had no idea what had been shouted, but it didn't sound troubled. It was presumably an instruction to the rest of the team, because they all began to move slowly into the dark building.

Drew followed last. Stepping to one side so that he wouldn't stand out as a target in the doorway, he paused for his eyes to grow accustomed to the gloom.

Inside, the building was largely a hollow shell, an enormous space which had at one stage housed manufacturing machinery, but which now echoed emptily. He could see the shadows of the other officers positioning themselves around the walls. Above them, there was some form of walkway running around the walls at the upper floor level—perhaps once intended for machine maintenance. Some pale light came in through the broken upper windows, but there was little to be seen.

Nergui and Doripalam stood poised at the far end, standing in front of a large double door, which presumably led into a storage room. There was a thin line of light coming from around the doors, indicating that there was illumination in the room beyond. It was difficult to be sure from where Drew was standing, but it looked brighter than daylight alone.

Doripalam signalled to two of the men to explore the walkways, reached by stairs in the corner of the factory space, although it seemed that the upper area was unoccupied. As far as

Drew could see, there was nowhere else for anyone to hide, other than in whatever space lay behind the double doors.

The remaining men gathered at each side of the doors. Drew followed the officers across the oil-stained concrete floor, and stood beside them. Nergui reached out and tried the handle of the left-hand door. It opened easily and a pale strip of light shone out across the concrete. Nergui raised his hand to Doripalam and another officer, who brought forward two handguns, handing one to Doripalam. Drew had not realised that the police were armed, but it was scarcely a surprise. He was slightly more surprised to see that Nergui himself was also holding a firearm.

Nergui motioned to the two armed officers to stand facing the door, so that between them they would be covering the whole area behind the door. Then shouting some kind of warning—probably the Mongolian equivalent of "Armed police," Drew thought—he kicked back the door. A bright light flooded out into the factory space, momentarily blinding Drew.

There was silence. Then Nergui said something and walked cautiously into the room. Doripalam slowly lowered his weapon, staring into the brightly lit space, a blank expression on his face. At first neither he nor the other armed officer made any move forward. Then they slowly turned to look at each other, and followed Nergui.

Another officer started to follow them, but a shouted instruction from Nergui caused him to stop. The rest of the team looked at each other in bafflement, but no one moved.

Ignoring the command—after all, he told himself, he was not part of Nergui's team—Drew stepped out from behind the police officers, and moved round until he was directly facing the doorway. Then he walked forward cautiously.

Nergui was standing in the middle of the room, staring fixedly at the object spread out before him. Doripalam and the other armed officer stood to one side, both gazing at the ground. There was a bright spotlight shining across the whole area, illuminating the ghastly scene. Drew wondered irrelevantly what the power source of the light was.

The object of Nergui's gaze was a decapitated body, propped against the wall in the full glare of the spotlight, like a grotesque museum exhibit. Fixed between its two hands, as if mimicking some parody of a ghost, was the victim's own head.

Drew stood for a moment, transfixed. To his side, some of the other officers had begun to cluster round the door, their curiosity finally getting the better of them. One of them, one of the younger ones, moved forward to look at the scene, and then backed away, a look of shock on his face, his hand over his mouth. He turned and moved rapidly towards the entrance, retching as he ran. Others began to move back similarly, as if the bright room were somehow contaminated.

Nergui looked up, and saw Drew. He nodded and beckoned Drew forward. Drew approached the room, uneasily but with less disgust than was evident amongst the police team. Although he had never seen anything quite like this, he had seen enough in his time to be able to cope.

"You do not need to come in," Nergui said.

"It's okay," Drew said. "I've seen—well, I can't say I've seen worse, but I've seen plenty."

Nergui nodded. "We both have. But, like you, I have never faced anything remotely approaching this."

Drew looked back at the officers outside, most of whom had now withdrawn from the room. "It must be a shock to your men."

Nergui allowed himself a pale smile. "You have no idea how much of a shock."

Drew looked around at the two armed men, then back at Nergui. There was clearly something else here, something he wasn't getting.

It was Doripalam who turned to Drew, a look of horror etched in his young face, his handgun hanging limply at his side. "You see," he said, "this is not just a brutal murder. Not just one of the most brutal murders I have ever seen. It is much more than that. We all know this man. He is a police officer. A senior officer." He paused, as though struggling for breath. "This is the brutal murder of one of our colleagues. And all set up here like some insane circus sideshow."

And the most terrifying thing, Drew thought, is that we appear to have come here as the invited audience.

SIX

"This is really very good." A long pause, broken only by the sound of their eating. "I'm sorry—I didn't mean to sound so surprised."

Nergui laughed. "No, it is understandable. My country is not known for the quality of its cuisine. We are a nation of warriors, not chefs."

"And, for that matter, senior police officers are not usually known for their culinary skills. I speak entirely personally you understand. But no, really, this is excellent."

"Well, thank you," Nergui said. "I will assume that your comments are more than mere British politeness. I enjoy cooking. It's something of a hobby of mine, but I rarely get the chance to try it out on others."

Drew looked round Nergui's apartment, wondering what clues could be gained to the character of the man opposite him. A few, no doubt, although he had the impression that Nergui was not a man who would expend much energy expressing his character through home décor.

Still, the apartment was comfortable enough, and surprisingly spacious. The narrow hallway led to a small but well-appointed kitchen, two closed rooms which were presumably bedrooms, and the large living and dining area where they were sitting. To Drew's inexpert eye, the furniture looked moderately expensive, and he wondered vaguely whether these heavy dark wood tables and plush crimson seats were manufactured locally or had to be imported from Russia, China or even further afield.

He had initially been surprised when Nergui had invited him over for dinner, as they were finally driving away from the factory after their gruesome discovery. The scene-of-crime and forensic teams were still working away, but the body had now been taken away for examination, and Nergui felt that there was little to be added by their presence.

"I thought," Nergui said, as they drove away, "you and Doripalam might perhaps join me for dinner at my home tonight? I would be honoured."

"Well, that's very kind of you." Drew glanced back at the dark silhouette of the factory. "But—well, are you sure? I mean, you mustn't feel obliged to be my host. I realise this has been a shock."

"A shock, professionally, yes," Nergui said. "We have never experienced anything like this before. Of course, we have had policemen killed in the line of duty. But nothing like this." Before Drew could respond he went on: "It is not that the victim was a personal friend, you understand. I knew him, had met him in passing a few times." Nergui laughed, with an edge of bitterness. "The last time, I think, I was reprimanding him a little because he had failed to sort out some papers I needed for a case I was working on. But I understand he was a good officer. And he was, I imagine, a friend to some of those who were with us today." He paused. "That is what is so horrific—that whoever did this tried to ensure that we would enter that place in force. He wanted to ensure that this body was found, not just by any passer-by, but by those who knew him best."

Drew shuddered. Nergui was right. It was a horrific thought, suggesting an extraordinary cold-bloodedness to the murder. It also raised the questions of what had motivated the murderer to behave in this way, and—even more chillingly—where this motivation might lead him next. "But why?" he asked. "Why would anyone behave like that?"

"Who knows? We appear to be dealing with some kind of madman, though I can't begin to conceive what kind. But we still don't know whether the victims, including this one, were selected randomly or deliberately targeted. Even in this last case, I suppose it is possible that the victim was selected randomly, but then the killer chose to expose the body in the cruellest and most spectacular way he could."

"But equally it may not be a coincidence that the victim was a police officer?"

"As you say. In which case, perhaps the previous victims were also not selected randomly."

It was like gazing into a pool of clouded water, Drew thought. Occasionally some object swam into view, and you began to feel that you could recognise the shape of it. But then the water clouded again, and there was nothing but greyness and uncertainty.

There was no doubt that even Nergui, calm professional though he appeared, had been shaken by the day's events. Nevertheless, he remained insistent that Drew should join him for dinner. "It is my duty as your host," he said. "But, more importantly, I would welcome the opportunity to spend the evening with someone. It is not a day to be alone, I think."

Drew was often grateful his domestic circumstances meant there was always someone to come home to. Sometimes he would share his experiences, but more often he would simply try to put them behind him. It made his working existence more bearable.

Ten years on from his marriage, he couldn't really envisage life any other way, and he wondered what it must be like for Nergui, coming home every day to this comfortable but sterile apartment. He also wondered why it was that having faced a trauma like today's, he could call on nobody other than his deputy and a total stranger.

As it turned out, Doripalam chose to excuse himself from the dinner invitation. Drew could not work out whether this was a tactful judgement on Doripalam's part or, more likely, it was simply that Doripalam had access to those domestic comforts which were so notably absent in Nergui's existence.

Still, Nergui was an excellent host. He had arranged an official car to bring Drew over to his apartment, and greeted him warmly at the door. He was dressed in what, to Drew's eyes, appeared to be a leisure version of the herdsman's robes, a brightly coloured flowing gown wrapped with a gold sash, his feet enclosed in finely embroidered leather slippers. Drew wondered if this was the typical dress of the average Mongolian at home, or perhaps simply a more overt expression of the dandyism which, in his professional life, Nergui appeared to confine largely to his choice of ties.

As he entered the apartment, Drew had been surprised to find that Nergui was cooking the meal himself. He had hardly struck Drew as the domesticated type, so it was incongruous to see him standing before a cooker, stirring and tasting the contents of the array of pans.

"There. It is fine. It is all under control," Nergui said, leading him into the lounge area. "Fifteen, twenty minutes, it should all be ready."

Nergui offered him a beer, and also produced two bottles of red wine for the meal. "It's not bad," he said, apologetically. "Bulgarian. It's difficult to get any better out here."

Nergui was a relaxed host, and Drew felt no discomfort even though they initially sat in an amiable silence. It was clear that Nergui had much on his mind, and he said little until he had served the first course—a spicy soup containing chicken and prawns. Drew expressed his compliments on the quality of the food.

"I'm afraid it is far from authentic local cuisine," Nergui said. "But then you should probably be thankful that it is not authentic local cuisine."

"I wish I could produce food like this."

"You don't cook at home?"

Drew shook his head. "Not really. I mean, basic stuff but nothing like this. My wife's the chef."

Nergui nodded. "You have children?"

"Two," Drew said. "Boys. Eight and ten."

"That must be exhausting."

"It can be. Especially for my wife, when I'm working long hours, which seems to be most of the time. So she tells me, at least."

Nergui smiled. "Does she work also?"

"She's a teacher. Primary school. Young children."

"Hard work, then. I imagine you don't have an easy time, if you are both working in these kinds of jobs?"

Drew thought about it. The question might have felt intrusive coming from someone else, but Nergui just seemed genuinely interested.

"It can be," Drew said. "We both end up working long hours at times. Sue has preparation to do. And I think the work is very tiring for her. But we seem to get through all right, most of the time."

"That is good," Nergui said, sincerely. "I enjoy living alone, but there are times when I envy people like you."

"Well, likewise," Drew laughed. "Sometimes a bit of solitude would be welcome."

"I'm sure," Nergui nodded. "I've never really known anything else."

"You've never—?" Drew stopped, embarrassed, unsure how he had been intending to finish the sentence. Been married? Been in a relationship? Anything sounded crass.

But Nergui seemed untroubled. "I was married once," he said. "Briefly. A long time ago."

"Oh. I'm sorry."

"Don't be. As I say, a long time ago. It was the reason I first went to the West."

"Really?"

"A long story. I met a young woman—a journalist from the US. This was what, fifteen years ago? I was working for the government here. My task was to show her around, look after her."

Something about the way Nergui spoke the last words made Drew look up. Again, it occurred to him to wonder about Nergui's background. What had been his role in the government, in the days when this country was still a satellite of the Soviet Union? And how precisely had Nergui been charged to "look after" the journalist? For that matter, had he similarly been charged to "look after" Drew? It seemed unlikely—Nergui was clearly the officer in charge of the murder case—but it also appeared that Nergui's current relationship with the police force was not necessarily straightforward.

"Anyway, you can no doubt guess how things turned out. We had a relationship. When she finished her assignment here, she left for the US and I decided to try to follow her. I didn't think it would be possible. Foreign travel was highly restricted in those days, and travelling to the US was almost unheard of. If I had been refused permission, I don't know how things would have turned out, whether I would have tried to leave somehow illegally. Probably not. I'm a very law-abiding individual, as befits my current role."

"But you were allowed to go?" Drew said, with some incredulity.

"I was very fortunate," Nergui said. "Things were just beginning to change here and in the USSR. This was the days of Gorbachev. There was a lot of optimism in the air, but also a lot of anxiety. We were already encountering pressures from commercial forces looking to exploit the resources we have in this country."

Drew wasn't entirely sure where this was leading. "You mean minerals?"

"We are a potentially wealthy country. There were already people visiting our country who we suspected were engaged in—well, industrial espionage, I suppose. The interest was in discovering what resources we had, and how capable we were of exploiting them ourselves."

"You're talking about commercial companies—multinationals?"

"Some of them. There was also support from various governments, of course—the US, China—preparing to get their fingers in the pie. The USSR as well, I think, saw the writing on the wall for its own future, and so was looking at commercial alliances as a means of protecting its own position here."

"So how did this affect your being able to leave the country?"

Nergui laughed. "Very simply, as it turned out. I had been involved in some work here in the field of—well, I imagine you would call it industrial development. It was primitive stuff, looking back, but we were concerned that, when we finally opened our borders properly, we should not be exploited by our more powerful and experienced competitors. When I decided I wanted to leave, I proposed the idea that I should go to study business studies at Harvard. I would be able to learn what our Western rivals did and bring the knowledge back."

"And the government allowed you to do that?"

Nergui looked momentarily embarrassed. "Ah, well, I do not like to—what do you say?—blow my own trumpet, but I had been a rather successful student during my time at university here. In academic terms, an outstanding student, I suppose. I was supposedly destined for great things in our government service, so it did not seem that outrageous an idea when I proposed it. A few years earlier it would have been impossible, of course, so I was very fortunate."

"So you went to Harvard?"

"I did the MBA, yes. My friend—my girlfriend, I suppose she was by then—was based in Washington. But, from here, I thought that would be close enough. It wasn't, of course."

"I'm sorry," Drew said.

"These things happen. Our marriage was an attempt to keep it alive, but I think we both knew it was going nowhere." He shrugged. "It's not the first time it's happened. It won't be the last. And it was probably all for the best. All of it, I mean. If it hadn't happened, well, I would have spent my whole life here. Which wouldn't have been a bad thing in itself, but I'm glad I've got a sense of what the world is like out there. It's a privilege shared by few of my fellow countrymen."

"I suppose not," Drew said. Various intertwined thoughts were drifting through his mind. He was trying to make sense of Nergui's story, which sounded just a little too neat, a little too pat in its narrative arc from love, through pursuit and parting, to self-consolation. Maybe it was just that Nergui had smoothed out the details and airbrushed out the pain and uncertainty that must surely have accompanied this story. Or perhaps the story itself was simply fiction, a cover to explain Nergui's visits to the States and the UK. Would it really have been possible to make such trips from here, even in the heady days of perestroika?

Which led inevitably to the second question. Just why was

Nergui telling him all this? They had just met, scarcely knew one another, had nothing in common other than their interest in five brutal murders. It wasn't even clear that their interests in the murders coincided. So why would Nergui unburden himself of all this personal material? Was it simply that he really did have no other friends he could share this stuff with? Was it just that he was taking his first opportunity in years to talk about himself with someone who could do nothing with the information?

It didn't seem likely. Nergui didn't strike Drew as someone fraught with unspoken sorrows. He had told his story in straightforwardly factual terms, no sense of welling emotion. It was as if he had merely thought that Drew might be interested. Just making conversation.

And then, of course, lurking behind all that was the ambassador's parting comment. Stick close to Nergui, but watch your back. What the hell had that meant? For a moment, Drew felt very tired and very far from home. He was a simple man—intelligent enough, certainly for his current job, but with no real interest in or aptitude for politics, large or small. He disliked game-playing, and it seemed like some games were being played here, even though it was far from clear who was involved. Drew very much wanted to trust Nergui, particularly in facing down the horrors they had encountered that afternoon, and his instincts told him that Nergui was trustworthy. But he knew that, so far from everything familiar, it would be madness simply to trust his instincts.

"So how did you end up in the UK?" Drew said, conscious that the silence had been prolonged.

"I finished the MBA, and then—well, I thought I'd carry on. I spoke with the authorities here, and it was generally agreed that I should get the most out of it while I was in the West. I ended up taking a doctorate in business administration at your

London Business School. It was hard work because I knew that I would not be able to stay more than a year."

"You completed a doctorate in a year?" Drew said. Maybe the story was fiction after all.

Nergui nodded. "As I say, it was hard. I'd already begun some of the research at Harvard, so I was able to build on that."

"Even so," Drew said, "that's impressive."

"Well, I don't know. I've always had an aptitude for academic work, research. It comes fairly naturally to me. These are skills I can still use in my work. You also, I imagine?"

Drew laughed. "Not to the same standard, I'm afraid. I have a university degree but nothing special."

"As I say, it's just a gift—a small one, but sometimes useful."

If Nergui was making this up, he was doing so very convincingly. There was no sense of arrogance or boasting about his achievements. If anything, he seemed mildly embarrassed, with something of the air of a golfer who has just hit a hole in one but doesn't know quite how he did it. And, if it was true, there was no doubting Nergui's intelligence at least.

"What did you do when you came back here?" Drew asked. "How did you end up in—your current role?" He realised, almost too late, that he didn't actually officially know what Nergui's role was.

"Another long story. But basically I came back as—well, what you would call an intelligence officer, I suppose. I was well-regarded, as you can imagine, especially with my newly gained experience and qualifications. By this time, we were beginning to approach something closer to what you Westerners would consider normality. People were actually being allowed to visit countries outside the Eastern Bloc. We had tourists coming here for the first time. Foreign investment began to enter the country. We even started to build some sort of relationship with China. So it was an ideal time for someone with my background."

While he was talking, Nergui cleared the dishes into the kitchen. He returned, a few moments later, carrying steaming plates. "Mutton," he explained. "I hope you like it."

Drew did like it, though he would have been hard pressed to describe the tastes. It was a spicy stew, which Drew would have characterised as Middle Eastern without really having much idea what it comprised. "Very good," he said, truthfully. "You were telling me about your career," he prompted.

"Well, it's not that interesting," Nergui said. "I progressed fairly rapidly up the ranks here, mainly just because I was in the right place at the right time. I was attached to the militia, but mostly working on intelligence projects alongside our Foreign Ministry, in the industrial and commercial field."

"When did you move over to your current role?" Drew realised that he was still dancing round the nature of this role.

"I joined the police when it was established as a civilian force ten years ago. Most of the new police force was drawn from the old government militia, as you'd expect, and at senior levels there was a need for those who'd had links with intelligence. We were not exactly overburdened with talent. As external interest in our country increased, we were encountering more and more instances of criminal activity—fraud, corruption, intimidation, industrial espionage, as well as more conventional crimes. Things were becoming more unstable in Russia. China was opening up to more commercial practices. You can imagine the growing pressure on this country."

Drew could easily imagine it. He still couldn't quite understand Nergui's role in all this, though. The links between the militia and foreign investment seemed obscure, and Nergui's subsequent movement into the police service didn't sound an obvious progression. Unless, of course, these were all simply different outlets for the intelligence services.

"What kinds of cases does the Serious Crimes Team normally get involved with?"

"All kinds. Major robberies, homicide, corruption. Anything that doesn't fall into the norms of day-to-day policing."

"But you've moved back to the Ministry now?" Drew prompted.

Nergui nodded. "Six months ago, yes. Not particularly of my own choosing. There were those who thought my talents were—underutilised as a policeman. The police force does not have a particularly good reputation in this country—justifiably in many cases I think. We have invested insufficiently in its development and it does not attract the highest calibre of employees. These days, there are more opportunities for our graduates in the private sector. But there has also been growing concern about national security, so I was—how do you say it?—poached by the Ministry. It was one of those offers I could not refuse."

"And what was your role in the Ministry?"

Nergui shrugged. "In general, dealing with cases that are perceived to pose a threat, in some way, to national security or stability. Not terrorism—we have a separate unit to deal with that, though it has not to date been a major problem for us, even with the breakup of the USSR. But things like major commercial fraud, corruption—anything that might pose a threat to, say, our economy, social stability or whatever."

None of this made much sense to Drew. It sounded very different from any concept of policing that he was used to. "And murder?" he asked.

"Not usually," he said. "But then we don't usually encounter murders quite like these."

"You really see these murders as a threat to national security? Is that why you've returned?"

"I have returned only because the Minister asked me to. It is embarrassing. Doripalam is a very capable officer, despite his youth. There's nothing I can teach him, I think. But the Minister is anxious. He is protecting his back. As for security—well, who knows? If we are simply dealing with a psychopath, then of course the answer is no. If there is something more rational behind the killings—like a vendetta or whether at least some of the victims were targeted—then, well, yes, it's possible. And there is also our concern for the stability of our country. Compared with many other parts of the old Eastern Bloc, we have survived the changes remarkably well. We have been through very difficult times, but our society has stayed remarkably stable. This is quite a safe country. But the kind of fear that could be stirred up by these killings—well, so far we have managed to keep the full details from being published and we have not indicated any linkage between the killings. But we can't keep this up for long. The press have been used to doing what the government tells them, but that is changing. I do not know, for example, how long we can prevent them from reporting that a police officer has been killed."

Drew nodded. "And what do you think will happen when people find out?"

"I do not know. There are many things that people fear. There are many interpretations they could put on these deaths." He stopped, enigmatically, as though unwilling to put his anxieties into plain words.

"And what about today's killing?" Drew asked. "Where does that fit into this?"

"It is intriguing, is it not? Horrific, but intriguing. As with your Mr. Ransom, the question is whether there is any significance in the choice of this particular individual?"

"You mean, other than the simple fact that he was a police officer?"

"Quite so." Nergui finished eating, and placed his fork and

spoon neatly across the bowl. "I do not like to say so, but today's murder may give us a little hope."

"Hope?"

"Or at least somewhere to start in our investigations. To date, we have had nothing. No leads. We thought Mr. Ransom might start to lead us somewhere, but it appeared not. Perhaps Delgerbayar might."

"Delgerbayar?"

"Our unfortunate colleague."

"So you think there might have been some significance to his death? Some reason why he specifically was chosen as the victim?"

Nergui leaned forward across the table, placing his fingertips together. "I do not know," he said. "But I do know, having asked some brief questions of his fellow officers today, that Delgerbayar had been acting oddly in recent weeks."

"Oddly in what way?"

"In a number of ways, apparently. Delgerbayar was not a particularly sociable person, I understand. People differ, of course. Our officers tend to be a gregarious bunch. You will generally find them after work throwing back the vodkas in one of our city bars. But there are exceptions to that, and Delgerbayar was one of them. He might join his colleagues briefly, but he would leave early in the evening. Nobody could ever recall seeing him at a party or a social gathering. I hope I'm not speaking ill of the dead, but he was generally seen as a rather—enigmatic character. He wasn't married, had no close family as far as anyone was aware. No one really knew what he did with his time. He had risen through the ranks largely because he was seen as a hard worker, I think, rather than through any great talent."

It was an interesting enough character sketch, but Drew wasn't sure where this was leading. "How had he been behaving oddly?"

"Well, out of character, let us say." Nergui smiled. "From what I hear, he had always behaved a little oddly. The first thing was that a couple of his fellow officers came across him one night in the bar in the Ulan Baatar hotel—another of our more upmarket places. It was only a coincidence that they were in there—the police don't tend to drink in the tourist hotels, as you might imagine. But they were there on duty, following up some petty thefts that had taken place in the hotel. And Delgerbayar was in the bar, sitting with a mixed group of Westerners and locals, apparently having a good enough time."

"Do you know who was with him?"

Nergui shook his head. "No, the officers didn't recognise any of them. They just thought it was an odd group to find with Delgerbayar—the Westerners looked well-off, business types. The locals also looked relatively prosperous—perhaps not the type you would normally expect to find associating with a police officer."

"Criminals?"

Nergui shrugged. "The term is a broad one," he said. "Maybe criminals. More likely those who have done well for themselves in our economy by—what is your phrase?—sailing close to the wind."

"But wouldn't you recognise those types?" Drew asked. "Surely they'd be well known."

"I would probably recognise them," Nergui said. "But in many cases—except for one or two larger celebrities—these kinds of people would not be well known to an ordinary police officer. Though our officers would probably be well acquainted with some of their employees."

"I understand. So, as you say, not the sort one would expect to find consorting with a senior police officer."

"No, but the two officers didn't really think much of it—it's not uncommon for officers to maintain some dubious contacts, particularly if they think they might extract some information from them." He smiled. "I've been known to do it myself. So it's quite possible that Delgerbayar's contacts were—well, if not exactly innocent, still quite legitimate."

"Do you believe that?"

"Who knows? With most officers, I would think it possible, though I might still be suspicious. From what I hear of Delgerbayar, it doesn't sound likely."

"And was there other strange behaviour?"

"Yes, and a more significant issue. Delgerbayar had been involved in an investigation into some illegal gold prospecting—"

"*Gold* prospecting?"

Nergui nodded. "Our country is rich in many minerals, including gold. The gold is, officially, being mined by a small number of companies which have acquired the appropriate rights. It is one of the ways you become wealthy quickly in this country."

Drew could imagine. Like much of the former Eastern Bloc, this now appeared to be a country where substantial poverty could co-exist very closely with extreme wealth.

"Not surprisingly," Nergui went on, "there are those who, lacking other resources, try to obtain their own small share of this wealth." Nergui's face betrayed nothing of his feelings—positive or negative—towards such people. "There are a lot of problems with people prospecting illegally for gold. In the right places, you can pan for gold in rivers. You will find small amounts, but those can still be enormously valuable—particularly to a poor family without other work."

"But these people can be prosecuted?"

"In principle, yes, very much so. In practice, the police often turn a blind eye, unless there is a direct complaint from one of the mining companies or the illegal activities are on a larger scale."

"So what was Delgerbayar investigating?"

"We'd had a complaint, apparently, from one of the mining companies about a small encampment that had been established near to one of their key sites. It wasn't clear how much gold was actually being found by this group, but they'd been there for some time and I think they'd become something of a visible challenge to the mining company. I think they wanted something done to make an example of them."

"What was Delgerbayar supposed to do?"

"There were two officers working on this, Delgerbayar and one other. The usual routine is that they would just give some sort of warning to the camp members, get them to move on. At most, they might formally caution them. But I don't think they expected to arrest or charge anyone unless there was active resistance."

"So what happened?"

Nergui leaned back in his chair. "Something strange happened. The day before they were due to visit the encampment, Delgerbayar disappeared."

Drew looked up in surprise. "Really?"

"He appeared briefly at headquarters and left a message for his senior officer to say that he had stumbled upon an important lead in the gold prospecting case and was therefore having to travel urgently south, to the Gobi."

"To the desert? Why?"

"He didn't say. It's difficult to see how there could have been any link to the prospecting case, which seemed like a trivial bit of business. He gave the name of a tourist encampment in the Gobi, where he said he was going to meet a contact."

"But surely he wasn't allowed just to disappear like that?"

"Of course not," Nergui said. "His senior officer was furious. It is likely that there would have been some disciplinary action taken, unless he'd come up with a very good explanation for his behaviour."

"But—"

Nergui anticipated the question. "But that didn't happen, no. He never came back—not alive, anyway. We don't even know for sure if he reached the tourist camp. So far, no one's admitted to having met him. He was booked on to a flight to the Gobi, and it looks as if he—or someone—may have travelled. But that's all we know. The next time we saw him—"

Drew nodded slowly. "Today. But it does sound as if there's a potential lead there."

"Exactly. Of course, it's possible that this is all coincidence and that the Gobi stuff wasn't linked to this—maybe it was just a young officer showing off, thinking he'd stumbled on something and going off without thinking through the consequences."

"It wouldn't be the first time, in my experience," Drew said, with a faint smile. "I might have even done it myself, if I think back far enough."

"But, from what I hear, that doesn't sound typical of Delgerbayar. If anything, he tended to be over-cautious. People were genuinely taken aback when he disappeared—I think most people assumed there was more to it. Some sort of domestic crisis or something. There were some who thought he'd had some sort of breakdown."

"So you have to assume a connection?"

"We do." Nergui sat back slowly in his chair. "I hope you enjoyed the meal."

"The food really was superb, Nergui." Drew realised that it was the first time he had used the Mongolian's name. He felt, just for a moment, as though he had fallen under a spell, as though the combination of the food and the alcohol and Nergui's openness had compelled him to lower his guard. He wondered whether this had been Nergui's intention, whether the unexpected openness about his background had been a deliberate ploy to gain his own trust.

Even as he felt this, he realised that the prospect didn't concern him unduly. He wasn't entirely sure whether Nergui could be trusted, but at the moment he felt some reassurance that at least they were in this thing—whatever it might turn out to be— together.

Nergui smiled faintly, as though reading Drew's thoughts. "Now," he said, "I have three questions for you."

"Go ahead." Drew couldn't read the Mongolian's expression, didn't know whether or not he was being serious.

Nergui ticked off the questions on his fingers. "Three simple questions. One—would you like some coffee? Two—would you like some of our excellent vodka with your coffee?" He paused, slowly tapping his third finger. "And three—would you like to travel to the Gobi in the morning?"

SEVEN

"We should have travelled business class."

"This is business class. You should see economy."

Drew laughed. This was like nothing he had ever experienced. He wasn't sure he would ever want to experience it again, but for the moment it was sufficiently different to be worth enduring.

He had never seen an aeroplane so crowded. It was a small propeller-driven plane, but it appeared to be more crowded than any 747 Drew had ever seen. It wasn't quite true that there were people standing but it felt as if there were. Certainly, most of the passengers seemed to be carrying more than their allotted allowance of cabin luggage, which appeared to be stuffed into any available place.

"I hope this is safe," Drew said, looking around them. As far as he could see, he was the only Westerner on board.

Nergui shrugged. "A better safety record than Aeroflot, anyway."

"That's very reassuring."

It was only a ninety-minute flight to Dalanzadgad, but this was quite long enough for Drew. He still wasn't sure that it was a wise decision to accompany Nergui. He had a suspicion that Nergui's decision to make the trip was prompted primarily by a desire to get himself and Drew out of Doripalam's hair, to give the young man the opportunity to get on with some serious police work without interruption.

As far as Drew could see, there wasn't a lot that he would be able to contribute to the investigation. On the other hand, it was a perfect excuse for a trip to the Gobi Desert, and it would have been a pity to have left this country without seeing it. Drew, who took his work very seriously, was uncomfortably aware that his visit to this country was a glorified public relations exercise, and he now felt additionally guilty about engaging in what was little more than a sight-seeing excursion. On the other hand, he told himself, he had not asked to come here. He was undertaking a task which his superiors felt to be worthwhile. And there was the small matter of having already been shot at, even if, as it had turned out, his life had not really been in danger. So maybe he should just sit back and enjoy this.

Although sitting back was not easy, given the state of the aeroplane seats. He had the impression that the passenger behind him was trying to insert a large cabin trunk in the space between their respective rows. He was also sure that he could hear the sound of a chicken clucking somewhere towards the rear of the aircraft.

"What's the schedule today?" he asked. This had all been very sudden. The previous evening, after he had found himself agreeing to accompany Nergui on the trip, Nergui had made a couple of official-sounding phone calls to organise the tickets and accommodation. Drew had returned to his hotel—again in an official car—at around eleven, and had then been up at six to prepare for the journey. He had retained his room at the Chinggis Khaan at Nergui's suggestion and left most of his luggage there, taking only his small shoulder bag with a change of clothes. There was only one return flight each day to Dalanzadgad so they would have to stay overnight. The intention was to stay in the same camp that Delgerbayar had been intending to visit.

"We get to Dalanzadgad at around ten-thirty. I've arranged to talk to one or two people from the airline to see if there's any record or recollection of Delgerbayar coming through. It's a bit of a long shot, but somebody caught that flight so we may be able to get some idea of whether it was Delgerbayar or not."

Drew wondered whether Delgerbayar would have been easy to recognise. Since the only time he had seen the man's face it had been detached from his neck, it wasn't an issue he particularly wanted to dwell upon.

"And then we go on to the camp. It's not too far—I've arranged for a jeep to take us out. I've set up an interview with the man who runs the place, and I've asked him if we can also talk to a few of the staff. You never know, someone might remember Delgerbayar."

Drew settled back in his seat, still trying to make himself comfortable. "This probably sounds a stupid question," he said, "but what exactly is a tourist camp?"

"Just what it sounds like," Nergui said. "There are a number of them, scattered about the Gobi. Permanent clusters of *gers* which people visit for vacations."

"Holiday camps?" Drew said. "In the desert?"

"Well, you could perhaps think of it as a large beach." Nergui smiled. "Though I admit it's a long walk to the sea."

"So who uses them?"

"They're still very popular," Nergui said. "Some of them cater for tourists from the former Eastern Bloc—we used to get a lot of tourists from there, when it was impossible for them to go elsewhere. But now it tends to be either international tourists—for them, it's part of the experience of visiting our country—or Mongolians from the cities who wish to visit the desert on their vacations. The place we're visiting caters mainly for foreign tourists."

"But—assuming that Delgerbayar's story was true or at least partly true—why would a contact have arranged to meet him in a place like that? Why not in Ulan Baatar?"

"That is part of the mystery," Nergui said. "I have no answer. It is a strange place to arrange an assignation. Assuming that Delgerbayar's story was true, then it's possible of course that the contact was a foreigner, maybe a tourist or someone posing as a tourist. But that still doesn't explain why they should have arranged to meet in such a strange location."

"Maybe they thought it would be a discreet meeting place?"

"That's quite possible. Of course, there are discreet places where one could meet in Ulan Baatar, but not many. In practice, the city tends to be something of a small village. Too many people know one another, frequent the same bars, the same restaurants. Delgerbayar was unlucky enough to be spotted in the Ulan Baatar. No matter where else he went, there was always the risk that he might be seen by someone."

"Which implies," Drew said, "that his contact—if there was one—was someone he didn't want to be seen with."

"Indeed." Nergui nodded, and not for the first time Drew had the impression that the Mongolian's thinking had already progressed several stages beyond his own. Nergui's face, though, was as inscrutable as ever. "Now," he said, finally, "you should enjoy the journey. It is not every day you have an opportunity to see the vast expanse of the Gobi."

This was true enough, but it was not easy to take Nergui's advice. Intriguing as the destination might be, the journey itself was anything but enjoyable. The takeoff had been unnerving—there had been at least a brief moment when Drew was convinced they were going to plough off the end of the runway into the cluster of sheds beyond. The ascent was little more reassuring, since he had the impression that the small aircraft was having to use every unit of its limited engine power to lift its heavy cargo. And now they were at what would normally be described as cruising altitude, the aeroplane was small enough to feel every buffet of air turbulence. Drew found no difficulty in declining the meagre meal of dried meats and biscuits that was proffered, but accepted the familiar small bottle of vodka that accompanied it with relative enthusiasm. Across the aisle, a group of young men, dressed in grey overalls, had already produced a larger bottle of vodka which they were consuming at an impressive pace.

Nergui glanced across at them and smiled. "Mongolians do not like to fly," he said. "We think it is unnatural. So we calm our fears with drink. Which of course does little for either our safety or our state of mind."

Nergui had clearly noted Drew's discomfort, and devoted his time to distracting stories of the desert, the nomadic herdsmen who frequented it, and other anecdotes of Mongolian life. Drew also had the impression, perhaps unfounded, that Nergui was attempting to distract his thoughts from the case that they were investigating.

The time passed quickly enough, though, even if it felt much longer in the pit of Drew's stomach. Before long, first the buildings and then the vegetation fell away, and Drew could see the vast expanse of the desert spread out before them. Drew had never seen a desert before and his expectations were conditioned largely by filmic images of the Sahara—empty wastelands of sand baking in the eternally noonday sun, a few palm trees, tents and camels.

Some of that he would undoubtedly see over the next twenty-four hours. But the landscape they passed over was surprisingly varied—they passed over hills, forested areas and green plains. As they flew south, the undulating hills slowly gave way to something closer to Drew's ideas of a desert. But even here he was surprised at how green the land looked. It was sand, for sure, but there had apparently been some rain over the preceding weeks, and a fine sheen of green, burgeoning grass, had spread across the landscape. Although the grass was sparse, from this altitude it bore a startling resemblance to a well-tended British lawn.

As they flew above the expansive landscape, far below Drew could see few signs of life. There were occasional clusters of *gers,* with the movements of animals that, from this height, might have been horses or might have been camels. Now and again, there was a fast-moving cloud of sand which Drew assumed was a vehicle of some kind. But otherwise there was little to be seen until they began to approach Dalanzadgad.

The descent was as unnerving as the ascent had been. It felt almost as if they were plummeting from the sky, though he had to assume that the pilot knew what he was doing. Drew felt his ears popping from the pressure change as the aircraft banked and then levelled, preparing for landing. Drew was never particularly good with aeroplane landings and this was one of the worst he had experienced. He was convinced they were simply going to plough directly into the ground, and so he was hugely relieved when their tyres hit the runway and bounced. The impact was a shock, but they—and the aircraft—seemed unscathed, bouncing speedily across the ground towards the airport buildings. Even then Drew thought they were still going too fast, but somehow the pilot managed to keep control of the aircraft and they pulled up safely at the stand.

There was no polite waiting for the pilot to turn off the seatbelt signs. As soon as the aircraft stopped moving, the crowd of passengers jumped up, as though co-ordinated, and began to scramble for their luggage in the overhead compartments. Somewhere behind, Drew once again heard the sound of a clucking chicken.

Only Nergui remained motionless in his seat. "There's no rush," he said. "We might as well relax."

Drew didn't feel too relaxed, but he was glad of the opportunity to recover from his airborne ordeal. "Is the flight always like that?" he asked.

"More or less. Not always that smooth." Nergui smiled gently, and once again it was difficult to be sure whether he was joking.

With remarkable speed, the crowd of passengers poured towards the rear entrance, and Drew and Nergui rose to follow. Outside, the sky was clear blue and the sun was already high. This late in the year, though, the temperature was cool.

Drew followed Nergui down the stairs and across the runway to the small concrete airport building. There were no passport or customs controls at what was exclusively a domestic airport. The arrival hall was anonymous, another example of Communist functionality. A couple of uniformed policemen were standing conspicuously in the corner, watching the disembarking passengers without interest.

Nergui walked over and engaged them in conversation, pulling his formal ID from his pocket to show them. Instantly, both men jumped to attention. They didn't quite salute, but they showed Nergui a respect which had been noticeably absent in their earlier demeanour.

Nergui beckoned him over, and spoke what were clearly a few words of introduction to the two officers. Both nodded towards him.

"They're going to take us to the airport manager," Nergui

said. "I don't imagine there's much he'll be able to tell us himself, but I think it's only courteous that we speak to him before we start bothering his staff."

They followed the police officers out of the main hall, and along a corridor to a small, sparsely furnished office. A small harassed-looking man was sitting behind a desk, scribbling figures down on a bundle of papers and occasionally stabbing numbers into a large, old-fashioned-looking calculator. He looked up impatiently as they came in.

Nergui spoke a few words and introduced Drew, who nodded politely. The manager brushed aside his papers and spoke brusquely to Nergui. Even without any understanding of the words, it was clear that he was not pleased to have them there. Nergui spoke a few quiet words in return, and the man rose, his chair scraping back across the polished wooden floor. He spoke angrily and stalked over to the window, which looked out on to grey concrete walls.

Nergui looked back at Drew and smiled faintly. "We don't seem very welcome," he said.

"I had that impression," Drew said. "What's the problem?"

"I'm not entirely clear," Nergui said, still smiling. "Our friend seems to be under the impression that we will disrupt the smooth running of his operation, and spread fear and anxiety among the passengers."

"You've told him we'll be very discreet?"

"Of course. But he doesn't appear to be reassured." The smile was still fixed on Nergui's face, but as he turned back towards the airport manager, his face returned to its familiar blank mask. He spoke a few more calm words to the manager, who once again responded angrily, stamping his foot petulantly on the floor.

Afterwards, Drew couldn't actually recall seeing Nergui move. But suddenly he was standing only inches away from the airport manager, his eyes blazing. Nergui spoke, still softly, not raising his voice. Drew had no idea what the words meant, but he could feel the sense of threat even from across the room. The manager blinked, and Drew reflected to himself that it was the first time he had ever seen the blood genuinely drain from someone's face. The manager's mouth opened once, twice, but no sounds came out. Nergui said something more, and the man nodded quickly, his eyes blinking.

Nergui turned back towards Drew and, like a light bulb being switched on, the smile returned. "That's fine," Nergui said. "Just a little misunderstanding, I think. We can see anyone we like, and our friend here will be only too pleased to make the introductions."

Drew found that he could barely speak himself. "That's very nice of him," he said, finally.

"Isn't it?" Nergui said. "But we're a friendly people."

Nergui led the way out of the office, and back into the main hall, the manager now scuttling along behind him.

"What was all that about, anyway?" Drew said, as he hurried along behind Nergui. "Just bureaucracy?"

Nergui spoke without looking back. He was heading towards a group of uniformed check-in staff, who were standing chatting by one of the desks. "I don't know," he said. "I thought at first he was just being difficult—you know, the usual petty official protecting his turf. But then I got the impression there was something else, that he might actually be frightened."

"I'm not surprised he was frightened," Drew said, deciding that there was little mileage in not being fully open. "You scared the life out of me, let alone him."

Nergui laughed. "No, before that," he said. "I was doing my usual, polite officer of the law piece, flattering him into helping. You know the kind of thing—?"

Drew knew it all too well. It usually worked okay with the petty official type.

"—and he was stonewalling. Not just being difficult, but looking genuinely anxious at the thought of helping us out. That was why I put the screws on a bit."

"You think he's afraid of something? Or someone?"

Nergui shrugged. "Possibly. Who knows?"

By this time, he had reached the group of check-in staff, who were looking at him with some curiosity, assuming that he was a passenger in search of information. Before Nergui could speak, the manager had caught up with him and interjected, gesturing backwards and forwards between Nergui and the others as he effected introductions.

Drew watched him closely. It was frustrating, tailing behind Nergui, unable to contribute meaningfully to any interviews, spending half the time wondering what the hell was going on. But the one advantage of his position was that he could at least watch carefully the expressions and body language of those that Nergui was addressing.

Nergui was right, he thought. This man did look more anxious than the situation justified. Even if one accepted the supposed reason—concerns about disturbing passengers and staff—this did not explain the gleam of sweat that had already appeared on the manager's forehead. It surely couldn't be the first time that the police had wished to investigate on site—this was an airport, after all. But as the manager hopped from one foot to the other, twisting his head and interrupting as though having to interpret to the staff what Nergui was saying, he did look scared. He was doing his best to conceal it, with over-eager smiling and laughing, but even some of the staff were regarding him oddly.

Nergui simply ignored him, talking steadily and calmly to the group of staff. After a few moments, he reached into his jacket and brought out the picture of Delgerbayar which he had copied from the police files. He showed it around the group, allowing them time to gaze fully at the face. Nergui had shown Drew the photograph during the flight. It looked to be a well-taken photograph, though Drew could not relate it to the white, bloodstained visage he had seen.

As Drew watched, one of the female staff in the group began to nod enthusiastically, talking hurriedly to Nergui. She was gesturing towards the photograph and then pointing towards a spot across the hall, close to the exit doors. As she pointed, she spotted a colleague walking slowly through the hall and called out to him. He looked up as she shouted, then hurried over to join the group. Drew wasn't clear what was going on, but it appeared to be important. Nergui was engaged in intense conversation with the woman, then, when the newcomer arrived, he turned and spoke rapidly to him also. The man was nodding and pointing over to the same spot.

Finally, Nergui turned to Drew and beckoned him to join them. Drew smiled vaguely at the group, who all simultaneously took a half step back as he approached. It was as if they didn't quite know what to make of a Westerner in their midst. There was no hostility in their response—just curiosity and a certain wariness.

"What is it?" Drew said. "You've got something?"

"Looks like it. I didn't really expect it. You have to ask the questions, but you can't really imagine that anyone would remember one passenger amongst hundreds a week ago."

"And do they?"

"Definitely. But only because Delgerbayar behaved rather differently from most other passengers that day."

"How?"

"It looks as if he arrived on the same flight we did today. He disembarked from the aircraft, made his way into here, and then over towards the exits, where we assume he looked around for someone who was meeting him."

"But how—?"

"It's not entirely clear what happened. Of course, nobody had particularly noticed Delgerbayar up to this point, even on the plane. We made enquiries among the cabin staff yesterday, but you saw how crowded the flights can get. Anyway, we assume that Delgerbayar got here and found the person he was due to meet. The first thing that anyone notices are some raised voices over by the exit doors. The whole room turns to look, and there are two men apparently having an almighty row. It's starting to turn into something physical—pushing and shoving, you know—when a couple of the airport police turn up to separate them."

"What happened? Did Delgerbayar tell them he was an officer too?"

"Not clear, but we can check with the local police and find out who was on that day, see if anything was said. But my guess would be not. In fact, surprisingly, Delgerbayar and the other man both turn hurriedly and walk out through the exit together. They were being watched by our friends here—" Nergui said, gesturing to the two airport employees, "—along with everyone else. It appeared that they both jumped into the same truck and sped pretty rapidly away from the airport."

"And they're sure it was Delgerbayar?"

Nergui nodded. "As sure as anyone can be in this kind of situation, I think. I pushed them quite hard on that and they've both looked carefully at the picture, and they're sure it was him. The others here weren't close enough to be certain, but these two both happened to be walking by the exits when it happened, so they were only a few feet away."

"So—we know he definitely came down here. And we know he met up with someone. Which suggests that at least part of his story was true."

"Though of course we don't know if his visit here was really connected with the gold prospecting business, or whether it was something else entirely."

As Nergui talked, Drew looked past his shoulder at the group of airport staff. The manager was hovering beside them, occasionally whispering something nervously. Drew raised an eyebrow to draw Nergui's attention to the scene behind him. Nergui picked up the signal instantly, but didn't turn round to look.

"He's asking whether any of them recognised the other man," Nergui said, quietly.

"I think your hearing is better than he realises," Drew murmured, smiling faintly.

"My hearing is very good," Nergui said. "I can hear them shaking their heads, and I almost think I can hear the relief in his voice. Or is that my imagination?"

"They're definitely shaking their heads," Drew said. "I don't know about the rest of it."

"Neither do I. But I think we need to keep an eye on our friend here."

Nergui turned to thank the manager and staff, smiling pleasantly at the group. Most of them looked excited to be part of some sort of official investigation, and a number wanted to ask more questions. Nergui made what were clearly polite noises, and then led Drew out through the exit into the sunshine.

"What did you tell them?" Drew said, when they were outside.

"Not much. Official investigation. Following up some routine lines of enquiry. The usual."

A jeep was standing, engine running, in what appeared to be the No Parking area immediately outside the airport building. As they emerged into the daylight, the driver jumped up then hopped out of the vehicle. Without hesitation, Nergui walked over and tossed his bag into the back. Drew followed and did likewise, then they climbed into the truck. Nergui spoke a few words to the driver, and they pulled out into the road.

Drew was struck that, even down here, ninety minutes' flight from Ulan Baatar, Nergui seemed to be recognised instantly. Drew considered himself lucky to be recognised if he stepped outside his own office.

There was little to Dalanzadgad—a few concrete-built commercial buildings around the airport, some residential blocks, a sprawl of randomly constructed wooden huts, and the inevitable *gers*. The town was primarily a gateway to the southern Gobi, rather than an entity in its own right.

The jeep quickly left the town behind, racing initially along metalled roads, then dirt tracks, and finally hitting the desert itself. They pounded along at high speed, scattering dust and debris. Nergui sat beside the driver, looking relaxed, enjoying the cool sunshine and the open space. For the first time, it struck Drew that this seemed the natural habitat for these people— even Nergui, city dweller, international traveller, seemed more at ease out here.

Drew was overwhelmed by the emptiness, the sense of space, the enormous blue spread of the sky. All sense of scale was lost here. Apart from the occasional hut or *ger*, there was nothing to provide perspective. Looking back, Dalanzadgad already looked both immensely distant and still strangely close. Ahead, there seemed to be nothing, just endless blank miles to the horizon.

The landscape seemed deserted. Once, they saw a distant figure on a motorbike speed by, miles away from them. Otherwise, there were no signs of life. Incongruously, the driver had turned up the volume of the vehicle's tape deck, so that the jeep was blasting American rock music as they drove.

After half an hour, there were the first signs of an encampment rising above the horizon ahead of them. It was impossible for Drew to tell how far away it was, but he could see a wire fence, a clustering of *gers*, and some larger wood-built buildings around it.

Nergui pointed. "That's the place."

"Plenty of beach," Drew shouted back, over the noise of the engine and the music. The camp seemed utterly isolated. "How do the tourists get out here?"

"They run buses from the airport. You'll be surprised how civilised it is when we get there."

It was a surprisingly long time before the camp drew near. As they approached, Drew saw that there were indeed tourists—a few of them, at least—sitting inside the fenced area. It was a surreal sight. In this deserted spot, apparently miles from any other life, tourists in tee shirts and shorts were lying on sun beds, reading novels, sipping beers, looking like holiday-makers on any beach anywhere.

"Doesn't look busy," Drew commented.

"Very late in the year," Nergui said. "If you'd come in the summer it would have been full. The weather's too cool now."

It was true. The sun was still blazing down from an un-clouded sky, but the temperature was only mild. The sunbathers were being optimistic, trying to make the most of the sunshine, but it was barely warm enough to be sitting outside.

The jeep pulled up to the gate, and stopped in front of what was clearly a reception area. Nergui jumped out and grabbed his bag from the vehicle, Drew following behind, and then turned and entered the building.

The wooden building was warm and dark inside. It was sparsely furnished, just a reception desk and a couple of low chairs. The man behind the desk looked up as they entered and smiled at Nergui, uttering some words of welcome. Nergui nod-ded back, and gestured behind him, introducing Drew.

"Mr. McLeish," the man said, smiling enthusiastically at Drew, "it is good to welcome you here."

"You speak English?" Drew said.

The man nodded, modestly. "A little," he said. "We have been receiving tourists from the United Kingdom and from the USA for a long time now—more than ten years. I have been trying to learn some of their—your—language."

"You speak it well, Mr.—?"

"Batkhuyag. I ask our visitors to correct me when I get it wrong." He laughed. "They are very happy to do so."

Nergui said a few more words to him in Mongolian. Batkhuyag nodded, and pointed behind him. "I have arranged a *ger* for you to use as a base," he said, speaking English, clearly for Drew's benefit. "I try to find the most—what do you say?—private one for you to use so that you can speak to anyone you wish to without being disturbed." He shrugged. "I really do not know if we can help you. The police down here came to ask some questions, but as far I am aware no one here was able to provide any real information. But we will help as much as we can. Please feel free to speak to anyone, to go where you wish." He paused, as if unsure how to formulate his next sentence. "I would of course ask that you try to disturb our guests as little as possible. I know you may wish to speak to them, but please come to me first so that I can prepare them."

Nergui nodded. "I do not know that we will need to speak to your guests. Would any of them have been here at the time that Delgerbayar—the officer we are investigating—was supposed to have visited?"

Batkhuyag nodded. "That was a week ago, yes? In that case, some of them would have been, although most are here only this week."

"Well, we will see how things go. We may wish to speak to some of those who were here last week, but I promise you we will be discreet."

"Of course," Batkhuyag said. "I should not have raised the issue. You know your jobs, I'm sure."

Nergui smiled. "If you've had the local police round here asking questions, I can imagine that discretion was not always evident?"

"Well, they are local men. They are doing their best, I'm sure. But I need to do mine, and the tourists are important to us."

"We want them to see our country at its best," Nergui agreed. "I will ensure that they do."

Batkhuyag led them back out into the open air, then through the cluster of *gers* towards the back of the camp. He gestured to a tent which lay separated from the others, close to the wooden building which served as a restaurant and meeting place for the camp. "I thought this would be best," he said. "We use it for staff during the busy part of the season, but it's empty now. You can use this to interview people and as your accommodation for this evening, if that's okay."

It was clear to Drew that Batkhuyag was doing his best to ensure that the hospitality of the camp was not unduly contaminated by the presence of the policemen. The *ger* was as far as it could be from the remaining tents, and was clearly not of the same standard as the tourist *gers*. But Drew didn't blame the man for seeking discretion. Subtlety wasn't a quality generally found amongst policemen, and he didn't imagine that the police here were any different.

Batkhuyag opened the door of the *ger* and showed them inside. The interior was dark but, to Drew's surprise, there was electric light. The place looked surprisingly comfortable. There was an ornately decorated table in the centre surrounded by rugs. Some hard wooden chairs had been placed, slightly incongruously, around it, but Drew imagined that those had been provided specifically for Nergui and himself. Around the far walls, there were two beds, again ornately painted. Sleeping here would certainly be an experience, but not necessarily an unpleasant one, he thought.

Nergui looked around and nodded, smiling faintly. "It looks fine," he said. "Most comfortable." It was difficult to be sure if there was a trace of irony in his tone. He gestured towards one of the seats. "You will join us, Mr. Batkhuyag?"

Batkhuyag looked surprised. "Me? I didn't really envisage—"

Nergui made a slight bow. "But, of course, Mr. Batkhuyag, you are the first person we wish to see here. I do not believe that anything happens in this camp of which you are unaware, no?"

Batkhuyag looked confused. It was, Drew had to admit, a neat question, a cunning balance of flattery and threat. "Well," Batkhuyag said, "I'm not sure I would say that—"

"Come now, Mr. Batkhuyag, there is no need for false modesty. I can see how well run this place is." Nergui casually lowered himself on to one of the wooden chairs. Batkhuyag had no choice but to follow. Drew pulled back the remaining chair and turned it round so that he could sit leaning on the chair back. He carefully positioned himself slightly away from Nergui and Batkhuyag. As far as he was concerned, this had to be Nergui's interview. He would intervene only if he thought there was something he could add.

Nergui leaned forward in his chair, his hands together. "Now, Mr. Batkhuyag, how much do you know about why we're here?"

Batkhuyag shrugged. "Not a great deal. Just what the local police chief told me when they visited."

"Which was?"

"That you were investigating some internal case involving one of your officers, who you believed had visited the camp a week or so back. They really just wanted to know if he had been here. They showed me his photograph."

"And had he been here?" Nergui said.

Batkhuyag shook his head. "Not as far as I'm aware. I didn't recognise the photograph."

"Is it possible he came without your knowing?"

Batkhuyag shrugged. "Of course it's possible. The day in question was one of our turnover days—one group of tourists coming, another leaving, some staying put. Things get very busy. We tend to get deliveries on those days, too. There's laundry being picked up for cleaning, new laundry being dropped off. Food deliveries. All of that. I couldn't swear that your—"

"Delgerbayar," Nergui said.

"I couldn't swear that he wasn't here for a while in the middle of all that. I'm pretty sure he wasn't staying here as a guest. Obviously, we had no one of that name, and that photograph didn't look familiar. Also our guests tend to stay for several days at least—as I understand it, your Mr. . . . Delgerbayar would have come down only the previous day. That would have been unusual, so we would have remembered."

"Did you ask any of the other staff if they recognised him?"

"A few," Batkhuyag said. "I mean, we didn't do it systematically or anything. The police weren't here long enough for that—I got the impression they were just going through the motions. Routine questions."

"That would be pretty much it," Nergui said. Watching the two men, Drew wondered about this. He didn't know how much the local police had been told. It was difficult to believe that they would be unaware of the brutal murder of a fellow officer. And why would they not have been told officially? Drew still had the sense of operating in an alien environment—superficially it resembled the world he was used to but it left him constantly wrong-footed. For Drew the murder of a fellow officer was still one of the most serious and dreadful of crimes. Partly this was because of the inevitable fear that it might be your own life on the line next time. But partly it was the recognition that if you tolerated that kind of assault on the forces of law and order, there was no possibility of holding any other line. It was difficult to believe that, if the police down here were aware of Delgerbayar's murder, they would have treated it casually.

"And nobody recognised him?"

"No, but that doesn't necessarily mean too much. We just asked a few of the staff in the restaurant and such like. They'd have been serving people meals, but they wouldn't necessarily get to know the tourists particularly well. On the other hand, around seventy per cent of our visitors are from overseas, so the staff tend to get to know the Mongolian guests better. They speak the same language, for one thing."

Nergui nodded slowly. "So it looks as if we can assume that Delgerbayar did not stay here as a guest, but it's quite possible that he did come here without your knowing."

Batkhuyag shrugged. "That's right. If he was here for a few hours, maybe meeting another guest, he could easily have come in and out without anybody particularly noticing, I think."

Nergui rose, and began to pace slowly across the tent. "I'm afraid we probably will have to conduct some more systematic questioning with your staff. And perhaps with some guests also."

Batkhuyag raised his head. "I am not in a position to prevent you," he said. "But can I ask you what this is all about?"

Nergui stopped pacing, and turned to look at him. Drew leaned back on his chair, his face studiedly blank.

Batkhuyag was watching Nergui closely now. "I realise that you may well not wish to tell me. I ask because if you are going to cause some disruption in the camp, I feel I have a right to know why."

Nergui remained silent. It was clear that he was not intending to assist Batkhuyag in taking this issue forward. At the same time, it was not at all clear to Drew how Nergui was going to handle this.

"I would ask only that you don't treat me as a fool," Batkhuyag said slowly. "I have lived in Ulan Baatar. I talk to people in the police. I am aware of your reputation. I am also aware that the police would not normally send someone of your . . . seniority to deal with an internal disciplinary matter. Or, indeed," he added, turning to face Drew, "an officer from the United Kingdom."

Nergui laughed suddenly. "Well, I'm very flattered that you think so much of me, Mr. Batkhuyag. And you are quite right that I should not treat you as a fool. I am sorry if my approach has seemed discourteous." Drew was reminded of the way Nergui had spoken to him as they had travelled back from the airport on the night of his arrival. This was Nergui the diplomat. It was not difficult to imagine him dealing with the British ambassador in the same manner—polite, but giving nothing away.

"We are not trying to deceive you, simply to exercise some discretion." He paused. Drew wondered if Nergui was trying to work out how to finesse all this, but he continued smoothly enough: "We are, as you rightly surmise, dealing with an extremely serious crime—it's a sensitive matter, and there are good reasons why I am unable to provide you with any more information at the moment. But, believe me, it is serious enough to warrant both my involvement and—because there are some Western interests at stake too—the involvement of my colleague, Chief Inspector McLeish." He gestured towards Drew, who noted the use of the rank with some internal amusement. Bullshit with a capital B, he thought, but it seemed to be doing the trick. "We believe there is a possibility that our colleague, Delgerbayar, has been involved in this, but we don't know precisely what his involvement is. That is why we are so keen to understand his movements down here."

"My information," Batkhuyag said, softly, "is that your Mr. Delgerbayar is dead."

Drew looked up in surprise. He had assumed from Batkhuyag's earlier words he had no inkling of why they were here.

Nergui's face remained blank. "And what information would that be, Mr. Batkhuyag?"

Batkhuyag shrugged. "People talk to me."

Nergui leaned back in his chair, lifting the front legs slightly off the ground. "Really? That's very interesting. You must be a sociable sort. Why didn't you mention this earlier?"

"I didn't think it was up to me. You were spinning me a line. That's your business. But I think it's better if we're straight with each other. I'm more likely to be able to help you if I know what it is you want."

Batkhuyag was clearly sharper than he appeared, Drew thought. But then you probably didn't run a place like this without being a little streetwise.

Nergui nodded. "You are no doubt correct, Mr. Batkhuyag. You will appreciate the need for discretion. But, yes, I can confirm that Delgerbayar is dead."

"Murdered," Batkhuyag said. It was not a question.

Nergui put his hands behind his head, looking relaxed. "Now, you do realise that your possession of this information raises some interesting questions for me?"

Batkhuyag said nothing. He was, Drew thought, giving nothing away unless he was likely to get back something in return. Funny, he thought, how these types are the same the world over.

Nergui frowned, as though he were working through some particularly abstruse conundrum. "The situation is this," he said, finally. "The news of our colleague's demise is not exactly public knowledge. Even the police down here do not know—at least not officially. But somehow the information seems to have reached you. I'm curious as to how that might have happened."

"As I say, people talk."

"Not really good enough, I'm afraid, Mr. Batkhuyag. You see, if I were the suspicious sort, I might come to the conclusion that the only way you could know about Delgerbayar's death would be if you were somehow involved in it."

"So why would I tell you and put myself under suspicion?"

"You tell me," Nergui smiled, coldly. "I would hate to have to arrest you while we try to sort that mystery out."

Batkhuyag did not look particularly troubled by the prospect. "I don't know what the police down here are supposed to know officially," he said, putting an ironic emphasis on the last word. "But I listen to what they say. They know about your Mr. Delgerbayar."

Nergui raised an eyebrow. "Do they?" he said. "And what do they know?"

"They come out here to drink, quite often," Batkhuyag said. "There aren't many places to choose from down here, and we get decent beer for the tourists. We don't encourage locals, but I turn a blind eye to the police."

"Of course."

"There was a bunch of them here last night. We have some music on most evenings—the usual traditional stuff for the tourists. Place gets full. There were some police officers and others here most of the night, knocking back the beer and the vodka."

"Mongolians?" Nergui said. "The others, I mean."

Batkhuyag frowned. "I'm not sure. There was a group turned up early on—a few police people I recognised and one or two I didn't. Others joined them over the evening. A few of the tourists, mostly Westerners—we've got a fair number of Brits and some Americans here at the moment."

"Is it usual for the tourists to drink with the locals?" Drew asked.

"It's not unusual," Batkhuyag said. "The language can be a barrier, but it's amazing how easily you can make yourself understood after a few vodkas. So, no, there was nothing particularly odd about that."

"So what were they saying?" Nergui asked.

"Well, I can't pretend I was listening closely," Batkhuyag said. "But I kept picking up bits of the conversation as I passed by."

"Of course," Nergui said, stony-faced. "You were working in the bar?"

"I do when we're busy. Anyway, I overheard them saying something about things up north, in the city. It was the usual stuff about how the Ministry doesn't know what it's doing, keeping people in the dark. You know."

"I know," Nergui said. "And they mentioned Delgerbayar?"

"Not by name. But I put two and two together. What I heard—what I thought I heard—was something about a policeman coming down here stirring up trouble. They said—I'm sorry about this but it's what I heard—they said, well, in effect that he'd got what was coming to him."

"And did they indicate why they thought that?"

"Not that I heard. Tell you the truth, I was a bit shocked. I mean, we complain about the police all the time, but you kind of expect that they'll stick together. Made me wonder what was going on. But also made me think that I'd be better off not enquiring too deeply."

Nergui nodded, his face still giving nothing away. "You're a wise man, Mr. Batkhuyag. Have you anything else to tell us?"

Batkhuyag shook his head. He looked less composed now than he had at the start of the interview, as though Nergui's response—or lack of it—had for the first time confirmed to him that he might be on the edge of something serious here. "Who else would you like to see?"

Nergui looked across at Drew, though Drew had the impression that this was more from courtesy than anything else. "I think we need to see any of your staff who were working in the bar last night or who might have been around on the day that Delgerbayar was supposedly down here." He handed Batkhuyag his open notebook and pen. "Perhaps you could write down the names, and then we can see people in order."

Batkhuyag thought for a moment, then dutifully began to write a list of names. "I think that's everyone, but if there's anyone I've missed, I'll add them." He rose to leave, but Nergui gestured him back into his seat.

"Two more brief questions," he said. "First, do you know the names of any of the guests who were with the police officers last night?"

Batkhuyag opened his mouth to speak, then stopped. "No, I don't," he said. "At least, there were a number, but I don't know who—"

"Just some names," Nergui said. "We will be discreet."

Batkhuyag looked from Nergui to Drew and then back again, clearly considering his options and realising how limited they were. "Okay," he said. "There were a couple I can be sure of. I'll ask them if they can spare a few minutes to see you— they've been off on a tour of some of the prehistoric sites but they should be back soon."

"Thank you," Nergui said. "And my second question—"

Batkhuyag had clearly already anticipated the second question. "I recognised the police officers, but I don't know their names—"

Nergui raised his head and smiled coldly at Batkhuyag. "Really?" he said. "Well, I suppose I could always take you down to the police HQ and get you to point them out to me."

"Look, a job like mine depends on discretion. If it gets around that I've been talking to you—"

"I can see that that would be a problem for you," Nergui said. "Just write the names down. I will tell no one."

Batkhuyag looked between them both again, clearly anxious now. Then he shook his head, and bent down to write the names on the pad.

EIGHT

They spent the remainder of the afternoon working steadily through the list of interviewees. It was necessary work—the kind of balls-aching routine that, in Drew's experience, dominated any major enquiry. But it was clear that they were making little progress.

The rest of the camp's staff were either much smarter or much dumber than Batkhuyag—or, quite possibly, Drew reflected, they were both. Either way, they were admitting nothing. No, they had no recollection of seeing Delgerbayar at the camp. No, they hadn't particularly noticed any strangers on the site that day, though it was difficult to tell with all the comings and goings. No, they had not overheard any conversations last night. Maybe there were some policemen in the bar last night—there often were—but, no, they couldn't honestly remember for sure. And in any case it never paid to get too close to the police.

"It's a waste of time," Drew said, as the final staff member had been ushered from the room. It was particularly so for him since few of the interviewees had spoken any English.

"It's always a waste of time," Nergui agreed, "but we have to do it. You never know when someone might let something slip. Look at Batkhuyag."

"He was being smart," Drew said.

Nergui nodded. "I like it when people are smart. It's when they make mistakes."

"He's just got a big ego. Likes to tell you what he knows."

"That will get him into trouble in a place like this," Nergui said.

"Maybe it already has."

Nergui frowned. "There are some patterns forming here," he said, slowly, "but I have no idea what to make of them. What are your thoughts?"

He sounded as if he was genuinely interested, though Drew suspected that he was being humoured. "I've no idea," he said. "What have we got? Delgerbayar makes his unscheduled trip down here, meets someone presumably by arrangement, gets into an argument with them, slips away when the police arrive and comes here, though we've no definite sightings. The person he met may or may not have been a guest here." It didn't sound all that much, now that Drew came to summarise it. "Then somehow, somewhere, he gets himself killed, and ends up, headless, in the factory where we found him." He plunged on, willing himself not to envisage that scene again. "And then we find that, within hours, although the news has been kept under wraps, the local police are gossiping about his death and apparently saying that he brought it on himself. It's not a lot."

"It isn't," Nergui agreed. "And we shouldn't necessarily make too much of the police down here. You're not likely to keep that kind of thing very quiet, especially when so many officers were involved in finding the body." He paused. "Which may, of course, be another reason why the killer set it up like that."

"But why would they think he had it coming?"

Nergui shrugged. "Maybe just the usual small-town resentment of HQ. Maybe they didn't like the fact that he'd invaded their turf."

"Or maybe they know something."

"Maybe. Which brings us to our group of tourists—those who were chatting to the police in the bar last night. We should talk to them next."

"It's not going to be an easy conversation," Drew said. "Especially if you're trying to keep Delgerbayar's death quiet."

"I think we should still keep it quiet. If the news is out there, I want to know who's spreading it, and I'd rather it wasn't me." Nergui paused. "Just a friendly conversation is all we need."

Nergui had asked Batkhuyag to track down some of the tourists. They were back now from their trip and were in their *gers* or out in the setting sun, resting before dinner. Moments later, Batkhuyag returned followed by two quizzical-looking men. Both were middle-aged, one short and overweight, the other tall and deeply tanned. The latter was wearing sunglasses and made no move to remove them as he entered the dim interior of the *ger*.

Nergui watched until Batkhuyag had backed out of the tent, and then gestured to the two men to sit. "Good afternoon, gentlemen. I am very grateful that you were able to join us."

The overweight man scowled faintly. "What's this all about? We're supposed to be on vacation." He was an American.

"I understand. I apologise for interrupting your leisure. I will be as brief as possible."

"That would be appreciated."

"You have been here a few days, that is right?"

"Four days. We're flying back up to Ulan Baatar tomorrow. It's an organised tour."

"I hope you're enjoying your visit to our country."

"It's very interesting. But I'd be grateful if you would get to the point." Drew was watching closely. It was clear that the overweight man had little time for small talk, but it wasn't clear if there was any agenda, beyond his desire to conclude their discussion. The other man, Drew noted with some interest, had still not spoken, but was watching the discussion with a faint smile playing across his face, as though he were nothing more than a disinterested observer of the interview.

"Of course," Nergui smiled. "As I think you have been told, I am a senior officer with the Ministry of Security here—"

"I was told you were a cop."

"In effect, I am. I'm on secondment to the Serious Crimes Team. My colleague here—" Nergui gestured towards Drew, "—is most definitely a cop. He is a chief inspector with the British police."

The overweight man looked across at Drew, baffled now. Whatever assumptions he had made about this meeting had clearly been overturned. "What's this all about? What's a Brit doing here?"

"It's a long story, Mr.—?"

"Collins."

"Mr. Collins. I won't bore you with the details, as I realise how precious your time is. We're investigating a potentially very serious crime in Ulan Baatar, which has also had an impact on some British interests there, hence Chief Inspector McLeish's presence. Sadly, it appears that the case may also involve one of our own officers who went missing a week ago."

"What does this have to do with us?"

"Nothing directly," Nergui said. "Except that we believe that, after leaving Ulan Baatar, the officer in question came here."

"Here? Why would he come here?"

"We do not know. As yet. He was seen at the airport, and we have some evidence that he came here. But we do not know what he did or who he saw. We are therefore interviewing a number of people—mainly staff, but also some guests—who may recollect him and shed some light on what he did here."

"And why do you think we can help?"

Nergui shrugged. "I have no idea whether you can or not. As I say, we are simply speaking to a cross-section of people. You have frequented the bar here in the evenings?"

"No law against that, is there? We tried that kind of law once. I wouldn't recommend it."

"On the contrary," Nergui said, "it is encouraged. Though perhaps some of my countrymen partake with a little too much enthusiasm. No, I simply wondered whether you had seen the officer in question in the bar?" He handed the photograph over to Collins.

Collins scrutinised it closely, then twisted and handed it to the other man, who looked at it very briefly without removing his dark glasses, and shook his head. "I'm afraid we can't help you," Collins said.

"No? Well, we have to keep asking. Thank you for your time, Mr. Collins and—?" He looked at the other man, who smiled and nodded back, but still said nothing. "We are very grateful to you. I hope you will enjoy the remainder of your trip. Have you had a chance to meet any of the locals down here?" He added the last question as an apparent afterthought.

"Locals? One or two—I can see what you mean about them knocking back the booze. We've had one or two lively nights in the bar." With the interview at an end, Collins sounded more relaxed.

"The local police use this place a lot," Nergui said. "We thought that might have been why our colleague came here. But they seem to know nothing about this."

"They—" Collins began, then stopped. "I don't know who we met. We couldn't really make ourselves understood. Except through the international language of the bottle." He looked back at the other man, and Drew wondered whether some sort of signal passed between them. But Collins had his head turned away and the other man had not removed his glasses, so there was no way of knowing. "Well, if you've finished with us, gentlemen, I think we'll go and prepare ourselves for another night of socialising and inebriation."

"Please, be our guest," Nergui said. "Have an enjoyable stay. Everything in moderation, as they say."

"Except moderation," Collins said, as a parting shot. The door of the *ger* closed softly behind him.

Nergui waited a moment, swinging softly on his chair, then said, "What do you think?"

"I think he's guilty as hell," Drew said.

Nergui nodded slowly, as though contemplating this opinion and giving his reluctant assent. "But of what?"

"Haven't a clue, I'm afraid. Probably nothing to do with this case."

Nergui laughed and rose slowly from the chair. "Come," he said, "we've spent enough time in the darkness going slowly round in circles. Let's at least step into the sunshine as we do it."

Drew followed Nergui out of the tent. At first, the light was blinding after the dim interior of the *ger*. Although it was still only mid-afternoon, the sun was already low above the horizon, casting long shadows across the desert. The day was growing noticeably cooler.

"It will be cold tonight," Nergui said. "Zero or perhaps lower."

They walked slowly out of the camp gates, and made their way across the sand, Nergui leading. There was no obvious destination. The undulating sands stretched emptily ahead of them.

Off to the left, in the far distance—it was impossible to tell how far—there was a small clustering of *gers*, but little else to be seen on the expanse surrounding them.

They walked a few hundred yards away from the camp, and Nergui stopped, looking back. "It looks very peaceful, no?"

"Miles from anywhere," Drew agreed.

"Miles from anywhere," Nergui repeated. "Miles from civilisation, certainly." He kicked the sand with his foot. "Desert," he said. "Emptiness." He began to walk again, heading away from the camp as if striding towards the desolate horizon. Drew followed, glad to be out in the air, but wondering where this was leading.

As though reading Drew's thoughts, Nergui stopped again, turning to face Drew. "I do not like this," he said, at last. "I do not like the pattern." He spoke as though commenting on an item of clothing or furniture, and for a moment Drew was unsure what he meant.

"The case?"

"The case," Nergui said. "I do not like the fact that we are down here in the Gobi. I do not like the involvement of the police. I do not like the systematic nature of these killings. I do not like the fact that—in the face of all that—we nevertheless appear to be dealing with a psychopath."

"We still can't be sure of that."

"No, we can't. Though I am not sure how else you would characterise such killings. But it is not just that. It is the totality of it that disturbs. It does not—how can I put this?—it does not fit together. And most of all, because there is a pattern here I still cannot read, I do not like the fact that we are down here, in this part of my country."

Drew was lost now. He watched Nergui, who was striding up and down the sand, as though he were unable to stand still for a moment.

"I don't understand. What is it you find so disturbing about this place? I mean, it's a desolate enough spot, but—"

"Desolate," Nergui repeated. "Yes, certainly. But it is the emptiness that disturbs me."

This was all becoming a little too philosophical for Drew's tastes. He would not have imagined that Nergui was a man prone to these kinds of imaginative fancies, but then he did not understand this culture.

Nergui smiled. "You think I am a superstitious fool?"

"No," Drew protested. "It's just—"

"I am expressing myself badly, trying to capture a feeling I have." He shrugged. "The famous detective's intuition. You have that?"

Drew smiled. "I think it's usually just a polite word for blind guesswork when I haven't a clue what's going on."

"That could well be the case," Nergui agreed. "But it is not entirely fanciful, I think, not in this case. We Mongolians are accustomed to the open air, to emptiness. It is our heritage. But today it feels to me as if we are surrounded by forces that are threatening that birthright. Do you know what lies that way?" He gestured towards the southern horizon.

For a moment, Drew was thrown by the apparent *non sequitur*. Then he turned to look where Nergui was pointing. The sun was beginning to disappear below the horizon, and the camp to their right was throwing huge shadows across the landscape around them. It would soon be dark.

Drew peered into the shadows. The line of the horizon was sharp against the deepening blue of the sky, but he could see nothing.

"You cannot see it from here, though it is not so very far," Nergui said. "Close to the Chinese border, down there, you will find one of our country's largest deposits of gold and copper, ready for exploitation."

"Not yet being mined?"

Nergui shook his head. "The deposits were discovered a few years ago. There are several different exploratory sites now, and there has been initial work carried out by various consortia—companies from Russia, Canada and the US, among others. Interest has been growing, as it's gradually become clear how substantial the deposits are. How much money there is potentially to be made. The Chinese are interested, as are the South Koreans. We are, as you might expect, nervous of the Chinese."

"If there's so much money to be made, why has it taken so long to get off the ground?"

"Mining is a risky and expensive business—we are talking about investment in the billions. I think, until the scale of the deposits was known, there was a nervousness about becoming involved. Perhaps there still is, but there is beginning to be a jockeying for position. Everyone wants to get in on the act. I am no geologist, but I believe there is much more out there." He paused. "This could transform our country. That is also a cause for nervousness. We are talking about a level of investment that is more than our gross national product—maybe several times more. If China or Russia were to make that level of investment—"

Nergui was pacing across the sand, beginning to walk back towards the camp. The sun had set, and darkness had spread across the desert with startling speed. Already above them, the sky was filling with stars.

"What do you think they might do?" Drew asked, walking behind Nergui.

"Maybe nothing. But it is not an altruistic state. We have spent decades being a puppet of the Soviet Union, and before that centuries as a satellite of China. I would not like those days to return."

Drew thought about Nergui's background in the industrial

sector, his experience in the US and Europe, his still unspecified role in the Security Ministry. It was not hard to see the connections in a society like this. "And you think that has something to do with this case?"

Nergui stopped and turned. The scattered lights of the camp were bright behind him. "I do not know," he said. "But we are here, in the Gobi, within striking distance of the exploration. We are here because we are following the trail of a murdered policeman who was supposedly investigating some trivial case of amateur gold prospecting. You are here because you are investigating the murder of a British geologist." He shrugged. "Of course, this may all be coincidence. But I feel something."

This all sounded fanciful to Drew, who had never had much time for the notion of the detective's intuition. His earlier response had been flippant but it had also been pretty close to the truth. He didn't often trust his own instincts. When he did, he had generally found it to be a mistake. Certainly, some of the people they had seen today, like the manager at the airport, had seemed evasive. But people often had something to hide, usually nothing to do with the matter at hand. Probably Batkhuyag was taking back-handers from suppliers, or even maybe from the police, for some scam or other. He was the sort who wouldn't want the police digging too deeply into his business, but it was likely that his fears had little to do with the case they were investigating.

"But what kind of connection could there be?" Drew said. "I mean, we're talking about brutal murders. The work of a potential psychopath. International mining companies may well have their ethical shortcomings, but I'm not aware they resort to that kind of stuff."

Nergui stopped as they approached the gates of the camp. "You are right, of course. I am probably just talking nonsense. It is hard not to be affected by the nature of the crimes we are investigating. It is hard not to see this as the beginning of the end of the world. The beginning of the end of our world, I mean. Things are changing here. I do not know what will emerge."

He stopped and looked back out towards the open desert. Far in the distance, it was possible to make out one or two lights, but otherwise, beyond the camp, the darkness was complete. The sky was heavy with stars now, sharper and brighter than Drew had ever seen. The absence of ambient light, the clarity of the air, made Drew feel that they really were poised on the edge of the galaxy, at the edge of the universe. And he felt, too, that at any moment they might begin to fall.

NINE

"Finally," Nergui said, "you will have an opportunity to sample some authentic local cuisine." He paused. "I apologise in advance."

Drew laughed. "I'm sure the wine and vodka will compensate."

"I am not sure about the wine, although I will see if I can influence our host. The vodka will be fine. But beware the airag."

"Airag?"

"Fermented mare's milk. It is an acquired taste. But you may prefer never to acquire it."

"Sounds—interesting."

"It tastes interesting. But we are not likely to be offered that here. You might be offered it if you visited a family in a *ger*, and I'm sure they arrange for the tourists to try it. People even distil airag vodka, which at least means that the inebriation compensates for the taste."

"You don't like it?"

"I love it, but I think you would not. But perhaps I am underestimating your Western tastes. In any case, as I say, we will not be offered that this evening."

They were sitting at the end of a bench table in the large tent that served as the camp's restaurant and bar. The space was already filling with crowds of tourists—most of them apparently English speaking, a mix of Americans, Canadians and British to judge from their accents.

"I still find it extraordinary that people come here as tourists," Drew said. "With all due respect, it's not an obvious holiday destination."

Nergui smiled. "No, only in the days when we had a captive market of those not allowed to journey beyond the iron curtain. We are working hard to promote our tourist industry, though—it is one of the ways we bring wealth into the country. These days, it is still mainly the serious travellers who come here, those who enjoy visiting the most faraway places. This is one of the last remaining wildernesses on earth. After all, it is little more than a decade since we had no Western visitors at all. Even now this place hasn't yet opened up in the way that Russia or Eastern Europe or even China have."

"It is an extraordinary place," Drew agreed.

"In a strange way, it is becoming even more extraordinary as the influences of the West begin to arrive," Nergui said. "We no longer know who we are. We were Communist, but never wholly subscribed to the creed. The Buddhists were suppressed but never really disappeared, and now they are stronger than ever. A large proportion of our people are still nomads and herdsmen. And many of those in the cities would like to be. But Western influences are growing. We are building our fancy business hotels. The large multinational corporations are investing in our development. We are sitting on vast resources which we and others would like to exploit. But we still drink airag. And we still eat this stuff."

As he spoke, the first course of the meal was being served, and a waiter dressed in traditional crimson robes was hovering at their shoulder. Nergui gestured him to proceed.

As it turned out, the meal was edible enough, though scarcely luxurious. The opening course was a salad largely comprised of tomatoes and cucumber. Then there was some plain grilled meat—the ubiquitous mutton, Drew thought, though it was difficult to be sure. Finally, some plain but not unpleasant cake. As the salad was being served, Nergui rose and walked over to the bar where Batkhuyag was standing chatting to another member of the camp staff. Nergui returned a few moments later, smiling and holding a bottle of red wine. "It's the usual Eastern European stuff," he said, peering at the label. "Romanian. But it will help the food down."

There was a water jug and glasses on the table. Nergui filled two glasses with the wine, and held his up towards Drew. "To peace," he said.

Drew returned the toast. "And to our—your—success in solving this case."

Nergui took a sip of his wine. "I think the two may well go together," he said.

"Thought you two gents would have found somewhere better to eat than this?"

Collins was hovering over them, a glass of beer clutched firmly in his hand. It was still early in the evening, though the meal was finished, but he already had the air of a not-quite-contented drunk.

"The options are limited," Nergui pointed out, smiling.

"You guys are staying here?" He swayed slightly, then carefully lowered himself to the seat. There was no sign of the man in the dark glasses.

"Just tonight," Drew said. "We fly back to Ulan Baatar tomorrow morning."

"Shame, shame," Collins said, sounding almost sincere. "We're having a good time down here, despite the lousy food." He gestured with the beer glass, narrowly avoiding tossing its contents across Nergui. "Beer's crap too, but at least there's plenty of it. And vodka."

"There is always plenty of vodka," Nergui said. "That is one blessing."

"No shit, sunshine." Collins beamed at them both, as though they were his new best friends. "Great stuff, the old vodka."

"Have you tried the airag?" Nergui said, sipping at his own glass of wine.

"Iraq?" Collins said. "We invaded that bastard."

"No, airag. It is our traditional drink."

"Thought vodka was your traditional drink." Collins seemed to be losing interest in the conversation, his gaze wandering around the room as though in search of more stimulating company.

"This is our other traditional drink," Nergui said. "You will be offered it on one of your tours. You must drink plenty. You will like it and it is good for you."

"Does it get you pissed?" Collins said.

"It is fermented," Nergui said, simply. "You can, if you wish, obtain airag vodka."

"Sounds wonderful. I'll get some to take home."

"Very wise. I'm sure it will be very popular in—where are you from, Mr. Collins? I mean, where in the USA?"

"Texas," Collins said. "Dallas. Where else?"

"Where else indeed? I apologise, Mr. Collins, it should have been obvious."

Collins stumbled slowly to his feet. "Good to see you again, guys." He staggered slightly, then regained his balance. "I'm back to the bar. Get you guys a drink?"

"That's very kind, Mr. Collins," Nergui said. "Not just at the moment, thank you. But we will join you at the bar, if we may?"

"It's a free country," Collins said. "Hey, is it a free country?"

"Nothing is free, Mr. Collins," Nergui said. "There is always a price."

Collins looked at him, baffled, then clearly dismissed Nergui's words as some kind of obscure Mongolian joke. "See you at the bar, gents," he said, lurching backwards.

"Do we really want to spend the evening with him?" Drew said.

"I can think of more edifying ways of relaxing, certainly," Nergui said. "But there are two good reasons why it might be a good use of our time."

"Which are?"

"He is on his way to being very drunk. And he does not have his minder with him."

"Minder?"

"Our anonymous friend in the dark glasses. Of course, I do not know if that is his role. But he joined our meeting today for some reason, and he seemed unduly reluctant to say anything at all."

"Probably just shy. Found your presence intimidating."

"Of course. That will be the reason. But, in any case, Mr. Collins seems far more talkative in his absence. It is probably worth our while to listen."

"We'd better not leave it too long, then. He looked as if he might well be comatose within the hour."

"Come then," Nergui said. "Let me buy you a beer."

Most of the tourists were still sitting at the tables, the babble of conversation rising as the evening progressed. Drew followed Nergui across the room to the bar, where Collins and a small group of other tourists were clustered. Batkhuyag saw them coming and moved over to serve them.

"Beers for us," Nergui said, "and perhaps we can buy Mr. Collins and his friends a drink."

Collins turned towards them, his face reddened by the alcohol. "Gentlemen," he said, loudly, "let me introduce the cops. This guy's come all the way from the United Kingdom. They're looking for one of their friends who's gone missing. Anyone seen him?" Collins looked around the group, as if he were seriously expecting a response. The others looked slightly embarrassed, and Drew suspected that they were probably looking for an excuse to leave Collins to his drinking. Drew didn't get the impression that the presence of two police officers was likely to reduce the group's discomfort.

"We're off duty now, Mr. Collins," Nergui said. He held up his beer. "As this demonstrates." Nergui was still wearing one of his dark suits but he was, for once, wearing his bright blue shirt open-necked and without an equally lurid tie. Drew thought he look almost relaxed.

"You guys really are cops?" one of the others said. His accent was American, from the southern states. "Collins isn't bullshitting?"

"Not this time." Nergui smiled. "But we are here to socialise now, nothing more."

"Cops are always cops," Collins said. "You bastards are never off duty."

"What makes you say that, Mr. Collins?" Drew said, smiling as politely as he knew how. He noticed that one of the group had already discreetly peeled away and was heading back to the dining tables. "Have you had many dealings with the police?"

Collins took a large swallow of his beer. "Jeez, I'm a businessman. Can't get you bastards off my back. You and the fucking IRS."

"So what line of business are you in, Mr. Collins?" Drew said. He tried to make it sound like nothing more than a social enquiry, just making conversation, but he was aware that his real curiosity was too close to the surface.

"See what I mean?" Collins roared, gesturing to the remaining two tourists. "Never let up, the bastards."

Nergui intervened smoothly. "Never mind," he said. "Tell us how you're enjoying our country." He turned to face the other two men, directing his conversation away from Collins. "This is your first visit?"

"Certainly is." This was the man who had spoken earlier. "It's a fascinating place."

"It's a craphole," Collins said, but the spleen had diminished in his voice.

Nergui turned. "I'm sorry you think so, Mr. Collins. It is, unfortunately, the only country we have."

The other two men guffawed, and Drew noticed them discreetly exchanging a signal that they should leave Collins to it. He watched as the two men moved away and walked back to join a group of mainly elderly men and women at one of the dining tables. He didn't get the impression that Collins was particularly welcomed by the rest of the tourists.

Collins shook his head and laughed. "You're right," he said. "I'm being a discourteous asshole. This country's okay. Not exactly Dallas, but okay."

"What made you decide to visit our country, Mr. Collins?"

He shrugged. "I travel a lot. Europe. Middle East. Far East. You name it. I enjoy travelling. Business or pleasure. I like going to interesting places. This is an interesting place."

"For a craphole, you mean?" Drew said.

"Hey, buddy, I was out of line. I apologised. Enough already."

"Of course," Nergui said. "I take no offence. You leave here tomorrow?"

Collins nodded. "Back up to Ulan Baatar, then into the north for a few days."

"Well, I hope you enjoy it all. Forgive me, but you do not strike me as the type who would normally be undertaking an organised tour of this kind?"

Collins signalled to the barman for another beer. "Spot on, buddy," he said. "But I wanted to see the place, and this was the only way to do it."

Nergui nodded. "It is still not easy to be an independent traveller here."

"Nope. I prefer to make my own way, usually, but I was advised against it." Collins seemed slightly more sober now, though he was still drinking the beer at a fast rate. "They told me it would make it harder to see the rest of the country."

"That is probably true. It is not so difficult now as it was. But we do not tend to make it easy for people to travel on their own."

"When do you cops ever make anything easy?"

"Well, that is not our job, Mr. Collins." Nergui smiled. "Your companion from this afternoon. He is not here this evening?"

Collins seemed to hesitate, though only for a moment. "Nah, he's gone off to bed early. Had a headache. Probably all that intensive questioning you put us through."

"We did not manage to extract very much from your companion," Nergui said. "He is a friend of yours?"

"No, met him on the trip. We get along pretty well, though. Drinking buddies. Not sure why he came along with me, but he happened to be with me when your friend"—he gestured towards Batkhuyag behind the bar—"asked me to join you."

"You never did tell us your line of business, Mr. Collins," Nergui said.

"No, I never did, did I?" Collins said. "And I wonder why you're interested."

"Just making idle conversation, Mr. Collins."

"In my experience cops never just make idle conversation."

"You seem to have a lot of experience," Drew said.

Collins laughed. "Yeah, too much experience not to be careful what I say to the likes of you."

"You are very astute, Mr. Collins," Nergui agreed. "I suppose that is necessary in the minerals business."

Drew tried hard to conceal his surprise. Collins's surprise, though, was obvious. "Jeez. Who the fuck told you that?" The belligerence was still there, but it was undercut now with a new hesitation. For the first time, Drew thought, Collins wasn't quite sure of his ground.

Nergui shrugged. "It is my job to know such things, Mr. Collins."

"I thought you bastards had put the KGB days behind you. What have you been doing, bugging my *ger*?"

"Nothing so crude, Mr. Collins. Your occupation was stated on your visa application. I thought it wise to make a few standard checks."

"Did you?" Collins said. "And what else did these—standard checks tell you?"

"Nothing to trouble you, I think, Mr. Collins."

Collins leant back against the bar and took another deep swallow of his beer. His eyes were darting around the room now, as if he were looking for someone to come to his aid. Behind them, the hubbub of conversation was growing louder.

Nergui was sipping his own beer very slowly. He smiled at Collins and then at Drew, who was watching all this with some fascination. He wasn't sure whether he should feel offended that Nergui had not chosen to share this information with him. "I hope I was not being intrusive, Mr. Collins. I made only the briefest of checks, looking at material in the public domain. But such things are always interesting."

Collins said nothing. He had drained his beer glass, and was clutching it in his hand like a lifeline. Drew wondered whether Nergui really had anything incriminating on Collins. He suspected not, but the fact that Collins was reacting in this way was telling enough.

"For example," Nergui went on, "you obviously know that your friend—your acquaintance from this afternoon—Mr. Maxon, I believe—also works in the minerals industry. And also lives in Texas, though in Houston. No wonder you get on so well. You must have a lot in common."

Collins shrugged, still watching Nergui closely. "We've barely talked about work," he said. "Don't think we're really in the same field. But I don't see it's any of your business."

"No, you are right. It is not." Nergui paused, as though thinking over the ethical implications of this. "It is, in part, my business to be aware of who is entering our country, and to understand why they are here."

"I'm a goddamn tourist, for Christ's sake," Collins said. "I'm here on vacation. What else?"

"I am not aware of anything else," Nergui said. "Unless you wish to tell me differently."

"Jesus, you people." Collins staggered backwards, as though the impact of the alcohol had suddenly overwhelmed him again. "You'll never change."

"How is that, Mr. Collins?" Nergui continued to sip on his beer, smiling.

Collins slumped against the bar. He looked up at the barman who, without being asked, placed another beer by his side. Drew wondered at what point they ought to suggest that Collins had had enough. It was difficult to be sure—his drunkenness seemed to ebb and flow with his moods. But his speech was definitely becoming more slurred now. "I don't know what the fuck it is with you people," he went on. "You have the chance to make something of this dump, but you want to keep control. You want to have it all your way. You'll go to any lengths to stop real money being made. You're all still bastard Communists under the skin."

"I'm not sure I really follow, Mr. Collins," Nergui said, softly.

"Oh, you understand well enough," Collins said. "Bastard Communist."

Nergui opened his mouth to respond, but a voice from behind them interjected. "Jesus, Jack. You had too much already?"

Maxon had appeared behind them, unnoticed. He was still wearing the dark glasses, even inside at night. With his eyes hidden it was impossible to read his expression, but there was the same thin smile on his lips. "I apologise, gentlemen. Jack can become a tad—aggressive when he's had a little too much."

It was the first time they had heard him speak, Drew realised. His voice was soft, emollient, the intonation of a salesman used to dealing with difficult customers.

"Do not worry," Nergui said. "Simply an exchange of views."

Maxon's smile was unwavering. "I've told Jack before. It's never a good idea to exchange views too forcefully." He paused. "Especially with the police."

"Wise advice," Nergui said.

"I think I'd better help get Jack to bed," Maxon said.

"Jeez, I'm okay," Collins said, waving Maxon away, but stumbling noticeably as he did so. "Fine for a few more yet."

"I don't think so, Jack," Maxon said. The words had the force of a command, rather than an expression of opinion.

Collins stared at Maxon, and for a moment Drew thought

the aggression was going to return. Then Collins shrugged. "Yeah, maybe you're right. Been a long day."

He thumped his now empty glass down on the bar and started to make his unsteady way towards the entrance, Maxon turning to follow him.

"Goodnight, Mr. Maxon," Nergui said. Maxon turned at the sound of his name, and for a moment Drew thought he caught a look of surprise before the blank expression returned. "By the way, Mr. Maxon," Nergui went on, "how are you feeling?"

"How am I feeling?" Maxon paused, and there was a slight, but definite edge of puzzlement in his voice now. He looked across at Collins, but he was turned away, fumbling with the door catches. "I'm feeling fine. Never better."

Nergui nodded slowly, as if he was giving this news serious consideration. "I'm very glad to hear that, Mr. Maxon. Very glad indeed."

TEN

After Collins and Maxon had left, Nergui and Drew had decided to retire early. They had a brief, friendly chat with some of the other tourists—mostly Americans, but with a scattering of Europeans too—but had recognised that they were unlikely to extract any further useful information from the group. So they walked back through the cold night air to the *ger*. Drew started to say something about Collins, but Nergui raised a finger to his lips. "We do not know where Collins and Maxon are sleeping," he whispered, very quietly. "Wait till we get to the *ger*."

It was a long time since Drew had slept under a tent. He had bad memories of a few seaside holidays in North Wales as a child, spending days listening to the endless drumming of rain on the roof, always feeling just too cold to be comfortable. But Drew had to acknowledge that this particular tent with its wooden frame and thickly padded felt walls was a long way removed from the flapping canvas monstrosities he had endured as a child.

The felt, Nergui had told him, was made by hand, the rolled cloth being pulled behind horses across the desert. In the centre of the *ger* was an iron stove, its chimney exiting through a hole in the middle of the peaked roof. The stove had been lit for them earlier in the evening, and the warmth in the tent now seemed perfectly adequate to repel the chill of the desert night. Even so, Nergui had told him that in the depths of the Mongolian winter, *gers* could only be made habitable by the collective warmth of multiple occupancy.

Inside, the *ger* was comfortably, if not luxuriously, appointed. The chairs they had used for the interviews were scattered around the floor. There were two narrow but comfortable-looking beds arranged around the walls, laden with blankets.

Once they were safely in the tent, with the door fixed shut behind them, Nergui said, "My apologies for not sharing the information about Collins and Maxon before. I had not intended to keep it from you. I called HQ earlier and asked them to look into the visa information. I picked up the message on my mobile just before we went into the restaurant."

"Don't worry. It made it much easier for me to keep a straight face. Like Collins, I didn't know how much you really knew."

Nergui laughed. "Not much more than I said, unfortunately. I had checked on the occupations they gave on their visa applications. I got Maxon's name from Batkhuyag earlier."

"Is there any indication of what exactly they do in the minerals business?"

Nergui shook his head. "Not really. In both cases the form just describes them as 'executives' and mentions the name of the employing company. I got HQ to check the company backgrounds, and discovered they're both part of a conglomerate involved in mineral prospecting and exploitation." He paused. "Mining, in other words."

"They both work for the same company?"

"In effect, yes. Different operating companies. It took a bit of digging on the part of one of my people to trace them back to the same parent. It's a US-based group which seems to operate in a whole range of sectors—mainly minerals like gold, copper, even uranium, all of which we have here. They also have various energy interests—oil, nuclear power."

"And they claim not to have known each other before meeting on this trip?"

"Collins claimed that Maxon was in bed with a headache," Nergui pointed out. "But he seemed to have made a good recovery."

"But if they are out here for a reason, why travel as tourists?"

"My guess is that it's because it's the easiest way to get around out here without arousing too much interest. We don't actively discourage independent travellers these days, but we don't make their lives too easy either. The government are keen to encourage foreign investment and links with external business, but we like to know what's going on. So if people are travelling here outside of one of the organised tours that we've now got pretty well-regulated, we tend to keep fairly close tabs on them. If they're here on legitimate business, then we usually know all about it in any case. If they want to travel for, say, scientific or social reasons, then we're happy to help so long as we know precisely what they're up to. We get a lot of visitors who have a specialist interest in things like our archaeology or geology, or even things like our music or folklore, but we usually arrange to work closely with them."

Drew again wondered just who Nergui was talking about here. Was this the police keeping tabs on people, or maybe some more shadowy government agency? But the implications were clear enough. "So someone who wanted to come out here and wander about on their own would arouse some suspicion?"

"Well, let us say, some interest, at least. Even if their intentions were legitimate, we would want to know what they were."

"And if their interests were not legitimate?"

"They would not get very far, I think."

Drew nodded. "So if you were looking to come out here for some illicit purpose, then coming as part of a tourist group might give you some cover."

"Absolutely. Of course, it would constrain your freedom of movement, but if your main aim was, for example, to make contact with someone or have some discussions, then it might give you enough scope."

"Which might explain why Delgerbayar came down to this place?"

"If they were meeting him. Or, more likely, if he was aware of a meeting taking place down here. Yes, perhaps."

Drew lowered himself on to one of the hard chairs. "Well, that closing little outburst of Collins's certainly suggested he was up to something."

"I was relieved," Nergui said. "I had almost given up on the possibility of taking advantage of his inebriation."

"But none of it makes any sense," Drew said. "I mean, even if Collins and Maxon are involved in something, it can only be some shady business deal. Why would that result in a series of brutal murders?"

"These things are not unknown. We are talking about some potentially very big deals here. There is a lot of money to be made. Those who were here early have gained some potentially major advantages. Others—some of them far from scrupulous—are now trying to muscle in on some of the opportunities."

"But multiple murder—"

"I agree. It seems unlikely. We have been aware of some cases of—well, shall we call them 'disputes' between different parties. And, I think, some of that has led to violence from time to time, though it is usually well concealed. But, no, nothing like this."

Drew was unsure what kind of world he was getting involved with here. In his experience, serious businessmen might well be unethical and even criminal, but they were rarely violent. If only because violence was too messy, left too many dangling loose ends. It was the real villains who got involved in violence, like the gangs fighting in the drugs feuds in inner-city Manchester or Merseyside. But most of these were small fry—little men with ideas far above their station.

At the same time, he could not ignore the fact that serious organised crime really did exist. It wasn't just the product of over-glamorised Hollywood movies. And over the borders from here, in both Russia and China, different forms of economic and social transition had created societies where such interests could thrive. It wasn't so far-fetched to assume that some of these forces might now be exerting some influence in this country.

If that were the case, Drew wasn't sure he wanted to be involved. This was unknown territory in every sense. In this world, he wasn't even sure where the boundaries lay between criminality, politics and business. It was already clear that for all his intelligence and charm, Nergui was like no policeman Drew had ever encountered. Stick close and watch your back. But from whom?

"But do you think it's possible," Drew asked, "that this is all connected?"

"I do not know," Nergui said. "All we can do is try to trace out the patterns and see where they might connect. We keep returning to mining, to minerals. But then it is the future of this country. It already accounts for more than half of our exports and has the capability to change the fabric of our society. So it is perhaps not unexpected that it should dominate our thinking at every level, or that it should attract some dubious interests. But whether that is sufficient to justify all that has happened? I do not know." He paused. "I am being fanciful again. But I have a sense of something working itself out. Something that is not straightforward. It makes me uneasy. I do not know where this is going."

It sounded like the mother of all understatements to Drew, but there was also a sense of something unspoken, some understanding that Nergui was reaching that he was not yet able or prepared to share. Nergui stared, blank-faced, at the floor.

"We should get some sleep," Drew said, finally.

"You are right," Nergui said. He looked up and smiled palely. "We do not know what tomorrow holds. We should sleep."

Drew expected that sleep would not be easy to attain, but he was wrong. The lingering effects of the beer and wine helped, and he fell asleep very quickly after climbing into the narrow bed. He was wearing an old track suit which he had brought in place of pyjamas. Nergui was wearing some similar old garment, which looked as if it might be military issue. Despite the chill of the desert night outside, the tent felt warm and comfortable. Nergui had turned out the electric light, and the darkness was almost complete, except for a very faint glow from the stove.

When he woke, Drew had no idea how long he had been sleeping. The tent was still in utter darkness, but almost immediately he had a sense that something had changed. He stiffened in the bed, trying to pin down the sense of unease that was rippling through him. Was there someone else in the tent? He lay still and tried to listen, but could hear nothing. Not even, he realised, the sound of Nergui's breathing.

He slipped out of bed, and fumbled his way carefully across the floor until his fingers touched the soft wall of the tent. Although his eyes were adjusting to the dark, he could see virtually nothing and the glow from the stove appeared to have extinguished. He thought he could see a faint shadow which might have been the low table. He stopped momentarily, wondering if he could hear anything, but there was nothing except the unnervingly loud sound of his own breathing.

Drew began to move forward, keeping his hand on the tent wall until he found the door frame. He ran his hand across the wood and fumbled until he found the light switch. He pressed the switch and the *ger* was flooded with bright light. The tent was empty. There was no intruder, no evidence of any disturbance. And there was no sign of Nergui.

His bed was rumpled but unoccupied. The sheets had been pulled back, as though Nergui had climbed out in a hurry.

Drew paused. Why was he getting so worked up about this? In all likelihood, Nergui had just gone off to the camp lavatories to relieve himself of some of the evening's beer.

But, somehow, Drew felt that wasn't the case. Something felt wrong. He looked around the sparsely furnished *ger* trying to identify anything out of place, something that might justify his sense of unease. But other than Nergui's overcoat being missing there was nothing.

Drew turned and pushed open the door. The cold night air hit him in the face, startling after the warmth of the tent. He stepped back in, grabbed his own coat and thrust his feet into his shoes. Then he pulled back the door and walked out into the night.

The camp was silent. For the first time, Drew thought to look at his watch. Just after three a.m.

The perimeter of the camp was studded with small spotlights to light the walkways, but otherwise everything was in darkness. There was no moon, and the sky above was dazzling with stars, an even more brilliant display in the full night. The thick smear of the Milky Way stretched out above.

Drew walked forward cautiously, listening for any sound. There was nothing. All of the *gers,* and the larger administration and reception buildings, were dark and silent.

He walked a few more steps, then turned the corner into the main walkway that led up to the administration building. At the far end, in one of the *gers* nearest to the reception building, there was a light. The door of the *ger* was open, and the light from the interior stretched out across the walkway.

Drew walked up the path, his feet making no noise on the soft sand. He drew level with the entrance to the *ger* and moved forwards to peer inside.

Nergui was standing just inside the door, his back to Drew, motionless.

"Nergui?"

Nergui turned, with no obvious surprise. "Drew," he said.

Drew walked forward, and looked past Nergui into the interior of the tent. He was, he realised, not surprised at what he saw. The bed nearest to the door was coloured deep red by spilt blood. A body lay face down on top, its large frame half sprawled across the floor.

Across the room, another figure was lying next to one of the other beds, the body twisted, the head at an odd angle. There was no blood this time, but it was clear that this figure was also dead.

"I felt it coming," Nergui said, quietly. "But I was too slow. I didn't take it seriously enough."

Drew stepped forward to look around the *ger*. "Who—?" He looked more closely at the blood-stained figure. "Collins," he said.

Nergui nodded.

"And the other? Maxon?"

Nergui shook his head slowly. "Batkhuyag."

"Batkhuyag? But why?"

Nergui shook his head. "I do not know. Perhaps they both said too much. But it is very strange."

"You think it was Maxon?"

"That is the obvious explanation. But it is very strange."

Drew wasn't sure what Nergui meant. "How did you find them?"

Nergui looked at Drew as though he had just asked an unexpected question. "You know," he said, "I am not sure. I woke up— I don't know why. I am a light sleeper, always, and I woke with a sense that something was wrong. That I should have acted before. That I was too late."

Drew thought back to his own awakening, his own sense of unease. "So what happened?"

"I put on my shoes and coat and came out. Just as you have done. I saw the light in here. The door was already wide open. And I came and found the bodies."

Nergui was as blank-faced as ever, but Drew had the sense that he was genuinely stunned by this.

"You didn't see anyone else?"

"No. I think I heard the sound of an engine as I walked up here. Maybe a motorbike. But it was a long way away, and I thought little of it."

"You think it was Maxon?"

"It may have been. But he could still be in the camp."

The thought chilled Drew. If Maxon was the murderer here, then it was likely that he had also been responsible for the previous killings. The thought that he might still be somewhere in the camp behind them was not pleasant. Drew turned and peered into the darkness, looking for any movement.

"We should call for backup," Drew said.

Nergui pulled out his mobile. "I already have," he said. "But they'll be a while. All we can do is wait here, I think. We need to watch the scene, and we need to ensure that, if Maxon is here, he doesn't make a break for it."

Privately Drew thought that he might not be too worried if Maxon did make a break for it. He certainly wasn't sure he felt like trying to stop him.

"You said it was strange," he said. "What did you mean?"

Nergui looked around. "Why should he do this?"

"As you say, maybe he thought they'd said too much."

"But why do this? Why here? Why now? At the worst, these two might have raised a few suspicions. We were leaving tomorrow, they would soon be gone. We had no evidence to detain them. Maxon wanted to remain low key, that was obvious. So why commit a brutal murder under our noses? Why turn himself into the only obvious murder suspect?"

Nergui was right. It made little sense. "Maybe they had a fight of some sort. Maybe Maxon really is a psychopath. And perhaps it didn't take much to set him off."

"It is possible. But there is something else happening here. I feel it."

Drew felt it, too. He could feel the cold air of the desert penetrating this space, entering his bones. He could feel the cold glare of the empty galaxies above his head. He could feel the blankness of Nergui's gaze, who stared at these bodies as if he himself had been the perpetrator of their deaths.

This last thought was unexpected and struck Drew almost

with the force of a blow. It was ridiculous, of course. The real killer was out there somewhere behind them, perhaps close at hand, perhaps far away. But watching Nergui's face, Drew was struck once again by how alien this world was, how little he understood. And he realised that out here, anything might be possible.

ELEVEN

"I'm very disappointed, Nergui."

"Of course. So am I. I take full responsibility."

Anxiety was etched into the Minister's face as he paced slowly up and down the room. He was a heavily built man, his dark hair thinning. He was wearing an expensive-looking Western suit, but he wore it uncomfortably, as though he would rather be wearing traditional clothes. "Naturally," he said. He smiled, though there was no obvious humour in his expression.

"I will of course tender my resignation, if you feel that to be appropriate. I should point out that Doripalam carries no responsibility for this."

The Minister laughed. "Don't be ridiculous, Nergui. I don't know that there's anything else you could have done. And even if there was something *you* could have done better, I'm sure that no one else could. Let's face it, at least you were in the right place at the right time."

"Not quite at the right time, unfortunately," Nergui pointed out. "And it was only luck that I was there at all."

"Nevertheless, the truth is, if you can't put an end to this, I'm sure nobody else can."

Nergui nodded in acknowledgement. He knew the Minister too well not to engage in false modesty. "You may be right," he said. "If so, the question is whether I can."

"And what do you think?"

"I honestly do not know."

"But you have some ideas?"

Nergui shrugged. "I do not know whether I would even dignify them as such. There are some patterns. Some leads we can follow. That is all."

"That isn't much."

"It is all we have."

"What about Maxon?"

"Another mystery. He is a Westerner, on the run in our country, potentially accused of a series of brutal murders. But he has vanished from the face of the earth."

"That's not possible. Not here."

"It is not. But it has happened."

"The US Government has shown no signs of involving itself?" The Minister presumably knew the answer to this already but he waited for Nergui's response.

"No. I suspect they may be slightly embarrassed." Nergui allowed himself a small smile. "It appears that Mr. Collins was a dubious character. The FBI had a large file on him, potentially linking him to a whole series of possibly fraudulent deals. Action had been taken against him by the US regulatory bodies in connection with various doubtful business dealings, but he had managed so far to avoid criminal prosecution. He also appears to have connections with organised crime interests. If we had known any of this, he would not have been allowed into the country. I don't think the US will be rushing to uncover any further dirty linen."

"Well, that's one relief," the Minister said. He slumped himself back down behind his large, virtually empty desk. "And you're sure we've kept the whole thing tightly wrapped up in the media?"

"As best we can. There was no way we were going to keep this completely under wraps, given it happened in the middle of a camp full of tourists. And, frankly, we also wanted to get Maxon's picture in the media as quickly as possible so he could be picked up. So we've implied that this was some sort of bust-up between American business associates, with poor old Batkhuyag getting caught up in the middle."

"With no link to the murders here?"

"No. Those haven't even been mentioned. Some people may make the connection, but with so little information I wouldn't expect it."

The Minister nodded. "Well, that's something. And what about your Englishman?"

"I'm not sure. His presence here is something of a token gesture. He wasn't planning to stay more than a few days. But I'm keen for him to stay a little longer, if his bosses can be persuaded."

"Why?" The Minister frowned. "Do we really want some foreign policeman peering over our shoulders, prepared to embarrass us?"

"I don't think that's a risk. He's a dedicated policeman, not—with all due respect, sir—a politician."

The Minister laughed. "But he's in contact with the British ambassador?"

"The ambassador is in contact with him. Which is no surprise. But I don't think that's a cause for concern. The truth is, we can make good use of McLeish's experience and expertise in this case. We don't have too much of that among our own people."

"That's true enough. Okay. I'll trust your judgement on this one, Nergui, for the moment at least." The Minister paused, leaning forward over the table. "But, Nergui," he said, after a pause, "remember—no more disappointments. We can't afford it. Not again."

"So what do you *think* is going on?"

"As I say, I really don't have a clue," Drew said. "Nergui keeps talking about patterns, but there's no pattern to it at all."

"So far as you can see."

"So far as I can see," Drew agreed, mildly irritated by the ambassador's implied superiority. Still, he imagined that the ambassador rarely implied anything else.

"But what about the mining connection? That seems to suggest some kind of link."

"Well, yes, but I've no idea what. There's not really much to it, when you try to piece it all together. Okay, Ransom was a geologist. Delgerbayar, the murdered police officer, was involved in some supposedly trivial gold prospecting case. Collins and Maxon were both working in the minerals industry. That's about it."

"Plus this strange convocation of visitors to the Gobi."

"Yes, and that." But at best, Drew thought, it was as if they had a few pieces from a much larger jigsaw puzzle. A couple of edges, a bit of sky, part of a face. But nothing that might make a picture.

"And this chap Maxon has really gone missing?"

"Apparently."

"That seems difficult to believe."

"That's how Nergui feels. He thinks it's virtually impossible."

They were sitting in the ambassador's personal lounge, a comfortable room with low armchairs, thick-piled carpet and glossy mahogany tables. It was late morning and autumn sunshine was incongruously bright outside the window. The ambassador sipped his coffee. "And do you believe him?"

Drew hesitated perhaps a fraction too long. "I think so," he said. "I mean, I've no idea what to make of any of this, but I've seen no reason not to trust Nergui so far." This was true. On the other hand, he also didn't know whether there was any positive reason why he *should* trust Nergui.

The ambassador did not look convinced. "Well," he said, finally, "is it safe to assume that Maxon is behind all of this?"

Drew shook his head. "No. Not necessarily. I mean, of course it's possible. He's been in the country longer than Collins—for nearly three weeks. And, interestingly, although he's now here as a tourist, it's not his first visit. He's been here, supposedly on business, a couple of times before—made visits to various of the mines in the north of the country. We're in contact with the FBI, but they're not telling us much. There's nothing to connect him to the murders here, so far as we can see."

"But if he isn't, then it looks as if we have two psychopaths on the loose simultaneously. Quite a first for this place."

"Assuming," Drew said, "that Maxon was responsible for Collins's and Batkhuyag's murders."

"You think there's any chance he wasn't?"

"I really don't know," Drew said. "I mean, if these two murders had happened in isolation, of course he'd be the obvious candidate in the frame. But it's still hard to see quite why he'd have killed those two at that point. And it's hard to tie any of that in with the earlier killings."

"Maybe they're not linked."

Drew shrugged. "Maybe not. In which case, as you say, we have two rampant psychopaths and one hell of a coincidence."

The ambassador nodded, making a show of stirring his coffee again and selecting one of the luxurious biscuits from the plate in front of them. "So what do you think they know?"

"Who?"

"Nergui's people. The Ministry. Intelligence. They must have more knowledge than they're letting on."

"I don't get that impression. But then I wouldn't, I suppose." He paused. "To be quite frank, I'm feeling out of my depth in all this."

"Out of your depth?" The ambassador raised his eyebrows. "An experienced policeman? You're dealing with a bunch of amateurs here. Other than Nergui, that is."

"It's not that," Drew said. "Though this case is like nothing I've ever had to deal with as a policeman. It's the politics. It's the sense that there's something else going on, coded signals I'm not picking up."

"Ah, the *politics* . . ." The ambassador sat back in his chair, smiling. "Well, I'm with you there. Even though it's my job."

Drew didn't bother to add that he saw the ambassador as part of the problem. He thought it was probably better to move on. "But to go back to your question, no, I don't get the impression they know more than they're letting on. Certainly not at the operational level, anyway. It's difficult to tell what Nergui might know, as I'm sure you've experienced. But I think he's as disturbed by this as anyone. More than most, in fact. And I think that's because he doesn't usually come up against things he doesn't understand."

"Well, that would make sense. I think Nergui's used to being in control of things. And I imagine he must be under a lot of pressure, though we'd never know."

"Pressure?"

"From his Minister. If all this has just been the work of some lone psychopath, that would have been bad enough in terms of its impact. If, as it appears, it's something more complicated than that, then the Minister will be getting very anxious."

Drew finally got around to taking a sip of his coffee, which was already growing cold. "Why?"

"Well, there's a lot of noble talk about, you know, protecting the fabric of society and all that—and I'm sure Nergui genuinely believes some of that—but for the Minister this is just our old friend politics once again." The ambassador paused, as if he were wondering how openly to speak. Drew had already decided that the ambassador's apparent willingness to take Drew into his confidence was simply more game-playing. He would share only what he needed to, Drew had concluded, in the hope of getting something back. "It's the problem with democracy, I suppose," the ambassador went on. "Since this country introduced democracy at the beginning of the 1990s, there have been many changes but the Communist Party has largely retained power."

"So what's the problem? Aren't the Communists firmly entrenched now?"

"To some extent, but there's a lot of public unrest. There are plenty who think the country's going to hell in a handcart. Who knows what's around the corner? A psychopath on the loose for too long wouldn't be particularly helpful to the career of the Minister of Security. But if it's something more than that—particularly if there are commercial interests involved in some way—well, that could really be a knockout blow."

"So the Minister will want this sorted?"

"One way or another, yes. And quickly."

"What do you mean—one way or another?"

The ambassador shrugged. "I'm sure you must encounter these kinds of problems from time to time. Politicians want solutions. They don't really care whether the solution really solves the problem, so long as they can be seen to have done something."

"That kind of thing doesn't usually get down to my level, I'm glad to say."

The ambassador smiled, coldly. "Then, young man, you should count yourself very lucky. Enjoy it while you can." He spoke as though Drew's privileged status might change at any moment.

It was only after Drew had concluded his meeting with the ambassador that he remembered that he and Nergui were due to have dinner at the embassy that same evening. The relative light-heartedness he had felt at finally getting away from the ambassador melted away. What he had said was true. He was increasingly feeling out of his depth in this world, unsure who to trust or what to think. The prospect of an evening between the ambassador and Nergui was not an enticing one.

And how long was he supposed to stay out here? The original plan had been for him to fly home at the end of the week, with only the possibility of a return. But then he had received a message on his mobile from the Chief Constable's office to say that Nergui had requested he stay here a few more days, with the Ministry picking up the expenses. It was made clear that in the interests of international relations—not to mention the PR—Drew should accept the request.

There was also a message from Nergui suggesting that they meet in the bar of the Chinggis Khaan for a drink before dinner. He had last seen Nergui during their flight back from the Gobi that morning. Drew had been feeling exhausted after their disturbed night and although Nergui had the same brightness and energy that Drew had noted from the start, he looked troubled by the events of the night.

Their conversation on the return flight had been desultory, partly because of Drew's tiredness and partly because there seemed to be little worth saying and the case was, in theory, being handled by the local police chief, but there was no doubt that in practice he reported to Nergui. The relationship had been obvious to Drew, watching their conversation at the murder scene, even though he could not understand what was being said.

Compared with the previous murders, these were straightforward. Collins had been stabbed repeatedly in the chest and back, and appeared to have died from the loss of blood. Batkhuyag had been strangled, probably with a belt. Although no precise time of death had yet been established, both had been dead for some time before Nergui had found them, which explained how Maxon had been able to make his escape. The working assumption was that Maxon was the killer, and only Nergui seemed to be treating this as anything other than simple fact.

Even before they had embarked on their morning flight back to Ulan Baatar, a full-scale manhunt was underway. The local police chief had confidently expressed the opinion that Maxon would be picked up by the end of the day. After all, he had pointed out, how easy could it be for a Westerner to hide in the Gobi?

Nergui had called as soon as their plane had touched down to see whether this prediction showed any sign of being fulfilled. The answer was no. No one had yet reported seeing or even hearing of Maxon or any other Westerner outside the tourist camp. Police officers on motorbikes were making the rounds of all the surrounding *gers,* but so far to no effect. Still, it was, as the chief kept repeating, early days.

Drew assumed that by the time they met that evening, Nergui would have something more concrete to report. As before,

Drew came down from his hotel room to find Nergui holding solitary court in the corner of the bar. Drew was pleased to note that he had already ordered the beers.

Before Drew could ask the obvious question, Nergui was already shaking his head. "Nothing," he said. "No news at all."

Drew sat down opposite Nergui and took a long pull on his beer. "When did you last check with them?"

"Twenty minutes ago. They've promised me they'll call as soon as they have anything to report." He smiled. "But I'm not sure I trust them to be assiduous enough so I'll probably call them again later. Just in case."

"Someone must have seen him."

"You would have thought so, wouldn't you? I don't see how a Westerner on the run can stay unnoticed in the middle of the Gobi for long."

"Is it possible he's being sheltered?"

"I suppose so. It's quite possible that there's some herdsman out there who's not heard the news—though many of them have shortwave radios, these days—and who's taken pity on him. But you'd have thought we'd have found something."

"Maybe he's not trying to hide. Maybe he's committed suicide or just ridden off into the desert."

Nergui nodded. "I suppose it's not beyond the realms of possibility, if it is true that he's responsible for these killings."

"You still think he might not be?"

"I genuinely don't know. It is the logical assumption. Although we then have to consider what the link is with the earlier murders, or we're left with two killers. But mainly it is that old instinct again, nothing more. I don't think it is as simple as that."

"You think the same person is responsible for all these killings?" It sounded ridiculous, Drew thought. But the alternative seemed even more absurd.

Nergui shrugged. "There is no point in speculating. But my instinct says no. Which is a truly terrifying prospect."

"I understand you've asked my bosses if I can stay on here." Drew realised too late that the statement sounded accusatory. He hadn't intended that, but maybe he was right to be annoyed.

Nergui nodded. "I'm sorry," he said. "I have been thoughtless. I should have asked you first. But I had the impression you were keen to stay a little while longer. And I was certainly keen to draw on your experience." He paused. "But I was forgetting about your wife and family. That was inconsiderate. I am sorry."

Drew wondered about trying to extract some moral leverage from Nergui's apparent embarrassment. But, in truth, he wasn't even sure how genuine this embarrassment was. Nergui struck him as a man who always knew exactly what he was doing. If he'd neglected to ask Drew first, this was probably because he didn't want to take the risk that Drew might decline. Much easier to go above Drew's head and get the deal done that way. Maybe in Nergui's position he'd have done the same. Maybe.

"Well, I think I've managed to square that side of it. Sue isn't best pleased, but I think she accepted that it isn't my choice. But what I can't really understand is why you want me to stay. I'm not sure there's really much I can add."

"You are too modest," Nergui said, in a tone that suggested sincerity about this at least. "Other than Doripalam, most of our men are amateurs or worse. We have never had to deal with anything remotely like this."

"Who has?"

"Well, you have much more relevant experience than any of us."

Drew wasn't convinced by this. His own suspicion was that Nergui wanted to have him around because he was a neutral third party. He imagined that Nergui's professional life was almost as lonely as his domestic life seemed to be. He had no obvious peers in the police, other than Doripalam, and the relationship there was uneasy. His relationship with the rest of the team seemed to be distant and untrusting. And no doubt his relationships with the Minister and his other political masters were far from straightforward. It was probably a relief to find himself working with someone who had no particular axes to grind.

"Well, I'll accept the compliment," Drew said. "To be honest, I'd be sorry to have gone back now. Partly because there's nothing more frustrating than leaving a case before it's resolved. And partly because I want to see more of your country while I'm here."

"I am surprised it holds many attractions for you any more," Nergui said. "The presence of corpses tends to take the edge off the tourist trail."

"Is that what your Minister thinks?"

"It is one of his concerns, of course. Our tourist trade is growing, partly because this is seen as being one of the last unexplored parts of the world. But also because we have a relatively safe environment."

"And the presence of a serial killer—or, worse still, two serial killers—doesn't particularly enhance that reputation."

"Quite. But I think his bigger concern—our bigger concern— is that there may be something more behind this."

Drew took a large drink of his beer. There seemed little point in holding back his thoughts. He was unsure what games everyone else might be playing, so there was probably some mileage in being completely straightforward. "My friend the ambassador thinks you know things you're not sharing. Is that true?"

"Me personally, or the Ministry in general?" Nergui said, without hesitation.

"Either. Both. I mean, I think the ambassador's concerns are with the Ministry. But from what I've seen, I think it's more likely that you might know something you're not sharing with anyone else. On your side or mine."

"Are we on different sides, then?" Nergui regarded Drew with something approaching amusement.

"You tell me. The ambassador clearly thinks we are. I hope not. But all this is new to me."

"Much of it is new to me also, Drew. I do not think we are opposing sides in this. But then I am not sure what the sides are."

It was only afterward, as they were walking through the clear night air towards the embassy, that Drew realised that Nergui had not answered his initial question.

The evening was already becoming chilly, and Drew pulled his overcoat more tightly around him. Nergui had told him that, as the winter approached, nights in the city became very cold—minus fifteen or more degrees. There was little cloud cover, and above the city lights and neon signs the skies were filled with stars. The main streets were well lit, and this early in the evening there were still plenty of pedestrians. The streets around the hotel were busy with cars and buses.

Away from the busier thoroughfares, though, the atmosphere of the city was very different. The side-streets were ill-lit, and in many cases disappeared into darkness only yards from the main road. As they walked briskly towards the embassy, Drew thought back to the first victim, the body dumped in one of these dark silent streets. Involuntarily, he glanced back over his shoulder. There were a few other pedestrians behind them, mostly swathed in heavy coats and hats, huddled against the deepening cold. For a moment, he had a sense of being watched, maybe even followed, though none of those behind were paying any obvious attention to himself or Nergui.

Nevertheless, he was glad when they reached the brightly lit gates to the embassy. As Nergui rang the bell, he looked back again. There was a figure standing, half in shadow, by the corner of the street opposite. It was only a silhouette so it was impossible to tell if he was looking in their direction. A moment later, he turned and disappeared into the gloom of a side street. Drew found himself shivering slightly, unsure if this was just the effect of the cold.

"Gentlemen, welcome. Do come in. It must be freezing out there."

Drew turned and was surprised to see the ambassador himself greeting them at the door. He wasn't quite sure what he had expected. During his daytime visits, there had been a receptionist and other staff dealing with visitors. In the evening, Drew had half-expected a butler.

He followed Nergui into the brightly lit hallway, and was surprised at the sense of relief he felt when the large front door was finally closed behind them.

"This way," the ambassador said. "We're in my private quarters. Much more intimate than any of the official rooms."

The ambassador led them along a corridor then up a flight of stairs. The door at the top of the stairs opened to reveal a small hallway, and then beyond that a comfortably furnished sitting room. A middle-aged couple were already sitting in armchairs, sipping sherries.

"Come in, come in, gentlemen. Let me take your coats."

Again, Drew had been unsure what to expect from the dinner. He had vaguely imagined some kind of formal arrangement— perhaps waiter-served around a polished oak table. However, the ambassador had been insistent on informal dress, so some form of intimate gathering seemed more likely.

"Let me do the introductions," the ambassador said, bundling their heavy coats into his arms. "Professor Alan and Dr. Helena Wilson." He gestured at the couple, who had risen as Drew and Nergui came in. "And Chief Inspector Drew McLeish and, from our host country, Mr. Nergui of the Ministry of Security. I'll leave you to get to know one another for a few moments, if I may, while I put these down and get you both drinks. Sherry okay?"

He disappeared back into the hallway. The Wilsons stood looking at Drew and Nergui for a moment. In Drew's experience, the mention of his police rank wasn't generally conducive to small talk at parties. But Nergui, as ever, was fully up to the moment. "Good evening," he said, smoothly, gently gesturing them back to their seats. "You both work in academia?"

Professor Wilson shook his head. "Helena does. I used to, but I've been seconded to the Civil Service for a couple of years now. Working for the government," he added, presumably for Nergui's benefit.

Nergui smiled. "Ah, so we are both government servants," he said. "What is your field?"

"I'm a chemist by background," Professor Wilson said.

"Ah. Very interesting." Nergui nodded, as though giving serious contemplation to this information. "I imagine there are few chemists in the Civil Service?"

"Well, not practising ones, no, except in the government laboratories. I'm a little unusual, I guess. I had a background in industry after completing my doctorate, with a parallel career in academia, so I bring a little commercial expertise to the policy field, as well as technical knowledge."

"I understand," Nergui said. "My own position is not dissimilar." He left the comment hanging in the air. "And you, Dr. Wilson, are you a chemist also?"

"Please call me Helena," she said, smiling. "No, I'm afraid I'm not a scientist at all. I'm an anthropologist by background, but for the last few years I've been working in the field of folklore and folk traditions. It's my fault we're here, I'm afraid. Alan's just tagging along."

"It's hardly a burden," he said. "It's fascinating. You have an extraordinary country here."

"You are very kind. You are here to study our folklore?" Nergui prompted.

Dr. Wilson nodded. "The music, mainly. But yes, all of it. I'm no expert in the field—I specialise in English folklore and folk song—but I was interested to find out more. So I used my sabbatical to arrange an exchange with the university here."

"And you have found material to interest you?"

"Very much. I was excited to hear the *khoomi* singing—hear it live, I mean. I'd only ever heard it on record. And you have a tremendous wealth of folk material—songs, stories."

"I am pleased to hear it," Nergui said. "I am afraid I can claim no expertise in the field, but of course I know songs and stories from my own childhood. Are these stories different from those in England?"

"There are parallels, and it's astonishing how often variants of the same stories recur throughout the world. But the stories here are distinctive. They reflect the geography, the history and the lifestyle here."

"Everything here is different," the ambassador said, entering the room with two more sherries. "This is like no other country."

"Have you been here long?" Drew asked.

"Three years now. They're looking to move me on, but I'm close enough to retirement that I think they might just quietly forget about me for the moment. This seems a decent enough place to wind down."

"There must surely be more comfortable postings?" Nergui said. "For all my loyalty to my country, I wouldn't claim that it is the easiest place to live."

"You're right but there are plenty of less comfortable ones too. This society is stable. The people are very hospitable. There is a wealth of history and tradition here which is different from anywhere else on earth. I can manage to get hold of most of the creature comforts I need." The ambassador held up his sherry glass in demonstration. "I'm very happy."

"Then you're very lucky," Professor Wilson said. "I don't think many could claim that about their work."

As though accepting a cue, his wife turned to Drew. "And you, Chief Inspector—"

"Drew. Please."

"Are you happy in your work?" She was smiling, but there was an undercurrent of seriousness that Drew couldn't quite pin down.

"I don't know if I've ever really thought about it. Mind you, I've never thought about doing anything else either."

"The ambassador told us why you are here. It's a dreadful case."

Drew exchanged a glance with Nergui. He wondered quite how much the ambassador had told the Wilsons. Had he just explained about Ransom's death—which had received some lurid coverage in the British press—or had he also discussed the wider series of killings?

"Well, I wouldn't take the press coverage too literally." Drew wasn't going to give anything away. "But, yes, it was a brutal killing. And it somehow seems worse when it happens to someone so far from home."

Professor Wilson opened his mouth as if he were about to say something, but then stopped and looked across at his wife. "We shouldn't pry," he said. "I realise that there must be things you have to keep under wraps."

Nergui smiled, his face as inscrutable as ever. "You are right," he said. "There are aspects of the case that we need to keep confidential, even in company as illustrious as this." There was no way of knowing whether the final comment was intended ironically.

"But you really have no idea of a motive?"

Drew shook his head. "As Nergui said, it wouldn't be appropriate to say any more. We're progressing with our enquiries, as they say."

"Of course, no. We understand. It's just a bit of shock when this sort of thing happens to a fellow Brit; it makes you look over your shoulder, particularly when you're in a place as—well, as alien as this." Professor Wilson glanced at Nergui. "I'm sorry, but you understand what I mean?"

Drew understood what he meant, all too well. Nergui simply nodded. "Certainly. Our country is very different from the West. We are becoming more Westernised in some ways—though less so in others, as the Soviet influence has declined. I can understand why you would feel very far from home." He sat back in his chair, as though musing on this idea. "Mr. Ransom's death was dreadful, and a real shock to everyone. All I can say is that, despite that, this is a very safe and stable country. Our crime rate is low, generally, and we have little violent crime."

"But you have had other murders?" Professor Wilson said. "Recently, I mean."

Nergui gazed at him expressionlessly. "This is a city. People get drunk, get into fights. We have the occasional mugging, the occasional assault. And, yes, the occasional murder."

"And do you think they're connected?" Professor Wilson said. "These occasional murders?" There was a definite edge to his voice now. Drew assumed that Wilson was a variant on the type of "concerned citizen" who could always be relied upon to write personally to the Chief Constable.

"I really don't think it would be appropriate to discuss this any more," Drew said. "I'm sorry, but you're putting us in a very difficult position." He was aware, even as he said this, that it was likely to be construed as a tacit admission that the murders were linked.

"I'm sorry, Chief Inspector, I had no intention of putting you in a difficult position. I was just interested to know whether it is safe for us to walk down the streets at night."

Nergui nodded, ignoring the undertone of sarcasm. "I understand your concerns. But this city is safer than almost anywhere else you could be, believe me."

The words were reassuring, and Nergui's calm demeanour was even more so. But Drew wondered whether Nergui's claim was true. And, more importantly, whether Nergui himself really believed it.

TWELVE

"What about you, Drew, do you believe in it?"

"No, I don't. Well, what I mean is, I'm quite happy to accept that there might be more things in heaven and earth and all that, so I'm prepared to keep an open mind in principle. But I have to say that I've never seen it work in practice."

"Have you ever used it?" Professor Wilson said. "In an investigation, I mean?"

It was nearly midnight, and they had become caught up in one of those conversations that only happen amongst strangers when too much alcohol has been consumed. Drew had noticed that the ambassador was adept at plying others with drink while minimising his own consumption. No doubt an invaluable tool of the trade.

"Not personally, no. But I've been involved in cases where it's been tried."

"What kinds of cases?"

"Oh, well, you know, usually missing persons—particularly

missing children. When there's a child missing, after a while the parents will cling to any hope—anything that might bring them some news, even it's bad. They'd rather know."

"But you've never seen it work?"

"No, never. I've always had mixed feelings about it. We wouldn't usually initiate it—though I know there are some senior officers who take it seriously—but we wouldn't stand in the way if, say, the parents wanted to try it. But I'm always afraid they're being taken for a ride. There are unscrupulous people out there, who'll take advantage even in a situation like that."

"So you think these people—mediums, whatever you choose to call them—are all charlatans?" There was something forensic in Professor Wilson's approach, as though he were a prosecuting barrister trying to get the better of a hostile witness.

"I wouldn't say that," Drew said, though privately he thought he would probably say exactly that. "I mean, some of the people I've encountered seemed genuine enough. In the sense that they believed in what they were doing, at any rate."

"But you never saw it work?"

"Never. There have been several occasions when we've all gone traipsing off, feeling slightly ridiculous, because one of these people had said we would find something in a particular location—a field or woodland or whatever. But we never did."

"But there have been instances where the police have been guided accurately by mediums, haven't there?" Helena Wilson said.

"I believe so," Drew said. "I've read press stories about them, and I've met some senior experienced policemen who give some credence to it. But it's not been my experience."

He wasn't entirely sure how they'd got into this conversation. It had started with some comments—apparently humorous—from Helena Wilson about her own "second sight." She had explained that she had grown up with a sense of being able to predict events or, on occasions, be aware of events happening elsewhere.

"It's one of Helena's hobby horses," her husband said. "As a man of science, I struggle with it a little."

"Rubbish, I'm not suggesting anything unscientific. I'm not even suggesting that it's necessarily true. It's not something I can turn on or turn off at will." This was obviously an argument that they had rehearsed on many occasions, and there was no rancour in her voice. "But I have had certain experiences, which I'd struggle to explain."

"What kinds of experiences?" Nergui said, sitting forward.

"Oh, well, you know, having a sense that something's going to happen before it does."

"Like predicting 9/11? There were, inevitably, people who claimed to have done that," the ambassador said.

She shook her head hard. "No, in my experience, it's something much more personal, much closer to home. It's the sense of—oh, I don't know, things like meeting someone and feeling that something bad is going to happen to them. And then it does—they have an accident or whatever."

"And this has happened to you?" Nergui asked.

"Yes, exactly that. I've also, on a couple of occasions, been aware of accidents or illnesses affecting people close to me before I've been told about them."

"That could just be coincidence," her husband pointed out. "It's the usual story. You factor out all the times you had that feeling but nothing happened."

"I can't argue with that. But I honestly can't recall having that feeling without some resulting event. Which doesn't mean that there haven't been plenty of occasions when I've not had the feeling but the person's gone ahead and had an accident anyway." She laughed. "I'm not making any serious claims for this, you understand, just telling you what I've felt."

"What about you, Nergui? Have you ever been involved in using mediums?" Dr. Wilson turned to Nergui.

Nergui shook his head. Drew had noticed that although Nergui appeared to be accepting and consuming wine and port along with the rest of them, he was displaying no sign of inebriation. Drew wished he could say the same for himself. He was finding it increasingly difficult to string a coherent sentence together. "I'm afraid not," Nergui said. "Though perhaps sometimes it would be better if we did. It might improve our success rate. I also think that attitudes are a little different here. We would not use a medium in the sense you describe, but many of my colleagues would see a spiritual dimension to their role."

"What sort of spiritual dimension?" Professor Wilson asked.

"It varies. Religion and spiritualism have a confused history here, mainly resulting from the Stalinist suppression of religion. So now we have some people who are genuinely Buddhists, others who have adopted some of the Buddhist or Taoist principles, some who are following older shamanist traditions, and so on. Not to mention the increasing number of evangelical Christians—one of the growing effects of Western influences. But I think it would not be unusual to find officers who used— well, let us call them spiritual methods, such as meditation, as part of their work. And some of that, I think, would not be too far away from what we have been talking about."

It was after midnight by now, and he looked at his watch. "It is late," he said. "We should perhaps be thinking about going home."

The idea of going home seemed powerfully attractive to Drew. The idea of returning to the Chinggis Khaan was rather less so, but he was conscious of increasing tiredness and inebriation. "I think that would be a good idea, if you'll excuse us."

The ambassador made a show of encouraging them to stay, but it was clearly little more than politeness. It had actually been a very enjoyable evening—not at all what he had been expecting, Drew thought. The Wilsons were not the kind of people he would normally spend an evening with, but their company had certainly been stimulating.

The ambassador led them back down the stairs to the main entrance hall. Outside, the air was icy, a thick frost already gathering on the street. Nergui had summoned an official car to take him back to his flat—Drew noted that such transport seemed to be available without difficulty to Nergui at any time of the day or night. They stood at the top of the steps, looking down at the car, its engine running in the empty street.

"Can I offer you a lift?" Nergui said. The Wilsons, like Drew, were staying at the Chinggis Khaan. "It's a cold night."

As the cold air hit him, Drew began to feel the effect of the alcohol. "If it's all the same to you," he said, "I think I wouldn't mind the walk. It's only five minutes."

The Wilsons looked at each other. "I wouldn't mind a lift," Helena Wilson said. "These heels aren't ideal for an icy street, especially after a few drinks."

"You're sure you don't want a lift, Drew?" Nergui looked at him closely. "You're okay?"

"I'm fine," Drew said. "Should have taken a bit more water with it, that's all. Fresh air will do me good."

He followed the others down the steps to the car. Nergui ushered the Wilsons into the back, and then climbed into the front by the driver. Helena Wilson started to close the rear door, then stopped, looking at Drew. "Chief Inspector. Drew," she said. "Are you sure you won't come with us? There's plenty of room."

"No, really, it's okay." He had started to walk away, feeling unstable.

"Drew," she said again. "I—" She stopped as if unsure how to go on. "Please. Take care, won't you?"

He turned, surprised by the sudden urgency in her tone. She closed the car door as the driver started to pull away, but was still watching him earnestly through the window. He thought, for a moment before the car moved, that there was a look in her eyes that was close to fear.

The car did a U-turn, and accelerated past him. He saw Nergui wave a farewell gesture through the front window. Helena Wilson was still watching him, looking back through the rear window. And then the car turned the corner, and was gone.

Drew straightened up, trying to maintain his equilibrium. He really had drunk much more than he had realised. That was the problem with whisky. The effects hit you suddenly, later. He stumbled slightly, and then began to walk slowly down the street, the large angular bulk of the hotel already visible against the clear night sky. The street was deserted and silent, white with the thickening frost.

He had walked only a few more feet when he heard a sudden tumble of footsteps behind him. He half turned, startled by the unexpected sound. For a moment, he caught sight of a shadow, the glint of something in the pale streetlight. And then he was pushed, hard, the force of the blow sending him sliding across the icy pavement. He tripped and stumbled, trying to regain his balance, as something hit him again. He rolled over, his eyes filled first with the glare of the streetlight, then with a jumble of stars and a looming shadow. And then with darkness.

PART TWO

THIRTEEN

"Nergui?"

Nergui looked up. Through the narrow window, he could see the sky lightening outside. He wasn't sure how long he'd been sitting here, reading through the case files.

"Brought you this." It was Doripalam, holding two mugs of coffee.

"Thanks," he said. "I need it."

"Well, I was making one," the young man said. "And I saw that you were already in." He placed the mug carefully down on Nergui's desk. "How was the ambassador's party?"

Nergui gestured him to sit down. "Alcoholic," he said. "But otherwise better than feared. We met a couple of rather odd Brits. He was a chemist who was also a civil servant. She was an anthropologist doing some work on our folk traditions. Or something like that."

"You're making my night at home sound more attractive by the second."

"Just bear that in mind when they come to offer you a job in the Ministry," Nergui said.

"That may be a little while yet."

"Well, the way this case is going there could be a vacancy before long. Not that I'd necessarily recommend you take it."

"That why you're in so early?"

Nergui looked up at Doripalam, wondering quite what was going through the younger man's mind. He was probably feeling some relief now that it was Nergui's reputation on the line in this case, but Nergui guessed that his feelings were likely to be more complicated than that.

"Not really. Didn't get home till late. Then I couldn't sleep so I thought I might as well come in. But all I've been doing is re-reading the files. I keep hoping that something new is going to leap out at me, but of course it doesn't."

"No news on our missing American?"

"Maxon? No, he's just vanished. Seems unbelievable. You'd imagine that a Westerner couldn't stay undetected for five minutes down there, but he seems to have managed it."

"Maybe he's dead too?"

Nergui nodded. The same thought had, of course, already occurred to him. He had assumed that Maxon had been riding the motorbike he had heard accelerating away from the camp before he found the two bodies. But maybe it had been someone else. Maybe Maxon had been another victim, not the perpetrator. Certainly it would be much easier to hide a dead body down there than a living Westerner. But it still wasn't a straightforward explanation. If Maxon was dead, how had the killer managed to kill him and somehow dispose of the body, alongside the other two murders? They had searched the tourist camp very thoroughly, and Nergui was as sure as he could be that Maxon wasn't there, living or dead.

But Doripalam was right. It was a possibility they couldn't

ignore. Though finding a dead body in the Gobi desert wasn't likely to be the easiest of tasks.

"I'm hoping he's alive," Nergui said grimly, "because he's one of the few decent leads we've got in this thing. If he's dead—if he's another victim—we're no further forward." He shrugged. "But I have a horrible feeling you may well be right. Nothing makes any sense here."

"I think everyone's getting rattled about this one. There are all kinds of stories flying about."

"Inevitably," Nergui said. They had done their best to keep the story under wraps as far as the general public was concerned. These days, it wasn't easy. The press was always keen to demonstrate its independence, and wouldn't take kindly to being excluded from a potentially major story. But the reporting of the initial murders had been low key, with no suggestion of any connection, and the Ministry had managed to ensure that none of the details were published. Delgerbayar's murder had been reported in a similar manner. It had been difficult to play down the Gobi murders, particularly given the need to try to track down Maxon, but they had not been linked to the murders in the capital city.

Nergui was unsure how long this relative quiet would prevail. While there were strict rules on police confidentiality, someone, somewhere, would eventually talk about this case to friends and family. Too many people—in the police, in the Ministry and other government departments—were aware of what was going on. And all of these people would themselves be anxious, perhaps feel the need to share their worries with someone else. Gradually the story would filter out, maybe in even more lurid form than the reality, if that were possible. And then the panic would begin.

Nergui knew that they had to make some progress, some real progress, before then. But for the moment progress continued to elude them.

"We're still working through all the routine stuff," Doripalam said. "All the door to doors, looking through all the missing person reports, combing the areas where the bodies were found—you name it. But it doesn't look promising."

"No. Mind you, with that stuff, there's no way of knowing. We just have to keep hoping."

"Anyone ever tell you you're too optimistic to be a policeman?" Doripalam said.

"Oddly enough, no. Though they've found many other grounds for disqualifying me for the role." Nergui smiled, palely. "There's no other way, though, is there? We can't give up."

Once the young man had gone, Nergui continued reading through the papers. He was painstaking, but there really was nothing new, nothing he hadn't seen before. He had combed through every detail, every nuance of the report. Maybe another eye would see something different, though he doubted it. But there seemed to be nothing more that Nergui could contribute.

He looked at his watch. It was already eight o'clock. He felt as if he had been up all night, which was almost the case. It wasn't physical tiredness, more a sense of mental, even spiritual, exhaustion, as if he really was at the limits of his endurance.

There was no one here that he could talk to, not even Doripalam. They'd kept their relationship positive, despite everything, but it wasn't the time to start unloading his personal feelings on the younger man. He had enough to cope with. Was it too early to call Drew? He thought not. Drew had given the impression that he was an early riser, so even after the previous late night, he would almost certainly be up by now. He picked up the phone and called the Chinggis Khaan, asking to be connected to Drew's room. He heard the ringing tone, but the call was not answered. He looked at his watch again. Probably Drew was at breakfast.

Eventually, the operator came back on the line. "I'm sorry, sir. There's no reply. Can I take a message?"

"Just let him know that Nergui called," he said. "He's got the number."

He put the phone down, feeling unaccountably anxious. There was no reason to feel concerned. Drew would be having breakfast or had gone for a stroll. It was even possible he was still sleeping and had not heard the phone.

But Nergui could not shake off a feeling of concern. It was that silly Wilson woman. Nergui was not, by the standards of his countrymen, a superstitious individual. But her talk of premonitions and psychic powers, however rational the articulation, left him feeling uneasy. There was something about the way she had looked at Drew as the car had driven away.

Looking back, Nergui thought that he should have insisted on Drew coming in the car with them. Not, he told himself, that there was any danger in the city at that time of the night. It was only a few hundred metres to the hotel, after all.

But the thought kept nagging at him. Maybe his fears weren't wholly irrational. After all, there was a killer—maybe more than one killer—at large in the city. There had already been an apparent attempt on his or Drew's life. And, of course, one policeman was already dead. In the circumstances, maybe leaving Drew to walk home wasn't his finest decision.

And there were more rational concerns. Drew had been pretty drunk. It was a cold night, icy underfoot. Maybe Drew had slipped, hit his head. Temperatures last night had fallen many degrees below zero. It was beginning to reach the time of the year when those without homes were all too commonly found dead in the streets in the early mornings.

Nergui rose and paced across the office. This was idiotic. He was behaving like a mother whose son is late coming home from a drinking session.

Despite himself, he picked up the phone and dialled the number of Drew's mobile, which he had scribbled on a pad on the desk. There was a long, empty silence while he waited for the roaming signal to connect. Finally, there was a click and the sound of the overseas ringing tone. The ringing stopped suddenly, and for a moment, as the familiar voice reached his ears, Nergui thought Drew had answered it. But then he realised that, from apparently immeasurable distances, this was simply the sound of Drew's pre-recorded voicemail message. "I'm sorry I'm not available at the moment, but if you'd like to leave a message—"

Nergui left a message, but somehow with no confidence that it would be picked up. His tiredness had fallen away, but it had been replaced by a yawning anxiety, an insuppressible sense that something was dreadfully wrong.

Blackness. Silence. Nothing.

Death must be like this. Perhaps, after all, he was dead. Or perhaps he had been buried alive. His body felt numb, and he couldn't tell if the numbness was internal or somehow imposed upon him.

But he must be alive. He was thinking. His mind was confused, uncertain, but he was slowly, step by step, piecing together a train of thought. Images. People. Voices. A cold white hard sheet. A burning orange light. Something unexpected. Something frightening.

Panic rose in him, though that surely must be another indication that he was alive. The dead didn't panic, did they? His breath caught in his chest. That meant he was breathing, at least, though for how long was another question.

He tried to hold his breath and listen. Could he hear anything? No. Nothing. Not even the beating of his own heart. Perhaps this was what death felt like, after all.

He was unsure how long he lay in this semi-comatose state. Maybe hours, perhaps only minutes. Gradually, though, he became aware that something was changing. The feeling was slowly returning to his body, the numbness slowly melting away. He could move his eyes, begin to move his fingers. He began, finally, to feel like a human being again. He was not dead. Or, if he was, death was much closer to life than he had ever imagined.

But the gradual return to sentience was neither pleasant nor reassuring. As the feeling gradually began to flow back into his limbs, he became increasingly aware of the pain. A dull throbbing ache that filled his arms and legs and head, the kind of painful lethargy that accompanies a serious bout of influenza. And more localised aches—bruises or contusions on his back, on his head. And on top of all this was a feeling of lassitude. Even in other circumstances, he would have struggled to rise from where he was lying.

As more and more feeling flooded back into his body, he became aware that his supine state was not voluntary. There was some kind of binding holding his arms, and something similar around his ankles. When he tried, painfully, to lift his head, he became aware of a cord around his neck, tight enough to throttle him if he tried to move more than a centimetre or two.

He realised—like a third party observing his own predicament—that he ought to be frightened. He had no idea where he was or what was happening here, his brain was not processing this at all. But one thing he could work out, what was happening here was clearly not good.

Slowly, slowly, consciousness came dribbling back. Why was he here? What was going on? Where was he? The questions came in no rational order, but at least he was beginning to formulate questions.

Suddenly, as if he had woken from a deep sleep, clarity hit

him. Whereas before there had just been a fog of sensation, now he could remember everything up to a point. He remembered the dinner at the embassy. He remembered the Wilsons, and the bizarre turn taken by their conversation. He remembered the strange behaviour of Helena Wilson. He remembered the car driving away into the frosty night. And then—

Then what? Himself drunkenly stumbling away. Something, someone crashing into him. And then nothing. And then this.

With full consciousness came a full sense of horror. He had no idea where he was or why he was here. But he was lying in the dark, with no sign of light or life, his limbs strapped down. And someone, for some reason, had brought him here.

FOURTEEN

"I'm sorry, sir. You can leave a message for him, but that's all we can do. I'm sure you appreciate—"

Nergui sighed and leaned forward over the reception desk. "No," he said. "I do appreciate that you're doing your job, but so am I. If you don't have the authority to do it, then can I speak to whoever's in charge here?"

"I'm sorry, sir. I mean, I understand you're in an official capacity, but I've been told strictly—"

It would never have been like this in the old days, Nergui thought. There was a time when one flash of your official card would have been enough to terrify the wits out of any functionary who got in your way. In those days, they knew what the Ministry was capable of. It was still generally unwise to cross the Ministry, but there was greater willingness to take the risk these days, particularly if Western currency was involved.

Nergui straightened up, smiling. Then he turned sharply on his heel. For a moment, the receptionist looked relieved, assuming that she had dealt successfully with a troublesome visitor. The look of relief turned to a look of panic as Nergui calmly pushed open the door that led behind the reception desk. "Now, if you'll just give me a cardkey to open Room 204, I won't need to cause the kind of fuss that might disturb your guests."

"You can't—" she said. "I'll call the police—"

Nergui shrugged, still smiling. "I've told you. I am the police. Please do tell the manager if you wish to. He can join me in Room 204. Now please give me a key."

She stared at him for a moment, then reluctantly took a card from the drawer beside her and ran it through the computer system. "That will open it now," she said.

"And if you or the manager should decide to call the police, you should mention that it's Nergui who has taken the key." He briefly flashed his pass again. "There, you see. If you tell them that, they will not be surprised and will not waste their time coming over here."

He let himself out from behind the desk and made his way across to the lifts. Out of the corner of his eye, he could see the receptionist hesitate and then pick up the phone. He hoped that she was only calling the manager.

He knew he was being foolish. There was nothing for him to worry about, and he could have waited and done this properly. But the sense of anxiety had continued to nag away at him. It was eleven a.m. now. He had called Drew's room repeatedly, but there had been no response. Drew's mobile appeared still to be switched off or out of range. There had been no word from him at all. Nergui had even tried to call the British ambassador, in case Drew had for some reason returned to the embassy the previous evening after the car had left. The ambassador, fortunately or unfortunately, had been tied up in a meeting and had not yet returned Nergui's call.

Finally, when he could see nothing else to do, he had come across to the Chinggis Khaan. The receptionist had called up to Drew's room, but there was, as before, no response.

It was perfectly feasible that Drew was deeply asleep or had decided to get some air. Maybe he was out exploring the city, doing some of the tourist activities while he had the opportunity. Maybe Nergui had simply missed him and he was already on his way to the police offices.

Or maybe, Nergui thought, he had not been back here at all.

The lift opened on the second floor and Nergui made his way along the corridor to Drew's room. He slid the card through the electronic lock, and pushed open the door.

The room was empty. The bed was undisturbed, though if the chambermaids had already visited the room, it was still possible that Drew might have been here this morning. The room itself was very tidy, with only a few personal possessions—a hairbrush, a paperback thriller, a still unpacked suitcase on the stand—to indicate that it was occupied.

Nergui pulled open the wardrobe doors. There were a couple of suits and several shirts hanging up. Nothing else. A pair of polished black shoes on the floor. Policeman's shoes, Nergui thought.

"Excuse me, sir, I must ask you—"

Nergui turned. A short, overweight man was standing in the doorway. He was balding and his hair was badly combed across in an attempt to conceal the fact. He was wearing an expensive-looking Western-style suit. Presumably the manager.

Nergui nodded politely. "Can I help you?" he said.

The manager looked nonplussed at Nergui's question and it took him a second to gather his thoughts. "I'm sorry, sir, but this really is—"

"Has this room been made up yet?" Nergui said. "Have the chambermaids been in here?"

The manager opened his mouth, clearly about to repeat his objections to Nergui's presence, then he stopped. "I can check for you," he said, finally. "Can I see your ID first, though, sir?"

Nergui nodded. "Of course." He smiled and pulled out his ID again. "Here," he said.

"That's fine, sir. No problem. You understand we have to be careful."

"Naturally."

He followed the manager back out into the corridor. A group of chambermaids were standing by the lifts, chatting. The manager approached them and spoke briefly, then turned back to Nergui. "They say that room's already been cleaned."

Nergui smiled at the group of women who were watching him with some curiosity. "Police," he said. "Room 204. Which of you cleaned that room?"

One of the women, young and pretty with dark hair, raised her arm shyly. Nergui looked at her. "Had the bed been disturbed?" he said. "Had anyone slept in it?"

She shook her head nervously. "No," she said. "The bed hadn't been slept in. I thought it was a bit strange, as the room was occupied . . . but you don't know—" She giggled slightly and turned away.

"Thank you," Nergui said.

The chambermaids giggled again, glancing back at him, then moved off together. Nergui turned to the manager. "Do you know who was on duty last night? On the reception, I mean. After midnight."

The manager nodded. "We lock the main doors at midnight, so people have to use the entryphone to get in. I'll need to check who the night porter was last night."

"Thanks. And can you make sure that no one goes into 204. I mean, no one. No chambermaids. No one."

The manager nodded, looking anxious. "I'm sorry," he said,

"but what do you think has happened? I mean, after the last incident, we're all a bit on edge."

"Trust me," Nergui said, "I'm as much on edge as any of you. As for what's happened, well, I haven't a clue at the moment. I'm hoping nothing's happened. But I'm fearing—well, I don't even know what I'm fearing, except that it's nothing good."

Back down in the hotel lobby, Nergui commandeered the manager's office as a makeshift base. The manager himself seemed only too pleased to hand over leadership to someone else.

While the manager was checking on the identity of the night porter, Nergui made another call to the embassy. The ambassador was still busy, as Nergui had expected, so he left a message for him to call back urgently. If anything had happened to Drew, it would be highly damaging if the ambassador was not advised of the situation immediately. He had also left a message for his own Minister, briefly setting out the current situation. In the circumstances, he recognised that this was probably the least welcome news the Minister could have received. Losing one Westerner might be an accident. Losing two—and one of them a senior policeman at that—might well be construed as criminal negligence. Nergui's was not the only career that was likely to be on the line here.

Oddly, Nergui felt remarkably calm. As soon as he had realised that Drew had not returned to his room the previous evening, his personal anxiety had melted away, replaced by an almost glacial attention to the minutiae of his duties. This was one of his strengths—the capacity to detach himself from personal emotions and lock himself rigorously into the requirements of his job. It was, he suspected, not a particularly attractive personal quality, but it was one of the factors that contributed to his professional effectiveness. In this case, though, he was conscious that his own emotions were buried not far below the surface.

The manager returned a few moments later with the night porter. He was a tall man, dressed in blue overalls. As the night porter sat down at the manager's desk, Nergui could smell alcohol on the man's breath. It was not clear whether he had slept since completing his shift early that morning.

Nergui nodded to him. "I do not need to detain you long," he said. "Just a few simple questions."

The night porter looked anxious. Nergui guessed that, in that line of work, there was always temptation to break the rules, or even the law in minor ways—drinking, petty theft. Probably the porter assumed that he had been caught out in some transgression and was about to be sacked, if not arrested. In other instances, Nergui might have been tempted to play that to his advantage, but that did not seem appropriate at the moment.

"You were on duty last night?" he asked.

The man nodded. "Came on at eleven thirty, worked through to seven."

Nergui paused, as though taking in this information. "Were there any disturbances last night? Anything out of the ordinary?"

The man shook his head. "Nothing. It was a quiet night." He looked nervously across at the manager. Nergui suspected that the porter had probably spent much of the night asleep.

"I dropped off an English couple after midnight. Did any other guests return after that?"

"Not last night. We don't tend to get many. If tourists go out to eat, they tend to be back before then. There's not a lot of late-night entertainment. The bar here's open till one, so if people want to drink they usually stay here."

"So there was no one else?"

"No one."

Nergui leaned forward across the table, staring intently at the porter. "You're absolutely sure of that?" he said. "This is very important. I'm not trying to catch you out. I just need to be sure."

The man nodded, more nervous now, but apparently telling the truth. "I'm sure," he said. "Nobody can get in without using the entryphone. Even if I was—" For a moment, Nergui thought he was going to say "asleep" but he went on: "Even if I was away from the desk for some reason, they'd have to wait till I got back."

"And it's not possible that someone else might have let anyone in in your absence?"

"Not last night. There was no one around. I was the only one on duty. The bar closed early—before midnight—because no one was in. So, no, I'm sure no one else came in after midnight."

"Okay, that's fine. That's all. Thank you for your help."

The porter looked surprised and relieved, as if he'd been reprieved from some major crime. He smiled and nodded, and looked across at the manager. "No problem," he said. "I'm here on site if you need anything else." He rose and hurried out of the room before anything more could be said.

"Assiduous chap," Nergui commented.

"He'd have been asleep most of the night," the manager said. "Probably half drunk. Or more. But I'm sure he's right. Even if he was dead to the world, it would just mean that the doors stayed locked. We've got video cameras over the entrance so we can check the tapes to be sure, but I think you can safely assume that nobody else came in here after midnight last night."

Nergui rose. "We may need to talk to other staff at some point. But if he was the only one on duty, I don't imagine anyone else can tell us much."

The manager shook his head. "I wouldn't have thought so. I mean, we'll give any help we can. What's this all about?"

Nergui hesitated for a moment. The manager would have no difficulty looking up Drew's name or recognising that he was a Westerner. He might even have some knowledge of who Drew was. "Look," he said, "this is all highly confidential. Nothing must leak out. I'm serious, if anything about this appears in the press, I'll be back here before you can open your mouth again. And you're likely to become closely acquainted with the inside of our magnificent prison facilities. So don't say a word to anyone. Not even gossip."

The manager was wide eyed. "I wouldn't—"

"Of course. But I can't take any risk on this one."

"You think this guest—this Mr. McLeish—has gone missing?"

Nergui was not surprised that the manager had already checked Drew's name. "We don't know," he said. "All we know is he didn't come back here last night."

"And is this connected to the previous—incident?"

Nergui was tiring of providing explanations, but he recognised the importance of treating the man with some courtesy. "Probably not. As I say, it may all turn out to be nothing. But, especially given the previous incident, we can't be too careful."

The manager nodded, with some enthusiasm. "Of course, of course. I understand. As I say, if there is anything more I can do to help—"

"We will be in touch. I am very grateful for your kind assistance today. I am sorry that I was so peremptory in dealing with your receptionist, but you will appreciate I was in a hurry. Please pass on my apologies."

Nergui thought that by now he had laid the politeness on

quite thickly enough. "But remember," he said, turning as he opened the door, "say nothing. To anybody."

Outside, the day was bright but cold. Nergui hurried across Sukh Bataar Square, pulling his coat tightly around him. As he walked he checked his mobile which he had switched off while interviewing the porter. There were two messages—one from the ambassador's secretary to say that he was now free and could Nergui call back, and, inevitably, one from the Minister. The latter was not a conversation he was looking forward to. He procrastinated briefly by calling the ambassador as he walked.

Eventually, he was put through. "What is it, Nergui? The message sounded urgent."

"It may be. You haven't seen Chief Inspector McLeish since we left last night?"

"No. I waved you off, saw him start to walk down the street. That's all. Why? Has something happened?"

"It looks as if he never returned to the hotel."

There was a long pause at the other end of the line. Nergui heard the vague swish of static, the sound of the ambassador's breathing. "How do you know?" he said at last.

"I've been trying to contact him all morning. Left messages. For some reason, I got worried and went over to the hotel. His bed wasn't slept in. The night porter on duty has no recollection of letting him in after midnight."

"It was—what, about twelve fifteen when you left here? But where can he have gone? It's only five minutes back to the hotel."

"I know," Nergui said, feeling an unavoidable sense of personal responsibility. "That's why we let him walk. I mean, there's no doubt some straightforward explanation—"

"I don't know what it could be," the ambassador said bluntly, echoing Nergui's own thoughts. "I mean, he doesn't know anyone here, so if he didn't come back to the embassy, there's nowhere else he's going to go. He was a little drunk—I mean, is it possible that he ended up going to the wrong hotel or something stupid like that?"

Nergui glanced up at the imposing silhouette of the Chinggis Khaan, black against the clear blue of the sky, dominating the city centre skyline. "It doesn't seem likely."

"He could have collapsed or something."

"Or slipped and hit his head. I hope that's not it, given the temperatures overnight."

"Christ, if we don't find him, this is going to be a major incident," the ambassador said. "How is it possible to lose a senior police officer?"

Nergui had no answer. It was an excellent question, and one he suspected the Minister would also be asking in the next few minutes. In his own mind, he was conscious of the political ramifications of the situation, but was growing more aware of his own personal feelings. He had grown to like Drew in the short time they had spent together. Nergui was more than capable of detaching himself from the emotions involved, but he realised that underneath, for the first time in many years, he was feeling genuinely worried about another human being.

"I'll get back to you as soon as we know anything," he said. "That's all I can do."

He delayed calling the Minister till he was back at the office, partly just to buy a few minutes and partly because he wanted to ensure that he was in as much control of the situation as possible. As it turned out, the conversation was easier than he had feared. The Minister's famous panic control mechanisms appeared to have kicked in, and he spoke calmly, even pleasantly.

"If you were anyone else, Nergui, I would have assumed that your message was exaggerated."

"I'm afraid not, Minister. I set it out as clearly as I could."

"You did indeed. So all you know is that he never returned to the hotel last night?"

"Well, we're as sure as we can be of that," Nergui said, trying to remain as objective as he could. "We know he didn't sleep in his room. The night porter on duty has no recollection of him returning after midnight. And it doesn't seem likely that he would have been able to enter the hotel any other way."

"So when did you last see him?"

"Just after midnight. I gave the others a lift back in the car, and Drew—Chief Inspector McLeish, that is—insisted on walking back to the hotel."

"Pity you didn't insist on giving him a lift."

Nergui didn't need to be told this. But then Drew had been adamant about wanting to walk, the hotel had been literally a few minutes away, the streets were deserted. No one could have predicted that anything would happen. But Nergui knew there was no point in going through all this with the Minister.

"Indeed, Minister."

"So what do you think could have happened to him? I take it that you're treating this as in some way linked with the other incidents?"

This seemed to be everyone's favourite euphemism at the moment, Nergui reflected. "Well, we have to recognise that there could be a link with the killings," he said. "But there's no way of knowing at the moment." He paused. "If there is a link, who knows what the implications might be? It hardly bears thinking about. But there could be a host of more straightforward explanations. People do go missing, and sometimes for the oddest of reasons."

"But they're not usually senior policemen on official visits to overseas countries."

"True enough."

"And, unless I'm missing something, it's not easy to come up with an explanation that doesn't have a potentially negative outcome?"

"Well—" Nergui hesitated. But the Minister was right. Even the simplest explanations—that Drew had fallen and hit his head, that he had collapsed, that he had been mugged—did not augur well for Drew's well-being. "I suppose you're right," he said.

"Which, in turn, doesn't indicate a particularly positive outcome for you or me, Nergui. Do you have any leads on this at all?"

"On the disappearance?"

"On any of it. This whole sorry mess." Nergui noted that, despite all his own reservations, the Minister had immediately elided everything into a single case.

"Some, but nothing substantive. Everything that happens seems to take us further away."

"We need to get somewhere on this, Nergui. And quickly. Especially after this. This is going to be a major incident. The British government will be all over us. The Western media will be all over us."

"I know."

The Minister, never one for niceties, ended the call without saying anything more. Nergui looked at the phone and nodded. "Don't hesitate to pass on any ideas you might have," he said to the now-dead receiver.

"Nergui?"

He looked up. Doripalam was standing in the doorway.

"I just heard. Is it true?"

Nergui shrugged. "It's true he's disappeared. What that means—well, your guess is probably a lot better than mine."

"I wouldn't have disturbed you, except—well, this is maybe

not the moment, but I've got a bit of an idea. It's probably stupid, but I wanted to check it out with you."

"What's your idea?" Nergui said. He knew that anything Doripalam came up with was unlikely to be a waste of time.

"Well, it goes back to Delgerbayar. You remember that he'd been involved in the gold prospecting case?"

Nergui nodded, wondering where this was leading. "Some small-time thing, as I understood it. Dispersing one of the illegal camps. He was due to go up there with another officer the day after he went missing."

"That's right. Well, I had a check back through the records. I don't think anybody picked it up, but I think Delgerbayar had already been up to the camp."

Nergui raised his head and stared at Doripalam. "What do you mean?"

"Just that. He'd been up to the camp before."

Nergui was sitting up and paying attention now. He was also cursing himself for apparently missing something that might have been important. "He wrote a report on the visit?"

Doripalam shook his head, looking slightly embarrassed. "Well, no, that's just it. There was no report. No one knew that he'd been."

"So why did you think he had?"

"I was having a look through the stuff that was cleared out of Delgerbayar's desk. I don't know why. Just clutching at straws, I think. We'd already been through it to see if there was anything important there. By the time I got to it, there wasn't much left apart from paper clips and old rubber bands."

"And?"

"Well, his desk diary was still there. Someone had already been through it but Delgerbayar wasn't one for making detailed entries so there wasn't much in there that was useful. Mainly just single names or abbreviations. Times of meetings, that kind of thing. Scribbled in there, usually. Obviously meant something to him, but wouldn't mean much to anyone else. But I went through it one more time, just in case anything new struck me. And what I noticed was that the phrase he'd written in the diary for the scheduled visit to the camp looked the same as something he'd scribbled in about a month earlier. I couldn't really read it, but in the end I became convinced the two words were the same."

"Doesn't sound like a lot to go on."

"It isn't. But I've checked back in the records—it looks as if Delgerbayar had various things officially scheduled for that day, but none of them actually check out. Nobody noticed, because most of them were just routine activities, but there's no question he wasn't where he was supposed to be."

Nergui looked at the younger man with some admiration. "And you accused me of being over-optimistic. I don't know what this means, but it looks as if it's worth pursuing, especially as we've got nothing else to go on. Who was it spoke to the people in the camp? I mean, after we found Delgerbayar's body."

Doripalam shifted uneasily on his feet. "Well, that's the other thing."

Nergui began to have a sinking feeling. "What other thing?"

"Well, I've checked back in the reports and, well, it doesn't look as if anyone went out to visit the camp."

"You're joking."

"Well, it's not really all that surprising," Doripalam said, looking uncomfortable. "The original job was a pretty routine piece of work—"

"Police as the paid lackeys of the mining corporations?"

"If you say so," Doripalam said. "After Delgerbayar's body was found in the city and there was all that stuff about his journey to the Gobi, it never occurred to us that the illegal prospecting stuff was relevant any more."

Nergui shook his head. "We never learn, do we? We tell ourselves that good policing is following up every avenue, no matter how trivial or potentially irrelevant. But then we all still manage to miss the obvious." He caught Doripalam's expression. "I mean all of us. It never occurred to me to think about the prospector angle, either."

"Well, if it's any consolation, it looks as if the camp had broken up in any case before Delgerbayar's death. The visit that was due to happen the day after he went missing never took place. So there's no reason why anyone should have thought that it was worth following up."

"Except you did," Nergui said.

Doripalam nodded. "So what do you think we should do about it?"

Nergui shrugged. "I think I need to get out of this place. I think we should go exploring."

FIFTEEN

"It shouldn't be allowed," Nergui said. "These are the people we should be treating as criminals."

Not for the first time on their journey, Doripalam regarded Nergui with some amusement. It would be interesting to observe Nergui's interactions with the Minister, he thought. They must have some lively political discussions.

"Look at it," Nergui went on. "It's a shambles. And here of all places."

Ahead of them, the grassy steppe swept up towards the smooth grandeur of the northern mountains. The rounded contours of these mountains were like nothing found in the west, Nergui thought. He remembered days spent walking up here in past summers, the grassy hillsides thick with wild flowers and darting butterflies, an extraordinary profusion of natural beauty.

But it was autumn now and late afternoon, the sun already hanging low over the mountains, reddening the slopes. It had been a long journey, and they were anticipating a further long trip back in the dark.

Their objective lay immediately ahead of them. The valley, as Nergui had accurately pointed out, was a mess. On the far side, there was a make-shift shanty town of *gers* and wooden huts, providing storage and accommodation. Closer to hand was the valley itself. Its sides were scarred and rutted with endless excavations, ripped randomly into the landscape. The summer's rains had turned the ground to mud, and now, with winter approaching, the earth was hard and frozen. On the far slope, a battalion of bulldozers and tractors worked away at the land, tearing rutted holes into the grass.

At the heart of the valley, the river was slick with spilled oil and other chemicals. Piecemeal dams and embankments had been built to shift the course of the river at various points, providing access to areas that had previously lain under water. From the sodden and disturbed state of the valley floor, it was clear that the river's path had been manipulated many times.

"It's not pretty," Doripalam acknowledged.

This was one face of the country's expanding minerals industry. Not all the production sites were as ugly as this, but there were increasing numbers of opencast excavations in the land north-east of the capital. Some of the production companies were relatively responsible, taking care of the environment where possible, giving consideration to the local flora and fauna, restoring the landscape once the work was completed. But others—a substantial number of others—paid little attention to such concerns. They came, took what they wanted, and left an unholy mess behind them. This, Nergui presumed, was one of those.

The worst part was that it was all legal. These companies had obtained their licences quite legitimately. The government was only too keen to do deals, so long as investment entered the country and the government was able to take its share. Most of the mines were joint ventures involving companies from Canada, the US, China, South Korea, Russia and elsewhere. These opencast mines were the cheapest option, the minerals simply ripped from the ground. Over the last decade, much of the production had been here in the north of the country in areas like this. Inevitably the resources would be finite, but for the moment there was abundance, and the country had experienced an extraordinary gold rush as producers had converged here to seize their share.

In principle, the licences were subject to regulation in respect of environmental impact, health and safety, and other human considerations. In practice, there was no will or ability to enforce this regulation. Bureaucracy, the producers would tell you, was the enemy of enterprise. And enterprise, as the government well understood, lay at the heart of investment and growth. Who cared if a few landscapes—or even a few people—were damaged in the process?

And, with an all too familiar irony, the forces of law and order were directed not towards these despoilers of the environment, but towards those who tried to gather up a few crumbs from their table. The illegal camp that Delgerbayar was supposed to have visited was some way downstream from here. The inhabitants were former herdsmen whose livelihoods had been damaged or destroyed by years of economic chaos and a sequence of harsh winters. They were attempting, with some success, to scrape a living by panning for gold in the riverbed. They emerged at night, once the floodlights were extinguished, scanning the valley with their feeble flashlights. They called themselves "ninjas," a reference to the cheap imported green plastic buckets they used for panning. As they worked their way across the valley floor, they strapped the buckets to their backs, in ironic homage to the ninja turtles of the cartoons.

No one with a grain of human feeling could blame them, but their actions were nonetheless illegal. The gold they found belonged to the ruthless predators operating in the valley before them. And the police were summoned like hired lackeys to do the producers' dirty work for them.

Nergui wondered vaguely why the encampment had broken up and moved on before the police had visited. It was quite possible that one of the mining companies had taken the law into its own hands, maybe irritated at the police's insistence on going through the proper channels. It would not have been the first time. But there was probably no way of ever finding out.

Their current interest lay not in the environmental chaos immediately in front of them, but in the cluster of *gers* that lay a mile or so beyond. It was here that, according to the records, some of those in the original camp had now retreated, hoping to find a livelihood among the fragments of gold. Nergui drove their Hyundai truck carefully past the pounding bulldozers and across the grasslands towards the encampment.

There was a group of men clustered around the *gers*, drinking beers and playing cards. They looked up, with some hostility, as the truck drew closer.

Nergui was unsure how to play this. The police were unlikely to be popular among this group, since they were seen as being little more than the hired hands of the mining companies. Except, Nergui reflected, that they weren't even hired. They did this dirty work for nothing.

But there was little point in hiding their identities as police officers. They had to give a reason for being here, and, if it came to it, it was always possible to indulge in a little official intimidation. Maybe, as so often, the simplest route was complete honesty.

Nergui pulled the truck to a halt and jumped out. Doripalam followed him, a step or two behind. Nergui thought the younger man was making a creditable job of not appearing nervous. Or maybe he was just more confident than Nergui.

The group of men looked at them, unspeaking and expressionless. Their ages were mixed—the youngest probably in his thirties, the oldest maybe late sixties. They were all dressed in traditional clothes, wrapped warm against the chilly air.

"Good afternoon," Nergui said, breaking the heavy silence.

No one spoke. Nergui sighed inwardly. This was not going to be an easy process.

"We're police officers," Nergui said. "We'd like a word."

The youngest of the men smiled thinly. "Well, well. I would never have guessed. I'm just surprised it took you so long."

Nergui shrugged. "I couldn't care less what you do down there. Someone may come to stop you, but it won't be me."

"Oh, someone will definitely come to stop us. And soon. And I couldn't care less if it's you or someone else. But that wasn't what I meant."

Nergui looked at the young man more closely. He sounded well-educated, much more articulate than most of the nomads he had encountered out here. He had, Nergui noted, already positioned himself as the spokesman for this group, despite apparently being the youngest of the men. The others seemed content to defer to his leadership.

"So what did you mean?"

"We've been expecting a visit from the police for some time now. It's taken you longer to get out here than I imagined. But I suppose it is off the metropolitan beat."

Nergui nodded, slowly. "You sound as if you're rather off the metropolitan beat yourself."

The man laughed. "It's still so obvious? After all this time. I thought I'd put all that behind me."

This was all getting a little too opaque for Nergui's tastes. He had a sense that he was losing dominance of the conversation. It was not a common sensation for Nergui, and his usual response, in professional circumstances, was to engage in some intimidation. He had a feeling, though, that this approach would not be effective here.

"Can we sit?" he said mildly. "I need to ask you a few questions."

"I should perhaps be careful," the man said. "If you're here in an official role, I might incriminate myself."

"Are there grounds for you to incriminate yourself?"

The man smiled. "You'll need a more sophisticated approach than that, I'm afraid." He gestured towards the *ger* behind them. "Come in. We can talk in here."

Nergui and Doripalam followed him into the dark confines of the tent. Inside, there were benches draped with blankets. He gestured the two officers to sit, and then squatted on the floor opposite them.

"My name is Cholon," the man said. "Tell me how I can help. Though I think I have an idea."

Nergui hesitated for a moment. "We are investigating a series of murders. Including one of a police officer called Delgerbayar."

Cholon did not appear surprised at this information. He nodded, as if absorbing Nergui's words, but made no response.

"We have reason to believe that this officer visited an encampment of illegal gold prospectors shortly before his death."

"This camp?"

"No, not here. Further downriver. But we also understand that some of the inhabitants of that camp are now living here. Is this correct?"

Cholon thought for a moment, as though about to respond in the negative, then he nodded. "That is so," he said. "A number of us, including myself."

"How long is it since you moved here?"

"In my case, about six weeks. But the camp finally broke up only about three weeks ago."

Nergui shifted on the stool, looking momentarily distracted. "Why did the camp break up?" he said, finally.

Cholon laughed. "The usual reason. Intimidation. Violence. Threats."

"From the mining companies?"

"Certainly not from any environmentalists." Cholon laughed. "Yes, of course from the mining companies."

"Did the camp receive any visit from the police?"

Cholon lay back, stretching out his legs across the floor. "Not while I was there. But I understand that someone—a senior officer—came after I had moved on. Doing the companies' dirty work as always."

"Delgerbayar?"

Cholon shrugged. "I don't imagine he was too keen to share his name with them. All I know is that it was the usual threats."

"This was an official visit?"

"You tell me," Cholon said. "Surely you know what errands you send your officers on."

"Suppose I were to tell you," Nergui said, speaking slowly, "that Delgerbayar was operating as—well, let us call him a freelance. Would that surprise you?"

Cholon smiled. "Nothing about the police would surprise me," he said. "And nothing about the mining companies, come to that. You're both capable of anything."

"I am sure that we—and they—are capable of many things. But I'm posing a serious question. Of course, there are corrupt police officers. The temptations are many. But you may be surprised to learn that the majority, the vast majority, are honest."

Cholon raised an eyebrow, an amused smile on his lips. "If you say so."

"I say so. But some of course are systematically corrupt. I do not know if any are directly in the pay of the mining industry—"

"I thought you were all in the pay of the mining industry. In practice."

Nergui shrugged. "We are obliged to obey orders. We are obliged to enforce the law. It may on occasions be a bad law."

Cholon snorted. "I'm sorry," he said. "I don't see where all this is leading."

"I thought you said you had some idea why we might want to talk to you."

"I—" Cholon stopped, then laughed. "So you do have more sophisticated approaches after all."

"You would be surprised," Nergui said, softly, "how sophisticated I can be. But let us go back to Delgerbayar. I will be straight with you. In visiting your camp, he was not acting in any official capacity. We do not know in what capacity he was acting. Did you have any similar previous visits from the police?"

Cholon nodded. "From time to time. Not just there, but wherever we were trying to prospect. The official visits—we had those too, but they were different. Then you'd just get a team of police turning up, with a warrant and a straightforward order for you to move on. You knew that if you didn't move within the defined time, you'd be arrested. So you moved. But the unofficial visits were different. That would be a lone police officer— usually armed. He would turn up with threats and innuendos, pretending he was just there to give you advance warning. Trying to help—but the message was always clear."

"Was it always the same officer?" Doripalam interjected.

Cholon shook his head. "No, I'm talking over a period of a couple of years. There were maybe two or three different officers—sometimes they turned up in pairs. The first time we thought it was a joke—that maybe they'd just failed or omitted to get the warrant for some reason and were trying to bluff their way through it."

"And what happened when you ignored them?"

Cholon stopped, suddenly. "That first time was two years or so ago," he said. "We were operating from a camp further downriver—a fair distance from here. Two officers turned up—no official paperwork, but warning us that if we didn't move things would become unpleasant. As I say, we thought it was a bluff. We've learned not to be intimidated easily. We're not going to back down just because someone in a uniform turns up—"

"I see that," Nergui said.

"So we just sent them on their way, and waited for them to come back with a warrant."

"And what happened?"

"They—the officers—didn't come back. But a couple of nights later, in the early hours of the morning, the camp was attacked."

"By who?"

"They were hooded, dressed in dark clothing. It was impossible to see their faces. They came armed with shotguns, knives, you name it. Attacked individuals—beat up some, injured others and—" He stopped.

Nergui watched him closely, saying nothing.

"—and they killed two of the group. Including my father."

"I'm sorry," Nergui said.

Cholon shrugged. "It is difficult to forgive them."

"You reported this?"

Cholon smiled. "In the circumstances, it did not seem prudent. We did not know for sure who attacked us—yes, the mining company was behind it, of course, but we did not know who had actually carried out the attack. We thought—and some of us still do think—that the police were in their pocket."

"We are not hired thugs," Doripalam said.

"Really? I've witnessed teams of police moving prospectors out of their camps, enforcing the law as you put it. Yes, this attack was more brutal than that, but the police can be brutal enough even on their official visits." He spoke the last two words with bitter irony.

"And you had further—unofficial visits?" Nergui said.

Cholon nodded. "As I say, from time to time. We took them seriously. The police came armed, but that was probably not necessary. We knew what could happen to us if there was any resistance."

Nergui reached in his pocket and pulled out the now dog-eared photograph of Delgerbayar. "Is this one of them?"

"This your Delgerbayar?" Cholon said. He peered closely at the image. "Yes, I think he could well have been one of them."

Nergui nodded slowly, putting the photograph back in his pocket. "Yes, I feared so," he said. He paused, adjusting his posture on the hard wooden stool. "And what happened to your brother?"

Cholon stopped and stared at Nergui. "My brother?"

"Your brother. Badzar. What happened to him?"

"How—?" Cholon leaned forward, wrapping his arms tightly around his legs. "I can see I have underestimated you."

Nergui smiled. "You are not the first. But tell me about your brother."

"I assume you don't need me to tell you, given your apparent omniscience."

"Humour me, Mr. Cholon."

"The way you've been humouring me?"

"Not at all. You have told me much that I did not know. Some that I did not wish to hear. But your brother. What happened?"

Cholon hesitated for what seemed a long time, as if he had

determined not to proceed. "Okay," he said at last, "I'll humour you. I presume you know the background?"

"I know some of the background. Let me tell you the little I recall, and then you can fill in the gaps. I first came across you, Mr. Cholon, or at least your name, in the late 1980s. You were something of a revolutionary, as I recall."

"Hardly," Cholon said. "Although perhaps, yes, in your terms I was a revolutionary. I considered myself a democrat."

Nergui nodded. "Campaigning against the government, against the dominance of the USSR. Some might have called you a freedom fighter. Or a terrorist."

Cholon snorted. "On a pitiful scale."

"There was sabotage. And a bomb."

"None of which worked. We were amateurs. Students playing at it. Copying what we had seen happening in China, in Eastern Europe."

"Nonetheless, you—and your brother—gained a certain notoriety at the time."

"My brother more than me. He was the one with the grand ambitions."

"So I recall. He was arrested?"

"Shortly before everything changed. The great tidal waves of democracy. The fall of the USSR. I'm still not sure what would have happened to him if that hadn't happened. He would still be in prison, I imagine."

"And what did happen to him? For that matter, what happened to you?" Nergui smiled. "You were a spokesman for your generation. Now you are an illegal gold prospector."

"Maybe not so different," Cholon said. "Doing my bit for freedom and the real redistribution of wealth."

"No doubt. But it's quite a shift."

Cholon shrugged. "So you say. Not much changed, to be

honest. My father had been a herdsman, a nomad. He had worked hard and moved back to the city, getting a job in one of the state manufacturing businesses. We were fortunate in getting a good education, going to university."

"The benefits of the old state against which you rebelled?"

"Possibly, but education is possible even in democracies, I understand? Anyway, things were going well until the economy collapsed."

"Brought down by the end of the Soviet Union."

"The irony didn't escape me. Though, as you well know, that is only part of the story."

"So what happened?"

"My father lost his job, and tried to return to herding, but those were harsh winters and nothing worked. My brother and I had to leave university, and we both decided that the best thing would be to follow our father back out here. Since then we have done our best to scrape a living."

"Until your father was killed?"

"As you say."

"Your brother is still out here as well?"

Cholon looked at him closely. "You are not so omniscient after all, then?"

"What do you mean?"

"I thought that was why you were here. I thought you were looking for Badzar."

Nergui noticed that Doripalam had drawn closer to them and was listening intently.

"Why should we be looking for Badzar?" Nergui said.

Cholon shook his head. "I said that I should not incriminate myself. Should I incriminate my brother?"

"That depends," Nergui said slowly, "on what your brother has done."

Cholon looked from Nergui to Doripalam, and then back again. "That is really not why you are here?" he said. "You are not looking for Badzar?"

"We were not here to seek Badzar. We weren't even here looking for you."

"But you knew I was here?"

"No. As you say, I am not so omniscient. I did not recognise you until you told me your name. But then I do have a good memory for the cases I've been involved with." Nergui stopped, as though he had finished. Then he said: "But you must tell us about your brother. What has he done?"

Cholon opened his mouth to speak, then stopped. There was a genuine anxiety in his eyes now. "I do not know," he said. "I do not know for sure."

A chill was beginning to creep down Nergui's spine. Once again he had a sense of something moving, circling, coming closer towards resolution. Behind Cholon he could see Doripalam shifting in his seat. There was an expression in Doripalam's eyes which Nergui could not read.

"What is it," Nergui said, "that you do not know for sure?"

Cholon stood up, slowly, as though his limbs were aching. He began to pace across the floor of the *ger*. "I thought that was why you had come," he said, again. "I—I dreaded you coming, but I also hoped that you would. So that at least I could know."

Nergui sat in silence, hoping that Doripalam would not break in with a question. Cholon needed space to speak, to articulate whatever thoughts were twisting inside his brain. Nergui knew this moment well from his interrogations. An inappropriate question would provide Cholon with an escape route, allow him to defer whatever it was he needed to say. Silence would allow him no exit.

"I need to know," he said at last. "I need to know what

my brother is capable of. I need to know if—if he can really be the one."

"Behind the murders?" Nergui said, his voice quiet.

Cholon looked up at him. "You are playing with me? That is it. You do know."

Nergui shook his head. "We know nothing, Cholon. But you need to tell us what you think."

"My father's death was a terrible thing," Cholon said. "It was not simply that he was killed. It was how he was killed. He was—butchered. The only blessing was that he must have died very quickly. But it was a horrible death—"

"Your brother witnessed it?"

"I think so. He would never say. But, yes, I am sure he saw it all."

"And what happened?"

"The death—the whole incident, but especially our father's death—affected us all very badly. I was thrown into—well, depression is what you would call it, I suppose. I found it hard to rebuild things, to carry on. I did not want to work. Everything seemed pointless."

"That is not so very surprising. In the circumstances."

"No. But it took me a long time, months, before I was able to move on. And even then it was not like before. But it affected Badzar far worse."

"Worse?"

"Very differently. I found myself unable to work, unable to move on. Badzar became angry. Furious. At the injustice. At the inhumanity of it. He wanted revenge."

Nergui was feeling cold now. The day was drawing late, and the sun would be setting outside. It would be an icy night, but the cold that flowed through Nergui's body was internal, the chill of fear. "What sort of revenge?"

"Initially, he went crazy. He went to the mining operations

down here—" Cholon gestured through the walls of the tent in the direction of the valley floor. "He was convinced—rightly, I'm sure—that it was the company behind what had happened. He stormed into their camp, found the office of the site manager, and attacked him. With his bare hands, but he did a lot of damage before they dragged him off. He had a knife in his pocket, though he had not used it."

"Was he arrested?"

"No. The man was battered and bruised but not seriously injured. I imagine that they did not want the police probing around too much into Badzar's accusations. He was thrown off the site, that was all. But they probably imagined they could get their revenge in some other way."

"And did they?"

"Badzar was too smart. He left here, kept moving. I didn't know where he was, though I heard stories of him joining other camps, other groups of nomads in the area. He had a motorbike and some money we had got for the gold." He paused, as if hoping that Nergui would interrupt. "And there were other attacks. Workers—managers, mainly—from the mining companies. There were several cases—attacks at night. Some were injured, in one case very seriously. One was killed."

"You think this was your brother?"

Cholon nodded. "I cannot be sure. The company blamed us, and we had to suffer more assaults from them. But, as far as I know, none of the attacks was reported to the police."

"Not even the killing?" Doripalam said.

"Not even the killing."

"So where is your brother now?" Nergui said. He was watching Cholon intently now, his eyes unblinking.

"Again, I do not know for sure. But I think he is in the city."

"Why do you think that?"

"I saw him last about a month ago. He turned up here one

day, on his motorbike. He looked . . . wild-eyed, disturbed. The way he talked was different. He talked slowly, as if he was drugged, and he talked about destiny and the need for action. He told me he was going away, and that I should not expect him to return."

"He mentioned the city?"

"Not specifically. But he borrowed some more money. He was not staying in this area. I do not know where else he would go."

"And you think he is responsible for the killings?" Every word was like a pebble being dropped into an icy pond.

"I do not know," Cholon said. "Genuinely, I do not. I don't want to believe that he could be capable of that."

"But you can believe that he was responsible for the attacks out here?"

"He is a disturbed man. I saw the look in his eyes. I heard the way he was talking. I do not know what he is capable of." Cholon stopped, as though he had finally run out of words. The silence stretched on. Finally he said: "But yes, in my heart, I think it is possible. It is possible."

SIXTEEN

By the time they emerged from the *ger,* the sun had already set. The sky was a deep mauve and darkening quickly. Glaring spotlights illuminated the waste of the valley floor, and the bulldozers were still slowly patrolling the landscape, tearing up earth and grass. Even at night, the noise was extraordinary, a ceaseless roaring echoing back from the surrounding hills.

"You will need to come back with us," Nergui said. "You will do that." It was not a question.

Cholon nodded. "If you think it will do any good."

"I do not know. We do not know that your suspicion is correct. But we have nothing else to go on. No other ideas. And time is growing short." He had not mentioned Drew to Cholon, and he felt again the rising fear that he had been trying to suppress throughout the day. "At the least, if your brother is in the city, we need to find him. And you may be able to help us in that."

"Perhaps. There are people I can speak to, who might have seen him, might have some idea where he is."

Nergui wondered whether he should be calling back to headquarters, getting officers out trying to round up some of these contacts, ready for their return. But he was worried that any sudden flurry of activity might drive Badzar to ground long before they arrived. At the same time, he could not guess at the possible implications of any delay. In the circumstances, the prospect of a four-hour drive through the night was not an attractive one.

In the event the drive was even worse than he had anticipated. There was only a single route from here to the city—it could hardly be dignified with the title of road—composed from years of horse and motorised traffic pounding down the hard earth. It was badly rutted along its length, the ground broken and pitted, and Doripalam had to drive carefully, peering into the light of the headlamps, to avoid being caught in any of the larger holes. In the darkness, it was impossible to gain any more speed, and Nergui found the slowness of their pace increasingly frustrating.

He sat in the back of the vehicle with Cholon. Cholon was chewing his fingers, looking anxious, with no evidence now of the superficial confidence with which he had greeted them earlier. It was as if he had been hiding some truth from himself, and now could no longer pretend.

"What do you know about the killings?" Nergui said. He was still trying to piece together the story in his mind, wanting to understand why Cholon should have harboured these suspicions. This could all, he thought, just be nonsense—evidence perhaps of Cholon's disturbed state of mind rather than his brother's. Perhaps they were merely chasing phantoms, in this endless, dream-like passage through the empty night.

"Only what I have seen in the newspapers. They get brought to us out here, though usually a few days old. I saw the story about the Westerner killed in the hotel but didn't think much about it. It seemed a world away. I saw he was working for the mining companies which didn't surprise me. It is a corrupt world."

Nergui listened, feeling every bump in the interminable road. "And you read about Delgerbayar's killing?"

"That was when I first began to wonder—I saw the picture of the policeman in the newspaper. I wasn't certain—just as I still wasn't when you showed his photograph to me—but I thought he was one of those who had visited the camps. And by this time I knew the stories of the attacks out here. So I began to wonder—I had seen the way that Badzar looked when I had last seen him. I was not surprised when you turned up."

"But you have no real grounds for suspecting that your brother is . . . involved in this?"

Cholon shrugged. "No, of course not. But I know my brother. We were close. I would not be here—I would not be betraying my brother—if I did not feel that something was dreadfully wrong."

Nergui sat back in his seat, watching the ceaseless passing of the rough terrain outside, just visible in the car lights. "You know there have been other killings?"

Cholon turned to Nergui, his mouth open. "Other killings? The same as the two I read about?"

"We do not know. Some of them have similar characteristics."

"Characteristics? What do you mean?"

Nergui paused, unsure how to take this forward. If Cholon was being honest—and there was no reason to assume that he wasn't—it was difficult to know how much of the truth he could bear. "The details do not matter," he said. "Let us just say that these were not straightforward killings."

Cholon looked at him as though about to ask a question. "I do not need to know," he said. "I do not know any more what Badzar might be capable of. I do not want to know."

"There have been a number of killings," Nergui said. "Three more in the city, as well as Delgerbayar and the Westerner, Ransom. Possibly connected. We do not know for sure. And there were two more murders down in the south, in a camp near Dalandzadgad. The last two were different, and we have a suspect who is not your brother. But we think there might be a link."

"I don't understand."

Nergui laughed mirthlessly. "Neither do we. Not at all. The common thread here is mining, mineral production, probably gold. That is the only factor that may link the killings, if they are linked at all. I do not know if your brother is involved. If he is, I do not know if he is the sole perpetrator of these killings."

"And I thought you were omniscient."

"At the moment, I would settle for knowing just one thing, anything, about this case with certainty."

The truck rumbled on, Doripalam still silent, leaning forward over the steering wheel as he peered into the sparse light from the headlamps, occasionally twisting the wheel jerkily to avoid a pothole. It was as if they were suspended in time, as if the awful reality outside the vehicle did not exist.

"There is one thing more," Nergui said at last.

"What?"

"There is a police officer, a detective, sent over from England. He came to investigate the death of Ransom, the Westerner." Nergui stopped, suddenly realising the weight of fear that lay in his heart. "He has gone missing."

"Missing? How can a visiting policeman go missing?"

"How could one of our own senior officers be brutally murdered? None of this makes sense. All we know is that the officer was walking from the British Embassy to his hotel late last night. And that he never got there."

"And you think—?"

"It is like everything else in this case. We do not know what to think. But we have to fear the worst."

"I cannot—I do not know what to say."

"You will appreciate," Nergui said, "that this is no longer simply a police matter, if it ever was. This will become a major diplomatic issue. I do not know what the outcome will be. But, whatever it is, we need to resolve it quickly. Do you think you can trace your brother?"

"I don't know. There are people he may have gone to. Places he might be. But it is all guesswork. I don't even know for sure that he is in the city."

It was becoming hopeless, Nergui thought. He was losing whatever touch he might once have had. The plodding methodical police work was going on in the background, but seemingly going nowhere, and still managing to miss the few things that might be important. And here he was, rushing off on pointless wild goose chases, desperate for anything that might give him a lead, clutching at any straw. But he was surely experienced enough to know that such leads were almost always illusory. He could almost feel this lead melting away as he reached for it. And increasingly his judgement seemed flawed. Perhaps he should have stayed up at the mine, spoken to more people, tried to find out precisely what it was that Delgerbayar had been up to. Instead, he had gone racing back to the city, for what? Someone who might have nothing to do with all this, and who could be anywhere. It was madness.

And underneath all that, he realised, as the truck rumbled on through the night, was something else, something that was driving him on into this insanity. It was the feeling, deep down in his bones, that Drew was still alive but that, unless Nergui could find some means of playing against the most extreme odds, he would not be alive for much longer.

*   *   *

Blackness. Emptiness.

He had no idea how long he had been here. Even with the return of consciousness, time seemed to have stopped. The sensations that should have given him some sense of progression—hunger, thirst, the aching of his body—seemed to have been suspended. He was aware of the hard surface beneath him, and of the imprisoning bands around his ankles, wrists and neck, but it was as if he were somehow detached from this reality.

Even the horror that had overwhelmed him when he had first realised his position had, for the moment at least, abated. Something—psychological, physiological, he did not know—had calmed his mind, allowed him to think rationally.

It was insane. The whole thing was insane. Why should anyone attack him? Why had he been brought here, wherever this might be? Why should anyone want to imprison him?

Was this a kidnapping? His policeman's mind was working automatically now, suppressing the fear, thinking back to his negotiator training, trying to work through the possible scenarios, the potential options available to him.

If this was a professional kidnapping, perhaps politically motivated, then his chances of survival and release were much higher. There would be some demand which the authorities might or might not be able to concede. There would be some form of negotiation. His survival would be guaranteed for a time, as the kidnappers would not lightly sacrifice their only bargaining counter. Perversely it was encouraging that so far he had been kept, literally, in the dark. If his kidnappers did not allow him to see their faces or have any information, they would have nothing to fear from his eventual release. Professionals, he reminded himself, whatever their motives might be, did not like to kill unnecessarily.

If the kidnappers were just small-time crooks who were aiming too high, his future was highly uncertain. If things became too difficult, they would simply want to cut their losses and get out. And central to cutting their losses, he realised, would be his own elimination.

Suddenly, the real panic struck him, blasting chills through his body like an icy wind. He arched his back, pushing and pulling against the ties that held his limbs, struggling and struggling and struggling, unable to make any headway. And then all his detachment collapsed, and he was nothing more than a mindless frenzy of wrestling bones and blood, as he felt himself lost in the blackness, falling into the worst nightmare he had ever known.

The end came equally suddenly. There was a sharp searing light, burning into his brain. He screwed his eyes shut tight, and the light was red, as hot as the sun, agonising in its brilliance, like hot wires against his eyeballs. He had no breath to scream any more, and all he felt was a desperate longing for the previous cool darkness. If that had been his death, then surely now he was entering the outer realms of hell.

But then his beating heart calmed, and the pain in his eyes and his head lessened. He still could not see, but he registered that this brilliance was nothing more than light, ordinary light. Black dots and shapes danced in the crimson brilliance, gradually settling back into order.

At last, after what might have been hours, he found himself able to move his eyes. His eyelids remained shut, and he realised that fear had rendered them immobile. Partly it was fear of the brilliance of the light. Mostly, though, it was fear of what sights might greet him when he was able to see again.

He forced himself to try to relax, to breathe more steadily, suppress his sense of panic. And finally he was able, very slowly, to open his eyes.

The sight that met them was unexpectedly banal. Above him, the source of the searing light, were four bright fluorescent strip lights set on wooden beams. Turning his head as far as he could, he could see concrete walls, metal shelving. Cardboard boxes with incomprehensible labels. Some items of anonymous industrial equipment, shaded with dust. A storeroom of some kind.

He was lying on a wooden bench, maybe a work bench. He twisted his head a little more, stretching his muscles to their limits to try to see his arms. His wrists were tied with plastic twine, coiled repeatedly around, fastened underneath the bench itself. His ankles and neck were presumably tied in the same way. He turned his head as far as he could. A water bottle—the kind used by cyclists and runners—had been taped to the bench beside his mouth enabling him to reach the nozzle. He twisted his head and, with considerable discomfort, managed to suck down some of the water.

The room was silent. He stopped moving and tried to listen. At first, he could detect no sound of any movement, other than the seemingly deafening beating of his own heart and the rasp of his own panicked breathing.

He forced himself to hold his breath for a moment, listening hard. And finally he thought he heard it, like an irregular echo of his own heartbeat. It was the soft but insistent sound of another's breath. He tried to lift his head but it was impossible. All he could see were the beams, the lights, the concrete walls.

But somewhere outside the constrained field of his vision, someone was watching him.

SEVENTEEN

By the time they reached the outskirts of the city, it had started to snow, thick flakes whirling in the glare of the streetlights. There had been some flurries earlier in the week, but this was the first serious snow of the winter. Perhaps it was as well they had travelled back when they did. Being stranded on the steppes in this weather would not be pleasant.

It was nearly one a.m., and the streets were deserted. For the first time, Nergui found the emptiness unnerving. Against the brilliance of the settling snow, the gloom of the unlit sidestreets seemed threatening. Nergui felt uncomfortable until they pulled into the enclosed car park at the rear of the police headquarters. Even then, he looked uneasily behind him as they bundled out of the truck and hurried through the snow to the entrance.

Inside, it was warm and reassuringly prosaic. There were one or two officers on duty, but most were lounging in the rest room, sipping coffee. Nergui led them through and up the stairs to his office. It was only once he was in there, settled behind his desk, with Doripalam and Cholon sitting opposite, that he finally felt fully secure.

What was happening to him? He had been doing this job, or something like it, for most of his adult life. He had a reputation for fearlessness. He was in the police building, surrounded by high-level security and staff who would jump at his every whim. And yet here he was, behaving like a skulking rookie, terrified of his own shadow.

For much of the journey there had been no network signal on his mobile. The networks were good in the cities and towns, but much more sporadic out in the countryside. As they had re-entered the city limits, his mobile had bleeped obligingly to let him know that there were messages for him. He gestured to the others to go and get coffees for the three of them, then sat down to listen to the messages.

The first, inevitably, was from the Minister. "Nergui, I don't know where you are," he said, an edge of threat in his voice. "I'm trusting that you know what you're doing. But things are starting to get seriously out of hand here. I'm stalling the British government as best I can, but I can't put them off for long. We need some answers, and we need them quick. Call me when you get in. Whatever time that is."

Nergui looked at his watch. One fifteen. He knew from experience that the lateness of the hour would be no excuse for failing to contact the Minister. He wasn't sure, though, that he had anything to report.

The second message, equally predictably, was from the British ambassador. "Nergui," he said in English, "I've been trying to get hold of that bloody Minister of yours. Seems to be permanently in meetings." Clearly, Nergui thought, the Minister was following the ambassador's own example. "I know the Foreign Office is in direct contact with him now, but I'd like an update. Nobody's telling me anything—" Even in these circumstances, it was difficult not to be amused by the plaintive tone. "Give me a call in the morning, Nergui. I really want to know what's going on."

That was one, at least, that could be safely left. Nergui waited, and listened to the third message. It was a voice he recognised. Batzorig. "Sir. You're probably out of mobile range at the moment—don't know exactly where you are. Can you give me a call as soon as you pick this up? I'm not sure, but it might be urgent. We've had a message left for us that I think you ought to—"

Nergui thumbed off the phone and jumped to his feet. In seconds, he was out of the door and jumping, three steps at a time, down the stairs to the rest room. He burst into the room, banging back the door. The three officers sitting drinking coffee looked up in surprise. Doripalam and Cholon were at the far end of the room.

"Where's Batzorig?" Nergui said.

"I think he's upstairs, in his office. He said to tell you—"

"So why didn't you?"

The officers looked confused. "Well, he didn't say exactly—"

"Forget it."

Nergui turned on his heel and stormed out of the room and then back up the stairs. Batzorig's office was at the rear of the building, down the corridor from Nergui's own. It was a large room he shared with three other officers, though he was the only one currently on duty.

He looked up from his desk as Nergui pushed open the door, and jumped to his feet. "Sir," he said. "Did you get my message?"

"Just a few minutes ago." Nergui sat himself heavily down opposite Batzorig. "What is it?"

"Well, it may be nothing, sir. But we received a message this evening. Just came through on the out-of-hours line, and I happened to pick it up."

"What sort of message?"

"Well, I was able to record most of it, sir." There was a facility for recording all incoming calls, no doubt a legacy from the days when surveillance was more commonplace, but still useful nonetheless. "As soon as I realised it might be important. I changed the tape so there was no danger of it being recorded over."

"Very good," Nergui nodded. Why was it that all these young officers felt the need to try to impress him? Had he been the same in his younger days? He feared that he probably had.

Batzorig held up the tape and slipped it into a cassette player he had set up on the desk. He had obviously been preparing carefully for Nergui's return.

For the first few seconds after he pressed the play button, there was nothing but the faint hiss of the turning tape. Then suddenly a voice, low and sibilant, cut in. "—Have something that might interest you. It may be possible to arrange its safe return. But this will require co-operation. I will call again at nine a.m. tomorrow." There was the sound of Batzorig trying to extract some more information from the caller, but it was clear that the caller had already hung up.

"What time did this come in?" Nergui said.

Batzorig consulted his notes carefully. "Just after ten," he said. "Seven minutes past, to be exact."

Nergui nodded. He wondered whether the caller had known he was out, had seen him leave with Doripalam. Had, perhaps, also seen him return.

He looked up at Batzorig. "Go and fetch the man I brought in. He'll be with Doripalam, either in my office or down in the rest room."

Batzorig hurried to do Nergui's bidding. Nergui sat, staring in silence at the tape machine. Then he leaned forward and pressed the play button again. He heard the same words:

"—Have something that might interest you. It may be possible to arrange its safe return. But this will require co-operation. I will call again at nine a.m. tomorrow."

It could be a hoax, of course. It was likely to be a hoax, in fact. Drew's disappearance had now been reported in the media, so they could expect their fair share of lunatic calls over the coming days. But something told Nergui that it was, at least, worth taking seriously. It didn't sound like a crank call—too short, too deliberate, too little desire to make an impression. There was something about the tone that unnerved him, a sense of emptiness, of uncaring.

The door opened and Batzorig returned, followed by Doripalam and Cholon. Nergui gestured Cholon to sit. The others hesitated, unsure whether they were part of this, but then came in and closed the door behind them.

"Listen to this," Nergui said. "Do you recognise the voice?" He had no desire to lead Cholon, but his question could mean only one thing.

He played the tape again, listening intently himself to the repeated words.

"—Have something that might interest you. It may be possible to arrange its safe return. But this will require co-operation. I will call again at nine a.m. tomorrow."

Cholon looked at the tape machine. "You mean is it Badzar?"

Nergui nodded, watching Cholon closely. He was still unsure how far Cholon could be trusted to give an honest response about his brother.

"Can you play it again?"

Nergui pressed the play button once more. He could recite the words verbatim by now, but they were still telling him nothing.

Cholon shook his head. "I don't know. It could be. It could well be. But I can't be sure."

Nergui played the tape yet again. The voice was obviously being disguised in some way—the deep timbre, the odd sibilance. But it did not sound as if it was being artificially distorted, other than by the phone itself.

"There's not much to go on," Nergui conceded.

Cholon stared at the tape player, as if the answer would emerge from the machine itself. "It's no good," he said. "I can't be sure. It doesn't sound like him, but there's something about it. Maybe I just don't want to believe it's him."

"Well, all we can do is wait until the morning. See if they call again." Nergui looked up at Doripalam and Batzorig. "We shouldn't make too much of this. It could well be a hoax."

He looked back at Cholon. "If your brother is in the city, we need to find him. Do you have any idea where he might go if he came back here?"

"There are a few people he might go to, at least to try to get somewhere to stay. Old friends from university days."

"Are they contactable by phone?"

"Most of them, yes, though I've only got the numbers of a few. They're generally working for the government, these days." He smiled wryly. "I'm not sure whether that's selling out or not."

Nergui looked at his watch. "It's late, but we can't waste time. Can you start phoning round? We'll probably get a better response if you do it, rather than making it an official police call."

"I'm not sure you'll get a particularly good response to any call at this time of night."

"We can't afford to wait till morning. We'll work with you. Maybe if you tell them that your brother's gone missing, that you're afraid he might be ill—"

"He has. I am," Cholon said. "Otherwise I wouldn't be here."

Doripalam led Cholon into another office where they could

begin the process of telephoning. Nergui didn't have high hopes of any result, but it was the only place to start. Batzorig excused himself with an offer to fetch the coffee that was presumably still waiting for Nergui downstairs.

Nergui looked at his watch. Nearly two. He couldn't put off ringing the Minister any longer. He had a suspicion that the Minister genuinely didn't sleep. No matter what time Nergui called, there was never any sense that he had been woken or disturbed by the call.

Nergui dialled the number, wondering what further ways he could find of articulating that, no, there was still nothing of any substance to report. The Minister's phone rang at the other end of the line, but there was no answer. In Nergui's experience, this was almost unprecedented. The Minister usually turned his phone off in the presence of the President, but there were few other exceptions to his rule of constant availability. After a few seconds, the voicemail cut in and he heard the Minister requesting him to leave his message after the tone. Nergui simply gave his name, noted the time, and invited the Minister to call back when he was free. He ended the call, feeling an absurd mixture of relief that he hadn't had to endure yet another content-free discussion with the Minister, and concern about what the Minister might actually be doing.

Before Nergui could allow himself the luxury of worrying further, Doripalam stuck his head round the door. "We've got something," he said.

"Really?" Nergui had not been expecting any serious results from the calls, let alone so quickly.

Doripalam nodded. "Cholon started with the most likely candidates. The real old friends. Struck lucky almost straightaway."

"What's the story?"

"Couple who were at university with Cholon and Badzar.

Same year as Badzar. He's a civil servant, she works for the tourist agency. They've got a small flat near the centre. Badzar just turned up, a few days ago, apparently, out of the blue, said he needed somewhere to stay until he was able to rent somewhere. They hadn't seen him for years, but put him up. Stayed a couple of nights, then disappeared."

"I presume their night has been well and truly disturbed by now," Nergui said. "Let's get over there and see if there's anything more they can tell us."

"Do you want Cholon?"

Nergui hesitated. "Might be as well," he said. "They might speak more openly with him there."

Nergui grabbed his coat and hurried back down the stairs. Doripalam went to fetch Cholon, and the three of them met at the entrance to the car park. The snow was coming down thicker than ever, the sky lost in the swirl of flakes. Already, since their return, an inch or two had settled on the truck.

"I carried on calling," Cholon said. "Managed to lose a few friends in the process, probably. But no one else had seen him. Most hadn't seen him for years."

"But we know he's here now," Doripalam said. "We know he's in the city."

Nergui shivered, telling himself it was due only to the blast of cold air that hit him as he stepped out into the night. The snow was coming down heavily, and the concrete underfoot was already becoming hazardous.

They climbed into the truck, Doripalam driving, and pulled back out into the city streets.

"Take it carefully," Nergui said. "We don't want to write off a police vehicle on top of all our other problems."

The roads were icy but Doripalam drove skilfully. Snow was a familiar problem and there were already snow ploughs and gritters out in the city, so the main roads were relatively accessible. By morning, much of the worst of the snow would have been cleared. The biggest problem was the lack of visibility. Doripalam peered forwards into the drifting snow, trying to spot any other vehicles that might be on the road. But, apart from the occasional snow-clearing lorry, the streets were deserted.

The flat was just a few minutes' drive away. It was part of a long, low-rise tenement, built of looming grey concrete overlooking a small park. Most of the building was in darkness, apart from two or three windows, one of which, Nergui assumed, was their destination.

They parked by the roadside, and Nergui led the way into the dimly lit entrance lobby, which to his surprise was unlocked with no sign of any security staff or concierge.

"Flat 23," Cholon said, from behind.

They made their way up the stairs to the first floor and along the dark corridor till they found Flat 23. Nergui knocked loudly. After a few moments, the door opened and a short, harassed-looking man peered out. He looked at them carefully for a few minutes as though deciding whether to welcome them or not. They he recognised Cholon and nodded, with a half smile.

"Come in," he said. "But please be quiet. The baby is asleep. She is easily disturbed."

They followed the man into a small, neatly furnished living room. A woman, presumably his wife, was sitting on the sofa, looking nervous. Nergui stepped forward, his presence filling the small room. "Thank you, Mr.—"

"Oyon," the man said. "And my wife, Odyal."

"I am sorry that we have to disturb you. Please be assured that we would not unless it was very important."

"I don't understand," Oyon said. "I thought that Cholon was looking for his brother—"

"That is correct," Nergui said.

"But I don't understand why the police—"

Nergui held up his hand. "It's a long story, and we don't need to bother you with most of it. But Badzar has gone missing and we have reason to believe that he may be very ill. We are trying to trace him as a matter of urgency."

Oyon frowned, as though trying to make sense of this information. It was clear that he realised that more lay behind this simple statement, but he also recognised that there was little point in pursuing it. "I don't know if I can help you very much," he said at last.

"When did you last see Badzar?"

Oyon looked across at his wife. "Just the other day. He turned up unexpectedly. Out of the blue."

"You had seen him before that? Recently, I mean?"

Oyon shook his head. "Not for years. I mean, we spent some time with Badzar and Cholon after university, when we were all working here. But we lost touch when—" He looked up at Cholon, suddenly embarrassed.

Cholon smiled. "We lost touch with everyone then. We were closer to you than to most. At least we exchanged the occasional letter. I kept meaning to visit you, but I never came back to the city."

"So it was a surprise when he turned up?" Nergui said.

"A complete surprise. A bit of a shock really. I mean, it was good to see him. Or at least it would have been—"

Odyal intervened: "He seemed like a different person. I would not have believed that it was the Badzar we used to know."

"Different in what way?"

"Well—" She looked awkwardly at Cholon. "I don't know when you last saw your brother, Cholon—"

"Only a short while before he came here. A few weeks ago."

"Perhaps he had changed over the years. Perhaps it would not have been evident to you?"

Cholon shook his head. "No. It was obvious to me, too. These changes had come about only in recent months. When I saw him again, he was . . . very different."

"At first, I was not even sure that it was really him," Oyon said. "He had aged—I mean, we have all aged but he looked much older than he should. He looked . . . disturbed in some way. I wondered about drugs. I was worried about his health so I am not surprised that you say he is ill—"

"His illness is not a physical one, I think," Cholon said softly.

"You mean that he is—" Oyon glanced at his wife, and then at the door leading into the baby's bedroom. It was clear that he was wondering just what sort of person they had been harbouring, why the police should now be interested in Badzar's whereabouts.

"We believe that Badzar may have had some sort of breakdown," Nergui said, smoothly. "We are concerned for his welfare. It would help us if you could tell us as much as you can about his visit here. Anything he said. Any indication of where he might be going."

Oyon sat back in his chair. "Well, let me think. He turned up the other night, Tuesday it must have been. Quite late, about nine. As I say, completely out of the blue. The doorbell rang, and when I answered it, there he was. He was dressed in clothes that looked . . . well, unsuitable for the time of year. A thin shirt, a jacket, no coat. He was carrying a small bag, a holdall. That was all. I suppose I must have stared at him at first, wondering who he was, because he said: 'It's me. Don't you remember? Badzar.' And, of course, as soon as he said that, I knew who he was, though I could still hardly recognise him. He looked so different from the person I knew."

"And what did he say?" Nergui prompted.

"He said he'd returned to the city on some business. I mean, we knew the story, how you—" He nodded towards Cholon. "How you had returned to the steppes with your father. But we knew very little else. He didn't explain what his business was, and, well, I didn't like to enquire."

"You thought it was something criminal?"

"Well, no, not really criminal. But I knew that he had had to make ends meet as best he could, so it would not have surprised me if he had been involved in some things that were . . . dubious. As a government employee, I thought it was best not to know."

"What else did he say?"

"Not much. He said he'd arranged to stay in the city for a few weeks and had organised some lodgings. But there'd been some sort of administrative mix-up and they wouldn't be available for a day or two. So he was throwing himself on our mercy, as it were."

"Did you believe him?"

Oyon frowned. "I'm not sure. I mean, it was a plausible enough story as far as it went. It seemed a bit odd that he should have made these arrangements but then had nowhere else to go other than to people he'd not seen for ten years. But Badzar was never the most conventional of individuals."

"So you let him stay?"

"Of course. What else could we have done? I mean, as you can see, we've hardly any room here, so all we could do was offer him the sofa, but that was okay for a day or two. We brought him in—gave him a meal, shared a few glasses of vodka. He relaxed a bit after that, seemed more his old self. We talked a bit about the old days. He was happy enough talking about university, but I had the impression that he didn't want to talk about what had happened after that."

"And he didn't give you any clues as to his business in town?"

"Not at all. I mean, he wasn't obviously secretive about it. But it never came up, and, as I say, I didn't want to enquire."

"And how long did he stay?"

"Just two nights. We didn't see much of him, to be honest. We saw him on Wednesday morning, as we went off to work. The baby goes to Odyal's mother when she's working. We gave him a key, and I had the impression he was out most of the day. We got back around six. He reappeared a bit later than that. We had another meal. He'd brought a bottle of vodka, so we had a bit more of that, and that was really it. He didn't give us the impression he was going to be going the next day, but again he was around till we'd gone off to work. When we got back, he wasn't here and the key had been left on the table there. We weren't sure whether to expect him back, but he never reappeared. To be honest, we were slightly annoyed that he hadn't bothered to come back to say goodbye. But, as I say, Badzar was always unpredictable."

Nergui nodded. "And he gave you no clues about where he was going?"

Oyon frowned. "Nothing very clear. I had the impression that it was somewhere nearby."

Nergui leaned forward. "Why do you say that?"

"I'm not sure." Oyon looked across to his wife for assistance. "It was something about the way he talked on that second night. We'd had a few drinks. It was all a bit more relaxed than it had been, though Badzar still seemed pretty tense. He was saying something about his journey here. He hitched a lift with some truck driver part of the way. Had everything set up here but then—what were his words?—there had been developments. I think that was how he described it. So he couldn't immediately move in where he'd planned. And he found himself on our doorstep—"

"That was it," Odyal said. "It was the way he said it. Almost, well, insulting. The impression he gave was that it wasn't so much that he'd been keen to see us after ten years, but that he didn't know where else to go and we were the nearest people he knew. We'd drunk a bit so I didn't really take it in, but I can remember feeling a bit irritated by the way he spoke."

"I think he realised what he'd said," Oyon said. "He'd drunk more than we had—was on the way to being drunk, really. He apologised a bit, said he'd not meant it to sound like that—that he'd actually come out of his way specially to see us. But I don't think I really believed him."

It was an interesting question, Nergui thought. Had Badzar started apologising because he was concerned he'd insulted old friends, or was it because he was worried he'd given something away about his proposed whereabouts?

"Is there anything else you can think of?" Nergui said. "Anything else he might have said? Any other impressions you formed? Even the most fleeting thought or idea might be useful to us."

"I don't think so," Oyon said. "As I say, he didn't talk at all about why he was here or what his business was. It was obviously something that was . . . I don't know, urgent, important to him. He seemed keyed up the whole time he was here. As if he was keen to be getting on with whatever it was he was having to delay."

"Did he seem threatened?" Doripalam said. "I mean, was there any sense that he was being pursued or that someone was looking for him?"

Oyon looked blankly at Doripalam. "I don't know. Is that why you're looking for him?"

Nergui shook his head. "We've no reason to believe he's in trouble. But we don't know why he's come to the city in this way. We don't know what he might be involved with. We're just trying to piece the picture together."

Oyon and Odyal were looking at each other, both clearly wondering what it was they had become entangled with. "I don't know," Oyon said. "I mean, he looked tense, as I've said, and unwell. But I didn't really get the impression that he was afraid. It was more that he was—I don't know—involved in some task that was proving challenging or demanding, maybe more than he'd expected. I can't put it any better than that."

"You've been very helpful," Nergui said. "I'm sorry if this has been an ordeal for you. And again I'm sorry for disturbing you at this time. We would not have done it if it hadn't been important. I'm sure you understand that."

"Of course, of course. I hope we've been of assistance." Oyon might have appreciated the importance of their visit, but he was also clearly very keen to get them out of the flat. It was evident that this was a visit that he wanted to put behind him.

"I'm sorry we've had to put you through this," Cholon added. "And I'm sorry if Badzar has caused you any difficulties. It would be good to come back again in different circumstances."

Oyon was ushering them gently but firmly towards the door. "It's always good to see you, Cholon. I'm sorry we've been out of touch for so long. Please, you're welcome here any time."

But, Nergui thought, there was little sincerity in his voice.

EIGHTEEN

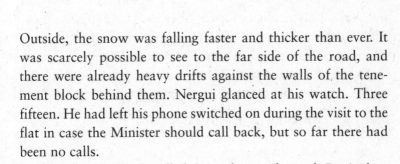

Outside, the snow was falling faster and thicker than ever. It was scarcely possible to see to the far side of the road, and there were already heavy drifts against the walls of the tenement block behind them. Nergui glanced at his watch. Three fifteen. He had left his phone switched on during the visit to the flat in case the Minister should call back, but so far there had been no calls.

The three men bundled into the truck, and Doripalam started the engine and turned the car around. The wheels were gripping but only just. If the snow continued, they would need snow chains until the roads were cleared.

"Back to HQ?" Doripalam said.

Nergui hesitated for a moment, and then nodded. An idea was beginning to form in his mind, coalescing around Oyon's final comments about Badzar's possible whereabouts. Perhaps it was possible that Badzar was really close at hand. Nergui looked back down the snow-filled street, his mind racing.

"Yes. For the moment."

Doripalam pulled back out into the road, and made his way cautiously back to HQ. At each corner, Nergui could feel the wheels sliding, as Doripalam battled to keep control. It was a night to be indoors. But Nergui had an increasing feeling that their activities were only just beginning.

As they turned slowly back into the HQ car park, Nergui's mobile rang. He thumbed the call button.

"Nergui. It's me." The Minister, of course.

"Minister. You called earlier, I think."

"Where are you, Nergui?"

"Just arriving back at HQ. It's early days, but we might have a lead."

"Excellent." The Minister sounded unexpectedly distracted, as if somehow his thoughts had already moved on from the murders. "Look, Nergui, I need to see you. Urgently."

"Now, Minister? But—" But what? It was only at that moment that Nergui realised that, in some dark corner of his mind, he had already begun planning other activities for the rest of the night, that he was already beginning to pursue a half-formed idea.

"Now, Nergui. As soon as you can get here. I have some things I need to discuss."

This did not sound good, but Nergui was past caring about the Minister's political positioning, even if this meant that he might end up as the sacrifice on this occasion. He looked at his watch. Three thirty.

"How soon can you get here, Nergui? I'm in my office."

"I'll come immediately. The snow's awful. Maybe ten or fifteen minutes."

"Make it ten." As always, the call ended abruptly.

Nergui turned to Doripalam. "I've got to see the Minister. I'll be an hour, no more. I've got an idea I want to follow up. I may be wasting everyone's time but we can't afford to delay. We should get snow chains put on the truck if we're going out again."

Doripalam nodded. "And I take it we are going out again?" There was a note of irritation in his voice.

"Trust me, Doripalam. I'm not keeping any secrets here. I've just got a hunch. I'll explain when I get back, though it's probably too half-baked to waste anyone else's time on other than my own. But I would be grateful for your support."

Doripalam looked at the older man for a second, then nodded. He twisted in his seat and looked at Cholon. "I should organise you some accommodation."

"What you're planning," Cholon said to Nergui. "Is this about my brother?"

"It may be."

"In that case, can I be part of it?"

Nergui looked at Doripalam, who shrugged. Nergui said: "I don't know what's involved and I don't know what kind of risk we might be talking about. And we can never afford passengers. So we'd be insane to let you come."

"I understand."

"But I think we're past the point of sanity on this. I don't know what we're doing any more. Chasing phantoms. So, yes, if you want to chase some phantoms with us, you can come. But do exactly what I tell you. I may be going mad, but I'm not completely reckless."

Nergui climbed out of the truck and slammed the door behind him. He watched as Doripalam and Cholon trudged slowly into the building. Then he pulled his coat around him and began to walk through the billowing snow towards the Ministry building.

*   *   *

After the impenetrable darkness, now incessant light.

Slowly, as he lay there, he had begun to regain a sense of his own body, the belief that movement was possible, that he was still alive.

He struggled at first, pulling against the bonds that held his wrists and ankles. But there was no give, no shifting of the cords that held him, only the burning pressure of the ropes against his skin. He was held firmly, tied with professional skill to the wooden bench.

The blind panic that had overwhelmed him in the darkness had passed now, but the terror remained. Somebody had done this to him. Someone was waiting, perhaps somewhere in this very room. Something, eventually, would happen.

There was something surreal about his predicament. Trapped, held by an unseen and unknown assailant, in a brightly lit industrial building. Moments went by when he really didn't believe it, when he half-expected to wake from a dream or somehow find that it was all an elaborate hoax. Then the reality hit him again, and fear chilled his heart. And at that point the silence would become the biggest threat of all, building around him like a tangible object, taking his breath from him. And he listened, straining his ears, waiting for whatever would happen next.

It was a long walk across Sukh Bataar Square, pushing against the buffeting of the strong winds and the frozen blast of the snow. The Square was silent and snow-covered, the statues shapeless under the gathering drifts. The snowstorm had settled in thickly now, and even the snowploughs and gritting trucks appeared to have given up on their work.

In normal conditions, the Ministry buildings were a five-minute walk away, on the far side of the square. Tonight, he had already been walking for ten minutes and still had some way to go. He pulled his shapeless old trilby down over his eyes, and his thick winter coat more tightly around him, and trudged on through the deepening snow.

As he walked, he wrestled with the thought that had begun to form during his interview with Oyon, putting his problems aside at least until he reached the Ministry, trying to work out the next steps in their search for Badzar.

Oyon, for whatever reason, had formed the impression that Badzar's destination was not far from Oyon's own flat. Nergui was inclined to trust that judgement. He had noted that Oyon seemed to be genuinely affronted that Badzar had turned up on his doorstep only because he was already in the neighbourhood.

Even it was true, there were still many places where Badzar could be holed up. There were numerous tenements around there, more concrete legacies of the old communist functionalism. Badzar could be staying with another contact, or could have rented a flat of his own, assuming he had the money to do so. More simply, there were also likely to be a number of unoccupied flats—those awaiting a change of tenant, even one or two blocks that were due for renovation or demolition under the government's continuing drive for renewal. Badzar could have broken into one of these.

But there was another possibility. The tenement block they had visited was on the edge of one of the industrial districts, close to where the concrete landscape of the city centre gave way to the sprawl of the *ger* encampments. In that area, there were some thriving businesses, some still state-owned, some the first fruits of burgeoning entrepreneurs. But, as throughout the city, there were many disused industrial units, left over from the period of economic madness when the country had adopted all the worst elements of free-market economics to disastrous effect.

And one of those disused units, only a half mile or so from Oyon's flat, was the factory where they had found Delgerbayar's body.

Was it simply a coincidence? After all, there were dozens of disused factories and warehouses across the city. Even if Badzar was holed up in one of them, why should it be that one? Surely he would not risk lingering around an area where the police had been engaged in a large-scale investigation.

Except, of course, that that could be precisely the point. There had been a tendency throughout this case to disregard the obvious because it was seen as irrelevant. They had thought nothing of Delgerbayar's intended visit to the illegal prospectors because it had appeared to be a red herring, just another part of the routine pattern of his life. So maybe this was similar. They had assumed that the location where Delgerbayar's body was found was simply a convenient stage set. It was just one of many large empty buildings, isolated from any domestic dwellings, with a suitably intimidating entrance and an appropriate setting for the body to be found. Nergui had had no doubt that the killer had chosen it with some care to maximise the impact of their find. But they had all assumed by the time the police reached the building, the killer would have been long gone.

They had searched the building rigorously, and subjected it to forensic testing where there appeared to be the possibility of finding any material or data potentially linked to the killer, but they had found nothing. There was no sign that the building had been occupied, other than by the spectacularly positioned corpse of Delgerbayar.

But Nergui had been working through the timescales in his mind. The day that they had found Delgerbayar's body was the same day that Badzar had appeared unexpectedly on Oyon's doorstep. Was it possible that, having committed the murder, he had set up the body as they had found it, and then moved to lie low with his former acquaintances for a few days?

He shook his head, leaning forward into the wind and snow, treading cautiously to maintain his footing. It was a ridiculous idea. Why would Badzar simply turn up unannounced? Wouldn't he have made some arrangements beforehand, arranged some safe place to stay? But that might be the reason. If Badzar was involved in this, he was leaving no pre-arranged trail, no plans, even assuming that his actions were premeditated at all. Oyon and Odyal would recall his turning up with some surprise, perhaps, but they had commented on his unpredictability. Under pressure from the Ministry, the story of Delgerbayar's murder had been suppressed and only limited information had been reported in the media, as Badzar could have predicted. There was no reason why Oyon and Odyal should have made any connection between Badzar's appearance and the murder.

Still musing on the implications of this, Nergui finally reached the anonymous concrete block that housed the Ministry of Security. The building was almost in darkness at that time of the night, lights showing in only a few windows. The front doors were locked, but Nergui had a key. He unlocked the door, struggling slightly with his gloved hands, and then stepped inside, snapping the lock closed behind him.

After the icy chill of the night, the warmth of the building struck him immediately. A profligate use of the Ministry's resources, he thought. He made his way slowly up the stairs towards the Minister's office on the second floor.

Most of the offices here, including Nergui's own, were bleakly functional—bare tiled floors, grey-painted walls, metal desks and filing cabinets, chairs built for sturdiness rather than comfort. The Minister's office, inevitably, was different. Nergui was unsure where the Minister had obtained his furnishings, since they surpassed even those used by the senior apparatchiks in the old days.

There was a light shining under the Minister's door. Nergui knocked and waited, knowing from experience that the Minister liked to keep visitors waiting, if only for a few moments.

There was the expected pause, then he heard the Minister's voice. "Come."

He pushed open the door slowly, and stepped inside. To his surprise, the Minister was not alone. A grey-haired man sat facing him, his back to Nergui.

He turned in his chair as Nergui entered.

Nergui raised his eyebrows. "Professor Wilson," he said. "This is a surprise."

Wilson nodded. "I was very sorry to hear about Chief Inspector McLeish," he said. "There is no more news?"

Nergui glanced briefly at the Minister. He had no idea why Wilson was here. He had understood that Wilson was not in the country in any kind of official capacity, but was merely accompanying his wife's research. Perhaps he was here to complain again about the lack of progress the police were making, particularly given Drew's disappearance. But it seemed unlikely he would be making an official complaint in the small hours of the morning. There was no helpful signal in the Minister's expression.

"Nothing we can make public, yet. There are some leads, but it's too early to say."

"Are you assuming that Chief Inspector McLeish is—?" Wilson left the sentence hanging.

"We're assuming nothing," Nergui said. "I remain optimistic for the moment."

Wilson nodded, clearly sceptical, but made no rejoinder. Nergui looked across at the Minister, wondering if he was going to offer any kind of explanation for Wilson's presence.

"You asked me to see you, sir?" Nergui was beginning to

find the situation irritating. There was no way of questioning the Minister's authority, but Nergui couldn't see why he was wasting time here when he needed to be getting on with the search for Badzar.

"You still don't seem to be making much progress, Nergui," the Minister said in English.

"We have some leads, sir," Nergui said. "I appreciate the urgency. In fact, you took me away from a potential investigation to bring me here." He presumed that the Minister had not just brought him over here to receive a public dressing-down.

"An investigation? What sort of investigation?"

Nergui glanced at Wilson. He had no intention of saying any more until he was at least clear why Wilson was here. "We're tracking down someone who we believe may be able to help us with our enquiries."

The Minister nodded. "That is why I called you over, Nergui. Professor Wilson may also be able to, as you put it, help you with your enquiries."

Without being asked—not always a wise action in the Minister's presence—Nergui sat down beside Wilson. "Really? In what way?"

Wilson coughed. "I'm afraid I was not entirely straight with you last night," he said. "My visit here is on a somewhat more formal basis than I indicated."

Nergui shot a glance at the Minister, who responded with a barely perceptible shrug.

"I understood that you were here to accompany your wife?"

"I allowed you to understand that. My wife's research is quite genuine, but it is not the primary reason I am here."

Nergui was growing tired of the game-playing. "I am sorry," he said. "It's been a long night already and I have much more to do. I don't particularly enjoy being lied to. I would be grateful if you could get to the point."

The Minister looked for a moment as if he was about to intervene, then he sat back. Wilson went on: "I told you that I worked for the British government. That much at least was true. I am here in that capacity."

"In what capacity, exactly?" Nergui could feel anger rising. He was unsure where this conversation was going but he did not like the feel of it.

Wilson sighed slightly. "As you may be aware, the UK government is one of the parties with an—" He paused as if seeking the appropriate word. "An interest, I suppose, in the development of the gold fields in the south."

Nergui looked from Wilson to the Minister, who was wearing his most accomplished blank expression. "I wasn't aware that the UK government had any interest in the gold fields," he said. "My understanding was that a range of commercial businesses were involved."

"That is correct. Our involvement is an indirect one."

"I'm afraid," Nergui said, "I really don't understand what that means."

Wilson nodded. "I'm trying to express this as delicately as I can. My position is a difficult one."

"I think so," Nergui said, "if you are in the country under false pretences."

"Well—" Wilson hesitated, and for the first time looked slightly unsure of his ground. "We will return to that, I'm sure. But let me try to explain my position. There is a substantial investment in the gold field development from a consortium of UK companies—"

"Along with substantial investment from a range of other international companies, I understand," Nergui said.

"Quite so. This is an entirely commercial transaction. The British government's role—my role, that is—has simply been to ensure that British interests are being protected."

"Which explains why you're here. It doesn't explain why your presence is so covert."

"We have had concerns about this project for some time," Wilson said. "In particular there has been some evidence of . . . well, tension between the partner organisations."

Nergui had been aware from his own professional interest that the project in question had not been proceeding entirely smoothly. The identification and potential extraction of the gold reserves had been more problematic than had initially been envisaged. Increased investment had been required, and while the size of the potential returns was still unquestioned, the timescale for realising them had become increasingly uncertain. Further investment had been sought particularly from the Russians, and Nergui understood that relationships between the parties had become strained.

"I'm aware of some of that," Nergui said.

"Were you aware that Mr. Ransom was also involved in this project?"

Nergui sat forward in his chair. "My understanding—" He glanced across at the Minister. "Our understanding was that Ransom was working for one of the companies prospecting in the north."

Wilson nodded. "That is correct. But he was a freelancer. He'd recently been recruited—covertly, to use your word—to provide some advice to the consortium in the Gobi. Primarily, as I understand it, to validate some apparently suspect data being produced by one of the partner companies."

"Were we aware of this?" Nergui asked the Minister.

The Minister gave a minute shake of his head. "We were not told," he said. "Ransom's visa was provided on the basis of his work in the north."

Nergui turned to Wilson. "So Mr. Ransom was also acting illegally. Was the UK government aware of this?"

Wilson looked pained. "We were not informed officially," he said. "But I can't pretend that we were entirely unaware. Mr. Ransom had something of a reputation as a troubleshooter in such matters."

"So are you telling us," Nergui said, "that Ransom's killing was in some way connected to the tensions you are talking about?"

Wilson shrugged. "I honestly don't know. But it was Ransom's death that brought me out here. We didn't know what was behind it, but it set alarm bells ringing. I wanted to find out more about the state of play in the consortium. Make sure that our interests were protected."

Nergui stared at him. He turned to the Minister. "I take it we were not aware of this either? Or did you just decide not to share it with me?"

"Nergui," the Minister said, "we were aware of none of this. Of course I would not have kept this kind of information from you. Not in the circumstances."

Nergui knew only too well that, in all circumstances, the Minister would share only what he chose to share. But it was difficult to believe that he would not have been open in this case.

"Which means," Nergui said to Wilson, "that you are also travelling illegally, in that you lied on your visa application about your reasons for entering the country."

"Not entirely," Wilson said. "I indicated on my application that, although I was accompanying my wife on her research visit, I would also take the opportunity to consult with the ambassador and other UK representatives about trade matters. I just didn't specify the nature of the consultations."

"Nergui," the Minister said, "I can see no point in raking over the question of whether Professor Wilson is here legally or not. I would have preferred a greater degree of openness, but that time is now past."

"I had no intention to deceive," Wilson said. "I merely wanted my entry into the country to be as low-key as possible. I did not know—I still do not know for sure—what interests are involved here, and I wanted, as far as possible, to observe without being observed."

"The fact remains," Nergui said, "that in effect you have withheld evidence that might have helped us progress more quickly in identifying Ransom's killer. Your information, at the very least, provides a possible motive for the murder, which to date has been missing." He paused. "If we'd been able to act more quickly, we might have prevented further murders. And," he added, "Chief Inspector McLeish might still be with us."

Wilson nodded slowly. "I know. I understand that. That's why I'm here. When I heard that the Chief Inspector was missing—well, I realised it was not appropriate for me to keep my silence any longer."

Appropriate, Nergui thought. Brutal serial killings, a potential kidnap. And this man talks about what is appropriate.

"Let me be straight," Wilson said. "My concern is a simple one. Some of the interests involved in the project are, I believe, dangerous ones. I do not know precisely who is involved, but we know the kinds of organisations. And I suspect that some of those involved would be more than capable of murder."

"So you think that Ransom was murdered because of his involvement in the project?"

"I think it's a possibility. Why he was killed, I've no idea. Whether he had some knowledge, some information—"

"And why was he killed in such a brutal manner?" Nergui said. "If these interests are as you say, then his killing would have been carried out professionally. There would have been no need for such a display. He would have been simply spirited away."

"Like Chief Inspector McLeish?"

Nergui nodded. "Exactly like Chief Inspector McLeish." Nergui paused for a moment. "Professor, I am sorry to be rude but I would very much like to speak to the Minister alone for a few minutes."

The Minister looked as if he was about to interrupt, but Wilson said, "Of course. I understand entirely. I will wait outside."

"Thank you," the Minister said, looking at Nergui. "We will just be a few minutes, I think."

As soon as Wilson had closed the door behind him, the Minister said, "I don't want to hear your views, Nergui. We have to take this seriously."

"I'm not suggesting for one moment that we don't take it seriously," Nergui said. "But I'm not at all clear what it means. Why should we trust Wilson?"

"He is here representing the British government."

"He's here under false pretences, carrying out unauthorised enquiries into a UK citizen who was also working here under false pretences. He has withheld information relevant to a major murder enquiry. And not through any ignorance, either—when I spoke to him the other night it was quite clear that he knew full well how serious this was. He's only spoken up now because McLeish's disappearance could expose a major scandal. So why should we trust him? We don't know what his agenda is. We only know that he's lied to us, to the authorities, from the beginning."

"Nergui, you're experienced enough to understand the politics behind all this. You know we've had concerns about the funding of the project in the south. We've turned a blind eye because of the importance of the project, that's all—we needed the investment."

"Of course, and we'll take money from anywhere if the price is right. I understand that well enough."

The Minister shook his head, looking as if his patience was

wearing thin. "Nergui, it is not your place to be questioning government policy. Your role is to maintain law and order—a role you've signally failed to carry out in this case, as far as I can see."

"It is not easy to carry out that role if information is being withheld from me."

"Nergui, you are drifting into dangerous waters here. Respected as you are, like everyone else you hold your position in the Ministry through my patronage. There are people out there who would be only too pleased to see you fall—"

"I take that for granted."

"I know your strengths, Nergui. I value your intellect, your honesty, your perception. These qualities are not common in an organisation comprised largely of incompetent yes-men. But I need you on my side."

"In that case, you have to trust me. I can't operate if I don't know who or what to believe."

"Nergui, believe me, I knew nothing of Wilson's story until this evening."

"I believe that." Nergui smiled. "If only because it must be a painful admission for you. It is disturbing to find that for all our intelligence work, there are things we are unaware of."

"It is very disturbing, Nergui. If there is any truth in Wilson's suppositions, it suggests we have a potentially very unstable situation in the south. If these people are prepared to act in this way—"

"But, I'm asking again, are we right to trust Wilson? He tells us that, for reasons unknown, he believes Ransom might have been murdered by—what? Organised crime? The Russian mafia? The triads? And they choose to kill Ransom in such a brutal way? I'm not sure if the story makes any sense."

"It depends on what might lie behind the murder," the Minister said. "If what we're seeing here is a series of eye-for-an-eye killings—the kind of gang feud that we speculated about—then maybe a high-profile killing makes sense."

"Well, maybe. But Ransom's was the fourth murder, at least as far as we know. So who are we suggesting started this round of killings—the Brits?"

The Minister shrugged. "I don't know, Nergui. I can't make sense of it. But you don't seem to be making a great deal of progress either."

Nergui nodded. "I can't deny that," he said. "I feel as if I'm grasping at shadows here. We have another lead, but I don't know how it would fit with any of this." He briefly outlined their visit to the illegal prospectors and their encounter with Cholon. "It may well be another waste of time."

"You have to take it seriously," the Minister said. "I'm not sure whether a lone psychopath makes any more sense than what Wilson's suggesting, but if there's half a chance it's true—"

"Then we have to stop him."

Nergui started to rise, but the Minister gestured him to sit for a moment longer. "But, Nergui, we also have to take notice of what Wilson says. As you say, we don't know what his agenda might be. We don't know if he's telling the whole truth or, indeed, the truth at all. But if there's any substance in what he's saying, then one of our major national investment programmes might be on the point of turning into a bloodbath."

"It's not much of a choice," Nergui said, rising. "A serial killer or a mafia feud."

"It may be worse than that," the Minister said. "It may be both."

NINETEEN

The weather had eased slightly by the time Nergui made his way back over Sukh Bataar Square. Snow was still falling, but less thickly than before, and Nergui could now see his way through the haze of streetlighting to the far side of the square. The landscape was heavily covered in snow, buildings and statues rendered shapeless by the drifts. There was no sign of human life across the vast area of the square, though a snow-plough was standing, apparently abandoned, in one of the main streets.

Nergui glanced at his watch. Four thirty. Time for the next leg on his goose chase. Nergui realised that he was operating almost entirely on instinct. It was a strange sensation. For all his occasional talk of intuition, Nergui's normal approach was one of painstaking rigour. He knew from experience that crimes were much more likely to be resolved through a systematic sifting of the evidence than through wild hunches or undisciplined guesswork. But in this case, though enormous efforts had been devoted to working steadily through every piece of evidence, the results had been virtually non-existent.

Not that this made Nergui's actions any more sensible or justifiable. He knew that if he had caught a junior officer racing across the country in the way he had been doing, he might well have been taking disciplinary action by now. He smiled, grimly. Everyone knew that the rules did not apply to Nergui, so he was unlikely to be challenged from within the police. But if he did not start to deliver some results soon, his position might indeed become untenable.

He was gratified to see, as he trudged back into the police HQ car park, that the four-wheel-drive vehicle had been prepared for snow travel, with chains and additional spot lamps. As he stepped into the warm building, he saw Doripalam sitting with Cholon in the rest room. He waved, and both men jumped to their feet and came out to meet him.

"Everything's ready," Doripalam said. "I got the vehicles prepared. We're ready to go when you are."

Nergui nodded. "You have firearms?"

Doripalam glanced at Cholon. "For you and me, yes."

"That's fine. I hope that they will not be needed, but we should take no risks."

"Should we take other back-up?"

Nergui shook his head. "It's your choice but I would prefer not. We may well be wasting our time. I would rather that we did not waste that of too many others. But we should have whatever resource is available standing by."

"I've arranged that."

Nergui smiled. He was beginning to suspect that Doripalam's approach to this case was much more rational, more cool-headed than his own. He turned to Cholon. "Are you sure you wish to accompany us? I don't know what kind of risks might be involved."

Cholon shrugged. "If this is my brother, then my presence may be helpful."

This was true enough. Nergui did not know what they were stepping into. But if they did find Badzar, it was conceivable that he would behave more rationally towards Cholon than to others.

"Okay," Nergui said. "But it's your decision. And you must do nothing unless we tell you to."

Cholon nodded, and the three of them trooped back outside to the waiting vehicle. The snow had almost stopped now, and the sky was clearing, with a few stars already visible. The weather would become colder before dawn, Nergui thought, the roads more icy and treacherous.

Doripalam climbed into the driver's seat. Nergui sat beside him, and Cholon climbed into the back. "Where are we going?" Doripalam asked.

"Back to the place where we found Delgerbayar's body. The disused factory."

Doripalam turned to stare at Nergui. "Back there? You really think we're likely to find something there?"

Nergui shook his head. "I really have no idea," he said. "I'm flying blind. If it were you behaving like this, I'd have you on a charge by now. But there's something—I don't know. It's close to the flat where Badzar stayed for those two nights. The timing of that coincided exactly with Delgerbayar's killing. I have a feeling about it, that's all it is. But I want to check it out."

"But the place was thoroughly searched after Delgerbayar's body was found."

"I know. But I think he may have been back there."

"He'd be taking a big risk."

"Maybe not. It's no riskier than anywhere else. Maybe less than other places. We assumed that the factory had no particular significance. We searched it thoroughly, then left it. We saw no reason to have it guarded or under surveillance. He might have realised that, once we'd finished our business with Delger-bayar, it was the last place we would return to."

Doripalam looked far from convinced, but shrugged. "Well, as you say, it's worth a try." He turned on the ignition and pulled the vehicle slowly out into the street. Even with the snow chains, driving was precarious and they could feel the heavy vehicle slipping slightly as they turned into the main street. Conditions would become worse as the snow gradually turned to ice under the clear skies.

The factory area was not far, but the journey took them close to thirty minutes as Doripalam fought to maintain control of the vehicle. Finally, they turned into the shadowy concrete yard outside the factory.

The sky had cleared fully now, and there was a nearly full moon shining brilliantly above the horizon. In the pale moonlight, the thick silent snow was eerie, deadening the sound of their movements. It lay thick across the yard, and had drifted deeply against the empty factory itself. Nergui jumped down into the snow, feeling it crunch under his feet. Even here, in the lee of the buildings, it was a good six inches deep.

He walked slowly across to the door through which they had gained entry on the previous occasion, Doripalam and Cholon following behind. Other than the sound of their own footsteps in the snow, the silence was absolute. The low moon lengthened the shadows, so that the side of the factory lay in darkness.

The door had been boarded up following their previous entrance. It appeared to be undisturbed but Nergui was aware that there were several other entrances around the building, which might allow access.

He turned towards Doripalam who was carrying the large crowbar they had brought in the rear of the truck. Doripalam was standing waiting, but Cholon had stopped some yards back, caught in the moonlight, staring at the massive building in front of them.

"Is something wrong?" Nergui half whispered, the sound of his voice muffled by the snow.

"I've just realised what this place is," Cholon said. "I came here only once or twice, and I did not recognise it in the dark."

"What do you mean?" Nergui moved to take the crowbar from Doripalam, watching Cholon closely.

"It's the factory where our father worked. It was when he lost his job here that we were forced to move out of the city."

Nergui nodded. With a slight sense of shame, he realised that his primary emotion was one of relief, an acknowledgement that the shadows he was chasing might, after all, prove to have some substance. He could see that Cholon's emotions, by contrast, were confused, his recognition of the truth battling with a realisation of its implications.

"We must press on," Nergui said. He inserted the crowbar behind the first of the nailed boards and slowly eased it away from the door. The doorway had been expertly sealed and it took some time to remove all the boarding to the point where the entrance was accessible. Finally, though, they had it cleared, and Nergui kicked the door open.

After the deadened silence of the landscape outside, the echo of the opening door was startling, booming around the enormous vaulted space beyond. Nergui waited a moment for the sound to die away, and then stepped carefully into the darkness. He waited again before preparing to turn on his torch, allowing his eyes to grow accustomed to the blackness.

As his eyes adjusted he realised that the darkness was not complete. The large factory room itself was unlit, but at the far end of the room was the faintest of lights hardly visible from this distance. Nergui squinted, trying to orientate himself to the shape of the building. It was, he realised, a glimmer of light shining under a door. The door of the room where they had found Delgerbayar's body.

The waiting. That was the worst of it. The knowledge that something was going to happen, but not knowing what or when. The sense that something or someone was waiting, just outside his vision, and might appear at any moment.

And the silence, the unearthly, unending silence. Other than the faint sounds of his own breath, his own heartbeat, he had heard nothing for—how long? He had no idea. It felt like hours, but was perhaps only minutes. There was no way to measure time. His body felt as if it was in suspended animation—he had long since ceased to feel any pain, any bodily needs or feelings at all. It was as if somehow he was existing beyond time.

And then suddenly the silence was broken. It took him a moment to register. Was it the sound of movement, of footsteps? He concentrated hard, trying to listen, trying to work out precisely what it was he had heard.

At first, he could hear nothing, then he heard it again, more clearly this time. It was the sound of someone, something moving somewhere close at hand. He strained to move his head to try to see something more, but the binding around his neck held as tightly as ever, and all he could see was the glare of the ceiling lights.

The sound grew louder. It was the sound of footsteps, not quite steady, not quite even, as though the person was dragging some heavy object. And there was something else, a scraping, something metallic being pulled along.

And then, for a breathless moment, there was silence once more. He could hear his own heart beating, faster and louder than before, the blood pounding in his ears.

For the first time since his initial panic attack in the dark, he was terrified. Up to now, his mind had detached itself from this reality and he had almost allowed himself to believe that the silence, the waiting, might continue forever, as if time really were suspended.

But the approaching sound of footsteps had brought him back to the reality of his predicament. There was no way out of this. He could not move. He could only lie here, his heart pounding, as he waited for what would happen next.

He strained his ears again listening for some clue, some indication. The footsteps resumed, uneven as before, backed by the strange metallic scraping, growing ever louder, ever closer. And then he heard something bumping against wood, a hollow echo. The footsteps paused again, and he heard, with a sickening emptiness in his stomach, the door at the far end of the room slowly being opened.

"It's the same room as before," Nergui whispered. "The room where we found Delgerbayar."

Doripalam and Cholon had clustered close beside him. The factory was icy cold, and they could feel the further blast of chilled air from the open door behind them. The three of them were looking down the length of the room. Nergui was holding a large spotlight, shining the beam down the dusty empty space towards the closed door at the far end.

The main factory area was as empty and deserted as before. Nergui had shone the torch around the large vaulted room, peering into the corners and up on to the ramps to make sure nothing had changed. At this time of the year, there were not even any rats scurrying in the corners. There was simply an eerie, hollow silence that seemed to close around them as they stood together in the freezing night.

Nergui turned to Cholon. "You don't need to come any farther. Go back to the car. If we're not out in ten minutes, radio for back-up."

Cholon hesitated. "I'd still rather come with you. If it is Badzar—"

"We don't know what we're going to find here." Nergui's mind was already conjuring up images of their last discovery in this place. "It's better if you go back and wait." Up to the point when he had spotted the glimmer of light from the far room, he had not really believed they were going to find anything here. It was a hunch, something that had to be checked out, but all his professional experience had told him that it was a waste of time. But his hunch had been right. There was something here.

Cholon paused a moment longer, but Nergui said: "Go. Now." Cholon nodded, and turned back to the open door. Nergui suspected he would wait outside, desperate to find out what lay behind this. That was okay—at least he would be in a position to radio for help if it should be needed.

Nergui nodded to Doripalam, and they began to make their way slowly along the length of the room. Nergui kept the spotlight trained ahead of them, trying to avoid it shining directly on the door so that there was less chance it might alert anyone in the room beyond.

By the time they reached the door itself, Nergui was convinced he knew what lay in the room. He wasn't sure what alerted him first—some instinct, perhaps, but then he picked up a smell he knew only too well. It was the smell of blood and decay. It was the smell that lingers when human remains have been left to rot. The smell of death.

He gestured silently to Doripalam to stop. Then he whispered: "Step back. I do not think we are in any danger here, but I suspect that what lies beyond that door will not be pleasant."

Nergui put down the spotlight and pulled out his pistol, his eyes locked on the doorway. Then he reached out and threw open the door, holding his breath, preparing for whatever lay beyond.

Even so, he was taken by surprise.

The room, as he had expected, contained no living creature. It was as silent and empty as when they had found Delgerbayar's body. And it was again lit by a spotlight attached to a car battery, providing the setting for another grotesque display.

But the centrepiece was different. There was no body on the table. Instead, there was a bloody mess, a horrifying parody of a butcher's tray. Nergui blinked, trying to take in what he was seeing. Finally, his breath coming in short bursts, he was able to decipher the extraordinary sight in front of him.

Lying on the table was a mass of severed human body parts. There were four hands, cut off at the wrist. And there were two human heads, their eyes empty and staring, placed precisely in the centre of the table.

Nergui turned to Doripalam, who had positioned himself behind Nergui and was staring, horrified, into the room. "I think," Nergui said slowly, "that Badzar has decided to fill in the gaps in our collection."

TWENTY

It was nearly eight by the time Nergui arrived back at police HQ. Doripalam had called out forensics to collect the body parts, and Nergui had waited, tramping backwards and forwards in the deep snow, until they and the scene-of-crime officers reached the factory.

Doripalam had asked for a full alert to be put out for Badzar's arrest, and officers were being called back on to duty to attempt a full-scale manhunt. At least now they had a clear suspect, but Nergui knew from experience how easy it was for a fugitive to hide out in this city. He was not hopeful that Badzar would be apprehended quickly.

He had sent Doripalam and Cholon back, telling them to get some rest. He had briefly informed Cholon what had been found in the room, but had not allowed him to see the grotesque display. As he spoke, he had seen the look of horrified emptiness in Cholon's eyes. It was no longer possible for Cholon to deny, to himself or anyone else, what his brother had been capable of.

"I'm sorry," was all that Nergui could say, but he could sense the years of uncomprehending anguish that lay ahead for Cholon.

Cholon began to walk, dead-eyed, back to the truck. Doripalam turned to Nergui. "You'll be all right here on your own? Do you think it's safe?"

Nergui shrugged. "I imagine so. I can't believe that Badzar would have hung around after setting up that little show for us."

"He's smart, though," Doripalam said. "How did he know we would come here? I mean—" He looked slightly embarrassed. "I mean, it was only a hunch on your part. I—well, I wasn't sure anything would come of it."

Nergui smiled grimly. "Neither was I, if I'm honest. But once the thought had occurred, I couldn't ignore it. But the truth is that that display could have sat there for a long time. The light was on a timer, and I suppose Badzar could always come and replace the battery at intervals if necessary. At this time of the year, the flesh wouldn't decay quickly. He could just wait until we—or someone—happened to stumble upon it." He paused. "And of course, if our phantom caller really is Badzar, then he might have used his next call to lead us here."

"But what's he up to? Why go to all that trouble to dismember the bodies, apparently to hide their identities, and then give us the missing body parts anyway?"

"I don't know, but I have a sense that this is moving towards some endgame." It was what he had felt all along, the sense of something moving slowly but ever more certainly towards a purpose, towards some sense of resolution. He couldn't square this feeling with the brutal and apparently random nature of these killings, but he now felt this sense of purpose more than ever. He shook his head. "There's something about this," he said. "I think endgame is the right word. There is some game being played here, and I have an awful feeling we're being treated as the pawns."

Doripalam nodded, clearly baffled by Nergui's speculations. "You don't want us to wait till the back-up arrives?"

Nergui glanced across at Cholon, who was leaning over the bonnet of the truck, looking like a man who had had all the life beaten out of him. "No, you need to look after Cholon. I can't begin to imagine what he's going through. Get him a hotel room, see if he can get some sleep, but keep an eye on him."

As soon as the truck had driven away, Nergui wondered if this had been a wise decision. There was no telling what Badzar might be planning. Perhaps he was observing him at this very moment, waiting until Doripalam and Cholon had driven away before moving against Nergui. Just as, Nergui thought, he might have been waiting for Drew on the night they left the embassy.

He looked uneasily around him. The yard beside the factory was silent and deserted. It was still dark, though the glow in the eastern sky heralded the approach of sunrise. In the distance, the city would be starting to come to life, the snowploughs out clearing the streets. But there was no sign of that here. Nergui flashed the spotlight around the yard, catching unnerving shapes and shadows as the beam circled. He moved himself slowly back against the wall of the factory, trying to ensure that there was at least no risk of his being caught from behind.

Nergui was far from being a nervous individual, but the next twenty minutes, until the back-up team arrived, were among the most uncomfortable he had ever endured. He stood, with his back to the factory wall, regularly arcing the spotlight beam around him, trying to minimise the risk that anyone might take him by surprise. He kept his hand in his pocket, resting on the cold handle of his pistol, ready to draw it at any sign of movement.

The snow was helpful to him because any figures crossing

the open area of the yard would be thrown into relief by the stark whiteness, and it was virtually impossible to walk silently across the crisp drifts. The moon had risen too, and the yard was bathed in its pale light, although there were still too many shadows and dark corners where an assailant could hide.

Nergui told himself he was being ridiculous. There was no possibility that Badzar would have hung around here, no chance that he had witnessed their arrival. The risks would surely have been too great. But, clearly, they were not dealing with a rational man. It seemed there was no limit to what he might do, no way of predicting his actions.

However much he tried to rationalise his position, Nergui could not shake the uneasy feeling that he was being watched. His mind went back to the arrow that had been fired at himself and Drew, and he realised how vulnerable his position might be.

He remained as still as possible, listening for any movement, any sound that might reveal the presence of another person. Now that the snow had stopped falling and the sky had cleared, there was a faint chill breeze blowing through the yards and alleyways between the factory buildings. He heard, once, the sound of something scattering, perhaps a paper blown in the wind, or maybe the echo of footsteps in the snow. He turned in what he judged to be the right direction, straining his ears, but could hear nothing more.

And then he heard another sound, off to his left. Unmistakable this time, the sound of scraping, snow being dislodged, someone moving. He directed the spotlight towards the sound, able to see nothing. The white sweep of banked snow rose towards a concrete wall at the far end of the factory yard. And then his spotlight caught something, raised upon the top of the wall—a shape, a shadow, moving swiftly, dropping behind the concrete. He tensed, shining the light backwards and forwards at the spot, but could see nothing more. Just the snow-covered top of the wall, perhaps a smudge or two where the snow had been disturbed.

He peered into the light, trying to see more. Perhaps it had been an animal of some kind, though that seemed unlikely on such a cold night. And in his heart he knew that someone had been watching him. Perhaps was still watching him.

Nergui shivered. The prospect that he was being observed by the person who had been capable of such unspeakable acts of murder and mutilation, who had perhaps been responsible for Drew's disappearance, sent a chill through his body. He crouched down, trying to present as small a target as possible, his eyes concentrating on the area where he had seen movement, but also constantly darting around the yard in case assault should come from another direction.

Finally his concentration was disturbed by a far more welcome sound. It was the noise of a car engine, closely followed by a second. Headlights flashed around the edges of the yard as two marked patrol cars pulled slowly to a halt in front of the factory.

Nergui rose, peering over the cars to see if there was any sign of movement beyond. Three police officers emerged from the front car. The rear car contained the pathologist and a specialist scene-of-crime officer.

Nergui spoke briefly to the three officers. "Come with me. I think I saw someone over there. It may be our man. But be careful. He's extremely dangerous."

He led the way cautiously across the yard to the snow covered wall where he had seen the movements. He flashed the spotlight across it. He had been right. The snow had been disturbed in the centre, as if someone had been trying to clamber over the wall. The wall itself was no more than six feet high, not difficult to scale in normal circumstances but made more treacherous by the drifted snow. There was no obvious gate or other entry point.

Nergui handed the spotlight to one of the other officers, and stamped his way through the snow drift to reach the wall. Aware that he might be making himself a sitting target, he reached up and pulled himself up till his head was above the top of the wall, ready to drop back if there was any evidence of a threat from the other side.

There was nothing, just a further area of snow-covered concrete, then the ground fell away into some form of wasteland— the ruins of some demolished building, though it was difficult to tell in the snow. On the other side were more factories and industrial buildings, tightly clustered.

Beyond the point where the snow on the wall had been disturbed, there was a line of jumbled footprints, leading down into the wasteland area. It was possible that they might provide some sort of trail, but Nergui suspected that the trail would be lost in the factory buildings opposite, where the narrow alleyways had avoided the worst of the snow.

"Was it him?" one of the officers asked.

Nergui shrugged. "I can't imagine anyone else being out here on a night like this. Get over the wall and see if you can make anything of the trail of footprints over there—anything at all from the footprints themselves. And then see if you can find where they lead. They probably just disappear on the far side, but it's worth a look. Take care."

The officers began to clamber up onto the wall. Nergui watched them a moment, and then began to walk back across the yard to where the pathologist and crime-scene officer were waiting. He nodded to them without speaking, and then led the way back into the factory.

Even for Nergui, returning to the scene, the display of body parts was still shocking. He could see the crime-scene officer visibly paling at the sight before them, and even the hardened pathologist appeared shaken.

"I'm assuming," Nergui said slowly, "that these items correspond to the two unidentified corpses already in our possession. That is, I am praying that we are not now faced with two further killings."

The pathologist nodded. "Let us hope not."

"And the second thing is to try to get some idea of their identities. If these were removed from the original corpses, then it should be much easier to identify them, I presume?"

The pathologist nodded, staring at the display with a mix of horror and bafflement. "There are no guarantees but at least we will have fingerprints, dental records. It looks as if the killer is trying to assist us."

"So it would seem," Nergui said. He turned to the crime-scene officer. "I want you to review every square centimetre of this place. Anything you can find—*anything*—may be critical. We think we know who we're looking for now, so we're going to need evidence to prove he was here. I can't imagine he's going to have left fingerprints, but there may be other forensic evidence."

He left the two men working in the room, still lit by the battery-powered spotlamp, and made his way back outside. The three officers had climbed back over the wall and were making their way back towards him.

"Nothing," one said, shaking his head. "The footsteps up at this end are too jumbled to make anything of. And over on the other side there's a whole network of sheltered alleyways that the snow hasn't touched. We followed the trail a few yards into the alleys, but then it disappeared."

"This man knows what he's doing," Nergui said. "He's not going to make it easy for us." He gestured back to the factory. "Two of you had better stay here, just in case." He looked around in the darkness. "I cannot imagine he is still in the vicinity. But then I didn't seriously believe that he was here in the first place."

He turned to the third officer. "We've got a full scale search going on of the area?" he asked.

The officer nodded. "As best we can. We only had the night duty on, but we're calling in as many officers as we can. The snow's not helping. They're gradually getting the streets cleared, but this is the first serious snowfall we've had this year so it's taking time to get it sorted. We've got patrol cars all round there now, but it's taken a while to get them in place."

"Okay. There's not much more we can do. If you take me back to HQ, you can get your car out with the rest."

As they drove back Nergui noted that most of the main roads were now largely clear. Lorries laden with huge cargoes of ploughed snow were ferrying along the major routes, trying to open as many as possible before the morning came.

Nergui looked at his watch. Seven twenty. The sky was lightening now in the east, and it would not be long before the sun rose. He would not be sorry to see the back of this particular night, but he was apprehensive about what the coming day might bring. The anonymous caller was due to ring back at nine. Was this a hoax or was it really Badzar? And if it was, what might he tell them?

Assuming that the limbs were those belonging to the original bodies, it looked as if Badzar was now trying to communicate something. Was this just coincidence, or did he somehow know that they had stumbled across his identity? If Badzar had been observing him over the previous days—which Nergui, with an inward shudder, increasingly felt to be the case—then it was possible that he had seen Cholon accompanying them. Maybe he had realised that Cholon had betrayed him. If so, they should ensure that Cholon himself was protected. He pulled out his mobile and dialled HQ, asking for Doripalam. It took Doripalam a few minutes to reach the phone, and when he eventually spoke he sounded breathless.

"I wanted to check that Cholon was okay. What have you done with him?"

"He's still here. I tried to persuade him to get some sleep, but he was keen to stay here, at least till the next call comes in. And I thought this might be the safest place."

"We need to keep an eye on him. It's possible Badzar has seen him with us."

"You think Badzar's been watching us?"

"I think he was watching us in the factory tonight. I think he was watching me after you and Cholon left."

There was an intake of breath at the other end of the line, as Doripalam took in the implications of this. "I'll take care of him. But I wanted to tell you, I've been doing some more digging since I got back here. There are some things I need to update you on."

Nergui glanced out of the car window. "I'm just a few minutes away. I'll find you when I get there."

The centre of Sukh Bataar Square was still thickly covered in snow, looking oddly pastoral under the smooth drifts. The roads around the square, though, were now clear. They turned off the square and pulled into the HQ car park.

It was only when he finally entered the HQ building that Nergui realised how cold he was. Through the glass he could see Doripalam sitting in the rest room with Cholon, a large pile of official files behind them. Cholon had finally fallen asleep, curled awkwardly in one of the large armchairs.

Doripalam jumped up as he entered, one of the files in his hand.

Nergui smiled faintly. "I need some coffee before I can take anything in. I'm freezing."

He filled the electric kettle that sat among the debris of used coffee mugs on the table at the end of the room and then turned back to Doripalam. "What is it?"

"A few things," Doripalam said. "I was wondering about Delgerbayar and where he fitted into this."

It was a good question. Cholon's description had suggested that, at the very least, Delgerbayar had been involved in some business on the side. It was, of course, one of the first questions they had asked in the light of his brutal murder, but there had been no indication of any wrong-doing on Delgerbayar's part.

"A thorough search was carried out of all Delgerbayar's files and materials after his death," Nergui said.

"I know that. It was all scrupulously clean. Maybe suspiciously so, knowing what we know now. But I had a look through the file again this morning, and something struck me. We'd asked for a copy of Delgerbayar's recent bank statements to see if there was any evidence of unexplained payments."

Nergui nodded. "As I understand it, there was no indication that he was on the take. The incomings and outgoings were pretty much what you'd expect for a man in his position."

"They were. But I had a closer look at the statements. Most of the payments were what you'd expect, but there were a number of small transfers of cash in from another account. Always just small amounts as if he needed to tide himself over to his next salary or whatever."

"Maybe he had another account," Nergui said. "A savings account or something."

"Well, yes, that's what I assumed. But I thought I'd better check."

Take nothing for granted. One of the first rules of investigation, Nergui thought, and precisely the one they'd been guilty of neglecting all the way through this case. "Not an ideal time of the day for checking bank details," he said.

Doripalam smiled. "No. So I called the manager at home."

"Bet he was pleased. What time was this?"

"About six. He was up already, at least. But he knew it was

a murder enquiry and, well, I mentioned your name so he was happy to help."

Nergui nodded. "There goes my chance of an overdraft. And he gave you the information without asking for authorisation in triplicate?"

"He did once I'd mentioned your name. It turned out there is another account. It was opened by Delgerbayar's father. The thing is, Delgerbayar's father died five years ago, though the bank weren't aware of that."

"And what was in this account?"

"I didn't push the manager to give me the exact amount, because he was beginning to feel a bit awkward about talking to me. But clearly a lot. The manager was told some story about the father being in some sort of export business. So most of the payments were in dollars. In cash, apparently."

"And the bank never thought to question this?" Nergui said. It didn't surprise him. The country had increasingly stringent regulations in place, having subscribed to international standards on money laundering. But they were frequently flouted. Nergui guessed that in this case a small proportion of the cash had also found its way into the manager's pocket. Maybe that was one small fry to deal with later, if they ever managed to deal with the big fish in this case.

"I think by the time he realised what we were talking about, he wished he hadn't been so helpful," Doripalam said.

"So Delgerbayar was on the take, and in a fairly big way. And it obviously made him at least one serious enemy. We need to get someone over to the bank before the manager starts destroying any evidence."

"I already thought of that," Doripalam said. "I didn't know who we could spare from the search for Badzar. I'd have gone myself but I wanted to stay to update you. In the end, Batzorig volunteered. He's gone over to the bank and told the manager to meet him there. Batzorig's going to go through all the papers with him and bring back anything he can find that looks remotely relevant."

"Sounds sensible," Nergui said, "though it may well be a waste of time. If the manager's smart, he'll have kept any written evidence of this to a minimum. And it was a clever move of Delgerbayar to use his father's account—that way the setting up of the account would have predated the introduction of the money laundering checks. It's quite possible that the manager can be faulted only in that he allowed substantial sums to be paid in without checking the source. And I bet that's true of every bank manager in the country."

"There are a couple of other things," Doripalam went on. "I did a bit of digging in one or two other areas as well. I thought it was worth doing a bit of checking on the mining company that Delgerbayar seems to have been involved with. Turns out it's a largely Russian-owned company. Got some state investment from us. It's part of the consortium involved in the Gobi project. In fact, the two biggest investors are the Russians and a US company."

"Strange bedfellows," Nergui commented. He looked at his watch. "How did you manage to find out all this in the space of about an hour?"

"Not difficult, actually. Did a bit of searching on the internet—got some basic information. Also got some data from government systems—not sure whether I was supposed to be on there officially, but I got one of the IT guys to do me a favour."

"You're making me feel old. This US company—wouldn't have any links to Collins and Maxon, would it?"

"You're not over the hill yet, clearly. Yes, part of the same group. Another operating company."

"And what about the Russian company?"

"MN Mining. It's based in St. Petersburg. They're part of a

wider group, but MN is exclusively focused on mining, primarily gold, in Mongolia. They've a major office in the city here. The Chief Exec is a Russian, Sergei Kartashkin, based here."

"And where does the US investment come in?"

"Well, that's where it gets interesting. To start with MN was established as a subsidiary here to carry out opencast mining in the north—the kind of stuff we saw yesterday. It looks as if they got some government funding from our end so it was essentially a joint venture. But then they began to chase some of the prospects in the south where more deep mining is needed. It's a much more expensive process—even establishing where the reserves are costs a lot, so they had to look for more investment. MN eventually became part of the consortium with the US company, a company from the UK and some South Korean interests."

"All supposedly legitimate?"

"Difficult for me to tell. It's more your area than mine," Doripalam said.

Nergui nodded. All kinds of money was flooding into the country, some honest, some much more dubious. There was a lot of incentive for organised crime to use this isolated republic as a route for money laundering, particularly if they could realise a return on their investment in the process. This didn't mean that the investment in this case was necessarily crooked, but a number of the Russian-based companies were known to have criminal links. Nergui was also aware that there were growing links—as well as significant tensions—between organised crime in Russia and its counterpart in the States. It would not be a surprise to find some unsavoury elements involved in this particular deal.

"Well, at least we now know that they've got interests in the south, which might begin to explain Delgerbayar's mysterious trip to the Gobi, given that he was on their payroll. And, given the background, even putting aside what we know about Collins and Maxon, I guess I'd be very surprised if they were entirely above board. I've no idea what all this is telling us, but we've started pulling at some interesting threads so maybe this thing might start to unravel. Though what it looks like underneath is anyone's guess."

Nergui looked at his watch. Eight forty. The promised telephone call was due in twenty minutes, assuming that the first call hadn't simply been a hoax. "Okay," he said, "we need to get everything set up for this call, if it comes. I want us to start trying to trace the call as soon as it comes in on the switchboard. Tape every word of it. I don't imagine he'll be careless if he's true to form, but we can't afford to miss a trick. You go and get things set up. I'll stick down here with Cholon for the moment."

Doripalam turned, on his way upstairs, but Nergui called after him. "Doripalam, you've done well. Very well. I think we're finally starting to get somewhere. Once we've seen whether our phantom caller returns, what do you think about a visit to Mr. Kartashkin? I feel in the mood for a business meeting."

TWENTY-ONE

At first they thought that the call wasn't going to come. Nergui had positioned himself at a desk which was secluded but within sight of the switchboard operator, so that they could signal to each other if necessary. Doripalam had set up the tape machine and was in contact with the telephone engineer who was going to try to trace the call. The attempt would probably prove futile. The call would almost certainly come from a mobile. Although it was theoretically possible at least to identify the area from which the call was being made, this would only be achieved if the caller was considerably more garrulous than on the previous occasion.

Nine o'clock approached and the small team tensed, waiting for a call on one of the external lines. If any other calls came through at the same time, the operator would put them on hold without warning to avoid distraction from the job at hand.

Nine o'clock came and went. At four minutes past, a call came in but it was only someone trying to report a stolen wallet. The operator, true to the plan, put the caller on hold and waited. "Hope he's still there when I get back to him," he commented.

"We don't know how long that might be," Doripalam said. "How long do we keep waiting?"

His question was answered almost immediately. They recognised the voice instantly from the night before. The tape was already running, and Doripalam had triggered the call trace.

"Nergui," the voice said. The operator signalled to Nergui, and then transferred the call.

"This is Nergui. Who is this?"

"I'm here to offer you help," the voice said. "I have something valuable which I think would interest you. I'm seeking only your attention in return."

"What do you mean?"

"As I say, I have something of value. I am seeking no reward except that you listen to me."

"This is nonsense," Nergui said. "I'm too old to be playing games. Tell me what you want or get off the line."

There was a long pause and for a brief moment Nergui thought that the caller really had hung up. Then he heard the faint sound of breathing down the line. Nergui held the silence, willing the caller to speak first.

"I have McLeish," the voice said at last. "The policeman. I want to meet you. Only you. I'll call again."

"How do I know you're—?" Nergui began, but the line had already been cut. Nergui slammed the handset down hard, frustrated at the lack of information. This could all still be a hoax, a stupid waste of time. He looked up at Doripalam who began to walk over, shaking his head.

"No chance of tracing it. Far too short. I think they'd got it pinned down to the south of the city, but that was about it."

"That would put him close to where we were last night," Nergui said.

Doripalam nodded. "It would, but it's not much to go on."

"He must have known we were trying to trace him. That's why he hung up so quickly," Nergui said. "He's a smart one."

"You don't think it's a hoax, then?"

Nergui shrugged. "Well, it could be. But he knew McLeish's name, and that's not been in the press so far. So if he's a fake, he's a fake with good connections."

"So what now?"

"We're no further forward. In fact, it feels like a step back because we don't know when or if he'll contact us again."

"He said he would."

Nergui nodded. "Well, if it's not a hoax, then I think we can assume he will. The question is how soon, and what happens in the meantime. We've got to keep the momentum here. Make sure that everyone available is on the search for Badzar. We want every building in that area scoured." He turned to the switch-board operator. "If our friend calls again, put him through to my mobile. We're going out—probably an hour or so."

Nergui stalked towards the door, grabbing his coat from the chair in passing. "Come on," he said to Doripalam, "we're going to pay a visit to Comrade Kartashkin."

After the sound of the opening door, there was silence. He tensed, straining his ears for what might follow, listening for the sound of movement, of footsteps. But there was nothing. At first, he thought he could hear the faint distant sound of breathing, but it was impossible to be sure.

Panic and despair overwhelmed him. He had been terrified of what might be about to happen, but at least there had been the prospect of some sort of resolution. This was worse. It was as if he was still held in suspension, endlessly paused, waiting for some change that would never come.

That, presumably, was the idea. This was a form of torture. He tried his hardest to suppress his rising panic and to concentrate. Someone had opened the door. Someone was out there. Someone was waiting.

He listened again, trying to distinguish some external sound from the beating of his own heart and the rasp of his own breath.

And then he heard the footsteps again, not close, still outside this room, the same unevenness, the same accompanying scraping. And something else.

The sound of a voice. Little more than a whisper, soft and sibilant. It was impossible to distinguish any words. It was impossible to tell if this was someone talking to himself or to a third party, though only one voice could be heard. It was as if someone was pacing up and down, waiting, counting out time.

And then the footfalls became more purposeful, no longer aimless pacing, but moving as if towards some goal. Were they receding? At this thought Drew felt relief coursing through his body. But he knew that this was ridiculous. Whatever respite he might be gaining could only be temporary.

He was right; suddenly the footsteps returned, growing louder, before he could draw in his breath again. The unevenness was still there, but he could no longer hear the sound of the scraping, just a slow purposeful footfall coming in his direction.

Then a change in the quality of the sound told him that whoever had been pacing around outside had at last entered the room. Watching him as he lay bound on the bench. All rational thought left him. He was helpless, consumed by a primordial terror, every instinct screaming to escape.

He tried to speak, but the words were trapped in his dry throat. He moved his arms and legs agonisingly against the plastic binding and tried again to lift his head, but still could see nothing but the roof and the lights.

The footsteps came closer and now he could hear the faint sound of breathing, the rustle of clothing. Someone was standing immediately over him, though still invisible to his constrained vision.

He held his breath. Expecting almost anything. A gunshot, a knife, a physical blow.

But there was nothing. The footsteps stopped. The faint breathing continued. Drew waited, his hands gripped white, for what might come next.

"I'm afraid he's tied up all morning." She ran her index finger slowly down the page of the desk diary in front of her, as though she needed to confirm her statement. "I might be able to find you a slot towards the end of the afternoon."

Nergui glanced at Doripalam, who looked back blankly. He smiled gently at the receptionist. "I don't think you quite understand," he said. "We're the police. We're investigating a murder. Several murders, in fact. We need to see Mr. Kartashkin now."

Her mouth had dropped slightly open at the mention of the murders, but she still didn't seem inclined to give way. "I've been told very strictly that he shouldn't be—"

But Nergui was already walking past her and up the stairs to the first floor. She jumped to her feet as though to try to stop him, but Doripalam motioned her to sit. "It's easier for everyone if you don't get involved," he said.

"But you can't just come—" She looked wildly around her.

"We can," Doripalam said, smiling. "We are. Incidentally, just to save time, where will we find Mr. Kartashkin?"

She stared at him as though he were insane. Then she shook

her head as though realising that there was little point in arguing. "He's in the Boardroom. Top of the stairs, first on the left."

"Thank you," Doripalam said. "See how helpful a little co-operation can be."

He bounded up the stairs after Nergui. Nergui had clearly caught the beginning of the conversation below, and so was now waiting at the top of the stairs, smiling back down at Doripalam. "Where did she say he was?"

"Boardroom. First on the left."

Nergui strode off again, just a few yards down the corridor to a sturdy wooden door. A well-polished brass plate confirmed that this was the Boardroom.

Nergui, not one to minimise the impact of his entrance, pushed down the handle and flung open the door.

Four men sat round a large mahogany table, files and papers spread between them. They were all staring in astonishment at the intrusion.

"Good morning, gentlemen," Nergui said. "Which of you would be Mr. Kartashkin?"

A large, bald man stood up at the far end of the table. "I am Kartashkin," he said calmly. "I trust that there is some good explanation for this intrusion."

"I believe so," Nergui said, smiling faintly. He produced his ID card from his top pocket and waved it airily in front of the men. "Ministry of Security," he said.

Kartashkin looked as if he was about to protest, then clearly had second thoughts. "I am not aware that our company is of any interest to the Ministry," he said calmly. "I have not gained this impression from the Minister."

Nergui smiled. "No, well, perhaps he does not share all his innermost thoughts with you. Perhaps you would like to give him a call to check?"

Kartashkin stared at Nergui's impassive gaze, then suddenly

looked down. "No matter," he said. "I am of course always happy to co-operate with the Ministry in any way possible." He looked around the table, smiling blandly. "Perhaps, gentlemen, you will leave me alone for a short while with Mr.—?" He glanced at Nergui.

"Nergui." Nergui smiled. "And my colleague, Doripalam. This should not take long."

The other men shuffled out, and Kartashkin sat smiling at Nergui and Doripalam. As soon as the door closed behind his colleagues, Kartashkin's smile vanished. "What the hell's this all about? I do not appreciate being invaded in my own offices."

Nergui's smile was as bland as Kartashkin's had been. "This is a very important matter, Mr. Kartashkin. We are investigating murder."

Kartashkin regarded him closely. "And what does murder have to do with me? I'm a businessman."

"As you say, Mr. Kartashkin. And a very well-connected one. We understand that at least one of our officers was on your payroll."

Kartashkin's head jerked up. "What do you mean?"

"What I say."

"That's ridiculous. We don't—"

"Delgerbayar, the officer in question, is now dead. Murdered. Brutally murdered."

Kartashkin rose to his feet. "I must ask you to leave. I'm not sure what you're implying, but it sounds like the most outrageous—"

Nergui slowly raised his hand. Kartashkin, imposing figure as he might be among his own colleagues, fell silent. "I am not trying to imply anything, Mr. Kartashkin. I am simply stating some facts and seeking your help with our enquiries."

Kartashkin slumped back down into his seat. "You can't prove—"

Nergui lifted his hand again. "Mr. Kartashkin, we are both adults. Let us not waste each other's time. You do not know what I can prove or not prove. I know that Delgerbayar was on your payroll. It may well be that other senior officers are also in your pocket. I do not know that, and at the moment I do not particularly care. But I do care about Delgerbayar because he is now dead, and I want to know why."

Kartashkin hesitated, looking from Nergui to Doripalam and then back, as though hoping that some other approach might be forthcoming. Finally, he said: "I don't know what you're talking about."

Nergui shook his head slowly. "That is disappointing, Mr. Kartashkin. I had expected a more intelligent response."

Kartashkin looked at the door as though expecting that someone would walk in and interrupt them. Perhaps, Doripalam thought, someone really would contact the Minister on his behalf.

"What are you proposing to do? Arrest me?" The words were defiant, but the tone much less so. Kartashkin had suddenly become a different figure from the blustering demagogue who had first greeted them. This was a man, Doripalam thought, on the verge of fear. But fear of what? This would not be a man troubled by the legal consequences of his actions. He did not seriously fear arrest. It might be that he was engaged in corruption far more serious than the bribing of a few police officers, but in this society foreign investment was always well beyond the law. Whatever he was afraid of was something far more troubling. As he watched Kartashkin, and saw sweat breaking out on his neck and forehead, Doripalam thought back to the board meeting they had apparently interrupted. They had caught only a glimpse of the grouping of men before they had responded to Nergui's interruption, but Doripalam had the impression, from the expressions and body language, that it had been some sort of crisis meeting.

Nergui nodded. "If I have to take you in to police head-quarters to get the answers I need, then so be it. It would be an unfortunate interruption to your day. I am sure you have much to get on with." Nergui glanced briefly across at Dori-palam, and it was almost as if the older man had been reading his thoughts.

Kartashkin shook his head. "I am not prepared to say any-thing on the record. If you want a formal statement, you will have to arrest me."

Nergui smiled softly. "But off the record?"

"I don't know." Kartashkin glanced at the door again. "This is not a good time. I am in the middle of things."

"We will keep you no longer than we need to."

"I . . . Well, we are facing some difficulties." He paused, clearly trying to think what to say. "You are right. Off the record. Delgerbayar was known to us. He did the odd bit of business on our behalf. Nothing corrupt—"

"I understand," Nergui said, his face blank.

"I do not know why he was killed. But I want to know why. We have been having some business troubles."

"You are involved in one of the Gobi projects, that is right?"

Kartashkin looked sharply up at Nergui, then nodded. "I think you know more than you are saying. Yes, we are involved in the Gobi."

"It is not going well?"

"It is proving more difficult than we envisaged, yes. There is enormous potential, but the initial investigations are proving difficult. It has required more investment than we expected. Considerably more." He paused, clearly wondering whether he had said too much.

"You are the major investor?" Nergui said. "Along with our government, I mean."

Kartashkin hesitated. "It's complicated," he said. "We were

the major investor, initially. It was virtually a joint venture between ourselves and your government, with a little investment and expertise from the US, the UK and Korea. But as the projected costs have risen, we've struggled to keep pace, so the other parties have increased their stake. Especially the US."

"The US government?" Nergui said.

Kartashkin shook his head. "There is government investment and support, as there is in all the partner companies, but this is a private company." He smiled, bleakly.

"But you have raised the required investment?"

"We have raised the required investment. But it has not been easy. There have been tensions."

"And murders?"

"We do not know if Delgerbayar's death is linked in any way—"

"Mr. Ransom, the Englishman, was also on your payroll, was he not?"

For the second time, Kartashkin raised his head and stared at Nergui. "You are playing with me," he said.

"Believe me, Mr. Kartashkin, I do not play where such matters are concerned. We know that Mr. Ransom was working for the consortium."

"He was working for our British partner. In the north. He was advising on the opencast mining—"

"Mr. Kartashkin, please do not underestimate me. We know that Mr. Ransom had been carrying out some work connected with the Gobi project. We understand that he had been called in to verify some disputed data."

Kartashkin's eyes were wide now. "In Russia, I think we have ceased carrying out secret surveillance on our citizens. I can only assume that this is not yet the case here."

"Assume as you wish," Nergui said. "But we do like to be aware when visitors to our country are acting illegally."

"Hardly illegally," Kartashkin said. "And you will need to take this up with our partner. It was they who requested—"

"He was working outside the terms specified on his visa," Nergui said. "But that is unimportant. We have two murder victims, killed in very similar circumstances, both apparently employed within your consortium. Such coincidences spark my curiosity."

"I do not know what is happening," Kartashkin said. "I am speaking the truth. I am out of my depth in this project, I admit it. I'm a businessman—a pretty hard-nosed businessman, I thought. I don't always do things by the book. But this is beyond me."

"What is beyond you, Mr. Kartashkin?" Nergui said.

"This project. There are people involved in this who scare me. On all sides." He glanced at the door again.

"Even on your own side?"

Kartashkin leaned forward, his hands clasped together. "Yes, even on my side. We're a legitimate business. But we needed more investment here to keep in the game. We've always walked a fine line."

"What do you mean?"

"We're based in St. Petersburg. It's not easy. Organised crime there is . . . well, it dominates the business world. Not all businessmen are criminals, but we all have to make accommodations."

"I understand. And you have been making accommodations in respect of this project?"

"More than ever before. We were desperate. We'd already sunk so much into this that if it had fallen through we'd have gone under. And there was increasing investment from the other partner countries, so we began to be afraid of being squeezed out. So we had to look for further investment at home."

"And you found it?"

"We found it. But only by doing business with people that we would not normally wish to go near."

Nergui nodded, and looked at the door. "Your colleagues," he said. "These are the people you are talking about?"

"Two of them, yes. The other one is my deputy. But the other two directors—"

"Do you believe they are responsible for the murders, Mr. Kartashkin?"

Kartashkin shook his head. "No. I mean, that would make no sense. Why would they want to kill Delgerbayar and Ransom?"

"So who did?"

"Well, this is what scares me. If we assume that the two murders are connected, then that suggests that they were committed by someone else in the project. Someone trying to harm our interests." He paused. "That, at least, is how my new colleagues appear to think."

Nergui nodded. "And they think this because this is perhaps how they would behave themselves?"

Kartashkin shrugged. "I do not know. But I know that they are taking the killings as—how do I put this?—as an affront to their honour. The way they talk disturbs me."

Nergui nodded. "I think you are a brave man, Mr. Kartashkin, to state your views so openly."

"I am anything but brave," Kartashkin said. "But I am trusting you with this. I do not want more bloodshed."

"I could insist on you coming back with me to give a formal statement," Nergui said. "And I may yet have to do so. But for now I think it is better if we treat our business as concluded. You have told me nothing."

Kartashkin nodded, the relief showing on his face. "Thank you. There is little else I can do, but I would help if I could."

"I would give you one piece of advice, Mr. Kartashkin. Get out of this. As soon as you can."

As they left the Boardroom, they saw two of the men who had left the meeting now standing at the far end of the corridor, watching them. Nergui made a gesture of apology. "I am sorry for disturbing your meeting. I hope that I did not keep you waiting for long." He walked slowly along the corridor towards the two men, who were watching him warily. One was tall, thin, shaven-headed. He wore dark glasses even indoors, in the middle of winter. His stare was blankly intimidating. The other was shorter, his hair combed tightly back, his eyes bright and blinking.

"Routine questions, I'm afraid," Nergui said. "We're investigating some illegal prospectors near one of your sites in the north. I just wanted to check whether you had actually met the prospectors, whether you could provide any information about them. But Kartashkin says no. Is that your recollection also?" He gazed impassively at the two men, a faint smile on his lips.

There was silence for a moment, then the taller man spoke, scarcely above a whisper. "We know nothing of this. We simply wish for the police to enforce the law."

"It is what we try to do," Nergui said. He nodded slowly, as though musing on his words. "But thank you. And my apologies again for the disturbance."

He turned and made his way down the stairs, Doripalam close behind, feeling the men watching him until he had walked across the reception and back out into the street.

As soon as they stepped back into the cold morning air, Nergui began to stride, with characteristic speed, back towards HQ. Doripalam hurried to keep up. "Nasty bunch," he said.

"Very. I was keen for them to know that Kartashkin had told us nothing."

"What do you think about Kartashkin? About what he said, I mean?"

"I feel," Nergui said, "as though he has provided us with another piece of the jigsaw, but I have no idea about how it all fits together. If it's true that Ransom's and Delgerbayar's deaths are somehow connected with the Gobi project, then where does Badzar fit in?"

"Maybe Badzar's working for one of the partner groups. Perhaps he's a hired killer."

Nergui stopped suddenly and turned to look at Doripalam. "It's possible, I suppose, but I can't see that it makes much sense. Who would hire a madman? And what professional killer would leave the bodies the way these were left?"

They crossed the road, stepping over the thick piles of greying snow left by the snowploughs. The roads were largely cleared now, and the morning traffic was becoming busier.

As they turned the corner back towards police HQ, Nergui's mobile rang. He pressed the receive button, holding the phone to his ear as he walked.

It was one of the junior officers. "We've had another call, sir. From our friend."

"Is he still on the line?" Nergui said. "I asked for him to be put through to the mobile."

"We tried, but he wouldn't hang on. Obviously thought it was a ruse to give us time to trace him. But he left a message."

"What message?"

"Said he wanted to meet you, sir. Just you. On your own. He's still claiming that he's got the British officer. Says he's prepared to release him but only if he can meet with you."

"Did he give us any reason to believe that McLeish is still alive?"

"Not really. Didn't stay on long enough."

"So what next?"

"He wants an answer from you, sir. As to whether you're prepared to meet with him. The implication was that if you don't, the British officer won't be alive much longer."

"Assuming he's alive now. Okay, we're only a few minutes away. Did he give you any indication when he would call again?"

"He said in fifteen minutes. And that we should be ready with an answer."

"In that case, I'd better try to come up with one."

He ended the call and relayed the gist of the message to Dori-palam.

"What are you going to do?"

"I don't know," Nergui said. "He's got us over a barrel, as he's no doubt fully aware. We can't just ignore this. The political ramifications are too great. But it would be crazy to go into a one-to-one meeting with a psychopath like this. Especially since we don't even know if he does really have McLeish or, if he does, whether McLeish is still alive."

"You could go in with some back-up."

"It would be a risk. If McLeish is there and alive, we don't know what Badzar would do if he thought we had him cornered."

"And it could all be just a hoax?"

"As you say. It could all just be some lunatic trying to make idiots of us. Not that that's been particularly difficult in this case."

They had arrived back at HQ. Despite the brilliance of the morning sun, the place still looked depressing, its dark concrete looming over them. The thick snow by the entrance was already grey from the tread of countless feet. Nergui did not feel at home here. He felt that the regular police resented his presence, were suspicious of his motives. But equally, he realised, he no longer felt comfortable back in the Ministry. He had always considered himself an astute political player, a survivor, but he was increasingly beginning to feel that this world was leaving him behind.

Inside, the offices were almost deserted, most of the officers engaged in the manhunt for Badzar. So far, he appeared to have slipped away without trace.

Nergui stopped by the telephone switchboard. "When do we expect him to call back?" he asked the operator.

The operator glanced at his watch. "Ten minutes," he said. "Maybe a little less."

Nergui nodded. "I'll be in my office," he said. "Put him straight through."

He led Doripalam into the office and sat himself down behind the desk, gesturing Doripalam to sit opposite. The files on the case lay untouched in front of him.

"I don't think I have a choice," Nergui said.

"What do you mean?"

"I think I have to do what he says," Nergui said. "Meet him. Alone."

"Even though we don't know whether McLeish is even still alive?"

"Especially because of that. The Minister can't keep a lid on this story much longer. The Western media are going to be all over us in the next twenty-four hours."

"The story won't be improved if we end up losing one of our senior officers as well," Doripalam pointed out.

"You're right." Nergui grimaced at the thought. "But, as I say, I don't think there's a choice. All I can try to do is minimise the risks. The risk to me. And the risk to McLeish, if he's still alive."

"And how do you do that?"

Nergui shrugged. "I've got my own talents in that direction. And I'll be armed. And I want you as back-up."

"Me? But I'm not sure I'm the best—"

"There are highly trained officers I could take with me, but I'm not sure who to trust here any more. I don't know who Badzar is working for, if he's working for anyone. And I don't know who or what he knows. I have a feeling that if I set this up as a formal mission, he may well know. And that may mean the end of things for McLeish."

"But I'm still not—"

"Doripalam, we've no idea what we might be letting ourselves in for here. We don't know what's driving Badzar. We don't know why he's suddenly decided to make himself known. It could be a trap. But why bother with a trap? We presume he's already got McLeish—if he's got demands, then he's already got more than enough leverage. If he wanted another victim, he could find one easily enough without putting himself at this risk. He could have killed me while I was waiting at the factory last night. I think it's more likely he wants something." He paused. "And maybe *he* doesn't know who he can trust, either."

Doripalam nodded and opened his mouth to speak. But then Nergui's phone rang. He picked it up, listened and reached out to switch on the intercom. "It's him," he mouthed.

The same sibilant voice emerged from the low-quality speaker. "Have you had time to think?" it asked, without preamble.

"What is it you want?" Nergui said.

"To see you. Alone."

"How do I know McLeish is safe?"

"You don't. You won't until you meet me. Now, please stop

wasting my time. Are you prepared to meet? Just you. If there's any other police presence, McLeish dies."

"If he's still alive."

"As you say. Yes or no?"

Nergui paused and glanced across at Doripalam. "Yes," he said. "Just tell me where and when."

TWENTY-TWO

Not quite silence.

Drew lay, straining every muscle to try to see or hear something, to try to gain some clue as to what was happening.

Someone was watching him closely as he struggled, in one more vain attempt, with the ties that gripped him. He didn't know how he could feel the presence of this other person.

But there was not quite silence.

It seemed like hours since he had heard someone enter the room, but was probably only minutes. And even though he knew that whatever happened next was unlikely to be pleasant, a part of him still refused to accept this, still somehow believed that his current state would continue indefinitely.

Why did his captor not simply get on and do whatever it was he intended? Why this endless torturing uncertainty? Was it simply an attempt to wear down his resistance? But why? Drew had nothing—no possessions, no information—that was likely to be of interest to whoever had kidnapped him in this country. If the intention was to extort some demands from the government, either here or at home, there was nothing obvious to be gained through this kind of psychological torture.

He continued to alternate between struggling with his bonds, and lying as still as possible, trying to gain some sense of what might be happening. But both activities were equally fruitless, nothing more than an empty gesture, a vain attempt to demonstrate to his captor that he had not yet ceased to resist.

And then, suddenly, unexpectedly, he felt the soft touch of a hand against his, the startling warmth of human contact. The touch was so gentle that at first he thought that he was imagining the sensation. But then he felt his hand being grasped firmly in another's grip, a strange feeling because the hand felt harsher, drier, than human flesh. He twisted his head, trying at least to see the hand, trying to see what was gripping his fingers.

And then he saw it. It was, indeed, simply a human hand clutching his own, but the fingers were enclosed in the kind of protective glove worn by those handling food in a shop or café. The kind of glove that might be worn by someone who did not wish to leave any trace of fingerprints.

Drew arched his back, trying to see more, but could still see only the hand and, beyond that, a wrist surrounded by a white shirt cuff. The hand was grasping his own tightly, pulling it hard to one side. He felt his heart beating loudly, his breath pounding through his chest as he wondered what would follow.

And then he heard something metallic, something heavy, being lifted from the ground. He could hear his captor's breathing, the slight strain of someone lifting something heavy, high above his head.

Drew tensed as he felt the momentum of the object through the air above him, his mind jumped back to the sights of the dismembered bodies, the thought of how those limbs had been removed. And as he felt the draught of air above him, he did not even have the breath to scream.

He felt, rather than heard, the heavy thump of metal on wood. He remembered, crazily, stories of those who had lost limbs initially feeling no pain, not even recognising that they had been injured.

But then his breath and his senses returned, and he realised that he was genuinely not hurt. He twisted his head to look at where his captor's hand was still gripping his own.

In the bench just by his hand, a large axe was buried a centimetre or so into the wood. His hand had been pulled back to avoid the axe, so the blade had instead cut neatly through the bindings around his wrist.

Drew opened his mouth to shout, though he had no idea what words he might utter to this still unseen figure who was unlikely to speak any English. Before he could speak, a handcuff was slipped around Drew's untied wrist. He felt his arm being pulled again, and was then aware that the other half of the handcuffs had been firmly attached to an object, as yet invisible to him. He twisted again in his remaining bonds but could still see nothing.

The figure moved behind him, and his other hand was gripped and pulled aside. Again, there was the swish of the axe falling through the air and he felt another bond fall free.

He tried to move, but the remaining bonds on his ankles and neck still held him firmly in place. He caught a glimpse of his captor as he moved rapidly around the room, a black shadow passing swiftly across his constrained vision. The figure was down at his feet now. Again, Drew felt the hand on his leg, holding his feet to one side as the axe fell again, severing the bond on his left leg. And then the same on his right. His legs were free, and only the tight binding on his neck still held him in place.

His captor moved slowly alongside the bench. Drew twisted his head as much as possible, and for the first time saw the figure who was standing beside him.

The man was unremarkable. He was of average height, stockily built, dressed in a cheap-looking, black Western-style suit. He wore a white shirt, open at the neck. He stopped now and stared at Drew.

He was wearing a black skiing mask which entirely covered his face except for two small eye-holes. And, whereas the rest of this figure was unexceptional, the eyes were striking. They stared fixedly at Drew, reddened, burning, unblinking. It was impossible to read the emotion that lay behind them, there was just an emptiness, a blankness, that seemed almost less than human.

Up to now, Drew's terrors had been substantial but unfocussed, nothing more than a fear of what might be impending. Now, though, the threat was real and immediate.

Drew lay still on the bench, his legs and right arm free, but his neck still pinioned to the bench. He shifted his head further, feeling the bindings cutting painfully into his neck, and saw that his left arm was fastened with the handcuffs to a ring on the end of a metal pole. Drew pulled hard on the handcuffs, but it was clear that the pole was set into some heavy, immovable base. It was this, perhaps, which Drew had heard his captor dragging along the floor.

The figure stood motionless, watching Drew. The axe hung loose in his left hand. And, in his right hand, held equally loosely, was what appeared to be a pocket knife, gleaming brightly in the room's stark illumination.

Drew stared back in terror, as the figure began to move slowly forward, raising the knife before his face. His eyes still seemed expressionless, empty of thought or feeling.

As the knife approached his face, Drew suddenly felt as if life and feeling were flooding back into his inert body. Too late, he kicked out with his legs, trying to thrust himself free, feeling the grip of the bond around his neck, preventing him from throwing himself off the bench. The knife rose above him, and Drew screamed, the echoes bouncing ineffectually around the walls and empty spaces.

Nergui had been here before.

How long was it? Three years, maybe four. Something like that. But the sights and sounds and smells—especially the smells—of this place had stayed with him ever since.

It was a place he would dearly have liked to forget. He remembered what he had seen here, at a time when he thought that his country was finally succumbing to irrevocable chaos. This place had seemed almost like a symbol of those miserable days, an image of the depths to which the nation had sunk and from which it had seemed unlikely ever to arise.

But things had changed, and Nergui supposed that this augured well for the future, even if his cynicism did not allow him to entertain excessive optimism. This place was as eerie and unnerving as ever, but its connotations were changing. Already the past was being put behind it.

Visually, the place was extraordinary, a tortuous tapestry of black twisted pipes and billowing steam. It was the entrance to a sewer pipe, a massive construct built in the Soviet days. The pipe network had been built to transport not only sewage but also steam heat from the then thriving factory units around to domestic buildings in the neighbourhood. It had not been a particularly efficient arrangement, in that substantial amounts of steam billowed out into the frozen air. But it did ensure, with characteristic Soviet ingenuity, that heat that would otherwise have been wasted—and which, in the West, would perhaps have been discarded without a thought—was transferred to a practical use.

But, with the collapse of the economy, the steam tunnels had been transformed into something more than merely practical. For some, in the most unpleasant and tragic circumstances, they had become life-saving. This area, only a few years before, had been overwhelmed by those with no other homes to go to—the majority of them children or teenagers.

Whatever their various backgrounds, the hordes of homeless young people had congregated here, trying to find some way of enduring the bitter cold of the icy Mongolian winter. The steam pipes had provided one source of warmth, and the homeless had come in their hundreds to shelter inside, braving the stench of the sewers in exchange for survival.

Initially, the authorities had largely turned a blind eye. If these people were able to fend for themselves, however harsh the conditions, then so much the better. But crime levels had risen, and the groups of semi-feral children became seen as a scourge by those in more fortunate positions. Pressure was placed on the police to deal with the problem, and Nergui recalled numerous raids on the area. Children were picked up in their dozens, and shipped off to shelters that were often only marginal improvements on the makeshift hovels they had left behind. Inevitably, many of those picked up simply ran away again within days, and the whole miserable cycle continued.

Gradually, though, things had changed. Crucially, the economy had slowly improved, and some foreign aid had been obtained to deal with some of the specific problems of homelessness. There was a growing number of decent children's hostels, many of them run by international charities. Work was now more plentiful, and many of those who had been homeless were able to fend for themselves.

Nevertheless, this still tended to be a place where the homeless would cluster, particularly as the winter approached. Many of the formerly thriving factories now lay abandoned, and it was possible to find shelter close enough to the steam pipes to stave off the rigours of the winter nights.

Now, though, the area looked deserted. Alleys ran off between the factories, deep in shadow. In the open areas, the ground was thick with snow, melting only where the steam continued to billow, filling the frozen air with a dense white fog. Nergui stepped slowly forward, straining his eyes. He could see only a few feet in front of him.

He glanced at his watch. Nearly three, as Badzar had stipulated. Behind him, across the city, the sun was already setting, and the shadows were lengthening between the buildings.

This was insane, he thought. He had sought no permission for coming here, nor even told anyone, other than Doripalam, where he was going. This solitary action went against every rule of policing. On the other hand, he did not see much alternative. The Minister, if he had been consulted, would probably have seen things the same way, though might have felt unable to say so overtly.

The proper thing to have done would have been to initiate a full-scale police operation. They should have surrounded the area, given Nergui full back-up, ensured that, whatever else might happen, at least there would have been no chance of Badzar escaping from this alive.

Instead he just had Doripalam, his gun, and his cell phone with Doripalam's number already dialled. They had agreed that if Nergui should call the number without subsequently speaking Doripalam should summon back-up immediately. But Nergui had no illusions that back-up would arrive in time to prevent Badzar's escape.

However, if the worst did happen and Drew was killed, the Minister could present this as a maverick escapade, not officially sanctioned. At worst, they would be back where they started, and Nergui would be left to take the responsibility, probably posthumously. At best, though, this might just conceivably produce the positive outcome that would never be achieved through more orthodox means.

The afternoon was already growing dark. Nergui pulled out his flashlight and shone it down the narrow alleyways, though the illumination was almost useless within the dense clouds of steam. He could make out only the cracked and stained concrete of the old factory buildings. Above, there were lines of smashed and boarded-up windows. Below, there was just scattered rubbish, the debris of abandoned industry, white shapes under the snow.

Badzar had not indicated precisely where he would be, or how he would make his presence known. He had simply told Nergui to come to this spot at three, and then to wait.

Nergui flashed the light up and around him, occasionally glimpsing, as the steam momentarily cleared, the dark towering factories. Once, far above, he caught sight of the densely starstrewn sky. There were no working streetlights down here, though behind him he could see a faint glow in the distance behind the mass of buildings. Through the mist, the sky was darkening from red to a dark purple as the sun disappeared. Soon, the darkness here would be thick and heavy, softened only by the continually billowing steam.

The atmosphere was getting to him, and the shifting clouds of steam created phantoms as he moved forward. He thought of the headless corpses and, despite the cold, the sweat trickled down his back. He told himself that if Badzar wanted him dead he would have killed him the night before. But the thought did nothing to calm his nerves.

Nergui carefully moved the flashlight around him, watching the thickening shadows, the constantly shifting clouds, trying to keep his back close to the wall. The only sound was the insistent hiss of the escaping steam, the rustle of his own footsteps in the frozen snow.

And then, without quite knowing how, he was aware of another presence. He peered forward into the gloom and the steam, trying to make out any movement. Just when he was almost convinced that he had been mistaken, he saw something, across the open space, at the entrance to one of the many alleyways. At first, it was nothing more than a movement, undefined, a sense of shifting space. And then it resolved itself into a shape, a silhouette, half obscured by the darkness and the drifting steam.

"Badzar?" Nergui called. He pointed his flashlight towards the shape, but the beam made little headway in the foggy night.

There was no immediate response. Nergui was sure now that the figure was that of a man, dressed in a long dark garment, but could still make out little more. His hand clutched at his pistol in his pocket and he began to move slowly forward.

He walked forward some metres, holding the flashlight steady, watching the black figure emerge slowly from the darkness. "Badzar?" he said again.

The figure remained motionless, apparently watching him without concern. It was still little more than a silhouette, the face featureless.

He took another step forward, and at last the figure moved, raising its hand. "Stop there." It was the same deep sibilant voice he had heard on the phone.

"Badzar. It's not too late to put an end to this." As he spoke the words, Nergui knew that he was lying: something had been set in motion here that lay far beyond his powers to resolve.

"Stop," the figure repeated.

Nergui obeyed, holding the flashlight out towards the figure.

As far as he could make out it was dressed in a long black coat, some sort of hood pulled over its eyes.

"What is it you want?" Nergui said. "Why have you brought me here?"

"The British policeman is safe," the figure said, as though answering the question. "He will remain so as long as you have done what I say."

"Where is he?"

"He is here. Close at hand. Are you alone?"

Nergui gestured with the flashlight. "Completely. As you can see."

"How do I know that?"

"How do I know you have McLeish?"

"You don't."

"Likewise, then. You have to trust me."

The figure nodded, as though considering this. He continued to stare towards Nergui, his face invisible. "I trust you," he said. "For the moment." And then he turned abruptly, and disappeared back into the darkness of the alley.

Nergui stared after him for a moment, then walked rapidly across the open yard to where the figure had been standing. There was no one there.

Nergui shone the flashlight down the alley. A trail of footprints disappeared across the icy snow. Nergui traced their path to where they ended at an open doorway leading into one of the factory buildings. For a moment, Nergui felt bizarrely reassured by the sight of the footprints—as, he realised, he had the previous night. It was as if he had to keep reminding himself that Badzar was, after all, only human.

He made his way cautiously down the alley, occasionally glancing behind him, in case this was some kind of trap. The silence had returned, and he could hear nothing other than his own footsteps.

There was no light showing beyond the doorway. The door hung open, and Nergui saw a broken padlock on the ground nearby. He stopped by the opening, conscious that he did not wish to make himself too visible a target. "Badzar. Stop playing games. Tell me what you want." He could hear his voice echoing in the empty spaces beyond the doorway, an unexpected contrast to the muffled snowbound world outside.

There was no response. Nergui switched off the flashlight, aware that it would only betray his position. He pulled out his pistol, thumbed off the safety catch and stepped forward into the darkness.

Once through the doorway, he stepped rapidly away from the door, moving himself along the wall so that his position would not be obvious. He stopped, his back pressed against the wall, and held his breath, listening for any clue as to what might lie inside this vaulted room.

There was nothing. The silence and the darkness seemed complete, other than the very faint greyness coming from the open doorway. He had no idea what was in the room, whether it was simply an empty abandoned space or filled with equipment of some kind. He did not know if Badzar was really in here, and if so whether he was here alone.

He stayed motionless by the wall, wondering what his next move should be. If there was no other response, he would have little option but to switch on the flashlight again. He felt absurdly exposed in here, recognising that Badzar was playing with him, leading him into a position where he had no choice but to reveal his position, to present himself as a target to an unseen enemy.

He pressed himself back against the wall, his pistol clutched tightly in his hand, his finger resting on the trigger, preparing for what might happen when he switched on the torch.

And then the decision was taken out of his hands, so suddenly that he almost fired involuntarily. The great vaulted space was suddenly flooded with light, rows of fluorescent tubes flickering into life along the roof beams.

Nergui tried to keep his eyes open, but was dazzled by the unexpected brilliance and for endless seconds could see nothing. He held the gun tight, wanting to be ready for whatever might be waiting, but aware of the risks of shooting into the unseen.

But nothing happened. And finally his eyes cleared, and he was able to look across the vast factory floor to what lay at the far end of the room.

TWENTY-THREE

The knife rose, the silver blade glinting in the bright overhead lights, then came down sharply. Drew's screams were still echoing round the vast empty room as the blade struck, the blade snagging hard against the tight cords.

Drew gasped, all the breath expelled from his body, his mind dazed, his terror now beyond even screaming. He felt, momentarily, the icy steel against his neck, then nothing more. It took him a moment to realise that he felt no pain, and several seconds more to accept that he remained unharmed, except for a mild tingling on his neck where the blade had grazed him.

He twisted his head, trying to see what was happening, and found that, for the first time since he had awakened in this place, his head was free. The stroke of the knife had, with consummate skill, sliced neatly through the cords that held him while barely touching his skin.

His captor was standing calmly, a few feet away, watching as

Drew twisted his body to see. Behind the woollen helmet, his eyes were unblinking.

Drew's body was aching and stiff from the lengthy period of captivity, and at first he was barely able to take advantage of his new freedom. He was held now only by the handcuffs which, as he looked around him, were attached to a ring embedded in a large piece of concrete. He pulled hard on the handcuffs and the block shifted slightly on the floor. It would have been possible to move it, but only with considerable effort. His captor must be considerably stronger than Drew himself, accustomed to moving heavy loads.

His muscles in agony, Drew pulled himself into a sitting position. His captor still stood watching, motionless, with the air of a scientist observing an experiment. Drew looked around him. As he had surmised, this was some kind of disused factory building. The room they were in was a storeroom of some kind, with empty metal shelves stretching around the walls. Here and there were abandoned items—a paint pot, some rusty-looking tools, a few pieces of wood and metal. Drew himself had been lying on a wooden workbench, set in the middle of the concrete floor.

The room was a relatively large one—maybe ten metres square—but through the door behind his captor Drew could see a further, much larger area. Probably the original factory floor, he thought.

It was as if, once his body had been freed, Drew had come to life again, returned from his state of suspended animation. During his captivity, he had been largely unaware of pain or other bodily needs. Now, suddenly, he was aware not only of the stiffness and aches arising from the discomfort of his imprisonment, but also of other pains—the bruises and grazes he had sustained while being attacked and kidnapped. But more immediately, he was acutely aware of a need to urinate.

He stared at his captor. "Who are you?" he said. "What do you want from me?" He was conscious that even if his captor was prepared to engage in dialogue with him, he was unlikely to speak English.

There was no direct response. His captor continued to stare at him. Drew pushed himself down from the bench and put his feet on the floor. His legs shook from the effort, but he forced himself to stand upright. "Why have you brought me here?" he said, in a last effort to make himself understood. He tried to move forward towards his captor, stretching himself away from the handcuffs as far as he could.

The other man still did not move. He was standing several feet beyond Drew's reach. As Drew tried to stretch towards him, he continued to watch, apparently with mild curiosity.

Finally, the man took a step back, still watching Drew. He turned suddenly and began to walk towards the open doorway. At the door, he paused momentarily, and looked back over his shoulder. "Come," he said in English. "This way."

Drew stared at him for a moment in astonishment. The words had been in English. The accent had sounded American, or at least the accent of someone who had learned English in the US. Drew watched as the man disappeared into the far room. Then, slowly and painfully, he tried to follow, dragging the heavy concrete block behind him.

He moved a metre or so along. Then he stopped and, with feelings mixed between relief and a sense of futile rebellion, he unzipped his flies with his free hand and began to urinate copiously across the concrete floor. It was only when he was finished and the liquid was running in rivulets across the empty room that he recommenced his slow progress towards the open door.

*   *   *

Nergui's sight cleared slowly, and he stared across the room through a haze of colours.

This was the old factory floor. It was a vast room, with a high vaulted ceiling crossed by metal roof-beams. Large windows stretched along each wall, although the majority of these were broken or boarded up. It was clear that the room had once contained some form of production machinery, but now, apart from a few discarded pieces of rusty metal, the large space was empty.

At the far end of the room, a man stood. It was the figure Nergui had seen in the darkness, dressed in a long black overcoat, with a hood over his head. Even in the bright light of the numerous fluorescent tubes, Nergui could barely make out the man's face in the hood's shadow, though it was clear he was a Mongolian.

"Badzar?" Nergui said.

"You know who I am," Badzar said. It was a statement, rather than a question. "I saw my brother," he added.

Nergui took a cautious step forward. It was not evident that Badzar was armed, but Nergui had already taken too many chances. "It's not too late to stop all this," he said.

Badzar shook his head. "I think it is too late," he said. "Not for me, but for others."

"Where's McLeish?" Nergui said. "The British policeman. You said you had him. Where is he?"

"He is not here," Badzar said. "It is not true that I have him. Not quite true." He held up his hand as Nergui started to speak. "But I know where he is. He is close by. He is, as far as I know, safe for the moment."

"As far as you know? What do you mean?" Nergui felt a small tremor of relief. He did not understand Badzar's responses, but they were bizarre enough to suggest that they could be true, that McLeish might after all still be alive. "Where is he?"

"Close by," Badzar said. He shrugged. "I am happy to take you there, though I do not know what will happen after that. I want an end to all this. It is not what I expected."

Nergui gently shook his head, trying to make sense of what he was hearing. Maybe it was simply that Badzar was insane, beyond all reason, disconnected from the enormity of what he had done, the crimes he had committed. But it did not feel like that. It felt, as it had to Nergui all along, as though something was emerging here, something he could not yet begin to grasp.

"It's easy for you to put an end to this, if that's what you want," he said. "Take me to McLeish. Hand him over. We can deal with things from there."

"It is not that simple," Badzar said. "It cannot be that simple again. There have been so many crimes and this is just the start."

Nergui took some more steps forward. Badzar did not appear to react to his approach, his hands hanging limply by his side. Nergui's hand was in his pocket, clutching his pistol.

"What do you mean," Nergui said, "just the start?"

Badzar shook his head. His face was visible to Nergui now, caught in the fluorescent lights. He was staring ahead, his eyes blank, his face expressionless. He did not look like a driven man, he did not look like a threat. He looked like a man who was lost, who had somehow travelled too far, too quickly, and now had no idea where he was. Nergui realised that Badzar was not staring at him as he had assumed, but was looking through him, beyond him, as if at something in the far distance. Nergui glanced behind him, wondering if this wasn't after all some kind of trap. But then it became clear to him that whatever Badzar might be staring at, it was not anything in this room. It was not anything that was visible to the human eye.

"What is it?" Nergui said. "What are you talking about? Where's McLeish? Take me to him."

Badzar blinked, and his eyes focused on Nergui, as if seeing him for the first time. "I'll take you to him," he said. "I want to take you to him. I think he is safe. At the moment."

"Quickly, then," Nergui said. He did not begin to understand what Badzar was saying, but it sounded as if, for whatever reason, McLeish's safety was far from guaranteed. "Take me to him."

Badzar stared at Nergui. His eyes were no longer staring into nothingness, but were now fixed on Nergui. The effect was no less disconcerting. "It was him, you see," Badzar said, as though responding to Nergui's instruction. "He was the one. He told me to do it. He helped me." He paused, his eyes pleading. "I would not have done it without him. Not in the same way. Not so much. Not so many."

"Who told you to do it?" Nergui said.

"He did. He led me into this. He told me it was the only way. And then we just went on. There was no way out. No way back."

"Who do you mean? Who are you talking about?"

"Him. He told me." Badzar was shaking his head now, repeatedly, obsessively. His eyes were still blank. "He told me."

"Where is he? Is he with McLeish?" Nergui looked around him at the empty, brightly lit room. He could not follow Badzar into his apparent descent into madness. Was there really some third party? Or was this just some bizarre symptom of Badzar's insanity? If so, there was no guarantee that McLeish was still alive, no guarantee that McLeish was here at all.

"He told me to call you. To bring you to him."

The words stopped Nergui, chills running down his spine. "He told you to call me? To bring me here?"

Badzar shook his head, looking impatient. "No, not to bring you here. That's just it. He told me to bring you to him. He doesn't know we are here yet."

"Where is he, then?"

"He's—nearby. I said I would bring you to him. But I wanted to talk. To tell you. That it was him."

"What was him?"

"Everything was him. Everything. He told me to do it. All of it. And he—was responsible."

"Who is he?" Nergui said again.

"He is nearby." Badzar stopped and looked at his watch. "We have no time. We have to go to him. Otherwise—"

"Otherwise what?"

"We have to go. Now. But I wanted to tell you."

"Take me to McLeish." Nergui pulled the pistol from his pocket. "Take me now."

Badzar looked down at the gun, but barely seemed to register its existence. "I need to take you now," he said again.

He turned and began to walk slowly towards the rear of the factory. There were wide double doors there, clearly designed to provide access for large machinery. To the right of the doors, there was a smaller entrance for everyday access. Badzar reached it, Nergui following close behind, and pulled open the door.

Nergui followed him out into a dark narrow alleyway. It was unlit, but Nergui could see both ways along its full length. Another factory building loomed over them.

"I will take you to him," Badzar said. He began to walk slowly along the alley, staring at the ground. Nergui followed behind, his pistol clutched in one hand, the flashlight in the other.

The alley opened into another open yard area, with a cluster of factory and warehouse buildings around it. The yard was covered with frozen snow, apparently undisturbed since it had fallen. Above them, the sky remained clear and star-filled.

Badzar walked slowly across the yard, leaving a trail of footprints in the virgin snow. By now, Nergui had no idea what to expect. It was clear only that Badzar was beyond any reason.

There was another, wider alleyway at the far side of the yard. Badzar started to walk down it, but almost immediately stopped and turned to his left. "Here," he said. "Here it is." He gestured towards the wall of the adjacent building. Nergui followed close behind and saw that there was a narrow doorway, that had been left ajar. "In here," Badzar said.

Nergui waved the pistol at him. "You first," he said.

Badzar nodded, and slowly pushed open the door and stepped inside. He walked a few steps forward, and Nergui followed carefully, still suspecting a trap.

Beyond the doorway, there was a short unlit passageway. At the far end were more double doors. They were closed, but around them shone a thin line of light.

"In there," Badzar said. "He is in there."

"McLeish?"

"Yes, McLeish is there. And he is there. I hope we are not too late."

"I hope so too," Nergui said. "You go in first."

He still had no idea what to expect, how to gauge Badzar's sanity. His greatest fear was that McLeish's corpse lay beyond this door. It was not clear what else might be waiting.

Badzar stepped forward and pushed open the door. Light flooded through the opening. Nergui paused, allowing his eyes to grow accustomed to the new brightness. He did not want to be caught out again.

Badzar stood, holding the door for him in a parody of conventional politeness. Nergui stepped forward slowly, holding the pistol in front or him, and entered the room.

It was another large abandoned space, this one probably an old warehouse, as the walls were covered in racks and shelving. As he walked forward in the brightly lit room, Nergui wondered irrelevantly how it was that these deserted buildings still had access to electricity.

Then he stopped. Badzar had paused a few feet in front of him, his arms limply at his sides as before.

The room was not empty. Drew was here, as Badzar had promised, and he was not yet the corpse that Nergui had feared. He looked, though, as if death might not be far away. He was sitting huddled on the floor at the far end of the room, his face pale and drawn, his eyes haunted. He was hunched forward, dressed in the clothes he had been wearing when he left the embassy. One of his arms was handcuffed to a post, the kind of device that one might use for tethering a dog or a horse.

And next to him was another figure, dressed in black, a black ski helmet pulled across his face, hiding everything but his eyes. He held a pistol loosely in his hand, the barrel pointing towards Drew.

The figure turned to them, and Nergui was sure that behind the mask, his face was smiling. "Good afternoon," he said. "You are just in time. Only just in time. I'd begun to think that you weren't coming." He raised the pistol in front of his face and looked at it, shaking his head. "So I will not need this just for the moment." He looked back up at Nergui, leaving the gun barrel pointing at Drew.

"But I'm glad you came," he said. "We've a lot to discuss."

TWENTY-FOUR

Nergui slowly lowered his pistol, but kept it in his hand. "I suppose I should have expected this."

"You're a smart man, Nergui," the masked man said, "but you're out of your depth here. I think we all are."

"Even you?"

"Yeah, maybe even me."

"Drew. You're okay?" Nergui looked across at Drew now, ignoring the masked man still pointing his pistol at Drew's head.

Drew nodded slowly. "I think so, for the moment."

"He'll be okay," the masked man said. "So long as you're sensible."

"Forget it, Maxon."

The masked man nodded slowly, then reached up to peel off the helmet. "As I say," Maxon smiled, "you're smart. Smart enough to help your friend McLeish here, if you're sensible."

Nergui shook his head. "It's too late, Maxon. Even if you get away from us, you won't get away from them."

"Smart again, Nergui. But you're wrong this time. I've been in this game too long to be caught out now. All I need is a little help."

"Not this time. It's gone too far."

"You've no idea how far," Maxon said. "It's beyond you now. This isn't about law enforcement or morality, it's about politics. Nobody wants the truth, they just want a politically expedient outcome. You can be a hero. You walk out of here with McLeish safe and the killer in custody." He gestured towards Badzar. "He's in no state to resist."

"And in exchange I let you get away?"

"You *help* me get away. I need shelter for a couple of days and help getting out of the country, that's all. I might manage it on my own, but with your help—with official help—I'll be safe." He shrugged. "Nobody loses."

"Except Badzar."

"Jesus, he's a killer. He's a serial fucking murderer. Why do you care about him?"

"I don't care about him. I want to see him given the treatment he deserves, whatever that might turn out to be. But I care about you. If he's a killer, what are you?"

"I'm a professional," Maxon said.

Nergui shook his head. "Maxon, you are, as you would no doubt say, a piece of fucking work. Okay, so what if I don't help you?"

"Then we all lose. Let's think about it, shall we? You don't play ball, first thing I make off with your friend here. You're back where you started."

"You won't get away for long. We're combing the city for you."

"Yeah, without any success till I gave you a small clue. Like telling you exactly where I fucking was. And the point is that I know exactly how much of a political storm is brewing about our friend. You've been able to keep the lid on it so far, but not for much longer. Soon as the Western media realise you've no idea where he is—or, worse still, if my patience runs out or my trigger finger slips—you're in deep shit. Particularly if it's made known that you had me in your clutches but let me slip away."

"This is insane, Maxon. Even if I do go along with this, what happens once you hand McLeish over? What's to stop us picking you up then?"

"Because I'll make sure you don't get McLeish till I'm well on my way. You didn't think I was going to just hand him over on your word as a gentleman, did you? No, it's quite simple. I take him away to another little hidey hole. You get me the clearance and the papers I need to get me out of here to some place of my choosing, and then I give you a call to let you know where to find him."

"You're crazy. Why would we go along with a deal like that? Easiest thing would be for you to shoot McLeish as soon as we're off the scene. That way it's minimum hassle for you, and we wouldn't know till it's too late."

"Jesus, you know, Nergui, you should be in my job. I'd never thought of that. Well, there you go. But as I see it, you've got no option but to trust me. But okay, you take Badzar with you, anyway. Gesture of good faith and all that. That way, if it all goes belly up, you'll at least have captured the dreaded serial killer. Sounds a smart deal to me."

"You're a bastard, Maxon."

Maxon shook his head, smiling faintly. "No, like I told you, I'm a professional."

"So how did a professional get mixed up in a mess like this?"

Maxon shook his head, impatiently. "There's no time for this crap, Nergui. I'm sure you've got the story all worked out for yourself."

"Some if it. You had a cosy deal going on the Gobi project.

Yourselves, the Brits, the Russians, Canadians, the Koreans. All amicable. All legit business." Nergui paused, watching Maxon. "Legitimate businesses, but a nice front for laundering money through an obscure country with the potential for substantial profits at the end. And our government maybe only too keen to encourage it. Once again, everyone a winner."

Maxon was watching him closely, though the aim of the pistol towards Drew never faltered. "Cut the crap, Nergui."

"But then things started to go off track. The explorations weren't going as well as expected. More investment was needed. The Russians and the locals kept telling you there were problems. Your people—and the others, the Brits, the Canadians—were suspicious. The figures didn't add up."

Maxon moved the gun closer to Drew's head. "Okay," he said. "Let me finish so we can all get moving and so that your friend here understands what this is all about. The Russians knew we weren't prepared to invest any more without a fucking good reason. So they announced they were investing more, demanding a bigger stake. We were being squeezed out."

Nergui nodded slowly. "But surely this kind of dispute could be resolved amicably? After all, our government is in charge of the project—they have the final say."

Maxon laughed, mirthlessly. "You know, Nergui, that might just have been the fucking problem. It's not for me to judge, but I got the feeling that there were some people there not batting on our side."

"So you decided to act on your own initiative?"

"It's my job," Maxon said. "I'm an enforcer. It's what I do."

"Except you didn't do it, did you? Where did you come across Badzar?"

"You're wasted in this business, Nergui. You're pretty professional yourself. You could make some real money. Yeah, I came across Badzar when he started launching one-man guerrilla attacks on our sites in the north. I was supposed to—discourage him. But then I heard his story."

"And your heart bled?"

"—And I thought he was more useful to us alive than dead. I brought him back to the city, initially. But then I managed to persuade him that I was on his side."

"You must have impressive powers of persuasion."

"Yeah, and not all of them involve violence. I reinvented myself as an agent of the US government looking to undermine Russian dominance of the mining industry here."

"Not so far from the truth, then?"

"The best lies never are. Badzar didn't exactly trust me, but he could see that we were working towards the same ends. And I also took the precaution of introducing him to one or two addictive substances. It's amazing how amenable people can be when you're the sole supplier of something they need."

"And your involvement was always deniable?"

"Exactly. Badzar had no real knowledge of me. Always useful if things go wrong."

"Which they did."

"On the contrary, they went better than we might have dreamed. It's just that the Russians were such stubborn bastards."

Nergui nodded. "The first killing—the dismembered body— that was one of the Russian team?"

"One of their geologists. One of those who'd been producing the dubious data. We thought that would give them a clear message."

"And they didn't report him as missing because that would have exposed the whole sordid arrangement. Instead, they just responded in kind."

Maxon nodded. "Pretty much so. We underestimated them, I guess. We thought that, compared to us, this was just a two-bit bunch who would back off at the first sign of trouble."

"Pretty naïve, Maxon."

"Yeah, well, I guess I'm used to operating in more civilised parts of the world."

"So the second victim—the one who was helped off the hotel roof—he was one of yours?"

"Same thing. One of our geologists. I think the message was clear."

"But you didn't take it?"

"Shit, no. I mean, this was a goddam battle of wills now. We directed Badzar very gently towards another of their team. Someone closer to the top guys."

"The body we found dumped in the ravine, and they responded by killing Mr. Ransom, who I take it was one of yours?"

"Exactly. Ransom had been doing some work for us, trying to verify the data that they'd been producing. He was our expert in that field. Poor bastard. He wasn't involved in any of this. Just doing his job."

"Another professional," Nergui said. "But I suppose you could say the same about the geologists you killed."

"Those bastards knew what they were doing," Maxon said. "They were in it to their necks."

"So how did our Mr. Delgerbayar get involved in this?"

"We didn't know how they'd got on to Ransom. He was basically a backroom guy that we'd had crunching data for us. Had barely been down to the Gobi and certainly wasn't anyone they'd see as a threat, unless they had some inside knowledge. Delgerbayar had been on the consortium's payroll for a while, but he wasn't just doing our dirty work, he was also helping out the Russians as well. They were paying him to do some digging about what was going on. He'd been up in the north asking questions, and then headed back south to talk to the Russians in the Gobi. He was getting rattled because he thought if there was a scandal his neck would be on the block. But it was clear he knew something about Badzar. That didn't worry me particularly—Badzar was always disposable—but too many people were beginning to know too much. Down south, everywhere was alive with rumour. We thought that Delgerbayar's death might make a suitable gesture. And it wasn't difficult to persuade Badzar."

"Why not?"

Maxon laughed. "Didn't you know? Delgerbayar was one of the leaders of the group who broke up the prospectors' camp. I don't know whether Delgerbayar actually killed Badzar's father himself, but it's possible. Badzar didn't take much persuading."

Nergui nodded. He could still see, in his mind, the grotesque vision of Delgerbayar's dismembered body stretched out in the factory where Badzar's father had once worked. The horror of the scene remained unchanged, but his response to it—his assumption of a clear distinction between victim and perpetrator—had changed forever. It was, he thought, the loss of another kind of innocence, long after he had assumed that cynicism had made him invulnerable to such shifts.

"And it was after that that we came across you in the Gobi?"

"Yeah, and you bastards scared the shit out of me. I thought that the Russians might have been on to Badzar, but I assumed I'd kept myself out of the picture pretty thoroughly. I headed down to the Gobi to brief Collins, who was liaising with our people down there. We headed out to the tourist camp to avoid being seen at the mines, and then you bastards turned up."

"Just coincidence. We were following Delgerbayar's trail."

"Yeah, because everybody heads to the same place down there when they're trying to be incognito. Jesus, Nergui, ever thought that maybe this country of yours lacks some leisure facilities? Anyway, I thought they were on to us. Good job I tend to jump to conclusions, because it turns out I was right. I spotted a couple of guys lurking round the camp, and thought I'd better make myself scarce. Collins was pissed in the tent. I invited whatsisname, the guy who ran the camp, in to join us for a few drinks. Then I slipped away, supposedly to the john."

Nergui raised his eyes. "You invited Batkhuyag in there deliberately?"

"Sure, so there were two guys. But also Batkhuyag had some inkling what was going on. He kept his eyes and ears open a bit too much. Another rumour merchant. I thought that, in the dark, it was quite probable that the killers wouldn't realise I wasn't there—they probably wouldn't know what I was supposed to look like. At the very least, it would buy me some additional time to get away. So that's what I did."

Nergui was still staring at Maxon. "I see what you mean by professionalism. But how did you manage to get out of the area?"

"I'd got Collins to organise me a motorbike. I think it was stolen. Anyway, I had that, with a decent supply of petrol, so I just headed north into the desert."

"Pretty risky at the time of year."

"Maybe. But what you don't know don't kill you. I was well prepared. Always am. I headed north—I'd got various equipment including good GSM navigation equipment with me. I just drove and drove through the night. Eventually got back here. Probably not thinking too straight by that point."

"Which is why you kidnapped McLeish?"

"No, I thought that through pretty well. I knew the Russians were after me. I suspected that your government wasn't likely to do me any favours. So I had to try to get out of here. Which wasn't likely to be easily achievable by any conventional means, as far as I could see. Then I thought of you and McLeish. You struck me as being, well, smarter and less corruptible than some of your compatriots and that McLeish would provide the leverage I needed."

"But how did you track him down?"

"Not difficult. I aimed to phone round all the major hotels asking for him, so I could see where he was staying. As it turned out, I hit pay-dirt first time at the Chinggis Khaan. I just waited there till he came out and followed him. Ended up at the embassy. I had a cold night waiting out for him to emerge, and then I thought it was wasted because he was going to get in the fucking car with the rest of you. But he didn't, and so here we all are. And now you and your friend can see how serious this fucking situation is."

"So where do we go from here?"

"Simple," Maxon said. "You take Badzar with you, claim the credit. Meanwhile, I look after McLeish while you make the arrangements to get me out of your goddam country."

Nergui glanced at McLeish. "I don't know if it's that simple," he said. "I'm still a policeman. I don't know whether I can go along with just letting you go. And that's putting aside the question of how much I can trust you in any case. If I let you out of here with McLeish, I can't expect to see either of you again."

"Jesus, what are the options here? I need to get out of your fucking country as soon as possible. Those bastards are only a step behind me. I'm not going to do anything to jeopardise my escape. But you need to act fast. And as for your fucking scruples, well, don't you realise you're the only one left who seems to have them? Your fucking government is behind the Russians on this one all the way. They just want to get the best deal. They happily got into bed with my people when that looked the most lucrative option, and now they've just as happily switched sides."

He paused, suddenly, and then unexpectedly smiled. He turned and gazed at McLeish, who was slumped against the concrete block, looking drained, beyond words. "And anyway,

Nergui, what are your fucking scruples worth? It's McLeish's life you're gambling with, not your own."

The last comment hit home. Maxon was smart, right enough. While Nergui had been talking, trying to buy time, Maxon had still been one step ahead, taking the opportunity to make sure that he and Drew understood the full significance of what they were involved with. Turning Nergui's own scruples against him. Pushing the only button that might make him co-operate.

Nergui shook his head and turned towards Drew, not knowing what he was going to say, let alone what he should do next.

It was as if Drew had taken Maxon's words as a cue. He suddenly seemed to gain new and unexpected strength and flung himself across at Maxon, dragging the metal post and concrete block behind him. Maxon staggered backwards, startled by the energy of the sudden lunge. His gun went off, firing randomly into the vaulted spaces above them. Almost simultaneously—and Nergui could never be sure what he had or had not seen—the factory space was plunged into sudden darkness. Nergui reeled at the total blackness, dragging out his gun but afraid to fire. He fumbled in his other pocket for his flashlight, which became frustratingly tangled in his coat.

Another shot echoed around the empty building, and then another. From somewhere just ahead there was a sharp cry of pain, and then a third shot. Then there was a long, agonising silence.

Nergui rolled across the floor till he felt the cold stone of the wall against his back. His ears and eyes were straining, trying to discern some movement, to gain some clue about what had happened. Finally, moving as silently as possible, he pulled the torch from his pocket and, throwing himself into a crouching position with his pistol held in front of him, he shone the light around him.

The room was completely silent now, eerily so after the echoes of the gunshots. Nergui carefully moved the flashlight beam around, and then realised that another torch was shining from somewhere across the room.

Ahead of him, Maxon lay on the concrete floor, blood pouring from a bullet wound in his chest. Next to him, Badzar also lay on the ground, his head apparently blown open by another bullet. Behind them, Drew was slumped against the concrete block. For a moment, Nergui thought that Drew had been hit as well. He was staring blankly into the light, his face white, his body shaking. Nergui realised with a deep sigh of relief that he was apparently unharmed.

Nergui shone his own torch back towards the approaching light. "Who is it?" he called, first in Mongolian, then in English.

The voice that replied was English, softly spoken, British. "I'm sorry to startle you," it said. "The darkness was a risk, but necessary." Nergui could make out a silhouette now, walking slowly towards them. He raised his pistol, prepared for anything that might happen. The approaching figure raised its own gun, but in an unthreatening manner. "Infrared sight. Seemed the best way."

Finally, the figure stepped into the beam of Nergui's flashlight.

"Wilson," Nergui said. "You realise I will have to arrest you for murder?"

Wilson nodded thoughtfully. "Whatever you say, Nergui. Though I think a simple thank-you might have sufficed."

TWENTY-FIVE

Outside, the snow had begun to fall again, thick and fast from the night sky. Nergui sat at an angle to the window, watching the falling flakes caught in the streetlights of Sukh Bataar Square, barely listening to the conversation.

"McLeish is all right, then?" the Minister asked, tapping together a sheaf of official-looking papers. As always, his desk was immaculately clear, except for an old-fashioned blotter and inkwell. Nergui suspected that the sheaf of papers was similarly decorative, something for the Minister to leaf through when he wanted to appear busy.

Nergui pulled himself away from the hypnotic swirl of the snowflakes and looked back at the Minister. "Physically, he's fine. We had the police doctor check him over. He sustained a few minor cuts and bruises in the original kidnapping, and he'd been without food or water for some time, but there wasn't any serious harm done. He's been patched up and given a decent meal, so he should be okay."

The British ambassador was sitting in the Minister's other armchair, flicking aimlessly through a thick file on his knee. Nergui had no idea whether the file had any significance, or whether this was just another piece of window-dressing. He was beginning to realise how little of this world he really understood.

"Still, I imagine it must all have been something of an ordeal?" the ambassador said.

"You might say that," Nergui said. This was, he presumed, another instance of that famous British understatement. Or possibly just crass stupidity. "He was very shaken. Who wouldn't be? As to the long-term impact, well . . . I'm no expert."

The ambassador nodded. "The police are well-versed in those matters. I've spoken with the UK Home Office. They've got well-established procedures for post-trauma counselling, all that stuff. We're having him flown back tonight on a specially chartered flight via Vienna, so we can get him out of here before the world's media cotton on to what's happened. He'll have access to the best treatment as soon as he gets back."

"That's good to hear," Nergui said, sincerely. "He's been through hell. I don't think we can begin to imagine what it was like."

"Though fortunately Maxon wasn't the killer," the Minister said.

Nergui turned to look at him, his mouth half open, biting back his instinctive response. "I suppose it depends on how you look at it," he said, finally. He paused momentarily, then continued. "Speaking of which, what happens to Wilson?"

The Minister hesitated, then looked to the ambassador. "Professor Wilson's been handed over to our custody. We'll take care of him," the ambassador said, smoothly.

"Which means what?" Nergui asked.

"Just that," the ambassador said. "We have it in hand."

Nergui looked from the ambassador to the Minister. Both faces were untroubled, giving nothing away. He shrugged. "Well, I'm sure I can depend on your country's integrity, ambassador."

The Minister nodded. "Quite right, Nergui. I think we can all be justly pleased at how this has all worked out, in the circumstances. Especially you." Nergui detected just the merest undertone of threat in the last two words.

"I did my best, sir. It was Doripalam who made the critical links. I can't in all honesty claim much credit. Or pretend that I wasn't lucky in the end."

"Well, these things are never straightforward, Nergui."

"No, sir, not with so many interests involved. It's not easy for a simple policeman."

The Minister stared at him. "I don't think I would ever class you as simple, Nergui. That may be your problem." He paused, then smiled broadly. "But I'm deeply grateful for what you've achieved here. McLeish is safe. We've removed a dangerous psychopath from the streets."

"Two dangerous psychopaths, I suspect," Nergui said.

The Minister shrugged. "Well, Maxon was a common criminal. The US had nothing on him officially but it looks as if they knew more than they were saying about his background. We're liaising with the FBI on that but they don't seem too surprised that he might have killed here. That kind of infighting isn't uncommon. I don't think he or his associate will be missed."

Nergui shrugged. "As you say, sir."

"You know, Nergui," the Minister said, "you're a good man. We'll be pleased to get you back in here where you belong."

"I'm sure you will, sir." Nergui smiled thinly. "And I'll be pleased to get out of Doripalam's hair, I suppose. He deserves some kind of recognition for this—he did a superb job." He paused. "But I'm thinking about my future. You might not think so, but I really am a simple man. I begin to think that I am much more comfortable with the kinds of crime I understand."

"I think the ambassador was a little put out," Nergui said. "Saw this as his territory."

McLeish smiled. He stretched out his aching legs as far as he could in the rear seat of the car. "I really couldn't face it," he said. "Another hour at the airport with that sanctimonious bastard congratulating me on my part in bringing a serial killer to justice." He laughed bitterly. "Lying motionless on a bench for two days."

"You did more than that at the end," Nergui pointed out.

"Probably would have just got myself shot if Wilson hadn't intervened."

"We don't know that Wilson did intervene," Nergui said. "Perhaps he was just holding the gun for a friend."

"Of course," McLeish said. "Jesus, what a world."

"Anyway," Nergui went on, "I don't know that Maxon would have shot you. I don't think he knew what to do. He was desperate, or he wouldn't have tried such a half-baked plan, but you were the only bargaining chip he'd got."

"And he was right to be desperate. Someone was right there behind him." McLeish paused. "I can't follow it, though. Do we assume that Wilson was working with the Russians?"

Nergui shrugged. "Who knows? I think we can assume it was the forces of stability and global capitalism. They don't care where the money comes from or goes to, so long as they get their share and nobody rocks the boat. Maxon had become a liability. Probably even to his own people. Or am I too cynical?"

"From what I've seen here, you're nothing like cynical enough. I just hope you can keep it up."

They fell into silence as the official car pounded through the empty night. As they approached the airport, they passed through one of the mining districts. Nergui stared out of the car window as they passed, watching the chaotic floodlit acres of heavy machinery, makeshift buildings, pipelines and trucks. McLeish turned back and looked at Nergui. "You know, when I first saw that," he said, "I thought it looked like a gateway to hell."

Nergui followed McLeish's gaze into the darkness. "I think perhaps you understand our country better than you realise," he said. "But I hope that you are wrong."